12/06

〜

"You're a mess, Kyla."

"You know what they say," she said with a cruel lift of her lovely eyebrow. "Men are attracted to women like their mothers."

The warmth of Zweli's green eyes chilled as he lightly ran his fingers over his bandage. "You aren't a thing like my mother. Even when she was dead stinking drunk, she was there when someone who loved her needed her. You're not capable of that, are you?"

"I went to you last night, you nincompoop!" she hollered.

He blinked and spent a moment floundering for words. "You…are you sure?"

"I'm n   f course, I'm sure."

"Why?

"I told

"Tell r

"Why   with her sleeve. "W   ospital at one A.M., a   ol' nurse with a mu

"Just s

A fresh   od before her, his arms open.

"You wear me out," he sighed when she made no effort to respond. "I'm too tired to fight you anymore and I love you too much to give up the fight." He turned and took one step toward the stairs before the weight of her hand on his shoulder stopped him.

"I love you, Zweli…"

〜

ONLY YOU

CRYSTAL HUBBARD

Genesis Press, Inc.

HUB

Indigo Love Stories

An imprint of Genesis Press, Inc.
Publishing Company

Genesis Press, Inc.
P.O. Box 101
Columbus, MS 39703

ISBN: 1-58571-208-6
Manufactured in the United States of America

First Edition

Visit us at www.genesis-press.com
or call at 1-888-Indigo-1

DEDICATION

This book is dedicated to Michael Boehringer, who first introduced himself to me by licking my shoulder in the middle of Madame Colvis's French class.

ACKNOWLEDGMENTS

I would like to thank Just Born Inc. for making Jolly Joes, the scrumptious grape-flavored chewy candies that sustained me during the writing of this book. I would also like to express my undying devotion to Dotty, Betty, Cindy, Melissa, Dulena, Bernadette, Gia, Maria and Ginny—The 29 Club—a group of Wakefield femmes fatales who impress me, inspire me, tolerate me and support me unquestioningly.

I would also like to thank Steve at McDonald's and his wife Carol, who generate such good buzz for my books. Every writer should have a muse like Steve, someone who never fails to offer encouragement and restore my enthusiasm when I'm most overwhelmed.

And finally, I owe an eternal debt of gratitude to Jeannetta Gladney, Angelique Justin, Genice Allen and Deborah Schumaker, women who have that rare combination of great brains, great senses of humor and great common sense.

PROLOGUE

Nigel's Italian loafers flattened a strip of the triple-padded ivory shag carpet as he paced in front of Kyla's white leather chaise. His hands were on the hips of his silky black robe, and his angry movements loosened the slipknot in his belt. When the belt slithered to the floor, the flaps of his robe fell open, displaying the hard muscle beneath the smooth, dark caramel skin of his chest when he stopped to toss his hands up at Kyla.

"I don't understand why you just won't sign on for the part," he complained. "Halle Berry let it all hang out, and she won an Oscar. What are you hiding, Kyla? Everyone has seen breasts before."

Kyla kept her whiskey-colored eyes on the emery board she was using to tidy up her fingernails. The repetitive motion camouflaged her rising anxiety. Nigel Chamberlain, her manager and agent of seven years, had harangued her all morning, demanding that she take a supporting role in a movie that could very well launch her film career. The script was good, as it should have been, since an Academy-Award winning screenwriter had written it. Oscar winners were on board to star in and direct the film, too. The role Kyla had been offered was brief but had a lot of impact. It also required the actress who played it to be nude the entire time she was on screen.

"Halle Berry had already proven her talent before she did any nudity." Kyla fought to keep her tone even. "If they want me so bad, then why can't they rework it so that I'm wearing at least a bra and panties?"

In frustration, Nigel fell heavily to his knees before her. "The director wants you because he knows you have the talent *and* the body to carry this part. Your body is a masterpiece. Don't you want to show it off?" He put his hands on the opening of her terrycloth robe and tried to tug one flap aside.

She smacked his hands away and scooted off the chaise. Nigel dogged her every step as he followed her about the huge, atrium-style living room of the rented condominium. She went to the bar near the glittering wall of French doors and poured herself a Pellegrino.

"What's the damn problem?" Nigel demanded. "They're just breasts!"

"These are mine!" Kyla clutched her bosom over her robe. "I don't want to share them with the movie-going public."

"Or anyone else, for that matter," he remarked snidely.

Kyla narrowed her eyes and contemplated pitching her water bottle at his head. Nigel "discovered" her in St. Louis in a Muny production of *A Chorus Line* and had signed her to an iron-clad contract, making him her manager and agent. From the moment she had stepped off the plane in Los Angeles, he had promised her the moon. He had gotten her steady work, but nothing remarkably challenging or artistically satisfying. As the years passed and the stars in her eyes dimmed, she had begun to see him for what he was: a narcissistic bully determined to make his name in the industry by turning her into something she didn't want to be. She had always dreamed of being an actress, but she wanted to do good, meaningful work. She wanted her talent, not her body, to be what audiences appreciated, and more frequently, Nigel made it plain that her body was what *he* most appreciated.

She gazed at the million-dollar view of San Francisco Bay offered by the sliding glass doors. The four-bedroom condo was a delightful perk and had come with her acceptance of the TV-movie role she had just filmed in the Palace of Fine Arts. She didn't know until after shooting had started that Nigel had arranged to share the condo for the duration of filming. Her part had finished shooting the day before, and her bags were already packed for her trip home to Los Angeles. She silently prayed for strength to get through a few more hours under the same roof with Nigel.

Clearly, he wasn't going to make it easy.

"You're pushing thirty, Kyla." He sidled up to her and twirled a strand of her hair around his finger. "How much time do you think you have left to make it in this business?"

She shrugged him off and backed a few steps away. "Maybe if I hadn't spent so many years with a lousy manager and an even worse agent—"

She should have put more distance between them because, before she could react, Nigel launched himself at her and struck her across the face. Stunned by the suddenness and ferocity of the blow, Kyla spilled to the carpet. She clutched the hot, throbbing handprint high on her cheek and, as Nigel ranted above her, swearing that she had made him do it, she thought of all the other wounds he had inflicted, the ones that caused pain beyond the physical. *You're too fat. You're too thin. You're too ethnic. You're not ethnic enough. You're too old.* After all the blows to her mind and soul, he had finally carried his abuse to the physical. Right there and then, Kyla Winters decided—as her late grandmother used to say—that she was full up.

She wobbled a bit as she found her feet. At age forty-two, Nigel still had the physique of the college football standout he'd once been. He glared at her as if she were to blame for his violent outburst. So used to controlling her, he didn't expect it when, after tucking a lock of her glossy hair behind her ear, Kyla balled up her manicured hand and gave him a fast and wicked right jab to the center of his face. A surprised grunt escaped him as he stumbled back a few steps, holding his spurting nose. He threw off his robe and charged at her, his black pajama pants slung low on his hips.

The murderous gleam in Kyla's eyes drew him up short. "I wish you would."

Her deadly calm convinced him that retreat would be his best option. "I want you out!" he yelled. "Now!"

"The studio rented this condo for *me*," Kyla said. "I'm the talent, remember? *You* leave."

"I made you," he sneered, snatching up his robe. "You're dead in L.A. without me."

"Good!" she shouted, and she meant it. "I'm sick of L.A. and I'm sick of you, Nigel. I'm sick of myself and what I let you turn me into."

"What are you gonna do without me, Kyla?" Nigel used a sleeve of the robe to staunch the flow of blood from his nose. "When I finish with you, no one will even hire you to do used car commercials."

"Nigel, I don't need you." She laughed, the honest truth of her statement briefly renewing her sense of self and freedom. "I don't need Hollywood, either. You know what? You stay. *I'll* leave." She started up the spiral staircase that would take her to her room.

"Don't come crying back to me when your ass is living on cat food and toilet water!" Nigel yelled after her. He staggered across the room to the bar and grabbed a handful of ice, which he wrapped in a bar towel before applying it to his busted nose.

"Worry about yourself," Kyla shouted down at him. "Have you forgotten that I'm your most successful client? When I go, so does what little cash flow you have."

"That's big talk from a scared little Missouri girl. I love you, Kyla. If I'm hard on you, it's only because I know how great you could be."

She kept climbing the stairs.

"You're going to end up old, alone, and pathetic!" Nigel emphasized his words with violent jabs of his finger. "You'll never find a man who treats you the way I do."

"Thank God," Kyla declared as she went into her room and locked the door behind her.

Two weeks after their angry parting, Nigel's words turned over in Kyla's head as she drifted into the rhythm of the road. Her Lexus, stuffed with all of her worldly possessions, hugged the asphalt as it sped along a lonely stretch of the dark Nevada highway. Though Nigel wasn't pursuing her, she hadn't been able to relax until she'd crossed the

California border. She thought about his angry curse, determined to exorcise it from her head by wearing it out.

You're going to end up old, alone, and pathetic.

"I'll get old, God willing," she murmured into the night, "but I won't ever be pathetic." She smiled and thought about her mother and her sisters, none of whom she'd seen in over a year, not since her last visit home for the birth of her godchildren, Claire Elizabeth and Samuel Zachary. "I won't be alone, either."

With their grandmother Claire's death three years ago, two of Kyla's sisters, Clara and Cady, had moved back to St. Louis. Cady had fallen in love with the doctor who had treated their grandmother, and she hadn't wasted a minute packing up her Boston apartment and relocating to St. Louis. With Claire's passing, Clara had felt the urge to be closer to her mother and sisters, and she'd transplanted her husband and children from San Francisco. Now that Kyla was headed home, only baby sister Chiara was still adrift in parts unfamiliar and far away. Longing flooded Kyla's heart and she stepped a little harder on the accelerator, eagerly anticipating her reunion with her family. She wanted nothing more than to walk into her mother's house and pull her family's love around her like a thick, warm quilt.

But there was someone else whose attention she suddenly craved. She put on her favorite CD and Billie Holiday's brassy rendition of "What A Little Moonlight Can Do" turned her thoughts to the time she had spent with Dr. Zweli Randall during the last stages of her grandmother's illness and after her death. A devout ladies' man and avowed bachelor, Zweli had shocked her with a proposal six weeks after their first meeting. She had turned him down for a number of reasons, the least of which being the fact that she'd still had aspirations of making it in Hollywood.

The more she thought of Zweli, the less appealing Hollywood became and Kyla relaxed, seemingly for the first time in seven years. And for the first time since she left San Francisco, she felt as if she were running *to* something, rather than away.

CHAPTER ONE

"Hey, sugar." Zweli leaned on the counter at the nurses' station, his dimples working overtime as he requested a patient's chart as though he were asking for a lap dance. The student nurse turned bright red, and when Zweli caressed the back of her hand as he took the chart from her, she burst into loud, nervous giggles.

"Dr. Randall?"

Zweli looked over his shoulder to see Dr. Keren Bailey motioning toward him. Zweli gave the student nurse a smile that sent a rush of color into her cheeks as he said goodbye and joined Dr. Bailey farther down the corridor. "What is it, Keren? A patient?"

"Nope." He stroked a hand over his bald head. "My sister-in-law is in town."

Zweli's casual smile froze. "Which one?"

"Guess."

"Chiara." Zweli swallowed hard and pulled at his shirt collar.

"No. Guess again."

Zweli's face went numb. "No," he said, dragging out the word. "Not…"

"Yes." Keren patted his shoulder.

Zweli stopped and leaned heavily against the wall. "Kyla Winters," he sighed. "I, um, haven't thought about her in months."

"Lie," Keren said.

"Okay, I haven't thought of her in weeks," Zweli amended.

"That's another lie."

"When did you get to know me so well?" Zweli rubbed his hands over his face. Keren knew his history with Kyla, and he also seemed to know that Kyla had become a permanent part of his heart and mind. She had returned to California after the birth of Keren's twins sixteen months ago, and Zweli hadn't heard from her since. She'd been working, he knew that. Perhaps she was involved with someone. Whatever she was doing, she hadn't communicated with him since the day they had stood together over a baptismal font as the godparents of Claire and Samuel Winters-Bailey. But Kyla's absence hadn't stopped him from thinking about her. And dreaming of her. And replaying in his mind the softness of her kisses and the feel of her body in his arms.

He was still the champion player of Raines-Hartley Hospital, but no woman had managed to pry his heart from the memory of Kyla Winters.

"How long is she staying?" Zweli asked.

Keren smiled. "She's back for good."

"For good?" Zweli repeated, slumping against the wall. "Kyla Winters is back for good…"

Zweli moved through the rest of his day in a daze. The smiles that weakened the knees of student nurses remained hidden. His ongoing flirtation with fellow cardiologist Dr. Barbara Shute stalled when he didn't respond to her none-too-subtle invitation to join her for legs and breasts at her place at the end of their shift. Zweli still cared for his patients with the same devoted attention, but an elemental change in him had occurred upon learning that Kyla Winters was back.

"Back for good," he mumbled to himself as he slowly strolled the produce section of Harold's Market after work. He palmed a pair of cantaloupes and invariably thought of Kyla. She had a slamming body, along with a fine mind and a devilishly sharp sense of humor to go with it. He hit her website often to look at her photos and catch up on what she was working on in Los Angeles.

His favorite photo was the one from the syndicated action series *Lifeguards*. Kyla, in a wine-red string bikini, posed against a tropical sunset. As he stood in the crowded market, Zweli could almost smell the coconut oil that made her honey-brown skin glisten in the photo; he could almost feel the soft kiss of the breeze that moved through the sun-gold strands of her long, dark hair. Although the role in *Lifeguards* had been small, the public had noticed Kyla. Just when her popularity was garnering her more lines per episode, the show had been cancelled. Zweli had been among those to write to the network, demanding that *Lifeguards*—and Kyla Winters in particular—be brought back.

Zweli put one of the melons in his carrying basket and moved on, still musing on Kyla. Instead of returning to television, Kyla had returned to St. Louis. He wondered how long she had been back, where she was staying, and—though he didn't want to admit it—whether she wanted to see him. "Who cares?" he suddenly said aloud as he stopped at the olive bar, drawing the attention of a young woman with long black hair and a bulbous lollipop propped between her gloss-slicked lips.

Kyla's the one who turned me *down*, Zweli thought, narrowing his eyes at a bin full of glistening Niçoise olives. *She's the one who left. So she's back. Why the hell should I care?* "I don't," he stubbornly mumbled.

"You don't what?"

Zweli finally noticed the woman standing close to him. Her words, spoken around her lollipop, had a cloying cherry scent.

"I don't know why I haven't asked your name," Zweli said smoothly, offering his hand and a smile that made the lollipop woman quiver. "Zweli Randall, M.D. And you are?"

"Cerise," she answered with a flip of her hair. She guided it to fall over one shoulder, drawing his eyes to the bosom of her red baby-doll T-shirt. The shirt was so tight, the words BUDDY'S GYM looked like BUDDY'SGYM. "It's French, for cherry." She slid the moist lollipop across her lower lip. "Do you like cherries?"

Zweli lapsed into a role he genuinely had no stomach for. "Who doesn't? In fact, I'm craving a ripe, juicy cherry right now. But I don't think they're in season."

Her sultry glance traveled over his chest. "I think you might find what you like at my place, Dr. Randall. Interested?"

Zweli allowed her to link her arm through his. He inwardly snickered at the ease with which he attracted women. Harold's Market was known for the quality of its meat, human and otherwise. Located a block away from the posh Buddy's Gym, it catered to the gym's fitness-conscious clientele and carried a wide variety of the freshest, most exotic produce, along with a huge assortment of vegetarian and whole foods products. Beautiful food for beautiful people was Harold's unspoken, but universally acknowledged, motto.

Cerise was certainly one of the beautiful people. Her burnt yellow complexion was softened by the red highlights in her hair, which fell straight to the middle of her back. Her black shorts looked as if they'd been sprayed on, and they fully exposed her long legs.

Kyla has nice legs, Zweli thought with a smile as Cerise led him through the produce department. Though a little on the thin side, Kyla's legs were long and nicely toned, strong and graceful, like a dancer's.

Cerise picked up an English cucumber as long as her forearm. "Now this," she smirked, running her shiny red talons along the length of the thing, "is what I call a cucumber." She giggled like a drunken chipmunk, but Zweli paid her no mind. He was still thinking about Kyla's legs, and how they'd looked in her five-inch heels on that fateful New Year's Eve when she'd torn out his heart and thrown it in his face.

Zweli's hand tightened around the handles of his grocery basket. He shook his head, trying to clear it of Kyla Winters. He hadn't seen her in over a year yet she plagued him like something from the Old Testament. He couldn't work in his office at the hospital without imagining that he smelled her citrusy perfume. He couldn't visit Keren and his wife, Cady, without holding his breath, hoping that she would mention her fickle-hearted actress sister. Worst of all, he couldn't drive his Alfa Romeo without picturing Kyla in the passenger seat of the roadster, her hair blowing in the wind, her short skirts offering him teasing glimpses of her thighs.

He couldn't pass a McDonald's without laughing at the stories Kyla had told him of her childhood manipulations to get a Happy Meal, and he couldn't watch *TVLand*, without hearing Kyla's voice singing the theme songs to every sitcom that aired from 1970 on.

"She really likes her television," Zweli muttered with a smile.

"Yes, I do," Cerise said. "I never miss my *telenovelas* on *Univision*."

"What?" Zweli turned his full attention to Cerise, trying to make sense of what she'd just said.

"You asked me if I liked television," she explained.

"Oh…sure. What are *telenovelas*?"

"They're like soap operas but a whole lot better," Cerise went on excitedly. "My favorite one is *Piel de Otoño*, and it's about a woman, Lucia Villareal de Mendoza, and her two friends, Rosario and Triana. Lucia, she was an orphan, and…"

Cerise's voice faded out of Zweli's consciousness as they continued through the store, which constantly reminded him of Kyla. In maintaining her "California ways," as Cady called them, Kyla put only the most natural and healthy foods in her body. Zweli had introduced her to Harold's, and she'd fallen in love with the wide variety of unusual fresh breads and produce Harold's offered. The two of them had been frequent patrons back when he thought he could make her his wife.

He absently grabbed two packages of firm teriyaki tofu and a head of bok choy and tossed them into his basket, which already contained an organic red onion, a package of bright green snow peas, and a large cantaloupe. Unwittingly, he had decided that a simple stir-fry—Kyla's favorite—would make a great dinner for him and Cerise. It never occurred to Zweli to ask Cerise if she liked stir fries, and even if it had, it wouldn't have been possible. Zweli got so lost in his reminiscences about Kyla that he failed to respond appropriately to Cerise's retelling of the loves and adventures of Lucia Villareal de Mendoza. Offended, Cerise had sidled away from him at the bakery counter to introduce herself to a muscle-bound man with spiky blond highlights and a pair of wraparound sunglasses dangling from the collar of his Buddy's Gym T-shirt.

Mindless of Cerise's absence, Zweli set his items on the checkout counter and smiled, happy that he was living his life perfectly well without Kyla. He paid for his order, dropped the change in the pocket of his jeans, and slung the bag over his shoulder as left the store. He whistled, so satisfied with his single life and his power over women that he didn't notice Cerise speeding past him in a convertible, banana-yellow Corvette driven by a man now wearing dark wraparound sunglasses.

"Yes, indeed, I still have it," Zweli muttered happily as he remotely deactivated the Alfa Romeo's alarm and set his groceries in the passenger seat. "Hell, I never lost it. What difference does it make that Kyla's back in town? It don't mean a thing to a man like me."

Zweli started the engine and revved it a few times before he realized that he'd forgotten something. Something important. He mentally retraced his path through Harold's, itching to know what he could possibly be missing. It came to him all of a sudden, and he slapped his hand to his forehead and said, "Low-sodium soy sauce. Can't have a stir-fry without that." He cut off the engine, hopped out of the car and ran back into the store trying to remember the name of the brand with the yellow and red label…the one Kyla liked.

One month after Zweli lost Cerise in Harold's Market to thoughts of Kyla, the real deal stood in the produce department, pushing the sleeves of her sweatshirt up to her elbows before rooting through a wide-mouthed barrel of pomegranates. The fruits were at the tail end of their short season, and she wanted a couple of nice ones. She hung over the rim of the barrel, her oversized sweatshirt forming a wide yellow drape that barred access to other shoppers. Kyla intently inspected the fruits, discarding this one because the skin was too red, that one because the skin was too pink, another one for being too light for its size and still another for being too heavy.

Her spandex-wrapped bottom thrust into the air, she was hanging by her waist over the lip of the barrel, sorting through the bottom fruits when she heard her name.

Her whole body flinched, her hands tightening on a pair of pomegranates as the deep, resonant voice registered.

"Kyla, I'd recognize you anywhere," the voice laughed lightly.

It was right behind her now, and Kyla felt her skin erupt in goose pimples. Kyla had been home for four and a half weeks, and she'd known that she'd have to face Zweli sooner or later. So much for later, she groaned inwardly as she withdrew from the barrel.

She fought the urge to swallow a mouthful of air when her eyes met his. The nervous warmth of a blush made the collar of her big sweatshirt feel too tight as she gazed upon the face she had seen in her dreams so many times in the past year and a half.

His dimples still had the power to make her knees soft and weak. His full lips formed a mouth that was almost too pretty for a man, but it softened the rakish, Clark Gableish lines in his forehead. He stared at her, casually but intensely, and a familiar surge of heat made her skin tingle. His sienna dreads were a fraction longer, but still short enough to really complement the clean-shaven planes and hollows of his high cheekbones and square jaw. His impeccable and truly unique fashion sense was still intact—only Zweli could pull off a leather St. Louis Cardinals bomber jacket with pleated Italian trousers, black leather loafers and a blindingly white silk shirt.

Zweli betrayed none of his surprised delight at seeing her. He'd instantly recognized her, despite being suspended in the barrel. Some women you'd know by their perfume, others by their voices. No woman on the planet had an ass like Kyla's, and, like an orchid or a sunset, Zweli considered it one of Nature's greatest works. For weeks he had suffered the itch of knowing Kyla was in town and been unable to realize any of his schemes to cross paths with her. Catching her at Harold's Market further proved one of his heartfelt beliefs: the best treats were the unexpected ones. "How are you?" he asked.

"You're fine," she exhaled before quickly correcting herself with, "*I'm* fine! I meant me. I'm…" She paused, taking a deep breath to settle her nerves. "I'm fine, Zweli. And you?"

He spent a moment teasing her with a dashing half smile that told her he could still read her perfectly. "I'm doing well," he finally said. "Work keeps me busy."

"Work and pleasure," injected the woman who stepped into view to wrap her hands around Zweli's right arm. "Hello, there." She flashed a brittle smile that belied the hostility in her ginger-ale eyes. "Dr. Barbara Shute. You must be a friend of Zweli's."

I could have been his *wife* right now, Kyla wanted to say by way of greeting the possessive minx hanging on Zweli's arm and every word. Instead, she said, "Zweli is practically family."

"I see." Barbara cemented her shoulder to Zweli's. She raised a fine, arched eyebrow and held onto his arm even tighter. "Do you have a name?"

Zweli noticed the hardening of a tiny muscle at the base of Kyla's jaw. Kyla Winters had the sweetest mouth, but it contained the sharpest tongue he had ever encountered. He pulled his arm free of Barbara's grasp and put himself squarely between the women. "Barbara, this is Kyla Winters. Keren's sister-in-law."

Barbara extended a finely manicured hand toward Kyla. "So you're the one," she said, the soft warmth of her features turning icy. "I've heard so much about Keren's sisters-in-law."

Kyla stood silently as Barbara's feral brown gaze traveled over her in what Kyla called the Witch Eye, that leisurely, toe-to-head visual evaluation that takes in every defect of another woman's person and dress. Barbara's narrowed eyes and pinched smile told Kyla what she already knew...that compared to Dr. Shute's designer after-work duds, she herself looked like a vagrant. Having just come from a hard workout at Buddy's Gym, Kyla was dressed in her sweaty, ratty best, bare of jewelry and makeup. Her hair was half in a ponytail and half out, and after her sojourn in the pomegranate barrel, the half that was half out now looked like the tail of a frightened raccoon.

Kyla—ever the actress—elegantly drew her shoulders back, tilted her head and leveled her gaze at Barbara. Zweli watched, mesmerized at Kyla's physical transformation from gym rat to noble empress.

"I'm afraid I haven't been in St. Louis for very long," she began, regally shaking Barbara's hand. "That might explain why I haven't heard a thing about you." She fixed her gaze on Zweli, mutely conveying her enjoyment of his discomfort.

Zweli took Barbara by her shoulder. "Well, now that we're all acquainted, perhaps we should let Kyla get back to her shopping."

Kyla nodded her head in a way that made Zweli feel as though he were being officially dismissed. He hid the sting by transferring his hand from Barbara's shoulder to the small of her back, a movement not lost on Kyla. "Well…it was nice seeing you," he said.

Kyla focused on keeping her smile benevolent when all she wanted to do was claw Zweli's hand from Barbara's back. "You too, Zweli," she offered sweetly before returning to her pomegranates. She gripped the rim of the barrel, determined not to look back at Drs. Randall and Shute. She was a strong actress, but she knew she wasn't strong enough to turn around and see him not looking back at her.

Kyla upended the bag containing her carefully selected pomegranates, dumping them into a ceramic fruit bowl, not caring if she now bruised them. She opened her mother's refrigerator and pitched in a pair of yellow squash, mindless of the carton of eggs that cushioned their landing. She stepped over her twin niece and nephew, who sat on the linoleum floor between the center preparation island and the refrigerator, and yanked a metal colander from its hook on the wall alongside the sink. Bumping her sister Cady aside, she emptied a bag of plump red grapes into the colander, propped it up in the sink, and started the water over them.

"Is something bothering you, Ky?" Abby Winters asked.

Kyla glanced at her mother, who stood on the far side of the prep island drumming her fingernails on its tiled surface.

"Bad workout?" Cady asked as she kneeled to hand sippy cups of water to her children.

"You little…!" Kyla hollered upon looking down at the twins. Samuel Zachary and Claire Elizabeth sat with Kyla's sack of apples between them. Sammy, juice dripping from his chin, was taking one bite from each of the apples his sister handed to him one by one.

"That's our cue," Cady announced before gathering a child under each arm and hustling them out of the room.

Abby tucked a silvery lock of her short hair behind her ear before she pushed up the sleeves of her Shetland sweater and began collecting the apples. "I'll make applesauce with these."

Kyla began loading the crisper with lemons, limes, oranges and a head of butter lettuce, each hitting the plastic drawer with a thud.

"The apples are my fault, honey," Abby said. "I told the twins that the first bite of an apple is always the best bite, and you know how Sammy's mind works. He's his mother all over again. I'll get you a new bag when I go out. Those are Galas?"

"Huh?" Kyla grunted.

"Your apples. That's why you're so mad, isn't it?"

Kyla slammed the drawer shut. "I'm not mad." She stood up and rubbed her temples. "At least not about the apples. I…" She spent a moment struggling against her better judgment.

"What is it then?" Abby asked.

Kyla crossed her arms over her chest and stared at the water splashing over her grapes. "I just saw Dr. Randall."

"Oh." Abby's eyes widened. "Ooh. Did you talk to him?"

"Yes. Just hello-how're-you-doin'. He wasn't alone."

Abby bowed her head to hide a tiny smile as she began putting away the rest of her daughter's groceries.

"He was with a woman, Mama."

"Some floozy, no doubt," Abby chuckled. "Cady says that Zweli's dates get younger and dumber every time he brings one of them to Sunday dinner."

"Zweli brings his dates *here*?" A combination of anger and jealousy made Kyla nauseous.

"Never the same one twice." Abby studied the Japanese nutrition label plastered on a clear plastic container of what looked like pickled dates. "Your sisters have a way of driving off Zweli's girlfriends. I think he brings them here just for the sport of it, the way Romans tossed good Christians to the lions." She harrumphed. "And believe me, not one of those girls was a good Christian."

Kyla involuntarily ground her teeth. "This one is a doctor."

"Is she pretty?"

Grudgingly, Kyla nodded. "I suppose. In a fussy sort of way. She has fussy feet. And fussy hair, fussy clothes, and a fussy face. She looks like she never sweats, and there I was looking like nobody's child." Kyla tugged the ponytail holder from her hair and gave it a cursory styling with her hand. It fell into soft waves scented with cucumber and melon.

Smiling, Abby shook her head. "I doubt Zweli saw you as nobody's child."

Kyla cast her eyes down so her mother wouldn't see the moisture filling them. "It doesn't matter, Mama. He's with someone now."

"That son-of-a-bitch," Abby grinned.

"Listen to the mouth on you." Kyla laughed around her tears as she embraced her mother.

"That's what Cady calls him, every time he shows up on Sunday with one of his floozies."

Kyla hugged her mother closer. "I blew it, Mama. I never gave him a reason to wait for me." She pulled away and grabbed a paper towel to wipe her eyes and her nose. "Oh, well. I guess I'll have to get used to it. Zweli's moved on." Fresh tears blurred her vision. "He's moved on. Right?"

Mesmerized by the reflection of candlelight dancing in the cozy glass oval of Barbara's dining table, Zweli ignored the stuffed chicken breasts sitting before him. Barbara's hand snaked between the candelabra and Zweli's wine glass to rest on his forearm. "Zweli?" she purred. She tipped her head to the right, capturing the candlelight in her dangling diamond pendant earrings.

Zweli's unblinking eyes were fixed on a fresh memory. Kyla had looked so damn adorable in her workout clothes. *And damn if she didn't have the nerve to be wearing the Northwestern sweatshirt she stole from me three years ago.* He chuckled lightly to himself.

"Zweli!"

The stab of Barbara's red fingernails, accompanied by her sharp voice, snapped him from his reverie.

"Retract, kitten," he said, drawing his hand back a safe distance.

"I've been talking to you for ten minutes and you've been in outer space," Barbara accused. She sat back in her white leather chair. "Is there something wrong with the food?"

Zweli picked at his plate with the tines of his fork. The wild rice and mushroom risotto was moist, fluffy, and had a wonderful sherry and sage aroma. The chicken had been broiled perfectly and the sautéed asparagus was probably the best he'd ever had. "The food is great, as always," he responded.

Barbara's eyes narrowed. She grabbed her wine glass before awkwardly crossing her arms over her chest. "You've been in a strange way all evening. As a matter of fact, you've been preoccupied and distant for the past month or so." She took a leisurely swig of her chardonnay. "Is there something we need to talk about?"

Zweli shrugged, his interest turning to the fine gold border of his dinner plate.

Barbara rolled her eyes and shook her head as she stared at the chandelier. "Let me rephrase the question. Is there some*one* we need to talk about?"

He set his elbows on the table and tented his fingers before his chin. "What are you getting at, Barbara?"

She abruptly leaned forward and set down her glass with enough force to slosh wine onto the tablecloth, and it dripped onto the thick white carpet as she lit into Zweli. "Your mind has been someplace else ever since we ran into that woman at the market this afternoon." She pointed an accusing finger. "I knew what I was getting into when I got involved with you, but I want to make one thing absolutely clear right now. I am not one of those horny little nurses you're used to trifling with."

"Put that thing away," Zweli advised, indicating her finger with a nod of his head. He tossed his napkin onto his plate. "Just so *you* know, I'm not one of the starry-eyed interns you're used to trifling with."

She took a quick, deep breath. "Look. I don't want to fight with you. I just want to know where we stand."

Zweli suppressed a groan.

Barbara crossed her left leg over her right. The jittery bounce of her left foot revealed the tension just under the surface of her forced calm. "I saw how you looked at that woman, Zweli. It was different."

He threw up his hands in frustration. "Different than what?"

"Different than how you look at every other pretty woman who crosses your path." Barbara's tone, now somber rather than wrathful, sent a flicker of shame through Zweli. "There was a time in my life when men looked at me the way you looked at the woman in the market. Time stomps along, I guess, and things change."

Zweli reached the limit of his patience. "For God's sake, Barbara, you're my age," he nearly shouted. "Thirty-four isn't old, and trust me, there are plenty of men panting after you. Take Harley Whitmire, for instance. He's started faking heart attacks just to be seen by you."

Barbara's dimples perked. "Harley's old enough to be my big brother." She scampered after Zweli, who headed for the foyer. "So you noticed. I'm glad you realize that I'm with you because I want to be, not because I have to be, Zweli."

He stopped, and Barbara collided with him. Turning, he said, "I'm not *with* you. I'm not *with* anybody. I see other people, I know you've seen other people. We're just friends."

Barbara's expression hardened. "Three dinners, two lunches and one weekend conference make us a little more than friends, I'd say."

"One of those dinners was a department function and the conference was just a conference." Zweli grabbed his bomber jacket from the narrow closet. "It's not like we shared a hotel room."

Barbara zipped in front of him to bar him from the front door. "I've put a lot of time and effort into us, Zweli. I don't know what it is between you and that woman, but I won't stand here and let it come between what you and I have together."

The jasmine candles burning in the mirrored sconces in the foyer cast Barbara in the softest, most beautiful light. Her warm brown skin and coffee eyes, her intelligence and her skill as a surgeon had been extremely attractive qualities, until now. In the presence of a brighter star, Barbara's appeal had paled. Now Zweli saw that Barbara's most irresistible quality had been her dogged pursuit of him and his fun at dancing out of reach. His shoulders fell. "Barbara, be fair. Are we really together?"

"That looks like it hurts," Keren said as he and Zweli carried their lunch trays to a table in the Raines-Hartley Hospital cafeteria. Since it was a Saturday, the room wasn't very crowded. Patients and their visitors far outnumbered the doctors, many of whom—like Zweli and Keren—were there on a sunny Saturday afternoon fulfilling their twice-monthly duties as on-site specialists.

Zweli would have preferred discussing the ills of one of his patients, rather than the purplish-black bruise in full blossom on his right cheekbone. "Yeah, it stings."

Keren took a seat facing the windows. "It kinda looks like knuckles."

"Barbara and I had 'The Talk' last night," Zweli said quietly.

"It's that time, huh?" Keren smiled. "That's quick. You two were together for what…a month?"

"We weren't together," Zweli insisted. "We dated, that's it."

"What was it this time? The 'My Life Is Too Complicated Right Now' talk? No, I don't think Barbara would go for that one. Did you use 'I'm Just So Overwhelmed by My Feelings for You, I Need to Slow Down?' " Keren stirred a pat of butter into his sweet peas. "Barbara would have laughed in your face over that one. I know. You pulled the classic out of the vault. 'It's Not You, It's Me.' "

"I asked her to honestly evaluate our relationship," Zweli said around a bite of pasta primavera. "She didn't view it the way I did."

Keren pointed at Zweli's cheek with his fork. "May I assume that's a parting gift from Dr. Shute?"

"Don't ever let anyone tell you that health-club kickboxing isn't the real thing."

"Well, who is she?"

"Who is who?"

"The woman you dumped Barbara for," Keren said. "You never leave without a successor in position."

Zweli pushed his tray aside and stared hard at his friend. "Is that how it looks to you?"

Keren set down his cutlery. "Well…yes."

Zweli spent a moment thinking back on his last few relationships. "There's been some overlapping, I'll admit, but…I didn't officially break up with Eliza before Marisol came along, so technically, I didn't have a backup in place that time."

"Eliza left for a six-month sabbatical in Sydney. You started seeing Marisol the next day, so—if we're talking technicalities—you were seeing two women at the same time."

Zweli thought harder. "Alessandra," he stated with a snap of his fingers. "Remember her?"

"The Italian internist."

"When I told her that I wasn't ready for a serious relationship, we broke up," Zweli said proudly. "I didn't have anyone waiting in reserve."

"Eliza came back two days before you did the 'Not Ready for Serious' with Alessandra," Keren reminded him. "She might not have been in reserve but she was definitely in cold storage."

Zweli dug deeper into his dating history to find at least one honorable parting. He gave up when his temples started to throb. "I'm a dog, man," he sighed. "I'm a lowdown, shiftless dog when it comes to women."

"There's more to your break with Barbara than you're giving up," Keren observed. "The 'I Thought We Were Just Friends Who Date' talk smells new."

Zweli slumped in his chair and let his head fall back. "I saw Kyla yesterday while Barbara and I were shopping for dinner at Harold's Market." He sat up and leaned over the table. "Everything was fine with Barbara until Kyla!" he insisted in lowered tones. "I don't know what happened, but when we got back to Barbara's place, I couldn't wait to leave. Barbara's attractive, she's smart, she's fun...but last night, she turned into a maniac. She practically wanted me to come out and say that we were going to be together forever."

"And, inconveniently, there's someone else you want to see."

"It's not like that, and you know it. Kyla isn't a backup." Honest emotion clogged Zweli's throat. "She never was."

"If you ask me, everyone since Kyla has been a backup."

"Seeing her again," Zweli started, "it was like she never left. You'd think that after being apart from her for so long, I'd be over her."

Keren took a few more bites of his spinach lasagna before he said, "For a cardiologist, you seem to know very little about the complexities of the human heart."

"What, you think I'm still in love with Kyla?" He snorted and tore at his buttered roll.

"Actually, that's exactly what I think. Now what are you going to do about it?"

"What *can* I do? She saw me with Barbara, and ol' Babs dug her hooks in."

"So."

"So? What will she think if I call her up and ask her out the day after she sees me on a date with another woman?"

"She'll think that you want to see her." Keren wiped up a smear of tomato sauce with his garlic bread. "End of story."

"That shows what you know about, Kyla," Zweli said through a dry, uncomfortable laugh. "She plays the game better than I do. I know, because I lost the first round on a technical knockout. That 'My Life Is Too Complicated' talk you mentioned? Guess who invented it?" He waited for Keren to respond, but when Keren just kept eating a hearty chunk of garlic bread, Zweli answered for him. "Your sister-in-law! That's the excuse she gave me the night I proposed to her. The next damn day she was on a plane to California."

"You sound bitter," Keren teased.

Zweli banged his fist on the table. "You're damn right, I'm bitter!" Mindless of the diners staring at him, he worked himself up into a full-fledged rant. "We may not have known each other for that long, but I know that I'll never find anyone who makes me feel the way she does. You know that I've looked. *Hard.* I've had moments over the years when I thought sheer insanity drove me to propose to her, but after three minutes with her yesterday, I know that I'm not the crazy one. She is."

Keren scrutinized Zweli the way he would a patient. "You need to talk to her."

Zweli fidgeted in his chair. "That ain't all I need to do to her," he grumbled under his breath. "Talk nothing. What she needs is some sense shaken into her. That was the first and last time I ever let that woman make a fool out of me. The next time I see her, I'm...I'm— "

"Cady and I are taking the kids to Abby's for Sunday dinner tomorrow night," Keren said over Zweli's mumbling. "You're welcome to join us."

"—gonna...okay," Zweli interrupted himself to answer. "What time?"

"About three. You can meet us there."

"Good," Zweli said decisively. "Kyla and I will have it out once and for all."

"Don't be too hard on her, Z."

"Why not?"

"Just...don't come at her from a place of anger. She doesn't deserve it."

Zweli uttered a noise of exasperation. "Are you speaking as my best friend or as her brother-in-law?"

Keren wiped his mouth, crumpled his napkin, and set it on his plate. "Both," he said before standing up and taking his tray. "See you tomorrow at three."

CHAPTER TWO

Troy Holtz took a seat between his aunts, Kyla and Ciel, at the dining table. "I don't have to sit in kiddie corner anymore," he said as he shook out a cream linen napkin and tucked it into the collar of his dress shirt.

"If Troy can sit with the adults, I should be able to, too," his younger brother, Christopher Jr.—C.J.—argued from a doorway of the small room off the dining room. The room, ordinarily used as a library, had been cleared of its dark green velvet brocaded loveseat and chaise to accommodate padded folding chairs and a card table set for five. "Mama," Ella whined to Ciel as she twisted the end of her silky, blue-black ponytail, "do I have to stay in here?"

"Yes!" Ciel answered in chorus with her husband Lee.

"Be good, children," Troy admonished, deepening his voice to paternal tones. "You should be seen and not heard."

"Knock it off, kiddo," Clara ordered her son. "Sixteen doesn't make you a man, and neither does sitting in here with the adults."

"Yes, ma'am," Troy said sheepishly.

Kyla rested an arm on the back of Troy's chair before leaning in to speak quietly to him. "Did your mom let you drive over here?"

Troy shook his head. "She said I haven't had my license long enough, and that it would be unfair to put the whole family at risk."

"I need to go to the hardware store to pick out some paint," Kyla said. "Want to drive me there after dinner?"

His amber eyes sparkling, Troy gave her a high five.

"What are you two up to over there?" Clara asked. She sat near the head of the long table with her husband Christopher, and she had a skewed view of her son and Kyla.

"I'm just arranging for a ride to Lowe's," Kyla said. "Would you please pass the mashed sweet potatoes?"

"That kid's been licensed for two weeks." A laugh issued from beneath Christopher's neat red mustache. "And he's already had two accidents."

"I backed into a parking meter and then tapped some guy's bumper when I was pulling away from the parking meter," Troy explained as he helped himself to the mashed sweet potatoes held by Kyla.

"'Tapped?'" Christopher raised his eyebrows. "That tap raised our insurance rates by two hundred dollars a year." He fixed his blue eyes on his oldest son. "You're lucky I didn't tap you when you came home with the car dented at both ends."

"We were just glad that no one was hurt," Clara said, laying a hand over her husband's. "It could have been worse."

"Yep," Cady said, nudging C.J. back into the kiddie room as she exited it. "He could have taken out a picket fence, a flamingo, a ceramic toadstool, and a whole family of lawn frogs on his first outing as a licensed driver. Perhaps that's why Clara's being so understanding. And silent."

The Winters women laughed at the memory the husbands and Troy knew nothing about. Kyla sat back to really appreciate the moment. This was the first family Sunday dinner since her return, and it was doubly special since it was the family minus the one-to-ten guests that were usually in attendance.

Abby wore one of her mother-in-law's old hand-stitched aprons, and she moved between kitchen and table like a well-trained French waiter. Kyla and her sisters, their husbands, and Troy lined the long sides of the dining table, a grand piece of Victorian black pine comprising the centerpiece of a dining room set that had been in the Winters family for almost one hundred years. Kyla couldn't quite see her nieces and nephews at the kids' table from her seat, but she plainly heard them, specifically Danielle screeching at Clarence to stop exposing his mouthful of partially chewed food. Cady and Keren took turns checking on their twins, who were making their booster-seat debut at the kiddie table.

Kyla's heart swelled with pure love for her family, and she was tempted to leap out of her chair to hug and kiss each one of them. To them, this was probably just another Sunday in just another September, but to Kyla, it was the beginning of a new life. She would be moving out of her family home soon, but never again would she be moving out of her family's lives. That thought made her so happy, she impulsively wrapped her arms around Ciel's neck in a smothering hug.

"You're choking me," Ciel squeezed out in a froggy voice.

"She's been ambushing everybody with hugs ever since she got back from Hollywood," Abby said, breezing past to set a steaming crock of mango-orange chutney next to the ham. "She nearly rendered me unconscious with one of those headlocks of love."

Kyla was reaching for Troy when the doorbell sounded.

"I'll get that," Cady volunteered much too quickly. She set her curls bouncing and her chair tottering on its back legs in her haste to answer the door.

"I wasn't expecting anyone else for dinner," Abby said.

Keren loudly cleared his throat. "I invited Zweli. I suppose I, uh, forgot to mention it."

The table quieted. The fine hairs at Kyla's nape stiffened. Keren had delivered the news as dispassionately as he'd announce the time, but the words had a tangible effect on Kyla. Suddenly sick to her stomach, she scooted her chair back to make a run for the kitchen.

"Kyla?" Cady's voice from the archway between the dining room and the foyer paralyzed her in mid-sprint. "Look who's here."

Kyla's muscles fought the mental command to turn around, but she managed to do it in time to see Zweli greeting Christopher and Lee with handshakes.

"I didn't know you were coming, Zweli." Abby rested a hand on one hip and leaned the other on the food-covered buffet. "And you're alone."

"I was under the impression that this was a family affair." Zweli backed toward the archway. He removed his wool jacket and hung it on the coat tree in the foyer.

"You're late," Keren said around a mouthful of turnip greens.

"No, he's not," Cady said. Her eyes on Kyla, she nibbled on a warm cheese stick dipped in her own personal side dish of mayonnaise. "He was here at three on the button."

"It took him this long to get out of his car and come into the house," Ciel added. "Cady and I saw his car at the curb when we took the kids their plates."

"You girls don't miss a trick, do you?" Zweli laughed. "I don't see my angels!" he called.

Four pairs of female feet thundered from the kiddie room and Zweli soon found himself enveloped by eight arms that tried to hug him at once. Kyla, watching, resumed her seat as her nieces, from eleven-year-old Danielle to eighteen-month-old Claire, nearly wrestled Zweli to the Persian rug, fighting for his attention.

"How's my pretty princess?" he asked six-year-old Ella, whose arms were locked about his middle. "Sleeping okay?"

Her dark head bobbed in a nod. "Mama used the spray you gave her."

Kyla gave Ciel a questioning look. "The kids watched *Monsters, Inc.* a few weeks ago and Ella kept having bad dreams about Randall," Ciel explained, moving her head closer to Kyla's and keeping her voice low. "Lee and I were having to get up every night to check under the bed and in the closet, and Ella kept insisting that Randall was there and that we just couldn't see him. So Zweli gave us a can of Monster-B-Gone. He made a label and slapped it on a can of strawberry-scented air freshening spray. We give the room a little spritz at bedtime, and Ella sleeps through the night."

Kyla pinched back a smile as she watched Zweli cup Ella's heart-shaped face. "Have you drawn me any new pictures in school?" he asked her.

"I drew a spider in a web." Ella wriggled out of his arms and ran into the foyer to retrieve the drawing from her mother's bag.

Abigail danced in front of Zweli, who inched his way toward the dining table. "I got a happy face on my spelling test," she announced proudly.

"Spell rutabaga," he said.

"Ruta...what?" Her head tilted as she wrinkled her nose. "That's not on my spelling list."

"It's on all the third-grade spelling lists," he teased.

Abigail giggled. "I'm in the *second* grade."

"Oh, that's right." He stroked his chin. "So in second grade a happy face is a really good grade?"

"It means I got all my words right."

"I got all my words right," Ella repeated as she handed Zweli a wrinkled sheet of white paper covered in heavy black crayon strokes.

"I bet you can spell rutabaga," Zweli challenged.

Abigail thought about it for a short moment. "R...u...t..."

"R, u, t...," Ella echoed, pitching her voice higher.

"Stop it, stinkhead!" Abigail swung at her sister, but Ella danced out of reach.

"I didn't give birth to any stinkheads, Abigail," Ciel warned. "Apologize to your sister."

"I'm sorry you're a stinkhead," Abigail said sweetly.

His hands on his knees, Zweli bent over to speak softly to Abigail. "No one likes to hear ugly words coming from such a pretty mouth."

A brick-red blush dusted Abigail's caramel cheeks.

"Thus spake the voice of God," Lee chuckled.

"I'm sorry, Ella," Abigail said earnestly. With Zweli's eyes still on her, she gave her sister a brief hug before they retreated to the kiddie room.

"Hey, Dani." Zweli swung Danielle off her feet, which sent her long, wheat-colored ponytails swinging. "What's good today?"

"I helped Grandma with the roasted potatoes." She straightened the wire-rimmed glasses that framed her big dark eyes. "I put the rosemary and dill on them, and I arranged them in the baking dish."

"Well then, I think I'll try some of those potatoes first." Zweli set her on her feet and glanced toward the kiddie room. "You all might want to get back in there and see what C.J. and Clarence are up to with Sammy Z."

Previous victims of Clarence's dinnertime sabotage, the older girls zoomed back into the kiddie room. Claire, no longer in the shadow of her taller kin, basked in Zweli's full attention. "How are you, peanut?" He set a warm kiss in the amber-gold curls at the top of her head as he scooped her up in one arm.

"Hi, Sway," she responded, pronouncing his name as well as she could.

"Sit down, Sway." Cady patted the vacant seat beside her, which happened to face Kyla. "Pull up a plate."

Zweli obliged her, and Cady picked her daughter out of his arms.

"You put peas in my straw!" screeched Abigail's voice from the kiddie room.

"Good one, Clarence," Zweli called.

"Don't encourage him," Ciel reprimanded Zweli as she left the table to break up the fight likely to ensue in the kiddie room. "He's been acting out horribly lately."

"It's transference," Lee said. "The Gooch is still riding him at school, so Clarence picks on his cousins because he knows no harm will come of it."

"You sound just like a child psychologist," Cady said.

"I only moonlight as a financial investment systems advisor," Lee teased.

"I thought you spoke to The Gooch's teacher," Zweli said, aware of the name-calling and bullying Clarence had been enduring since the first day of school. The Gooch's taunts of "Smart Boy" and "Shorty" had steadily escalated into nastier names and devious little pranks.

"We did, and on Back-To-School night we talked to Mr. and Mrs. Gooch," Ciel said. "I mean Mr. and Mrs. Russom. The teacher thinks it's a case of immaturity on The Gooch's part, and the Russoms think Clarence is just being 'too sensitive.' "

Abby brought an extra plate and cutlery to the dining room. She stood by the buffet and firmly said, "What you need to do is stop calling that child The Gooch and keep a record of all the things he says and does to Clarence. Send a copy of it to the school principal, the Russoms, and the superintendent of the school system. That should be enough to scare the Gooches and their little Goochling into better behavior." She smiled at Zweli and her voice softened. "Just tell me what you want and I'll fix your plate for you, honey."

Kyla sat stunned at the sway "Sway" held over her female relatives. From baby Claire on up to Abby, every one of them adored him. She made herself president of that fan club as she looked at him across the wide table.

"Did you drive the Alfa Romeo?" Troy asked Zweli, who nodded. "Can I drive it later?"

"No," Clara said in sync with her husband's "Hell, no."

Cady handed Claire to Keren, who allowed her to eat sesame-ginger green beans from his plate. She crossed her forearms on the table and caught Kyla's gaze. "One by one, Mama's ducklings are finding their way back to the pond."

"I can't wait for Chiara to find her way home, too," Abby said anxiously. "She was here for only two days last Christmas, and I don't think she's planning on coming home at all for the holidays this year."

Cady raised her crystal goblet of ginger ale to Kyla. "We'll lure 'em back one at a time. Welcome home, little sister."

Beverages rose in a toast to Kyla. Zweli's still-empty glass hovered a second longer than everyone else's. "Welcome home, Ky," he said.

Once she looked at him across the table, she couldn't look away. He held her gaze even as Abby set a plate heaped with food before him.

I've missed you, Kyla wanted to say. With Zweli there at the table, it really did feel like her family had assembled to make a perfectly ordinary Sunday almost a holiday.

Zweli's dinner steamed pleasantly under his nose, but he couldn't turn his gaze from Kyla. She wore no makeup or jewelry. With her long hair in a sleek ponytail, and dressed in an elegant but understated black, long-sleeved dress, she looked sexy and sophisticated without even trying. Zweli wished that he were sitting beside her, to reacquaint himself with the perfumes of her skin and hair.

"Abby, why don't you join us this time?" Keren asked his mother-in-law. His inquiry was as much a part of Sunday dinner tradition as Abby's reluctance to give up her waitressing duties. "Don't you ever eat on Sundays?"

She waved her hand and picked up an empty bowl that had contained a fluffy mountain of cheese and chive mashed cauliflower. "I spent the whole day preparing food. The last thing I want to do is sit down and eat it."

"Hold on there, Mama," Cady started. "You weren't the only one in there after church, peeling, chopping, dicing, spicing, skinning, and stirring. Clara, Ciel and I helped to."

"You did a wonderful job on the fried okra and the oven-barbequed spareribs, Cady, and I thank you," Abby said with a curtsy. "The oven did most of the work on the ribs, though," she added under her breath before taking the empty bowl to the kitchen.

"I do what I can," Cady called after her mother. "I wonder how much cooking *you* could get done with twins running underfoot."

Abby popped back into the dining room. "If you'll recall, Miss Mother Of The Year, I helped your Grandma Claire prepare Sunday dinner with five little children running underfoot for years. When it came time to eat, every time I'd sit down to my plate, some little voice would pipe up. 'Mama, can you get me some more juice?' 'Mama, can you get me some more corn?' 'Mama, can you get me this?' 'Mama, can you get me that?' I haven't sat down for Sunday dinner with my children since Jimmy Carter left the White House.

"Monday through Saturday, I don't have to worry about feeding anyone other than myself, so come Sunday, I look forward to cooking for you all, and making sure that your plates stay full."

"And I don't mind getting here early to help," Cady said.

"Kyla was the biggest help today, if you're keeping score," Abby said. "For someone who doesn't know how to turn on a stove, Kyla does a wonderful job of putting together flavors and textures. She made the squash medley. It never would have occurred to me to use coriander and Italian parsley, and she used low-fat chicken broth in it instead of butter."

"Kyla's help would also explain the smoked turkey in the greens," Keren said as he set a wriggling Claire onto the floor. "Mom normally uses salt pork."

"What did you use the pomegranates for?" Zweli asked.

"Snacking." Kyla dropped her eyes and toyed with a thin lock of hair that had escaped her ponytail. "While I was helping Mama cook. Otherwise, I'd have eaten a whole dinner just tasting the dishes we prepared."

"Everything is wonderful," he said.

She looked at him and his heart banged against the wall of his chest. In the waning light of the afternoon sun, she had an ethereal, somber beauty that pulled at his heart and reminded him of Keren's words from the day before: *Don't be too hard on her, Z.*

"You haven't tasted it yet," Kyla said, tipping her head toward his plate. "How do you know it's wonderful?"

"It's always wonderful. Your mom is the best cook in town."

"That's what Greedy kept saying," Troy laughed. "That woman could *eat*."

"Who's Greedy?" Kyla asked.

"One of Sway's magnificent seven," Clara said with an eager smile. Zweli's eyes slowly closed in a wince.

Kyla looked from Zweli to the faces of her sisters, each of whom tried too hard to look innocent. "Is someone going to let me in on the joke?" Kyla asked.

"Greedy is one of Zweli's old girlfriends," Troy said as he cut into a thick slice of baked ham. "She's one of the seven worst he's ever brought here." He shrugged. "I thought she was kind of pretty, though."

Ciel smacked him on his shoulder. "That is why you should be in the kiddie room, big mouth," she whispered fiercely.

Kyla narrowed her eyes a bit at Zweli. "I'd like to hear more about Zweli and his magnificents."

"There was Ticktock," Cady said, grinning. "She had this thing with her jaw. It clicked when she chewed. It sounded just like the ticking of a clock."

"She had a temporomandibular anomaly, and it was real funny when you kept humming 'Hickory Dickory Dock' at the table, Cady," Zweli said wryly.

"I was just amusing my children," Cady laughed.

"Then there was Flash," Clara said.

"She had some serious bling bling on her grille," Troy laughed behind his loosely curled fist.

"She had braces," Clara explained, "and she was so worried about getting food stuck in them when she ate. So she would keep her lips open a little bit when she chewed, and you'd see all that metal catching the light. Imagine a pair of wind-up chattering teeth with tinsel tangled up in them. That's exactly how her mouth looked."

"Lord have mercy," Abby said from the kitchen. "I didn't know my girls could be so catty."

"Yes, you did," Ciel said. "We get it from you. You're the one who nicknamed Greedy."

Abby flew from the kitchen. "Let me tell you about Miss Greedy! She came to dinner with Zweli once, and she had the unadulterated audacity to show up here again the next Sunday, uninvited and alone, with a plastic container to take home a doggie bag."

"Or a doggie box, as the case happened to be," Lee corrected.

"That woman could eat like a man," Abby remarked before disappearing once more.

"Sling Blade was the worst," Cady said. "I haven't seen an underbite like hers since my last visit to the Museum of Natural History."

Zweli turned on Cady. "It wasn't that pronounced, and I never would've noticed it if you hadn't started grunting and mumbling like Billy Bob Thornton in that damn movie."

"Ummm hmm," Cady growled.

"I liked Huggies the best," Troy said, his dimples perking in a wide grin.

"No wonder, since she was practically your age," Clara said. "Where did you find that one, Zweli?"

He sighed. "She's a Rams cheerleader. I met her after a game last season."

"I miss Huggies," Troy said dreamily.

"You must miss the kiddie room, too," Ciel hissed. "You can go right back in there if you can't sit in here and behave."

"Do you remember Got to Go?" Cady laughed so hard she almost tipped over her glass of ginger ale.

Lee crossed his arms and legs and pursed his lips in an exaggerated impersonation of an impatient woman. " 'Zweli, we got to go,' " he mimicked in a nasal falsetto. " 'When you said we were going to dinner, I thought you meant someplace *real*.' " He scowled and scanned the room with staccato head motions. " 'I've never heard of a man bringing his woman to a family dinner when it's not even his family. We got to go!' "

Clara wiped away tears of laughter. "That woman sat in the living room all during dinner. She left by herself after Zweli gave her cab fare."

While her family enjoyed their hilarious walk down memory lane, Kyla recounted the number of magnificent dinner companions. "Who's the seventh?" she asked.

"We forgot Crazy Ass," Ciel said.

The laughter diminished to a few dark snickers. "I take it back. Sling Blade wasn't the worst," Cady said. "Crazy Ass wins that contest."

"Crazy Ass," Christopher repeated dreamily, picking at the corner of his mustache as he stared at nothing.

Clara gave him a shove.

"Crazy Ass seemed to have something to prove," Ciel said. "She was something of a flirt."

"That's how she got her nickname," Cady said to Kyla. "She brought her crazy ass up into this house and had the nerve to try and feed my husband a fried chicken liver."

"Oh, I remember that," Ciel said, covering her mouth with her fingers. "Then she tried to give Lee a backrub right here at the table." She turned to Kyla. "After dinner, when we were having coffee in the living room, she bent over right in front of Christopher, and she was wearing this short skirt and stockings, and not a stitch of underwear."

"Be fair, Ciel," Zweli said. "She was wearing a G-string."

"A G-string is not underwear," Ciel said.

"A G-string is for entertainment purposes only," said Clara.

"She just couldn't handle being in a room with so many beautiful women," Zweli said easily. "She had some insecurity issues."

"How did you know that she was wearing a G-string?" Kyla asked.

Holding Kyla's icy gaze, Zweli didn't miss a beat. "Christopher told me."

The table erupted in laughter, and almost against her will, Kyla joined in. She was glad Zweli was there and that he'd come alone, but she wanted to pinch herself for letting her guard down. His charms weren't confined to the women in her family, and they never would be. She'd be stupid to forget that. Especially when he looked at her with his heart in his eyes, the way he was now.

"Hey," Zweli called, trotting out of the house after Kyla and Troy, "where're you going?"

"Aunt Kyla's letting me drive her to the hardware store." Troy caught the car keys Kyla tossed to him, and then sprinted to the silver Lexus parked a few houses down.

"Time for a little home repair?" Zweli shoved his hands into his pockets. He had to, or he would have thrust his fingers into Kyla's hair to renew his memory of its softness.

"I'm picking out paint for my apartment," she said. "I'm officially moving on Friday and I want to start painting on Sunday."

"So you found a place." He rocked on his heels, waiting for her to volunteer the whereabouts of her new apartment. "Is it nearby?"

"It's on Kingshighway, near Forest Park." She studied her fitted black suede boots to avoid Zweli's gaze. If she looked into his eyes, she knew she'd fall into their jade and coffee depths and never find her way out again.

"Is it close to the hospital?" He took a step closer to her.

She pulled her black wrap closer about her shoulders to ward off a shiver that wasn't caused by the chilly evening. "It's close to Cady and Keren, too." She lifted her head to see what Troy was up to, but found herself staring at Zweli. "It's…"

"What?" he smiled.

"…got a bedroom," she finished, half in a daze. She shook herself out of it. "And an eat-in kitchen, central air, a balcony, and video surveillance," she rattled off as she hurried down the four steps that led to the sidewalk.

He followed her. "Do you need any help moving?"

"No, I'm all set. I recruited the troops." She covered half the distance between the house and her car. Troy was in the driver's seat, rocking the car to whatever music he'd put in the CD player.

"Kyla, wait." Zweli caught up to her, took her arm and turned her away from the car. He ran his hands along her upper arms, which kept her from fleeing. "Things don't have to be like this between us."

"Like what?" She met his gaze straight on.

He swallowed hard. In the odd purple light of the sunset, Kyla's dark honey eyes seemed to glow as if lit from within. No matter how annoyed or angry she was, the ugliness of the emotion never compromised the beauty of her eyes. They always had the gentle calm of a doe's, but as he gazed into them now, he was discomfited by the somberness in them. In that moment, he realized that something other than a longing for home and family had driven her from California.

"Things don't have to be awkward between us," he finally said. "All that stuff back there, about the magnificent seven...your sisters were exaggerating."

A single note of laughter escaped Kyla. "No, they weren't."

Zweli dropped his eyes. "Okay, they weren't, but those women weren't..." There was no way to finish the sentence without sinking further into the mess he'd created with his scattershot dating style.

"They didn't mean anything to you?" Kyla offered. She drew away a bit, afraid that she'd sounded as hopeful to Zweli as she had to her own ears.

Exactly, Zweli wanted to say. Instead he went with, "They were just friends."

"What's Crazy Ass's name?"

"Why?"

"Call me curious."

"I don't see what her name has to do with anything. I haven't seen her since I brought her to dinner."

"What's Greedy's name?" Kyla stepped out of Zweli's reach.

"Kyla, why—"

"You don't remember their names, do you?"

He uttered a short sigh of impatience. "They weren't memorable women."

"Or maybe there've been so many of them, you don't bother to learn their names." Kyla's mouth formed a perfect, petulant pout that Zweli itched to kiss. "What in the name of Heaven would possess you to bring dates to dinner with *my* family?"

"Self-defense!" he shouted in a fit of irritation. "Do you think it's easy for me to be in that house, to even be around Keren and Cady, and not think about you? I love your family like they're my own, but every time I was around them, all I did was wonder where you were and what you were doing. I had to arm myself against the memory of you, Kyla. That's why I brought those women here. Funny thing is, all I ended up doing was shooting myself in the foot."

Kyla's brow wrinkled in confusion. "How so?"

Because being with another woman in the company of your family made me see how much I still want to be with you, he thought. But what he said was, "No woman looks good in the company of the Winters sisters. You know that."

Kyla's stomach clenched. "Yeah. It's the story of my life," she mumbled before turning and heading for the car. "I'll see you, Z."

"Don't run off again," he called after her.

She stopped and slowly turned to face him. "What do you mean 'again?' "

"You ran from me three years ago when I proposed and you ran out on me again after Claire and Sammy were christened. If you're really here to stay, stay and talk to me."

"I didn't run out on you. I had a job in L.A.," Kyla said through gritted teeth. "I was trying to make something of myself." She whipped around and took three angry steps to the car before turning back to Zweli for a parting shot. "I was working, you jackass! I wasn't busy trying to date every woman in St. Louis! Where'd you find them anyway? They sound like rejects from the Ripley's Believe It or Not Dating Service."

"That the best you can do?" Zweli said calmly.

"Their *online* dating service," Kyla sneered.

"All right, woman, that's enough!" he erupted. "I admit it was stupid to bring dates to your mom's house, but what alternative did you leave me? I love your family, and you know what? They love me back. I want to share my life with them, and part of my life is dating." He threw an arm toward the house. "*They* understand that. Why can't you?"

"Because—" she started, but then bit her tongue before she blurted something she couldn't take back.

His eyes narrowed in his hunger for what she would say. He closed the short distance between them and laid a hand along her face. "Because what, Ky?" he asked gently.

"Because..." Her eyes searched his, mutely willing him to understand her feelings.

He grinned. "Because you're still in love with me, aren't you?"

"Because it's bad form," she snapped. She started for the car. "And at no point in our relationship did I ever tell you that I loved you!"

Troy must have been watching, because he hopped out of the driver's seat, trotted to the passenger door, and opened it. Kyla got in and he chivalrously waited until she'd collected the fringed tails of her wrap before he closed the door. With a neat salute to Zweli, he returned to the driver's seat.

Zweli watched as Troy lurched into the flow of traffic, then braked suddenly to avoid hitting what looked like the shadow of a tree.

Watching Kyla's man-sized nephew drive off with her made it too easy to envision some man driving her away after Sunday dinner with the family he'd come to view as his own. With hot pangs of jealousy souring the delicious meal he'd just consumed, Zweli went back into the house to find out more about Kyla's upcoming move.

CHAPTER THREE

"I like this." Cady leaned back to study the area of the living room wall she'd just finished painting. "I never would have guessed Cream of Wheat would make such a nice background color for this room."

"It's Tropic Sand, not Cream of Wheat." Kyla gave her scrawny black kitten a nudge as she passed Cady, carrying a freshly stirred can of paint. "The paint stylist at the hardware store said that pale, off-white colors could make a small room look bigger."

Christopher, a physicist-turned-carpenter upon his family's return to St. Louis, harrumphed. "Far be it for me to contradict the advice of a paint *stylist*, but the only way to make this room seem larger would be to knock out this wall." He used a knuckle to rap on the wall separating the living room from the kitchen. The hollow sound that resulted made him shake his head. "From the sound of it, we could probably push through it with our bare hands right now."

"I didn't invite you people over to insult my new living accommodations," Kyla said defensively.

"You invited us because you needed cheap labor." Keren softened the jibe with a kiss to Kyla's forehead.

"I don't mind spending a Sunday afternoon helping Aunt Kyla." Troy merrily slopped paint onto his roller and slapped it against a wall.

"He's been as high as a kite since you let him crash your car last Sunday night," Christopher called into the kitchen, where Kyla was painting the doorframe.

"It was only a little tap," Troy said.

"Against a Hummer," Christopher said, "and you're lucky the driver didn't call the police."

"Aunt Ky talked him out of it," Troy smiled. "He asked for her autograph and her phone number, too."

Cady joined Kyla in the kitchen. "Did you give it to him?"

"Of course not. The guy recognized me from *Lifeguards* and he drives a Hummer. He was an egotistical, macho stud wannabe seeing me as my character, not as a real person."

"What was your character's name again?" Lee asked. He put his hand to his ear and tilted his head toward the rest of the room.

"*Kati, with an 'i*,'" everyone answered as one.

Kyla laughed. "That has to be the worst catchphrase in the history of television. It said so much about what my character was supposed to be."

"I thought your character was a stripper who wanted to do something to benefit mankind, so she traded her G-string for a one-piece thong bathing suit and a CPR mask," Cady said.

"Kati saw her brother drown after he fell off of a dolphin watch cruise ship," Kyla corrected. "That's why she became a lifeguard."

"That's what I liked best about Kati," Troy said. He swiped his forearm across his jaw and managed to smear paint along his chin. "She had such concern for others."

"Then how come you never watched the show past the opening credits?" Christopher tossed his son a damp cloth to wipe his face. "Once Kati's slow-motion beach run was over, you switched to MTV."

"I watched the show," Troy insisted guiltily as he turned back to his painting. "Sometimes."

"My favorite episode was the one where Kati and those kids got trapped in the underwater cave," Lee started. He set down his paintbrush and dropped into a dramatic crouch. "There were sharks waiting in the water, an undersea sulfur leak spraying toxic fumes in the cave, and the oxygen in the tanks was running low." He cupped one hand over his nose and mouth and took a loud, dramatic breath from an imaginary oxygen tank. "Kati and all five kids had to share air, then the chubby kid with the inhaler started to go into some kind of seizure—"

"I lived it," Kyla said quietly to Cady. "I don't need to have it reenacted."

"Lee's just playing around." Cady put her paintbrush in a bucket of water in the sink and began washing her hands. "He and Ciel and the kids never missed an episode of *Lifeguards*. I think they have them all on tape."

"Great," Kyla said woodenly. "The boxed DVD set of Season One will be out in time for Christmas."

"Does *Lifeguards* really embarrass you?"

Kyla picked up her paint-speckled kitten and hugged it to her chest as she leaned back against the edge of the sink. "It was a good job, but it wasn't what I went to Hollywood to do. I became a black Chrissy Snow, and it was good for the show. Sucked for me, though. Every job I went up for after that was the same damn thing. Kati with an 'i' is the rookie barrister at an eccentric San Francisco law firm. Kati with an 'i' is the gum-popping girlfriend of a master car thief in the Bronx. Kati with an 'i' is the lovable yet incompetent nurse at an inner city hospital."

Cady scratched between the kitten's ears. "Someone actually made that last show?"

Kyla nodded. "It was cancelled before the pilot even aired, but the actress who took the dumb nurse part is now starring in a show about a single mother who works as a waitress by day and a private eye by night. She was nominated for a Golden Globe last year."

"Did she win?"

"No."

"Then who cares?"

"I care, Cady." Kyla's voice broke. "I worked so hard for crumbs out there. It makes me so angry and sick and…and…"

"Jealous?" Cady laid a gentle hand on her sister's shoulder.

Kyla slumped. "Yes. I hate to admit it, but sometimes I'm so jealous that it makes my insides hurt. I never had the right formula, Cady. Success out there is built on talent, timing, and opportunity, and not necessarily in that order."

"You've got scads of talent, Ky. You always have. Do you remember the time I broke your Baby Alive doll?"

Kyla laughed dryly. "You banged her against the banister. Her head popped up, but it didn't pop off, and the workings of her robotic throat were exposed. Her mouth kept making dry sucking noises and I had nightmares for about a week."

"Well, that's beside the point," Cady said quickly. "I went to you, and I had the doll behind my back, and I said that I had some bad news for you. You were only five, but your face wrinkled up, your bottom lip began to tremble, and you brought your hands to your face. I showed you the doll and you fell to your knees, wailing and clutching at your hair. You took Baby Alive and cradled her and wept over her. You were rocking back and forth, muttering about the good times the two of you used to have. Then Clara came and said that she'd just made chocolate pudding, and zip!" Cady snapped her fingers. "Just like that, the tears stopped, you dropped Baby Alive on the floor, and you went into the kitchen and pushed your face up to the eyebrows into a big bowl of pudding. You were five, and you gave the performance of a lifetime. That's why we started calling you Susan Lucci behind your back. Your tears never worked on us after that, by the way. We knew that most of the time, you were just hamming it up to get us in trouble with Mama."

"Acting is the only thing I've ever been good at," Kyla said. "It's the only thing I truly love, and I hate that I'm giving it up."

"Who says you have to give it up?"

"Cady, I'm too old to—"

"Hold on there, kid," Cady warned. "Remember that I'm older than you are before you finish that sentence."

"By Hollywood standards, I'm too old to keep knocking on doors that won't open."

"Is that why you came home?" Cady asked. "Because you gave up in California?"

Kyla turned and reached for a roll of paper towels. She tore one off and used it to mop her sweaty brow. "I needed a change of scenery. I needed something familiar. Something comfortable."

"Something…," Cady lifted an eyebrow, "or someone?"

"Damn these radiators!" Kyla loudly evaded the inquiry and stepped into the living room. "Christopher, isn't there something in that fat toolbox of yours that you can use to turn down the heat?"

"I'm a wood stylist, not a plumber." Christopher shook sweat from the damp ends of his red hair. "Your landlord has to know that your heat is stuck at eighty degrees. If the previous tenant hadn't told him, he would have found it out during his walk-through before he rented the unit to you."

"He said that I needed a new thermostat, and that he'd have it installed before I moved in." Kyla squatted at Christopher's toolbox and sorted through it.

"What are you looking for?" Lee asked.

"This." She lifted a wrench that was longer than her forearm.

"You can't fix a thermostat with a wrench," Christopher said.

"No, but I can fix my lyin' ass landlord," Kyla said.

Cady quickly moved to block the door. "Kiddo, you have just a little too much aggression right now, even for you."

Kyla dropped the wrench. The thing landed on the glossy hardwood floor with an eardrum-shattering bang. "Fine. I'll call him before I go downstairs and bust in his front door."

"What's gotten into her all of a sudden?" Keren asked Cady once Kyla was out of earshot.

"I sort of brought up He Who Must Not Be Named," Cady whispered.

"Zweli?" Keren said.

"No, Lord Voldemort." Cady gave her husband a teasing kiss before crossing the room to take the phone from Kyla.

"Dammit, he's not answering!" Kyla hollered as she handed the phone over to Cady. "I know he's down there."

"Hi, Mr. Landlord," Cady said sweetly into the man's answering machine. "I'm calling from Unit 10E and we have a little problem that I was hoping you could solve. We're melting up here. It's a lovely, sixty-eight degree September day outside, but it feels like the middle of July in 10E. Kyla mentioned that a new thermostat was to be installed prior to her taking possession of this unit, but we happened to notice that the installation hasn't taken place just yet. I'm so sorry to interrupt your weekend, but we were hoping that you could give us a call and let us know when we can expect that new thermostat. You have Kyla's number, but if I can be of any service, please call me at the law firm of Brown, Fuller, King & Winters-Clark. My name is Ciel Winters-Clark, and my number there is—"

"Cady!" Keren interrupted.

"Wha—Hello, Mr. Landlord," Cady said into the phone. "You're home after all. Here's Kyla."

Kyla took the phone, floored by her sister's audacity. *Cady would have made it in Hollywood*, she thought as she put the phone to her ear.

Three hard knocks on her front door brought Kyla into the living room. "That was quick," she remarked.

"When your landlord said he'd be up soon, I guess he meant as soon as he hung up the phone," Lee said. "Remind me to impersonate my wife the next time someone ticks me off."

Kyla straightened her T-shirt and cutoffs before opening the door. "Thank you so much for—" It wasn't the landlord. "Zweli," she said, stunned, as he stepped past her and into the apartment.

"Hey, everybody," he greeted.

Kyla slammed the door and went after him. "What are you doing here?"

"Someone might have mentioned that we were painting your apartment today," Keren confessed, taking Kyla's arm as she tried to pass him. "Zweli offered to help."

"If I'd wanted him here, I'd have invited him myself, Keren," she griped.

Cady stepped up to speak low near Kyla's ear. "I invited him. It's been a week since your last falling out. I figured you needed another chance to…do whatever it is you two do."

Kyla snorted and aimlessly kicked the recently painted baseboard with her bare foot.

"Look," Cady said. "You and Zweli have a lot of unfinished business that you need to take care of if for no other reason than to give me and Keren some peace. We've got you on one side, irritable and pining, and Zweli on the other side, impatient and heartbroken."

"Irritable and pining?" Kyla cut in.

"More like loud and mean," Keren mumbled.

Cady took Keren's arm in a loving yet protective grasp. "What he means is that you've been a little on the belligerent side since you saw Zweli at Mama's house last week." Before Kyla could angrily interrupt, Cady calmed her with, "We totally understand how difficult it must be. You just moved back home, you're getting your bearings, and you have this unresolved business with Zweli. You guys never had a real finish. Sex always complicates things, even when it's ancient history."

Kyla blinked in surprise. "Zweli and I never had sex." She glanced at Zweli, who had already stripped off his long-sleeved shirt and was painting in his white T-shirt alongside Lee and Christopher. She also noticed that Troy had inched his way closer. Intent on eavesdropping, he didn't seem to realize that he was now moving his paint roller mindlessly within the empty space of the kitchen doorway.

"Troy," Kyla began evenly, "if you ever want to crash my car again, you might want to give minding your own business a try."

"Yes, ma'am," he said before briskly snapping back to his original position.

Kyla stood almost head-to-head with Cady. "Zweli and I never slept together. He…" She grabbed the tail of Cady's T-shirt and pulled her into the kitchen. "He turned me down."

"Zweli?" Cady asked incredulously. "Zweli Randall?"

"It was right around when Grandma died. I was feeling so…so…"

"Numb," Cady finished softly.

"Yes. And…" Kyla stared at the ceiling as she sought the right word.

"Alone," Cady offered with a knowing glance at her husband in the other room. "I was at that place, too, for a long time. I know the furniture."

"I made a pass at Zweli. He said no. When I look back on the whole thing, I realize that he did the right thing. I didn't want him so much as I wanted to feel something other than pain and grief."

"Remember when Grandma Claire died?" Kyla asked softly.

"Won't ever forget it," Cady sighed.

"It was after the Raines-Hartley holiday party. It was late, and Zweli and I were sitting in the hospital cafeteria drinking some awful vending-machine coffee. We meant to stay just for a little while, to sort of decompress after the party, but we ended up spending the rest of the night there, just talking. I don't even remember him saying anything about himself. He mostly just listened while I sat there, rambling on, me-deep in conversation, so to speak. When I think back on it, that night shouldn't have meant anything, but…I don't know…"

"But it meant everything, didn't it?"

Kyla nodded. Tears threatened to spill over her lower lashes, but she blinked them away.

Cady aimed her sister toward the doorway. "Go in there, grab a paintbrush, and start painting. That's all you need to do right now. The rest will write itself." She gave Kyla a little push in Zweli's direction.

Kyla had taken two hesitant steps when a knock sounded on the door. With an audible sigh of relief, she raced to it, and once again, it wasn't the landlord.

"Food!" Troy cried in delight as the aroma of fresh-baked pizza entered the apartment along with the deliveryman. He dropped his roller in a shallow pan of paint and hopped over a bunched drop cloth. "I'll take those," he offered. The Angelo's Pizza deliveryman slid a stack of pizza boxes from an insulated carrier while Kyla retrieved her handbag. Troy took the pizzas and set them on a box in the middle of the living room as Kyla paid for them.

"Thanks, lady," the deliveryman said, acknowledging the fat tip Kyla had given him. He started away, but doubled back before Kyla had a chance to close the door. "Hey, you look familiar, lady," he said. His eyes roamed over her, taking in her denim cutoffs and her sleeveless white T-shirt. His gaze stopped at her breasts, and Kyla suddenly wished that she was wearing one of her utility Playtex Living Bras instead of the cute La Perla number she had on. "You're Kati!" he finally said.

"With an 'i'," she recited along with him.

With a smile that showed every tooth, the deliveryman blushed as he said, "I bet you get this all the time, but can I have your autograph? I'm gonna need proof if I go back to Angelo's and tell everybody that I met Kati from *Lifeguards.*"

Kyla quickly glanced over her shoulder. Her relatives were pushing boxes together to form makeshift tables and chairs. Autograph seekers were a part of Kyla's life, but judging from the way Zweli stood to one side staring at the deliveryman through narrowed eyes, it was a part of her life that he wasn't keen on.

Let me make this quick, Kyla thought as she accepted the deliveryman's pen. He turned to let her use his back as a writing board. "What's your name?" she asked.

"Javier. But you can write it to Javy. Yeah. Write, 'To Javy, my number-one stud.' That'll make the fry cooks back at Ange's crazy."

Kyla hurriedly scribbled the autograph on the back of Javier's delivery receipt and then handed it back to him.

"Thanks, Kati," he said, looking at it. "I mean Kyla." He winked. "With an 'a.'"

Kyla gave him a polite, rehearsed laugh. Behind her, she heard a noise that sounded remarkably like a grunt.

"It was nice meeting you, Javier," she said.

"Javy." He took her hand and gave it a hard shake. "And believe me, the pleasure is all mine."

His eyes went to her chest again and Kyla took a short step to the side, making sure Javy had a good view of her strapping brothers-in-law.

Zweli stepped full into view. "The pizza's getting cold, Ky."

"Thanks, honey," she said loudly.

"Honey?" echoed several curious voices faintly behind Kyla.

"Thanks again, Javy," Kyla said. "I'll, uh, see you."

"Oh, you bet you will." Javier grinned from ear-to-ear as he backed away. "I'm going to make sure that I get all your deliveries from now on."

A chill skipped along Kyla's vertebrae even as she nodded pleasantly and closed the door. She rested her forehead against the door and engaged the deadbolt, and made a mental note to have a police bar installed along with the new thermostat.

"You look funny."

She lifted her head to see Zweli standing at her right shoulder. "That one had The Look in his eyes."

The left side of Zweli's mouth lifted in a grin. "What look?"

Kyla started for the pizza. "The I-Want-To-Store-Your-Head-In-A-Cooler-In-My-Basement look."

"He seemed harmless enough." Zweli opened a pizza box and took a slice of the steaming, gooey pepperoni pie inside.

"They all seem harmless, at first." Kyla started opening pizza boxes.

Zweli looked down to see a four-legged puff ball winding its tiny body in and out of his ankles. "Hey, puss. What's your name?"

"Cicely Tyson," Kyla said.

"Why did you name her *that*?" Troy laughed.

"Because she's so sleek and dark?" Lee guessed.

"No, because her is such a gweat widdle actress," Kyla answered in baby talk, scooping up the kitten and rubbing its tiny nose against hers.

"I've been meaning to ask you what happened to Esther Rolle," Cady said.

"She died while I was in San Francisco, filming that stupid TV-movie." Kyla set the kitten on the floor. It immediately returned to

Zweli's ankles. "She was twelve years old when I got her from the animal shelter four years ago. She had a good run."

Kyla found the pizza she wanted. It was sitting alone on top of a box marked KITCHEN.

"You really have left California behind," Cady said. "I haven't seen you eat pizza in years."

"This one is buffalo-style chicken tofu with soy cheese," Kyla said. "You can take the girl outta California, but you can't take California outta the girl."

"Even so," Cady said, "it's good to see you eating again." She bit into a giant triangle of olive and mushroom pizza. She had to wind a long string of melted cheese around her finger to break its connection between her mouth and the rest of the slice. "The thing I used to hate about your visits home was that you'd never eat anything other than brown rice and vegetables sautéed in fat-free chicken broth."

"The thing I hated about her visits was that I never heard about them until the day after she'd gone back to Cali," Zweli said. With a pointed stare at Kyla, he used a white paper napkin to wipe a dab of pizza sauce from his mouth.

"Well," Troy began around a jaw full of pizza, "maybe Aunt Ky felt funny around you. Sex complicates relationships."

Christopher began to choke.

"I've only *heard* that sex complicates relationships," Troy told his father as he slapped him on the back.

"Knock it off, before I start slapping back," Christopher coughed.

"I'll get you some water," Kyla offered.

"I've got some right here." Christopher took a long swig of the bottled water he'd brought with him. "Kyla, I think Troy and I should be heading out. He's got homework due tomorrow that he hasn't even started."

"How did you know?" Troy asked.

"Kid, you always have homework that you start at the last minute on Sunday," Christopher said. "And every Sunday, your mother and I are pulling our hair out, trying to help you get it done. I've been through the tenth grade once and that was enough. I shouldn't have to go through it again."

"You wouldn't have to help me so much if you let me go to public school," Troy grumbled.

"You think so, huh? You and I have a lot to talk about on the way home," Christopher said warningly. "Say your goodbyes."

"You mean goodnights, don't you?" Lee asked.

"It depends on how our father-son tête-à-tête goes," Christopher answered.

"We should be heading out, too," Cady said. "Mama's probably ready to throw Sammy out of a window, and Claire is probably scared to death that she'll actually do it."

Keren collected grease-stained paper plates from Cady and Lee and stacked them on his before tossing them into the cardboard box Kyla was using as a temporary trash can. "The last time Abby kept the kids, Sammy cut Claire's hair while she was napping."

"He can use scissors?" Kyla marveled. "He's only a year and a half old."

"We're lucky he used scissors and didn't go for the knife drawer in the kitchen," Keren said.

"My godson is a natural-born surgeon," Zweli said.

"*Our* godson," Kyla corrected. "And maybe he'll grow up to be a hairdresser."

"Not in this lifetime," Zweli replied.

Lee picked up his sweater, which he'd draped over a box. "We're going to leave you two to argue over your children. Will we see you at dinner Sunday, Zweli?"

Zweli looked at Kyla, who stood with her arms crossed over her chest, scowling. "I'm not sure," he answered cautiously. "Something tells me I may not survive the next five minutes."

Zweli made it through the next two hours with Kyla, most likely because she didn't speak to him. Working side by side, they finished the living room before moving to the bathroom. It took forty-eight minutes to give the bathroom its first coat of Seafoam Splendor, and Kyla was acutely aware of Zweli's presence as they worked in the close confines of the miniscule room.

As she did the edgework around the mirror, standing back-to-back with Zweli, she couldn't tear her gaze from his reflection. She watched the easy grace of his long arm muscles working beneath his caramel skin as he stroked the paint onto the wall. His T-shirt hugged the broad shoulders that tapered to a trim waist.

It's not fair, Kyla thought. *Men become more beautiful with age while women like me just fall apart.*

When she caught her own image in the mirror, Kyla saw the inaccuracy of her thought. Since leaving California, she'd put on a few pounds and they'd given her face a fullness that made her look more youthful. Her eyes seemed brighter, probably because she was sleeping at night rather than spending up to sixteen hours a day in heavy makeup under bright hot lights on a film set. Her hair was an utter mess, but it was nothing that a comb and brush couldn't fix. Winters women aged well, and Kyla was pleased to see that she was no exception to that.

But when Zweli turned around and caught her smiling at herself in the mirror, she saw the true definition of beauty. *No wonder I liked Seafoam Splendor,* she told herself. *It's the same damn color as Zweli's eyes.*

He stood so close now. Despite the heat of the room, she still felt the warmth of his chest through the few inches separating them. She met his eyes in his reflection, and the unmistakable heat she saw there made her tingle.

She shook herself free of his image and stepped outside the bathroom. "You, uh, didn't have to stay."

"I didn't mind."

"I think it might be best if you left now." She took three steps down the short corridor and went back into the living room. Zweli followed her, but he turned into the kitchen and started water running in the sink.

"Mind if I ask why you're kicking me out?"

"I'm tired, Zweli." *I'm tired of thinking about you all the time, and tired of wondering where your true heart lies.* "When I'm tired I always let my defenses down."

He used paper towels to rub the remaining paint from his hands. "And you think you need to protect yourself from me?"

"Don't I?"

"I'm just trying to be friendly."

"There's an undercurrent of hostility towards me every time I'm around you," Kyla accused. "I don't enjoy it, and I certainly won't put up with it here in my own home."

"Home?" he laughed. "You call this shoebox a home? The walk-in closet in my bedroom is bigger than this place." He exited the kitchen and in six long strides he was standing by the living room windows, which were floor-to-ceiling affairs covered by musty brown plaid drapes that had been abandoned by the previous tenant. "You don't have anything that makes this place even remotely inviting, like a sofa or a television or a sound system."

Kyla marched over to the drapes and yanked on the cord that controlled them. The drapes leaped apart and shimmied to either side of the windows, revealing a vista-view of the sun setting beyond the lush greenery of Forest Park. "It's tiny, but it gets great light," she said defensively.

He refused to acknowledge the lovely spectacle before him. He waved an arm, encompassing the kitchen and dining areas. "You don't have dishes or cooking implements." He began walking toward the one room he had yet to see. "I'll bet you don't even have a bed—"

He shut up immediately upon seeing the huge four-poster occupying most of the floor space in Kyla's bedroom. Zweli had dated an antiques dealer for three months and had learned enough about the trade to know that the maple-stained ash bed frame was a genuine piece of art. "This is some bed," he said. "Frame," he quickly amended. "Bed frame."

"It was my grandmother's." Kyla smoothed out a tiny wrinkle in the pale satin duvet covering the queen-sized mattress. "It's been in my family for over a century. One of my great-greats made it. He was a doctor, but he liked to work with wood as a hobby."

Zweli ran his fingertips lightly over the figures of wheat and flowers carved into the headboard.

"His name was Jacob Winters, and he grew up on a ranch in Juniper Falls."

"Missouri?" Zweli used a finger to trace the long details carved into the post nearest him.

"Yep. His father, Quentin Winters, died in the Civil War at Fort Pillow. Arsonists killed his mother and grandmother in Juniper Falls a few years after. He and his sister were taken in by the white rancher who'd served in the war with Quentin. The rancher was a doctor, and supposedly that's why Jacob went into medicine."

"Your family has such a rich history. It's one of the things I love about it."

"Cady could tell you more about us Winters folk than I can." She crawled across the bed to the unpacked box marked CLOTHES that she was using for a nightstand. Lying on her stomach, she rifled through a shorter box full of papers and folders. "I've got some chapters of the book she's been working on for the past couple of years. It's supposed to be Grandma's biography, but it's really the story of the whole Winters family. It's really good, too. Cady dug up some really interesting stuff. One of my great uncles was a darts champion on Whidbey Island."

"Where's that?"

"Off the coast of Washington state. My people really got around."

Zweli grunted an acknowledgement. He stared at Kyla's backside, and the sight was so pleasing it left his mouth too dry to speak.

With a thick sheaf of dog-eared papers in her hand, she scooted back to Zweli's side of the bed. "These are just the first five chapters.

The book starts with the purchase of a slave in Mississippi, who was renamed Ismael Winters by his Irish owners. There are so many layers to Cady's book. Ismael's story illustrates the sociological aspects of how insidious slavery was by showing how easily the oppressed came to this country and became oppressors themselves. She actually managed to track down a letter written by Ismael's owner, talking about how much he hated the English because Britain had enslaved his Irish ancestors.

"Cady also ferreted out a red-headed Italian sailor who spent some time in the Gulf Coast region of Louisiana with a woman who later married into the Winters family. She had a child that was rumored to have been fathered by this Italian, but the baby was totally accepted and raised as a Winters."

"So you're part Italian?"

"I guess. One hundred and fifty years dilutes the genetic pool somewhat."

Zweli sat beside Kyla and looked down at the chapters resting on her lap. "Cady won't let me read it until it's finished. She says—"

"What?" Kyla asked softly, her gaze probing his.

He looked at his hands and fisted them to keep from laying his palm on the burnished gold skin of her thigh. "She says the book won't be finished until our chapter is written."

"Hmm."

"That's it? 'Hmm?' "

"I don't know what to say." She set the chapters on her pillow. Swallowing back a lump of anxiety, she said. "Maybe Cady knows something that I don't."

"Your sister is a very perceptive lady. Sometimes it's easier to see something for what it truly is when you're on the outside looking in."

"I guess I'm trapped on the inside because I'm as blind and disoriented as a star-nosed mole above ground," Kyla admitted. "Why are you here, Zweli? Why were you at my house last week, and why—"

He stopped her litany of questions with a soft kiss to her lips. She drew a long, shivery breath that left her light-headed as she turned slightly into his chest. It occurred to her to move, to get off the bed before she got into trouble. But touching her only with his lips and the softness of his breath, he held her in place.

This wasn't the breathless, hungry kiss she had fantasized about sharing with him. Although no less passionate, this kiss was more dangerous in its sweet simplicity. In the way that a whisper could have more impact than a shout, Zweli's tender kiss gave her neither the will nor the reason to withdraw. She wrapped her arms around his shoulders and pulled him with her onto the bed. She gave herself completely to his kisses, which grew more eager, more insistent, as her hands moved over his back and shoulders.

A hot coil of tension tightened within her as every part of her yearned for the man in her arms. She slid her knee along his outer thigh, and when he shuddered in response, she slipped her hand into the back of his jeans.

Zweli released a short, choppy breath. For a moment, he felt sixteen again, with no control over his responses. Kyla made it all but impossible to remember that he was a full-grown, experienced man who knew how to give as good as he got. His whole body hardened with the effort it took to hold back, to enjoy this moment that he had awaited for such a long time.

He half-covered her body with his and plunged his fingers into her hair. The thick dark strands were as cool and soft as corn silk, and as Zweli nuzzled the soft place at the base of her ear, he delighted in her citrusy vanilla scent.

"You always smell good enough to eat," he chuckled near her ear. He tasted her earlobe, and her toes curled.

She cupped his face. He turned his head just enough to kiss her palm as she said, "I can't imagine that you're still hungry. You just ate a whole pizza."

As if on cue, Zweli's stomach growled. He eased down her body, kissing his way to the low neckline of her T-shirt. Just as his fingers tugged at the springy fabric covering her right breast, his pants began to buzz.

With a loud groan of frustration, he reached into his back pocket and took out his beeper. He glanced at the digitized number in the text box and frowned. "I have to call the hospital."

"The phone in the kitchen is hooked up. Is everything okay?"

Instead of answering, he went into the living room. Following him, Kyla saw him lift his long-sleeved shirt from a box and grab his cell phone from beneath it. He dialed in the number from the beeper while Kyla waited quietly. When the other party answered the call, the volume on Zweli's phone was loud enough for Kyla to hear a woman's voice.

"I hate to interrupt whoever you're doing on your night off," the voice began.

"Is this call about a patient, Doctor?" Zweli asked in a hard voice.

" 'Doctor,' huh…it's like that now, Zweli?" the woman said.

He grimaced. "The patient, Barbara."

"Ephraim Davis coded two hours ago. The team worked on him for fifty-one minutes but couldn't get him back. I pronounced him. I'm sorry, Zweli. I know he was one of your favorites." Barbara gave him a few seconds to absorb the news before she continued. "I know how you must be feeling. Why don't you meet me at the Stagecoach Inn after my shift tonight? Just for drinks. And if something more comes of it, well, maybe it'll help take your mind off Mr. Davis."

A ball of coldness formed in Zweli's chest as he rubbed his eyes with his thumb and forefinger. "I can't." He hunched his shoulders and spoke more quietly into the phone. "Listen, I have to go. Thanks."

He hung up over Barbara's next words, which sounded angry.

Zweli's vacant expression dulled the needles of jealousy pricking at Kyla. "Is your patient okay?" she asked.

Shaking his head, he sank onto the nearest heavy box. "It's always the good guys," he sighed.

She went to him and closed her arms around him, cradling his head to her chest. His arms went tight around her middle. "I have to go to the hospital," he said. "It's important, otherwise I'd stay right here and—"

"I understand." She tipped his face toward hers and kissed the corner of his mouth. "Go."

He slowly stood and grabbed his shirt and car keys. "I'm sorry, Kyla. One of these days we'll get our timing right."

"Maybe that call was a sign." She smiled wanly as she accompanied him to the door and opened it for him. "Maybe it kept us from doing something in haste."

Standing in the corridor, he leaned back into the apartment. Expecting a kiss, her breath caught in her chest. Zweli brought his mouth close to her ear, but it wasn't for a kiss. "That call was just that…a phone call," he whispered. "And I promise that when we do 'something,' it won't be in haste."

Raines-Hartley Hospital was less than a mile from Kyla's apartment building. Zweli arrived at the hospital in five minutes, but he couldn't bring himself to leave the car. Idling in the farthest spot on the roof of the parking garage, he stared, unblinking, at the city streets five stories below.

The cold emptiness he'd felt upon first hearing the news of Ephraim's death was thawing into grief. Losing patients was a part of medicine, and Zweli was usually equipped to handle the losses. But Ephraim affected him differently. "Eph," as everyone had called him, was a thirty-eight-year-old father of two who had beaten the odds for a long time. He had a congenital heart anomaly that should have killed him before his twentieth birthday, but he'd lasted twice as long as anyone could have predicted, and he hadn't wasted a second of the time he'd had.

Zweli thought back on all of his conversations with Eph and his family, and he admired the man that much more. Eph hadn't spent his life watching the clock, waking up each day wondering if it would be his last. He'd spent his time living. He'd found and married a woman he'd called his "dream come true." He had a son and daughter who adored him, and he owned a delivery business that he'd started in college, a business that had grown to pull in enough to pay for two sets of private school tuition, yearly vacations to Florida and Hilton Head Island, a completely tricked out Lincoln Navigator, and a six-bedroom colonial in one of the poshest sections of West County.

Zweli found himself envying Eph's short life, not because of material possessions but because of the life and love Eph was leaving behind. His life had meant something. His time on Earth might have been short, but every moment had counted, and he'd had a beautiful family to share it.

Eph had everything, Zweli thought. *Everything I want.* He tightly gripped his steering wheel. "Even if you have it for just one day, it makes all of life worth living," he said aloud. "And I want it with Kyla."

Zweli got out of the car, slammed the door shut and activated his alarm. Practicing his remarks in his head as he went, he walked briskly to the cardiac care unit. The sooner he spoke with Mrs. Davis, the sooner he could return to Kyla.

CHAPTER FOUR

"I'm here to see Dr. Randall," Kyla told the nurse sitting behind the reception desk in the cardiac care unit.

The woman wore a whimsical penguin-printed surgical tunic that contradicted the bland light in her pale eyes, which studied Kyla over the top of bifocals. "Is Dr. Randall expecting you?" she asked flatly.

"No, but—"

"Then he's with a patient." The nurse dropped her eyes to paperwork on the desktop. Without looking at Kyla again, she slapped a pink memo pad in front of her. "Leave your name, a number, and the reason for your visit, and I'll make sure the doctor gets the message."

Kyla began to feel uncomfortable. "I'm not a patient or anything like that," she explained hesitantly. "I'm…well…"

The nurse folded her hands on the desk and leaned toward Kyla. "Let me guess. You're his sister?"

"No." Kyla took a step back.

"His cousin?" the nurse supposed.

"I'm not family," Kyla managed, feeling sicker by the second. "I'm just a friend." *For how much longer remains to be seen.*

The nurse pinned her with a skeptical stare before tapping the pink pad. "Leave a message. Dr. Randall will get it."

Kyla picked up a ballpoint pen and pulled the memo pad nearer. "Dr. Randall has a lot of sisters that visit?"

Her eyes still on her work, the nurse said, "The man must have grown up in a shoe. His sisters are all pretty, they're all young, and I've never seen the same one twice."

Kyla tapped the end of the pen against the memo pad twice before setting it aside. "I don't have a message after all. I'm sorry for interrupting you." She turned to leave and took a step that left her square in the path of Dr. Barbara Shute. "Excuse me," she said, hoping she wouldn't be recognized as she tried to sidestep the doctor.

Barbara stepped neatly into her way. "It's…Kyla, right? You must be here to see Zweli."

"He's busy," Kyla said with a brittle smile. "I was just leaving."

Barbara took her arm. "I just saw him. He's with a patient but he should be finishing up soon. I'll take you to his office."

Even though Kyla pulled against her, Barbara looped her arm through Kyla's and dragged her back the way she had come. "Well, what do you know?" Barbara said, halting ten yards away from a small lounge area near the elevators. "There's Zweli now."

Territorial pride rushed through Kyla at the sight of him. His light wool trousers and shirt were impeccably tailored, as usual, and his shoes were the height of Italian fashion. Since he wasn't wearing his white coat at the moment, he looked more like a male model than a doctor. Kyla was so taken by his handsome appearance, she didn't notice the woman he was talking to until Barbara pointed her out.

"Oh, my. That's not a patient," Barbara said with exaggerated surprise.

Kyla's jaw clenched. Barbara wasn't much of an actress, so Kyla easily saw how much she was enjoying the little scenario she'd ushered her into.

"That's so Zweli," Barbara laughed lightly.

"What's so Zweli?" Kyla asked, regretting it as soon as the words left her mouth.

"Hitting on the wife of a patient he lost last night," Barbara whispered behind her hand.

Kyla couldn't hear what he was saying, but her eyes dissected every nuance of movement between Zweli and the petite, mocha-skinned woman he spoke to. Zweli was much taller than her, which probably explained why he lowered his head and leaned in when he spoke to her. The woman clutched crumpled tissues to her nose and Zweli took another step toward her. When he began stroking her upper arms, Kyla's stomach clenched.

"Zweli's always had great timing," Barbara said. "The man knows when a woman is ripe for him, and he won't give up until he gets what he wants. But I guess you know about that better than anyone else."

"What the hell is that supposed to mean?" Kyla was ready to snatch off her shoes and earrings and give Barbara a good old-fashioned ass-whuppin' right there in the cardiology ward.

"My dear," Barbara said with a sugary smile, "you're the one that got away. Love is a game and no one plays it better than Zweli. Except you, perhaps, because the man has been positively unpredictable since we ran into you." She lowered the tone and temperature of her voice. "I know you don't want to marry him, or else you wouldn't have refused his ring. Why don't you just sleep with him and get it over with, so the rest of us can get back to business as usual?"

Kyla quivered with rage. She wanted to choke the smarmy grin off Barbara's face and to put her foot through Zweli's stomach. She settled for a little performance.

"Zweli and I are just friends," she said merrily. "I'm not his type." She gave Barbara a deliberate wink, then started away.

"Wait a minute." Barbara pursued her. "What's Zweli's type?"

"He likes big, flat, billboard asses," Kyla said airily. "The bigger the better." With a short wave of her fingers, she made her way toward the elevators at the opposite end of the corridor. She looked over her shoulder to see Barbara self-consciously tugging the back of her white coat down over her backside as she walked toward Zweli.

"Open up, Kyla!" Zweli matched each word with a fist against Kyla's door. "I know you're in there because I can see your shadow under the door."

A loud creak of a floorboard signaled the disappearance of the shadow at the seam where Kyla's door met the floor.

"You're behaving like a damn teenager," Zweli said. "You came all the way down to the hospital to see me. Why didn't you have the receptionist page me?"

"She didn't have time," Kyla shouted through the door. "She was too busy fielding messages from all of your sisters and cousins!"

"Look, I had a life while you were gone. I won't apologize for it because it has nothing to do with what you and I have now."

"What do we have, Zweli? It can't be much, considering the way you were groping that woman in the hallway today."

"What...?" he started, but then it occurred to him. "You saw me with a patient's wife. Her husband died last night. I was consoling her."

"You're good at that, Zweli. I know from experience."

He bowed his head, touching it to Kyla's door. "That's a low blow, Ky, and you know it."

She stood with her hands fisted in her tiny foyer. It *was* a low blow, but she didn't care, not after discovering that Zweli had run around like a howler monkey in heat while she was in California.

"You never answered me yesterday," Kyla said, her anger and hurt putting a tremor in her voice. "I asked you why you came here, and why you've made yourself a part of my family's life."

"You know the answer," he said through clenched teeth. "You've known for a long time."

"All I know is that you have something to prove. You always have to win, don't you?"

He tugged at the sides of his head. "Woman, I don't know what the hell you're talking about, and if anyone should be angry here, it's me!"

She flung open the door. "Oh yeah? Why's that?"

She wore a pair of loose-fitting jeans and a light, boat-necked sweater. She was barefoot, and her hair hung in chic disarray about her face and shoulders. She managed to look as fresh as a high school girl and as furious as a harpy all at the same time. Even as he marveled inwardly at how lovely she was, he held onto the volcanic emotion mounting within him.

"Why, Zweli?" she demanded. "What gives you the right to be angry at *me*?"

"Because you left!"

The words erupted with more force than he had intended, enough to make Kyla jump back.

"I'm sorry." He moderated his voice to lessen the chance of a neighbor calling the police. "I didn't mean to yell at you." He moved closer to the doorway, but she didn't invite him in. "When I proposed to you, I was sure that you'd say yes. I was sure that you felt the same way about me that I felt about you."

Kyla listened silently, even though the sound of her own heartbeat threatened to drown out his words.

"When you said no, it made me temporarily insane," he went on. "Or maybe it wasn't temporary, considering that I still have very strong feelings about your rejection. Let me ask you a bonus question of my own, Kyla." He met her gaze squarely, and he was surprised to see apprehension swimming in the amber pools of liquid light fixed on him. "Why did you say no? You never told me, and I sure as hell haven't been able to figure it out on my own."

She had replayed that night in her mind so many times, she had worn holes in the memory. The one thing that refused to fade or fray was her reason for turning down his ring. But with him standing in her doorway, looking at her as though he were lost and she was home, she wasn't sure she could speak over the lump painfully blocking her throat.

She tried to clear her throat but the lump refused to budge. "It doesn't matter now, Zweli. It's water under the bridge."

"That's not good enough, Ky. It's almost as bad as the 'My Life Is Too Complicated' speech you gave me three years ago."

"I don't want to hurt you."

"You won't."

"Zweli…"

"Kyla." He flashed his dimples in a rakish smile that did little to mask his naked yearning. "Nothing you can say could hurt me more than the no you shot at me three years ago."

"I turned down your proposal because I thought you were playing a game. I thought you were putting on a show for your friends. It never occurred to me that you were being serious."

Her quiet admission hit him hard enough to knock the air clean out of his lungs. When he could breathe again, he worked out a peculiar, nervous laugh. "I was wrong, Ky. You found something worse than that no."

"I warned you." She spoke almost too quietly for Zweli to hear. Almost.

"I have the worst taste in women," he said. "I always have. But I always I managed to stay one step ahead, to keep from putting anything real at stake. Until I met you." He tossed his hands up in surrender. "You're the only woman I've ever known who's as greedy and selfish and self-centered as I am. You stole my heart and took it with you when you left. The heart is a funny muscle, Ky. It's as delicate as it is tough. I thought we'd found a place where we could begin again yesterday, but apparently you just wanted attention."

She blinked. Then her mouth fell open. Any sympathy she might have felt for him vanished. "You're worse now than you were three years ago! The only difference between now and then is that now I know how far you'll go to get what you want. I saw you with that woman today, Zweli, and just two weeks ago, you were with that crocodile-faced Barbara Shute! You're a hard man to resist. I knew it three years ago and I know it even better today. Yesterday was a mistake and it won't happen again. I won't be your big fish, Zweli."

"You'll just be the one that got away," he said tonelessly. He scrubbed a hand over his dreads as he slowly backed away. "I learn something from each of my patients, Kyla. The thing I learned from the man who died last night was to stop fooling around and get busy living the life I want. I've known a lot of women, but I've loved only one. You. Only you." He shoved his hands into his pockets and took a few more steps backward before he turned all the way around and headed for the elevators.

It's a line, she vehemently told herself. *He always knows what to say and when to say it.* She closed the door and leaned against it until she no longer heard his footsteps in the corridor.

Sunday afternoon didn't come soon enough for Kyla. She was the first to arrive at her mother's house to help prepare dinner, but the arduous work of helping her mother cook for fifteen or more people did little to keep her mind off the one person she most hoped to see.

"Mama," she started, forcing her tone to remain light, "I don't suppose you heard from Zweli last week."

Abby pressed back a smile as she peeled the skin from a steaming sweet potato. "As a matter of fact, I didn't. Was I supposed to?"

One shoulder rose in a shrug. "It's just that Cady and Keren haven't heard from him, either."

"Well, that seems odd."

"I thought so, too." Kyla put some muscle into prying the snowy white meat of a coconut from its hard, hairy shell.

"Are you two fighting again?"

"Yes, and he's the one who started it. He just can't seem to get over the fact that I didn't want to marry him."

"He seems to have gotten over it all right to me," Abby remarked. "I wonder if he might bring two dates to dinner today."

"He's coming?" Kyla couldn't hide her glee.

"Heavens, I don't know." Abby took up another freshly boiled sweet potato to strip of its skin. "Zweli's always welcome here. If he comes, he comes. If he doesn't, he doesn't. You know, Kyla, I think your toasted coconut shavings will really complement the flavor of my mashed sweet potatoes."

"I picked it up in Costa Rica," Kyla said absently. "I was there on location once, for *Lifeguards.*"

Kyla wished that she could be as blasé about Zweli's attendance as her mother, and she wished it even harder once her sisters and their families began to arrive for dinner. Even after everyone but Abby had sat down for the meal, Kyla remained positioned opposite the wide dining room window to take advantage of the panoramic view of the street. By the time Kyla was ready to accept the fact that Zweli wasn't coming, it had grown dark and her sisters were clearing the table while Abby laid out desserts on the buffet.

Clara, Ciel, and Cady had retreated to the living room for a rowdy game of team Monopoly with the children while Abby, Keren, Lee, and Christopher did the dishes. Kyla found their laughter and muffled conversations comforting as she stood alone at the dining room window, willing Zweli to arrive in a burst of noise and color.

And excuses, Kyla's inner cynical voice whispered. *He'll come in with apologies to Abby and kisses for the rest of the girls, and all the while he'll smell of another woman's perfume.*

"Shut up," she muttered to her inner voice. She was being unfair and she knew it. Zweli had been honest with her about his goings-on in her absence. And he'd never disrespected her by giving her the impression that he'd been with another woman immediately before or after spending time with her.

And that kiss...that one, candy-sweet kiss that had almost led to the consummation of every moment of longing she'd ever spent on Zweli had revealed one of his biggest secrets: It didn't matter what woman had come after her because none had managed to replace her.

She was as sure of it as she was of the fact that Zweli's absence was her fault. There was a language to kissing, and she and Zweli had always understood each other, perhaps too well. Which only made Zweli's absence that much more hurtful.

He knows I wanted him to be here, Kyla thought. *That's why he isn't.*

"Why don't you come and have some coffee in the living room," Abby offered, removing her apron as she rounded the dining table. "Watching for him won't make him appear."

"I'm not—" Kyla swallowed the lie. "I must have been thinking out loud."

"You're a good actress, Kyla. Ordinarily, you do a wonderful job of hiding your true emotions. But when you let your guard down, like now, it's like your forehead is clear and I can see exactly what you're thinking and feeling."

"I threw him away, Mama," Kyla said, nearly choking on the disappointment she'd tried to suppress all day. "That's why he isn't here."

"Then go get him," Abby said simply. "He never goes far."

"You make it sound so easy. Like all I have to do is call him up and say, 'No hard feelings. Come on over and have a life with me.' "

"It is that easy."

"Then why have you been single for so long, Mama? Why didn't you get on with your life after Daddy died? Why didn't you meet someone else and start over?"

"For the same reason you've been eyeballing that window all night, little girl," Abby said before leaving Kyla with a wistful, somber smile.

Kyla watched her mother's back as she went into the living room. As a child, she'd never given much thought to her mother's romantic life, or absence of it. But as a woman, she now understood how someone could love a man so much that upon losing him, no one else could take his place.

"Not me," Kyla muttered, her gaze still fixed on the street. "I won't be a slave to the memory of Zweli Randall."

She made a decision and threw her shoulders back as she grandly marched into the living room. "Fix me up," she demanded, staring in turn at each of her sisters. "I need a date."

"Quit wiggling," Cady ordered. "You're shaking the fringe, and it's throwing off my measurement."

Kyla looked down at her sister, who was on her knees hemming the dress Kyla was planning to wear for Halloween. "I don't mean to shake it. It moves when I breathe."

Cady plucked a straight pin from her pinched lips. "Can you stop breathing for a minute?"

Kyla took a deep breath and held it, which stilled the shimmy of the six-inch gold fringe covering her dress.

"That's better," Cady mumbled once she'd set the hem at Kyla's mid-thigh. "I might be able to get this done right now and you can wear it on your big date tonight." She placed a few more pins before saying, "You can breathe now."

Kyla exhaled loudly. "Why do you keep calling it a 'big date?' "

"It took Clara two weeks to find this guy, and trust me, it wasn't easy. She couldn't fix our baby sis up with just anybody. This guy had to meet some very specific requirements before Clara would even consider fixing him up with you."

"Like what?" Kyla asked.

"He had to have a car."

"That's it? If he has a car, he's good enough for me?"

"He had to have a nice car," Cady clarified.

"Well, what kind of car does he drive?"

"A Mini Cooper."

"Cute."

"I had one of my contacts in the St. Louis police department check him out," Cady said. "He doesn't have a record. He's never even had a speeding ticket."

"Is that good?" Kyla wondered. "All normal people get speeding tickets at some point, don't they? Should I be worried about this guy?"

"Trust Clara." Cady stood. "And don't forget that she's just looking out for your best interests."

"I'm starting to feel like Laura in *The Glass Menagerie*," Kyla said. "Like some pathetic shut-in who can't work up the guts to get hold of her own life and her own men."

"You're not a 'Laura,' Ky." Cady stuck her leftover pins into a tomato-shaped pincushion. "You're an 'Amanda,' but without the over-inflated ego and the tendency to allow exactly one moment in the past to define the rest of your life."

"I love that play," Kyla said.

"Me, too."

"Tell me more about my Gentleman Caller."

"His name is Sterling."

"I already knew that much. We spoke on the phone when we made our plans, but he was at work so he couldn't really talk. Tell me something else about him."

"I can't." Cady set her pincushion on the edge of her living room table before unzipping Kyla and helping her wriggle out of the form-fitting dress. "I don't know anything more about him."

Kyla slid into a black dress of wool jersey and smoothed it over her strapless black bra and silk panties.

Cady's eyebrows bounced. "Black silk on a first date? Go 'head, girl!"

"I just wanted to feel pretty," Kyla said. "Sterling won't be unwrapping any treats tonight."

"Or any other night," Cady giggled under her breath.

"I heard that." Kyla stepped into her black heels and followed Cady into the bathroom. "What was that supposed to mean?"

"It means," Cady began as she stood to look in the mirror above the sink, "that I think you're wasting your time with Sterling."

"I was wasting time with *Zweli*," Kyla insisted. "Sterling might turn out to be the best thing that ever happened to me. If nothing else, I hope to just go out and have a good time with a man who doesn't try to play me at every turn."

"Uh huh," Cady grunted. After wetting her finger in the sink, she wrapped a few of her curls around it, giving them springy new life.

Kyla studied her sister's outfit, admiring the burnt orange sweater dress that perfectly complemented Cady's figure and complexion. "Are you going somewhere?"

Cady nodded. "Millicent Raines invited Keren and me to a fundraiser at the Saint Louis Art Museum. It's a silent auction. Keren had to be there earlier and I had to file a story, drop the kids off at Mama's, and hem your dress. My ride should be here any minute. What time is Sterling picking you up?"

Kyla glanced at her watch. It was almost seven. "In about five minutes."

"You'd better get moving, then." Cady went to the living room closet and retrieved their coats.

"He's picking me up here," Kyla said merrily.

"Why here?"

"I didn't want him to know where I live in case he turns out to be crazy."

"Oh, wonderful," Cady scowled. "So he'll know where my defenseless children and I live?"

"And where your tall, strong, fearsome husband lives," Kyla said. "Sterling's picking me up in the lobby. I didn't give him your condo number or your name. You and the kids are probably safe."

A loud knock startled them in spite of Kyla's words. "Who is it?" they both said.

"Zweli."

Kyla stared wide-eyed at the door. "What's he doing here?" she mouthed at Cady.

"Would you get that for me?" Cady whispered innocently.

"It's your house," Kyla snapped back. "You get it!"

"Hello?" Zweli sang from the other side of the door.

Kyla went to the door and swung it open. "This is ridiculous, even for you," she started, her mouth working on automatic even as her eyes devoured the sight of him. She hadn't seen or heard from him in two weeks, and she'd missed him. She missed him even more now that he was standing in front of her in a blue-gray wool business suit that made the gold and jade sparks in his eyes crackle.

He had no right to look so relaxed and handsome on the night of her first date with some other man, and his unintentional audacity angered Kyla. "Some women might be flattered by your showing up out of nowhere on an important night, but I'm not one of them," she ranted. "You've had two damn weeks to call or visit or whatever, but you decided to ignore me up until you knew I was going out with someone else. Well, guess what, Zweli?" She didn't wait for him to guess. "The sooner you get used to the idea that you and I will never be together, the happier we'll both be. My date will be here soon, and I want you to leave before he arrives."

Zweli thoughtfully stroked his chin as he took a short step closer to Kyla. She looked fantastic in a clingy black dress that showcased her figure without really showing anything. Her thick auburn hair fell softly to her shoulders, nicely framing her face. Even with her fine eyebrows drawn in fury and her bow-shaped mouth molded into a pout of aggravation, Zweli couldn't help thinking he'd never seen her look more beautiful.

And she was about to waste it on another man, a fact that sent a niggling current of jealousy moving through his chest.

"I'd be feeling a little stupid right now if I'd come here to see you," he said glibly, "but as a matter of fact, I didn't know you'd be here." He brushed past her, nudging her aside. "Cady, are you ready to go to the museum?"

Cady approached. Zweli took her coat and held it for her. "Are you staying?" Cady asked Kyla as she shoved her arms into her coat.

Kyla nodded, her eyes on Zweli and her mouth hanging open in indignation.

Cady reached forward to close her sister's mouth. "Lock up when you leave, 'kay?" she said before leaving, arm-in-arm, with Zweli.

"You set me up," Zweli accused. "You knew that I'd run into your sister. If I'd known Kyla was at your place, I wouldn't have agreed to cart your sneaky butt to this shindig."

"You can't avoid her forever, Zweli." Cady led him into the gallery housing the exhibits for the fundraiser and allowed him to take her coat, which he then presented to the coat check girl. With a flash of her dimples and a flip of her hair, the pretty brunette issued Zweli a claim check. He took it, sparing little more than a glance at her as he handed her a folded bill, thanked her, and stepped away from the counter.

"What was that?" Cady asked.

"What was what?"

She looked back at the coat check girl, whose eyes bored holes into Zweli's back. "Nothing," she said.

Zweli paused at a giant Plexiglas panel hanging from the ceiling, with several pieces of artwork mounted on each side of it. "I don't recognize any of these works."

"They were all done by exciting new artists," Cady said.

Zweli peered closer at one of the nameplates. " 'Pig With One Eye, One Smile, One Leg and Lots of Tiny Toes,' " he read aloud. "Created with orange marker on manila paper. By Rosie, Age 3." He looked at Cady. "Three?"

"It's kid art," she smiled. "All the proceeds are going to the Home For Little Wanderers. I'm bidding on Rosie's 'Pig.' "

"This is the first time I've been to a museum and can say the art looks like it was done by kids without offending anyone. They're not half bad, either." He strolled to the next panel, murmuring a polite "pardon me" to a voluptuous woman in a sequined dress who was standing in his way.

"Oh, pardon *me*, by all means," she cooed, giving Zweli a come hither look that meant she would have no problem honoring any request he made.

"Cady, come look at this one," he said, ignoring the woman completely. "It's called 'Mommy Playing in the Sun with Her Children.' It looks just like you and the twins."

Cady went to him and grabbed his sleeve. "Are you okay?" she asked quietly.

"Yes. Why?"

"The coat check girl and Lola Falana over there sent very strong signals your way, and you failed to receive. Where's the flash-talkin' flirt I've come to know and love so well?"

Zweli kept his eyes on the pencil rendering of a round-headed, pointy-haired mother and her equally round-headed children. "You sound like Kyla," he sighed. "You disappoint me, Cady. I assumed that you knew there was more to me than chasing women."

"Good heavens," Cady said. "You really are in love with her, aren't you?"

"I'm bidding on this one." Zweli indicated the pencil drawing with a tip of his head. "I can appreciate this artist's *oeuvre*. See how the sun has so many rays?"

"That's the sun?" Cady peered closer. "I thought it was a big hairy spider hanging over a pizza."

"This isn't a pizza, Cady, this is the mother." Zweli pointed out features that possibly could have been eyes, a nose, and a smile filled with jagged teeth. "And these three smaller pizzas, these are the children. This artist has captured the elemental beauty of a mother at play with her children. Look at the joyous smile on the mother's face. This could be you and the twins, or—"

Cady's silence caught Zweli's attention. He turned to see her staring across the room, an enigmatic smile gracing her face. Following her line of sight, Zweli found Keren at the end of it, standing in a small group of doctors with Albert Raines and his wife, Millicent. Keren was speaking, but his eyes were fixed elsewhere, on his wife. Zweli watched a blush tint Cady's face, making her glow under her husband's intent gaze. She seemed to radiate with the bright heat of her love and passion for Keren, and it was alluring. A beautiful woman in love…there was no more powerful aphrodisiac. Zweli realized right then that he would give anything to have Kyla look at him the way Cady was looking at Keren.

After nearly four years of marriage and two children, they're still like newlyweds, Zweli thought with a twinge of envy.

He knew that he shouldn't be surprised. When a Winters woman fell in love, she stayed that way. He didn't know the details of Clara and Christopher's courtship, but he knew that they had married sometime between graduate school and their postdoctoral work. After eighteen years, they still petted and whispered to each other like a couple of teenagers on prom night. Ciel and Lee had been sweethearts since the ninth grade, but had waited until Ciel's graduation from law school before jumping the broom. They had been together for so long, they were practically the same person. They had a shorthand communication that no one else could translate, and their private jokes were so private, even their children didn't understand them. The willful Kyla and the wandering Chiara were the only unmarried Winters women, and Zweli was sure that once they settled down, it would be forever, same as their older siblings.

"I need brain surgery or an exorcism to get Kyla out of my head," he mumbled to himself. *Only she's not just in my head*, he thought. *She's everywhere.* "I sweat that woman."

"Then why haven't you called her?" Cady offered, her gaze still locked on her husband.

"We had a fight. Again. Every time we start to get close, she finds some reason to get mad at me. I thought she was too smart to buy into Barbara's bull. Kyla knew she was being played, but it gave her a reason to find fault with me all over again. She all but said I wasn't good enough for her, but I think the real reason she's provoking these fights is to keep me at a distance."

Cady mouthed a few words at Keren, who nodded, before she turned her full attention back to Zweli. "Kyla does that to all of us when she's under a lot of stress. She's always been that way. You remember what it was like when Grandma Claire was in the hospital. Kyla picked fights with each of us, just about every day."

"So what do I do?" Zweli started making his way to the bidding tables. "You can't reason with a person who's completely ruled by emotion."

"Ignore her." Cady moved along the table, searching for the paper bearing the bids for 'Pig.' "That's what I always do. She'll come to her senses and make up with you."

Zweli bent over the page for 'Mommy Playing In The Sun With Her Children.' No one had yet bid on the drawing, so he wrote in a three-figure sum that he hoped would scare off any other interested parties. "I don't know, Cady. You're her sister. Kyla will always come and make up with you. I'm just some man. She can afford to lose me."

Cady used the black felt-tipped pen mounted beside 'Pig' to tamper with the decimal points of previous bids. She moved each of them one or two places to the left, making sure that her bid was now the largest. "There," she said, capping the pen. "I'm not playing around here. I'm gonna get my 'Pig.' "

"You don't have any shame, do you?" Zweli asked.

"I don't have a drink, either. Let's scrounge up a couple of cocktails before we steal Keren away from Albert and Millicent."

"I, uh, think I'll wait here until the bidding closes."

"Why?"

"There's a nice cross breeze over here. And it's less crowded."

Cady's smile flashed in sudden understanding. "You want to protect your bid on 'Mommy.' "

"Shh!" he whispered sharply.

"I'll get you a drink," Cady laughed. "Keep an eye on my page, too. I don't want Mr. Fifteen Dollars changing his bid back to one hundred and fifty."

Zweli glanced at the page for 'Pig.' Even before tampering with the other bids, Cady had outbid her nearest competitor by two hundred dollars. "That's one pricey 'Pig.' "

"It's worth every penny, too," Cady said. "There's something about Rosie's 'Pig' that really hits home with me."

"I hear you," Zweli said. Cady went for drinks while Zweli searched out 'Mommy.' A small group of patrons crowded around it, and Zweli's competitive juices began to run faster. 'Mommy' had hit home with him, and he wasn't about to lose it. Something about that drawing tied in directly with the loss of Eph Davis and Zweli's own desire to build a life with Kyla. Eph was gone and Kyla was too, if she was dating other men.

Zweli turned and moved the decimal point on his bid one space to the right. His arms crossed over his chest, he stood near the page. He wouldn't lose 'Mommy,' too.

"So Sterling," Kyla said as she pulled her water goblet and plate closer to her edge of the table, "you're a scientist. A physicist, right?"

Sterling Bancroft had picked her up an hour late and he was hopelessly overdressed for Miso, the macrobiotic restaurant he'd chosen to take her to. He sat across the tiny, casually laid table, his gangly legs so long that his jittery knees frequently banged the table's underside, setting the cutlery and glassware jumping. He had already stained one leg of his wool slacks with the cup of twig tea he'd sent flying earlier, and his constant pulling at the wet spot was becoming more than a little distracting.

"You think I'm a scientist?" Sterling sniggered. "That's cute. I'm a nuclear physicist. Got the Ph.D. to prove it." He vigorously rubbed at the tea stain with the spring water-soaked napkin the waiter had brought him. "Clara is more of a scientist than I am. She does more hands-on research, more hands-on lab work, than I do. She's quite bright, really, if I do say so myself. And if I say so, that's saying a lot." A loud, braying laugh erupted from him, which earned shocked stares from neighboring diners. Sterling adjusted his thick, dark-rimmed glasses. "I'm sure Clara told you that I've won our office MindOlympics three years running now."

"No." Kyla forced her plastic smile to remain on her face. "Somehow Clara neglected to mention that."

"I'm a math guy, basically," Sterling said around a laugh that sounded more like the snort of a pig searching for truffles. "Although that's really putting it mildly, in terms most lay people can readily understand."

Kyla bristled. "I've heard of math before." She tented her hands over her plate of adzuki beans and butternut squash.

"Yes, I'm sure." He picked up his knife, curled under his upper lip, and studied his teeth in the blade. Loudly sucking at his upper teeth, which were capped with porcelain veneers the size of Chiclets, he used the nail of his pinky finger to pick at the fleck of spinach stuck between his incisors. "But have you heard of Wedderburn's Theorem?"

"Wedderwho's what?"

"It's brilliant." Sterling brought his pleasantly steaming plate to his face and took a long loud whiff of it. "Boiled collard greens with millet, couscous, quinoa and sweet corn," he moaned. "This should really hit the spot. I've been so irregular lately." He clicked a button on his watch, which looked like something from the prop shop of a James Bond film. "It's been thirty-eight hours since my last bowel evacuation and I'm really starting to feel the pressure of my yin being out of sync with my yang." He guffawed at top volume, and the sound blew Kyla back a good two feet.

"I'd rather hear more about your theorem," Kyla said, choosing the lesser of two evils.

"Yes, right." Sterling used his pinky finger to burrow deep into his right nostril. Completely oblivious to Kyla's grimace of horror, Sterling elaborated on the theorem. "It's not mine, actually," he said, wiping his pinky on his napkin. "It's named for Joseph Henry MacLagan Wedderburn. Fascinating mathematician. He was interested in determining the structure of algebras over arbitrary fields. He proved two theorems. One: that every simple algebra is a matrix algebra over a division algebra, and two: that every finite division ring is a field."

"I never liked algebra," Kyla said curtly as she cut into her steamed squash. "I was more of a geometry kind of girl."

Sterling took an enthusiastic bite of his greens. "Wedderburn's theorem on finite algebras gave a structure of all projective geometries with a finite number of points!" His dark brown eyes round in excitement behind his glasses, he seemed to wait for Kyla to share in his enthusiasm.

She wasn't entirely sure that he was even speaking English. "Hooray?" she mustered weakly.

"One of the best proofs of Wedderburn's Theorem I've ever read was written by Theodore J. Kaczynski." Sterling took a ballpoint pen from the breast pocket of his white dress shirt and began scribbling on his napkin. "In it, Kaczynski postulated that we let F be our finite skew field with F* as its multiplicative group."

The savory taste of Kyla's adzuki beans died on her tongue. "Sterling, Ted Kaczynski was the Unabomber."

"I know," he said matter-of-factly before returning to the proof. "If we let S be any Sylow subgroup of F* or—"

"Sterling." She set down her fork. "He killed three people."

"But he was a brilliant mathematician," Sterling argued.

"Why don't we talk about something else?" Her tone left no room for argument.

Sterling scratched at his neat, closely-trimmed afro. He smiled, baring his oversized teeth and flaring his giant nostrils. "Clara tells me it's been a while since you had a date."

Kyla reached for her green tea and downed the whole cup in three long swigs. "Clara spoke out of turn. The truth is, I've actually been seeing someone. Sort of. Well—"

"You don't have to explain." His hand darted forth and grabbed hers. She snatched her arm back and her hand easily slipped from his sweaty grasp. "I didn't mean to startle you, Kyla. But I have to tell you, this isn't the first time I've found myself in the role of rebound boyfriend."

"Boyfriend?" she coughed.

"I don't mind it." He laughed, and it sounded like a jackass singing the last line of 'The Star-Spangled Banner.' "The role suits me. You see, I try not to get too involved with members of the opposite sex. I've found that abstinence and the conservation of my bodily essences keeps my brain working in tip-top condition."

Kyla shuddered. "Oh God."

Sterling stared at her through heavy-lidded eyes, the left side of his smile cocked lasciviously. He absently picked at a blemish near his ear as he said, "I knew you'd be pretty, Kyla, because your sister is really quite attractive. But you're one of the most beautiful women I've ever met, not to mention been fixed up with. It's been a few months since the last time I spilled my seed, as they say, and I don't have any projects due at work until the end of the month. What would you say if I said we should get out of here and go back to your place? We could stop for a box of antiseptic wipes on the way, unless you already have some."

"Check, please!" Kyla called.

"Yes, ma'am!" Sterling said eagerly. "I'll get the waiter to box this to go. Do you have hypoallergenic pillows? Because I'm deathly allergic to feathers. And any kind of animal dander, especially cats, although the allergens from cats come from their saliva and not their hair. Well, it's the hair, but only because cats use their tongues to clean themselves."

"You're not coming home with me, Sterling," Kyla said firmly.

"That's okay. You can come to my place. My mother's out playing cards tonight. Sometimes, she doesn't come home until after midnight."

Kyla tossed a few bills on the table, more than enough to cover her share of the check and tip. "Goodnight, Sterling." She scooted her chair back and stood.

"Aw, c'mon," he whined. "I missed my weekly Dungeons and Dragons game for the first time in twenty years to take you out tonight. We don't have to have sex if you don't want to." He stood and spoke to her in a low voice. "I could come over and just, you know, try on some of your clothes. Do you have any silk panties? If not, I have my own in the car. I have to keep them there so my mother won't find them."

"I have to go home now," Kyla said slowly, cautiously. "If you hurry, maybe you can make your little game after all tonight."

The waiter brought the check and Kyla asked him to escort her to the door.

"Okay then, Kyla," Sterling shouted after her. "I'll see you around then. Bye! It was nice meeting you!"

She retrieved her coat and left the restaurant, calling for a taxi on her cell phone as she ran down the street as fast as she could.

CHAPTER FIVE

Kyla stood on her mother's doorstep with a hot dish of herbed leeks burning her hands. She'd rung the doorbell twice, but no one had answered. Her sisters' cars lined the street in front of the house, so she knew there were people at home. She banged on the glass in the door with her fist, her mood growing more and more sour by the second.

"It's about time," she snarled, expecting one of her sisters when the door was finally opened. "I burned my fingerprints off holding this stupid casserole dish."

"I'm sorry to hear that," Zweli said as he held the door wide for her.

"Y-You," Kyla stammered, her anger receding. "Hi."

"Hi."

"Hi."

"You said that already."

"Yeah." She stepped past him into the foyer. "Hold this, please." She set the casserole dish in his hands before removing her coat and hanging it on the coat tree. She took the dish from him and started for the kitchen.

"It's good to see you, Ky," he called after her.

"You too," she responded without turning around. She passed the living and dining rooms and headed straight back to the kitchen, where her sisters and her mother bustled about. She set the dish in the sink and leaned heavily against the edge of it, her hands braced far apart in front of her as she stared out the wide window.

"What's the matter with you?" Abby asked as she breezed by with her hand cupped beneath a dripping spoon of roast beef gravy.

"I just spent ten minutes knocking on the door with steaming leeks burning my hands," Kyla said. "Why didn't you tell me that you'd invited Zweli to dinner?"

"I didn't think my guest list was any of your concern," Abby said. "I invited Reverend Kurl, too."

"The way I saw it, Reverend Kurl invited himself," Ciel said as she untied her apron. "Mama made the mistake of being the last one out of the church today, so she got stuck feeding and watering him."

"Is he here?" Kyla asked.

"He's already sitting at the table." Clara took a can of beer and a frosted mug from the refrigerator. "This is his second 'refreshment.' "

Narrowing her eyes, Kyla aimed a finger at Clara. "I need to talk to you about that creature you fixed me up with."

"Sterling?" Clara said sweetly.

"He was anything but," Kyla snapped.

"What a nice name," Abby said. "Sterling." She slipped on insulated mitts and reached into the oven for a gigantic roast. "What do his people do?"

"Cross dress, among other things," Kyla answered.

"No!" Clara exhaled, her eyes round pools of delighted disbelief. "Does he really?"

Kyla accepted the relish tray her mother pushed on her. "When he wasn't twitching, picking, wiggling or hee-hawing, he was propositioning me. Apparently, he has his own women's underwear collection that he keeps in his car, so I'm sure he found ways to amuse himself once I walked out on him." She took the relish tray to the dining table, with Clara close on her heels.

"Kyla, Kyla, Kyla!" Reverend Kurl proclaimed, his weathered hands striking his knobby knees with each utterance of her name. "Your mama tells me that you been home for weeks, and I ain't seen you in my church yet. I know you ain't avoidin' the Lord's house now, are you, girl?"

"No, Reverend," Kyla sighed sharply through a glassy grin. "I've been busy moving, looking for work and—"

"Ain't nobody too busy to take time out for the Lord," the Reverend cut in. He looked at Kyla sideways through his big, thick glasses. "You been out there in Hollywood with all them schemers and sinners. Probably no one in this house needs church more than you."

The house seemed to go very quiet. Every person in the house over the age of three had at one time or another been the victim of Reverend Kurl's accusations regarding schemers and sinners, and each of them had humbly succumbed to his bullying and hastened to attend church services.

Kyla had never responded well to bullying. All the adults would have watched her response if Abby hadn't rounded them up and corralled them into the kitchen to take the food to the table and the buffet.

Kyla placed one slim hand on the dining table and leaned on it. "I'm not avoiding the Lord's house, Reverend. I love the serenity and balance church provides. What I've been avoiding are the hypocritical posturings of a man who probably practices every sin he constantly preaches against."

"What's she sayin'?" the reverend asked.

Kyla raised her voice. "I'm saying that you are—"

"So kind to express your concern about Kyla's immortal soul," Zweli said, finishing her sentence before she said something she might regret. He took her by the shoulders and turned her toward the kitchen. "Kyla burned her hand earlier, so I'm gonna take her into the kitchen and take a look at her, to make sure she's okay. Will you excuse us, Reverend?"

Without waiting for an answer, he hustled Kyla into the kitchen against the flow of traffic out of it. He guided her to the sink and started a slow stream of cool water. Placing her hands under it, he gently stroked her palms with his thumbs.

"There's nothing wrong with my hands," she said quietly.

"I see that."

She turned to look at him, to really drink in the sight of him. She was so tempted to rest her head on his shoulder, to fall asleep breathing in his clean, fresh scent. "I didn't know you were here. I didn't see your car."

"I traded in the Alfa Romeo yesterday." He turned off the water and dried her hands with a kitchen towel.

"What are you driving now?" Kyla asked dryly. "A sporty new Jaguar? A Bentley?"

"An Explorer." He took her hands and began to pat them dry as though they were fine porcelain. "It seats seven. It's very…very…"

"Family oriented," Kyla said. "Lee drives an Explorer."

"Well, he's the one who recommended it."

"I'll bet Troy's disappointed."

"He got over it fast enough." Holding one of her hands, Zweli set the towel on the counter. "I let him drive it around the block."

"What did he hit?"

He softly stroked Kyla's palm. "A handicapped parking sign, but Christopher hammered it back into place."

Kyla moved closer to him, so close that his clothing brushed against hers. "Any damage to the car?"

"No."

Cady burst into the kitchen. "Unless your hands have burned off, will you two come on? Reverend Kurl is ready to say grace."

Kyla broke away first, leaving the kitchen to go into the dining room where two empty seats had been reserved far from Reverend Kurl. Zweli offered one to Kyla before taking the other. She didn't hear a word of the Reverend's lengthy blessing for the gifts they were about to receive, or his plea to the Lord to steer His lost sheep back into the flock of the Mt. Tabor Baptist Church. She was oblivious to all but the presence of the man beside her.

At least until after the food was served, when Cady's voice sliced through her reverie like a steel blade through soft muscle. "So, Kyla," she said. "How was your date last night?"

"It was interesting."

"Think you'll see him again?" Cady asked airily.

"Doubtful." Kyla took a big bite of steamed dill cauliflower. "He's been beamed back to his home planet."

"You've always been so picky, Kyla," Abby said. "I'm sure he was fine."

"If 'fine' means blowing his nose into his napkin, then using his fork to sort through his own mucus right there at the table, then yes, Mama, Sterling was fine."

"Well…maybe he had a cold, honey," Abby said.

"Mama, you're crazy."

" 'Honor thy mother,' " Reverend Kurl directed, spraying his neighbor with bits of roasted pork tenderloin. "The Devil got a good hold on you, girl. You need to come to church and let me lay hands on you, and I'll drive the Lord of Flies out of you. You'll be singin' sweet songs to Jesus after I'm done with you. It's been a long time since I had to work the devil out of a body as stubborn as yours, yessir."

"You wouldn't happen to be related to Sterling Bancroft, would you?" Kyla asked dryly.

"You'll have a better time with Ethan," Ciel said.

Kyla swept a glance at Zweli, whose expression remained unreadable through all the talk about her dates. "Could you come with me for a second?"

They excused themselves and returned to the kitchen. "I don't know what's gotten into my sisters, but they should know better than to talk about my dates in front of you."

Zweli held her gaze as he said, "I don't mind."

Her mouth opened, but no words came out.

He worked out a smile. "What you do is your business."

"You don't care that I'm dating?" The question sounded like an accusation.

He dropped his gaze and shook his head. "Look, I'm glad we had this chat, but my dinner's getting cold."

"Are you dating that woman I saw you with at the hospital?" Kyla hated the shrewish tone in her voice.

"I haven't seen her since the day you saw me in the corridor with her. I told you. She was my patient's widow, not a potential girlfriend."

"Well, who are you dating?"

"No one, Kyla. I'm interested in you. Only you."

"Then why are you being so damn calm about me going out with other men?"

He stroked a thumb along her cheekbone, and she felt something deep inside her turn liquid. "Because all I want is for you to be happy." He left her then and went back into the dining room. Kyla, bewildered, stood alone in the kitchen for the longest time.

Traffic on Lindell Boulevard was heavier than usual for a late Sunday evening, and Zweli idled at a red light mere blocks from his condominium complex. His new car gave him a whole new perspective on driving, particularly on the other drivers. He could easily look into neighboring cars. To his left, on the far side of the intersection, a couple in a westbound Honda seemed to be having a spat. The long-haired woman in the passenger seat sat as far as she could from the male driver, her features hard and her mouth working stiffly as her eyes shot withering looks at the driver. The driver, his face unreadable, maintained a death hold on the steering wheel, and stared fixedly through the windshield. The woman kept on yelling at him and the driver rolled his eyes; his cheeks puffed out in what could only be a long, exasperated sigh.

To Zweli's right, a different story was unfolding. A man and woman practically sat on top of each other in the front seat of a late-model Buick. The woman drove, or was trying to, while her companion did his best to distract her. Zweli imagined the giggle that likely accompanied her sibilant body movement when the young man's hand slipped over her thigh and under her short skirt. He watched her knuckles whiten as she gripped the steering wheel tighter when the young man brought his face to her neck.

Zweli was curious as to how far the young couple would go, and he might have sat there and watched had the mad honking of the cars behind him not spurred him through the green light. The Honda continued its journey west and passed Zweli as he headed east, keeping pace with the Buick. Zweli thought about how perfectly the two couples represented his relationship with Kyla. Fussing and fighting on one hand, passionate and loving on the other.

There seemed to be no middle road.

Dinner at Abby's was almost always the highlight of his week, and this time had been no exception, but for the fact that his delicious dinner was sitting in his stomach like a glob of wet cement. Although he still felt weak and queasy after his performance with Kyla, he was pleased with it. He'd almost fooled himself into believing that he didn't care what she did or with whom she did it.

Judging by her quiet demeanor the rest of the night, he'd fooled her, too.

For the rest of the drive, he ignored the goings-on of the other drivers as he made his way home and pulled into his assigned parking space. With his plastic container of leftovers tucked under his arm, he went into his apartment building and, forsaking the elevator, climbed the stairs to his seventh-floor condo.

His condo was one of his favorite places, filled with furniture and accessories he had painstakingly acquired from designer showrooms, estate sales, antique shops, and art deco galleries. The décor was an eclectic mix of classic and modern, all in line with his dedication to form, function, and, above all else, beauty.

His security alarm was programmed to open the living room draperies to a picturesque view of the Gateway Arch and to turn on the wall-embedded sound system when he came home and punched in the entry code. Tonight's musical selection was Lena Horne, circa 1941. Lena's sweet, silken voice wrapped around Edward Heyman's evocative lyrics to "Out of Nowhere," which had always been one of Zweli's favorite songs. When that song gave way to "Prisoner of Love," Zweli felt that he finally understood what the songs meant.

They weren't just strings of words sung beautifully. The songs told the story of his life with Kyla. Zweli stood in the middle of his living room, bathed in Lena Horne's voice, spellbound by the words that described the power Kyla had over him. He couldn't move until the song was over, and then he went to the counter that separated his all-white kitchen from his living/dining room.

On top of a crumpled white Saint Louis Art Museum wrapper sat 'Mommy Playing in the Sun with Her Children.' He picked it up and brought it into the living room, then sank into the sleek softness of the black leather Le Corbusier sofa and put his heels on the charcoal glass top of his Isamu Noguchi cocktail table before propping 'Mommy' on his knees.

The young artist couldn't know that her work had become the object of Zweli's most heartfelt desire. Zweli studied the drawing in the warm glow of his soft track lighting, and he wondered if the child had drawn what she already had or what she most wanted.

He lightly touched the glass covering the art, and in his mind he gave the piece a new title: 'Wife Playing in the Sun with Our Children.'

"Daddy, you can't keep answering the door dressed like this," Abigail whined into her headset microphone as she adjusted the neon pink straps of her sequined top. "Why couldn't you be somebody normal, like Spiderman?"

"Put a cork in that whine," Lee advised his firstborn, "before I make you put a coat on, Li'l Kim Lite."

Lee stood in the doorway of Abby's house, dressed in a short-sleeved plaid shirt, baggy black trousers pulled up to his armpits, and a molded wig of black plastic with a swoop of hair sticking straight up off his forehead. The master of mimicry, he screwed up his face and altered his voice and said, "I do believe you're going mental, I must say."

"Who...*what*...are you supposed to be?" C.J. asked his uncle, and in so doing, voiced the question on the minds of everyone under the age of thirty on Abby's front porch.

"I'm Ed Grimly," Lee said.

C.J. spat one end of his long, spiky pirate's mustache from his mouth. "Who's that?"

"Martin Short did the character on *Saturday Night Live* back in the '80s," Kyla told her nephew.

"Oh," said C.J. "Who's Martin Short?"

Troy, who, as Neo from *The Matrix,* was dressed in head-to-toe shiny black "pleather," took off his dark glasses. "Was Ed Grimly the one who gave his office co-workers all those crazy nicknames?"

Lee stood aside to allow his costumed relatives into the house. "No, that was Richard the Copy Room Guy, and he was played by Rob Schneider. Ed Grimly was like the goofy, poorly dressed cousin of PeeWee Herman."

"Who's PeeWee Herman?" Danielle asked as she swept into the living room in a pink gown fit for a genuine medieval princess.

"You kids don't watch enough television," Lee grumbled as the children stampeded into the living room.

Cady, dressed in a rust-colored suede-like top and matching miniskirt, her hair teased into a helmet of brown spikes, laughed over a bowl of candy corn packets. "Lee, you watch too damn much television. And if you had let me make your costume, you might have been something relevant to the twenty-first century."

"Ciel wouldn't let me be Chaka Khan," Lee argued. "Maybe I'll let you costume me next Halloween. You did such a good job with the kids this year."

Christopher tore off his pirate's tricorn hat and pulled his sword from the scabbard at his waist. "Cady did mine, too."

"And mine." With a saucy flip of her hair, which had been styled in a high ponytail at the back of her head, Clara turned in the white leather-like vest and matching skin-tight pants Cady had sewn for her.

Ciel, in a clingy black and white pantsuit dominated by polka dots, posed next to Clara. The polka dot motif was repeated on the wide headband keeping her dark hair back, and the flounced cuffs on her sleeves and pants belled prettily as she moved. "I think I'm going to wear mine to work on Monday," she said.

Lee wrapped an arm around his wife. "You have to love a world that would allow Ed Grimly to go home with all this at the end of the night."

"Let's see you, Kyla." Christopher offered his hand to take the trench coat she wore over her costume.

Kyla opened her coat and the light in the foyer seemed to change. Gold fringe sparkled all over her body, throwing sparks over the walls and the cherrywood flower table. When she raised a hand to smooth back her long, sleek hair, she shimmered.

Lee gave her a wink. "You look like a *Solid Gold* dancer."

Kyla joined her sisters in the living room.

"What are you guys supposed to be?" Christopher asked. "Strippers?"

Clara rolled her eyes and hung her arms over her husband's shoulders. "When we get home, I'll show you what love's got to do with it."

Ciel grabbed the protrusion atop Lee's plastic wig. "If you're nice to me, maybe later I'll shake your tail feathers."

"I left a good job in the city," Cady said. "Boston, to be exact."

Christopher still looked lost.

"We're Tina Turners, Chris," Cady said. "You don't see it?"

Kyla decided to show him. She slinked to the center of the archway dividing the living room from the foyer. She began shrugging her shoulders and tap-stepping to music she heard only in her head.

Lee snapped his fingers and launched into his best Ike Turner impersonation. "And we're rollin'…rollin' now…"

Kyla took the cue and set her sleek dark locks and her gold fringe flying in a dance that would have made the object of her imitation proud.

"Holy Proud Mary," Zweli exhaled, his gaze roaming over Kyla as he stepped toward the archway.

Kyla froze. It took her hair and her fringe a few seconds to freeze along with her.

Zweli stood there in a long, black coat that could only be genuine leather, tiny black oval shades and black boots. He looked like an action figure come to life, a tall, dark hero too good to be real. "Who are you supposed to be?" Kyla asked, even though the question circulating in her brain concerned more of a why than a who.

Troy sidled up to him and answered. "He's Morpheus."

Zweli took an abrupt stride to Kyla, stopping so close to her that she could see the shine in her eyes in his shades. In a low rumbling growl that made her skin prickle, he said, "Will it be the blue pill or the red pill?"

Her mouth worked to form an answer, but it was hard to speak with him standing near enough to kiss. He let her off the hook when he turned to address the room. "Who's ready for some serious trick or treating?"

A chorus of "I am!" rattled the house.

"Will the Tina Turners be joining us?"

"We are," Clara said, indicating herself and Ciel.

"I've already been out with Raggedy Ann and Andy," Cady said as she herded her children away from a giant bowl of sweets. "I'm going to take the twins home and dunk them in the tub before Keren comes home from work."

Zweli took a good look at the black yarn wigs and blue-and-white striped stockings Cady had made for her children before he peered at her costume over the tops of his tiny shades. "Do you plan on greeting him at the door in that outfit?"

"You betcha," Cady grinned. "It matches the Tarzan costume I made for him from the scraps of my costume."

"So it's just treats and no tricks around the Winters-Bailey house tonight, huh?"

"Oh, there'll be tricks. I've got the movement of a Chinese acrobat in this costume."

"There are children present!" Kyla whispered sharply. "Knock it off, you two." She glared at Zweli. "Why are you here, anyway?"

"I trick or treat with Cady and the kids every year," Zweli said. And because he was still annoyed by her decision to date other men, he added, "You'd know that if you'd been here."

Kyla opened her mouth but snapped it shut before an insult took flight. Zweli was right. He was the one who had stayed, who'd been an active participant in her family's traditions. It wouldn't be fair of her to try to drive him away with insults. And the last thing she wanted to do was to see him go.

"I'm sorry, Ky," he said, sure that her contemplative expression was the result of his waspish comment.

"Forget it," she said lightly. "It's my first Halloween with my nieces and nephews, and Cady worked for weeks on our costumes. I just want to show them off and have a good time tonight."

He smiled and slipped her hand into his. "Then let's roll."

"Look at them," Lee said, pausing by Kyla and Zweli. "We told the kids to stay together, and they're running from house to house like a pack of junkies. You'd think people were handing out rock cocaine instead of Snickers and Skittles."

"Even Mr. Cool's in a frenzy," Zweli laughed. He pointed to a house where Troy was leaping over the luminaries lining the brick walkway to the front door. As his mother—Tina Turner circa 1984—tried to slow him down, Troy steamrolled his way past a group of much younger children to have a handful of miniature candies dropped into his black sack.

"Gotta run," Lee said, hiking his pants up to his armpits. "Clarence is headed for The Gooch's house, and I know he's got about a half dozen StinkShooters hidden behind his tabard."

"His what?" Kyla asked.

"That sister of yours put a hidden pocket behind the front panel of Clarence's Grim Reaper costume," Lee explained as he started away.

"She gave him some StinkShooters right before we left the house, and if I know Clarence…"

"The Gooch's house will have to be evacuated and fumigated before the night's over," Kyla finished.

"Catch you guys later," Lee said, and he ran off to intercept his son.

Kyla scanned the crowds of children that had come out on the mild night. Most of them were in black, but her nieces and nephews stood out in their bright pink satins, red velvets and gold braid. Even Clarence's hooded Grim Reaper costume had a silvery-gray shimmer that made him look like a part of the night without blending wholly into it.

Assured that her nieces and nephews were in the company of responsible Tina Turners, a pirate and an Ed Grimly, Kyla slowed her steps to put more distance between her family and herself and Zweli. The action wasn't lost on Zweli, who enjoyed the simple thrill of holding Kyla's hand.

She glanced up at the silver sliver of the All Hallow's Eve moon and took a deep breath of the clean night air. Two blocks from her mother's house, she could still detect the faint aroma of Abby's popcorn balls on the breeze. Abby had been making the treats every Halloween for over three decades, and the children of the children with whom Kyla had once trick or treated now lined up across the porch and down the steps to get one of Abby Winters's orange-tinted popcorn balls.

"When we were little," Kyla started, "my sisters and I used to go out twice every Halloween. We'd make the rounds once, in one costume, then go home and change into another costume and go out again." She pointed to a three-story brick house with no porch light on. "A woman named Alice Crumb used to live there. She made the best oatmeal raisin cookies to give out on Halloween. I think she died a couple of years ago."

"What kind of costumes did Cady make for you guys back then?" Zweli asked.

"Cady didn't learn to sew until she was in high school. Grandma made our costumes when we were little. I didn't realize it when I was a kid, but she was amazing. One year, she made five princess costumes and five clown costumes."

"Which did you wear first?"

"The clowns. We didn't care who saw us as clowns, but all the older kids were out by the time we'd finished our first run of the block. We wanted to look pretty during the peak run."

"Whose idea was it to be Tina Turner this year?"

"You really have to ask? It was Cady's idea, of course." Kyla stopped to pluck a big, golden-orange maple leaf from a branch overhanging the sidewalk. "She thought it would be funny. Halloween is her favorite holiday, and she thinks of the craziest things. She made dinner for the kids tonight—toasted skin grafts with chocolate-covered blood clots for dessert. That's cheese pizza and chocolate-covered cherries to us folk over the age of twelve."

"Your sister amazes me."

"Yes, well, you'd be surprised at how many different ways people say that about her."

"You amaze me, too." Her hand tensed in his and he knew that he was wading a bit too close to dangerous waters. "You know," he started, changing the subject, "I was always a Rerun for Halloween."

Kyla laughed and stopped near a mailbox. "From *What's Happening*? I can't wait to tell Lee."

"No," he chuckled. "I was always whatever my older brother had been the year before. If he was Batman, I was Batman the next year. I had hand-me-downs for every occasion. My younger brother, Yawu, always got a new costume because he was so much bigger than me."

"I never knew that you were a Jan," Kyla said.

"A what?"

"A Jan Brady. The middle child of three. What's your older brother's name?"

"Kwaku."

"Interesting."

"I can trace my ancestry back to Ghana on my father's side," Zweli said. "Just as you Winters girls recycled the names Zacadia and Claire, the branches of my father's family tree are nutty with Kwakus, Zwelis and Yawus."

"They're beautiful names. How did you get the Randall?"

"British occupation," Zweli supposed. He removed his shades. "That's where my green eyes come from, too."

Now that he'd exposed them, Kyla couldn't look away from the jade fire in them. "Do your brothers have such pretty eyes?"

He shook his head. "It's the only feature that ever got me any attention from girls."

Kyla stiffened slightly and resumed walking.

"Kwaku was always the handsome one," Zweli said. "And Yawu was the baby. He had that built-in cuteness that no one could resist. I was a skinny little stringbean up until my freshman year of college."

Glancing at his wide shoulders and his long, well-formed legs wrapped in black leather, Kyla couldn't picture him as anything other than the earthbound god he appeared to be right now.

"I had bad skin, too," he admitted. "And no athletic ability whatsoever."

"What happened to turn froggy little Zweli into a prince?" Kyla hugged her arms to her chest in a shiver.

"Time, I guess." He took off his coat and bundled Kyla into it. "Maybe I had the chance to grow once I left home. I didn't get much sunlight standing in the shadows of my brothers. Kwaku's in advertising. He's been married since Methuselah came off the mountain, and he's got four kids. Two girls, two boys. Yawu's still playing the field. He's in public relations with the Indiana Pacers."

"Wh-Who... Wh-What... What do your parents do?" Kyla finally managed. It was hard to think up conversation with Zweli's hands moving along her upper arms over the coat. She wanted to plunge her face into the coat and drink in deep gulps of his scent, but she couldn't, not with him standing so close to her that she could taste the dimple in his chin if she wanted to.

And I really want to, she admitted to herself. But then Zweli suddenly looked away, removing the temptation of his delectable dimple.

"Hey, Kyla," he said. "Where is everybody?"

She took in the empty stretch of pavement before and behind them, and the long, black wrought-iron fence beside them. "I think we kept going straight a block or two back, when we should have hung a right with everyone else." An ornate stone gateway across the deserted street caught her attention. "That's the way to the ruins. Come on!" She took off in a trot and started across the street.

Zweli followed close behind her. "St. Louis has ruins?"

"You've never been to Tower Grove Park?" She threw a smile at him. On the opposite curb, she stopped and pointed to a sprawling white building with a single needle-like spire piercing the night sky. "That's Tower Grove Baptist Church on the corner there. Mama sent us there when we were little. Clara never had to go because she was in Catholic school. Since she had mass every morning, she didn't have to go to church on Sunday with the rest of us."

Kyla grabbed his wrist and looked at his sleek Tag Heuer. "The park closes at ten so we'd better make this quick."

"Make what quick?"

But Kyla had taken off through the stone gateway and he had to hurry to catch up to her. She left the main paved path and moved onto the grass, behind the cover of a stand of tall hedges. In his long black coat, she disappeared into the shadow of a willow that had to be at least eight stories tall. When she rounded the corner, Zweli saw it…the ruins of Tower Grove Park.

"It's pretty here, isn't it?" Kyla said breathlessly.

Zweli looked in amazement at the mock classical ruins. The rough-hewn, sand-colored bricks surrounding a wide reflecting pool with a delicate stone fountain had an orchestrated look of antiquity about them. The air was still, turning the pool into a mirror that provided an upside-down image of the fountain, the giant willow, and the star-filled bowl of the Halloween sky. Despite the cool of the evening, Kyla took off his coat to add her gold shimmer to the scene before him.

"I've seen mock ruins like this in old Victorian parks in England, but never here in the United States," Zweli said.

"This one was built with stones from the Lindell Hotel," Kyla said. "It burned down ages ago. The park itself was designed and built by Henry Shaw. It's a kid's paradise. When we were coming here instead of going to church, we'd pretend to be genies under the Turkish pavilion, or Chinese princesses under the Oriental pavilion. We even acted out the Trojan War here once when Clara had to read it for school."

Zweli snickered. "Oh really? Who played Achilles?"

"Chiara." Kyla laughed as she strolled close to the water's edge. "She was little but she definitely had the spirit of an invincible warrior. Cady was Hector and I was Helen." She kicked a tiny stone into the water, sending ever-widening ripples gracefully across the skin of the pool. "Stupid ol' Helen."

"Some women are worth dying for," Zweli said quietly.

In his thick, ribbed black turtleneck, he melted into the night. His voice echoed across the pool and seemed to envelop Kyla.

"You were telling me what your father does for a living," she said, abruptly changing the topic of conversation.

"He's an accountant now. My brothers and I put him through college once we graduated. But up until I was in the fourth grade, he had the coolest job of anyone's parents." Zweli began circling the pool, to meet Kyla on the other side. "He drove a street cleaner."

"What did he do when you were in the fourth grade?"

"He still drove a street cleaner. Only none of the kids thought it was that cool anymore."

"What about your mother?"

"She still thought it was cool."

The left side of Kyla's mouth curved in a reluctant smile, and Zweli suddenly itched to kiss that sensuous tilt.

"I meant what does your mother *do*."

His shifted his gaze from her eyes to somewhere above her nose. "She has a small boutique that sells gourmet chocolates. But years before that, she drank. And yelled. And occasionally, she hit." He sat down on a low formation of stones bordering the pool, and Kyla joined him. "My mother's family owns a very successful restaurant in New Orleans. She came from fairly substantial money, and when she was nineteen, she was supposed to spend the summer after her freshman year at Tulane working as a hostess at the restaurant. She met a kid named Jackson Randall in the kitchen one day. He washed dishes by day and took accounting classes at night at a community college."

"From accounting student in New Orleans to street cleaner in Indianapolis," Kyla said. "How did that happen?"

"Kwaku," Zweli said with a sad chuckle. "My mother found out she was pregnant before the summer was out. Her parents flipped. They tried to make her get a private, 'medicinal' abortion, but she refused. She was in love." He rolled his eyes. "She and my father ran away to his grandparents up north, in Indiana. They were husband and wife and the parents of a baby boy by their twentieth birthdays."

"It sounds like a fairy tale."

"It was, if you listen to the way my father tells it. His version leaves out the part where he worked his ass off at two jobs to support us until I was in junior high. And the part where my mother became a drunk." He raised his face to the starlit night. Shadows partially covered his face, so Kyla couldn't fully translate his expression. She scooted closer to him, and draped his coat over the both of them.

"I remember it, sort of," Zweli began. "My mother would have a cocktail, as she called it, with my father when he came home from work. She worked her way up to having cocktails with breakfast, then lunch, then dinner. It got to the point where I never saw her without a bottle within reach. She deteriorated so fast, when I look back on it. She went from this beautiful, elegant, laughing mother to a shrieking, shrewish, drunken mess who always smelled like alcohol and sweat."

Kyla took his hands and threaded her fingers through his. Zweli was her playful prince. She was unaccustomed to this brand of sadness weighing his voice and dulling the shine in his eyes.

"When your father died, your grandparents gave Abby every kind of support she needed to make sure that you and your sisters turned out well," Zweli said. "My father kept our family intact all by himself. That man would come home from one job at six A.M., make lunches, and get me and by brothers off to school. He'd go to his second job, then come home to sponge my mother up before we came home from school. He made dinner while we did our homework. He must have learned a few things at the restaurant because he was a really good cook. We were the only kids I knew who ate gumbo and shrimp étoufée on a regular basis.

"At bedtime, one of our neighbors would come over and keep us while my dad was at his night job. My father cooked, cleaned, mended ripped pants, took us trick or treating, never forgot a birthday…the one thing I never saw him do was sleep. When I have children, I hope I'm half the father he is."

Kyla stared at the knot of their clasped hands. "If you want to be, then you will be."

"I want a houseful of children," he said.

She shuddered. "Not me. Every time I hear a baby cry, I can feel my ovaries shriveling."

His heart sank a little at her confession. "But you're so good with your nieces and nephews. The twins adore you, especially that little bad ass, Sammy Z."

Kyla thought back on the times she had spent with Claire and Sammy since her return. One of her most perfect moments had been spent with Claire asleep on her chest, the little girl's head tucked under her chin, the two of them sharing the same air. Sammy had been awake at her feet, sloppily coloring her toenails with a light blue Sharpie, but that had made the moment even more precious. "I suppose it's different when the kids are related to you," she conceded. "Or when they're your own. I'd be lying if I said I've never thought about having children.

Since I moved back home, I've been thinking about it more than I like to admit. Seeing my sisters with their families…I guess it's contagious."

Zweli swung one leg over the stone wall, straddling it. He moved a little closer to Kyla, framing her between his knees. When he opened his mouth to speak, she sensed the direction his question or comment would take, and words tumbled from her own mouth to derail him.

"Why didn't your mother's parents help financially?" she asked. "She was still their daughter and you and your brothers were their grandchildren."

"They cut my mother off when she ran away. My father wouldn't have taken a dime from them even if they had offered. Even when things got as bad as they could get, Dad didn't ask anyone for help."

"How bad did it get, Zweli?"

He closed his eyes and vividly saw a memory that he hadn't thought about in years, but one that was a part of him. He opened his eyes to a night that was too pretty to taint with the story of how far his mother fell.

"Zweli?" Kyla placed a gentle hand on his face.

"Yawu got sick at school and they called my mother to come pick him up. She walked to the school and into the principal's office. She was so drunk, she'd forgotten to put shoes on. Her hair was a tangle, her face was dirty and her nightgown was stained. She was loud, belligerent. Yawu was only eight and he was so embarrassed, he told the principal that the crazy-drunk lady in his office wasn't his mother. I was eleven, and I was called down to the office to sort the matter out. I denied her, too."

Even now, twenty-three years after the fact, Zweli stung with the pain of his betrayal. Kyla felt it and took him in her arms. "Kids do goofy things," she told him. "She was the one in the wrong, not you. You can't hold a child to an adult standard of behavior."

"The school called my father. He came and took the three of us home. It was weird, like he finally saw my mother the way we did."

"How was that?"

"Like she was garbage." He withdrew from Kyla's embrace to switch roles with her. He pulled her close and she settled against him, her back to his chest. "My father didn't get mad or yell or cuss at her. He took her home and put her in the tub, dosed Yawu with cough syrup and put him to bed with cartoons on, and then he sat at our little kitchen table and he cried. I stood in the doorway watching my father sob into his hands.

"He has such big hands, and they're so calloused, he can reach into the stove without an oven mitt to pull out baked potatoes. Those work-roughened hands never hit me. He has a deep voice, like James Earl Jones, but he never used it to tell me to shut the hell up and get out of his face. He was everything my mother wasn't."

"He must have really loved her."

"That's what makes it so sad. He did love her. We all loved her. We lived for the rare moments when she was sober. When she seemed happy. My mother rarely smiled, but when she did, we all got drunk on it. Showing up crocked at school to pick up Yawu, though, that was the last straw. Dad waited until her next sober patch, and then he gave her a bus ticket to New Orleans."

Kyla sat up and faced Zweli. "He sent her to her parents?"

"He would have, if she hadn't made him a promise."

"To stop drinking?"

"He made her promise just to try. It took almost a year, but she did it. She's been sober for twenty-one years. She's finally the person she wanted to be all along."

"What do you mean?"

"I didn't see it when I was a kid, but I get it now. My mother gave up her youth, education, her family, and her career ambitions to become a wife and mother. She gave up too much of herself for life with my father. Alcohol was her escape."

"'They began to sag like a heavy load,'" Kyla murmured.

"Hmm?"

"Langston Hughes. He wrote a grocery list of things that could happen to a dream deferred. 'Does it dry up like a raisin in the sun? Or fester like a sore—and then run. Does it stink like rotten meat? Or crust and sugar over—like a syrupy sweet? Maybe it just sags like a heavy load.' Your mother's dead dreams began to sag like a heavy load. I know what that feels like."

"You achieved your dream, Kyla. You're an actress."

"Alfre Woodard is an actress." She stood, taking his coat with her. "Lynne Thigpen was an actress. Me? I'm just a performer. I was still an aspiring actress when we first met. I graduated to frustrated, and now I'm completely disenchanted.

"That sounds like self-pity."

"It's worse. I have a new answer for Mr. Langston Hughes. I know what happens to a dream deferred. It becomes a slow-acting poison that kills the dreamer's soul, little by little, until she becomes an empty shell, just taking up space."

"I didn't know you were so pessimistic."

"Yes, you did."

"Well, you seem worse since your last go-round in Hollywood."

"Yeah…well…" She shrugged. "Drugs scare me, chocolate is fattening, liquor ruins your skin and your health, so pessimism is the only addiction open to me."

Zweli stood and took two steps to stand before her. "Pessimism gives you wrinkles." He caressed her cheek with the backs of his fingers, which sent a pleasant shiver through her that Zweli mistook for a chill. When he moved to wrap her in his coat, she let him.

He reached inside the coat to lock his hands at the small of her back. The fringe of her dress tickled the back of his hands while the heat of her body warmed his palms. "My mother made the mistake of thinking her dreams had been destroyed. If she hadn't climbed out of the bottle, she wouldn't have her own boutique now. She wouldn't have her family. Maybe you should trade your pessimism for patience."

Kyla traced one of the thick ribs of Zweli's turtleneck with her fingertip. "I've shown incredible patience, especially tonight."

"What are you being patient about?"

She placed her hands flat on his chest and slid them up to his nape. "I've been very patiently waiting for you to kiss me." She brought her mouth to his, but Zweli slightly tipped his head back, leaving her lips to graze his dimpled chin. "We've been together for hours without fighting. We should make the most of it."

With every cell and fiber of his body straining to keep his hands from straying from the safe territory of her back, he said, "I agree."

Kyla took one of his wrists and directed his hand to her backside. Her words softly filled the cup of his ear when she stood on her tiptoes to say, "You're the Prince Charming I always fantasized about when I played in this park."

Zweli wrapped his arms tightly around her. The otherworldly setting was beautiful and quiet, and with Kyla exactly where he was sure she was meant to be, he bowed his head to whisper into her ear. "Then marry me."

She would have bolted if he hadn't been holding her so closely. "Wha…" she started.

He dropped to one knee. With the feathery fronds of the big willow undulating on the same breeze that had sent Kyla's fringe dancing earlier, he took her hands and kissed them. "Marry me, Kyla. Marry your real-live prince."

For the shortest second, she felt as though she'd slipped into one of her girlhood fantasies. She had always suspected that the ruins had magical properties, and now she was sure that they were conspiring with the innate sorcery of Halloween to force Zweli into this latest proposal.

The longer it took her to answer, the more Kyla realized that it would take more than magic to get her to appease the yearning in Zweli's face.

"I can't," she said.

"Why not?"

"I-I have a date tomorrow night," she stammered.

He freed her hands. He stood, slowly, and scrubbed his hands over his face.

"I'm sorry," she said.

"Don't be." He wouldn't meet her eyes. "I got caught up in the moment. I'm the one who should apologize."

"It's okay."

"Let me walk you back to Abby's," he said. "It's past ten."

"Thank you." She pulled the coat closer around her shoulders as they began walking away from the ruins.

The streets they had traveled to get to the park now seemed too quiet and the patches of darkness too deep. Zweli walked close to her, but he kept his hands in the pockets of his trousers. Kyla would have liked to hold his hand again, but she didn't press him.

I can't ask him for his hand when I keep refusing him mine, she thought.

CHAPTER SIX

The restaurant was small and Kyla had been seated too close to the entrance. Every time the door opened, cold air whooshed at her from behind and the entering customers bumped her table, elbow or leg as they moved past her. The torture of waiting seemed to stretch out infinitely now that her date, Ciel's choice this time, was twenty minutes late. Kyla would have spent the time debating whether or not she should leave if her mind hadn't been wrapped so tightly around Zweli.

Last night was going so well, she thought. *Why did he have to go and ruin it?*

He'd been so quiet on the way back to Abby's house, and once there, he'd given her a quick peck on the cheek before climbing into his new SUV and driving off. She would have preferred another argument to his quiet acceptance of her latest rejection.

She entertained the possibility that he didn't care about her anymore, but she quickly realized how idiotic that was. He wouldn't have proposed if he didn't still care. If he didn't love her.

Kyla watched the people on the street beyond the plate-glass front of the restaurant. The temperature had plummeted in the past twenty-four hours, but the cold of the new November hadn't stopped the loving couples of St. Louis from parading before Kyla. *Is everyone in love in this town?* she wondered as she watched couples walk by hand in hand, arm in arm and shoulder to shoulder. One couple stopped right in front of her to share a ruby-nosed kiss, and Kyla made a retching sound that made the diners nearest her turn.

Kyla stood and put her coat back on. She was tying a knot in the black trench coat when the door opened in her face. "Kyla!"

She looked over her shoulder, certain that the blue-eyed, pony-tailed man blocking her way was looking for some other Kyla.

"Kyla Winters," he said, his toothy smile widening with each word, "you look just like the pictures on your website."

Damn that website, she said to herself as she pulled her mouth into a smile. *Yet another one of Nigel's stupid ideas that I'm still paying for.*

"Are you Ethan?" she asked.

He took one of her hands and shook it in both of his. "Ethan Ault, at your service. Were you leaving?"

"No, I just got here," she lied. She untied her belt and peeled off her coat.

"Mmm, mmm, good!" Ethan grunted through his smile. "I love a lady in black!" He leaned back and exaggerated the action of looking her up and down. Kyla felt the eyes of the other patrons following Ethan's as they roamed from the tips of her suede boots, along her fitted wool slacks and her snug turtleneck.

"This table looks good." She quickly dropped into the seat she had just vacated.

"Sure," Ethan said. "I didn't know we could just seat ourselves. Cool."

"You've never been here before?"

"Once, but not at night." He laughed and feigned a shiver of fright as he looked out of the window. "This isn't exactly my neck of the 'hoods."

Her forehead creased in confusion. Hazel's Soul Food Kitchen was on the corner of Delmar Avenue and North Kingshighway, the nexus where the edge of the city met the fringe of the suburbs, where low-income residents, no-income Washington University students and bohemian middle-to-upper class suburbanites converged to enjoy the shops and restaurants lining Delmar. There was no greater diversity than that found in the neighborhoods surrounding Hazel's.

Kyla raised a suspicious eyebrow. "Where do you live?"

"Sunset Hills. I've got a four-bedroom split-gambrel and a forty-foot in-ground pool." He took off his jacket and held it up. "Do you like it?" he asked, displaying the puffy silver coat. "It's vintage FUBU." He hung it over the back of his chair.

"You don't seem like a defense attorney."

"Never judge a book by its cover. That's the first thing you learn as a defense attorney. Sometimes the cats that look like the biggest rough-necks are the innocent ones. Boy, I sure learned that lesson the hard way."

Kyla wasn't sure she wanted to know the details. "Do you know what's good here?" She picked up one of the menus tucked between the napkin holder and a vase of fresh Gerbera daisies.

"I only had coffee and sweet potato pie the one time I was here. I don't know much about the food. I picked this place because I thought *you* would like it."

It was on Kyla's tongue to ask him why he'd think that when a group of young people entered the restaurant. Judging from their slouchy Euro-fashionable clothing, worn backpacks and uneven ratio of boys to girls, Kyla assumed they were Washington University students. They crowded around the table across the aisle from Kyla and Ethan, and she overheard a boy with a strong Irish accent commenting on a motorcycle parked in front of the restaurant.

Ethan leaned toward them. "The bike's mine," he said, sounding exactly like the Lucky Charms leprechaun. "She's sweet, t'isn't she?"

"Is it a Harley?" the young Irishman asked.

"No, it's a Yamaha," Ethan smiled, "but I took off the decal, so it confuses people."

"Do you have an accent?" Kyla asked once his attention returned to her. "I thought I detected one when you came in, but it seems to come and go."

"I was born and raised in Arkansas," he said, and this time he sounded exactly like Bill Clinton.

"You have a real knack for accents."

"I've found that it helps put people at ease," Ethan said as the waiter appeared. "I don't even know I'm doing it most of the time."

"How are you two tonight?" the waiter asked pleasantly.

"S'up, man?" Ethan greeted dispassionately before hunching over his menu.

Kyla bristled at his linguistic morph into Eminem.

The waiter chuckled and passed a hand through his long, needle-thin braids. "I can come back in a few minutes, when you're ready." He went to the table of students and began taking their drink orders.

Ethan leaned across the table to speak to Kyla, a peculiar smile on his face. "It's brothers like that that drive me crazy."

"Why?" Kyla sat back in her chair, annoyed by his use of the word 'brothers' and the way he was suddenly trading 'that' for 'dat.'

He grinned. "You didn't notice the way he was looking at you?"

Lookin' atchoo? Kyla repeated in her head. "No, actually." She snapped open her menu and pretended to study it. "You know, you smile a lot. Has anyone ever told you that it might seem rather…off-putting?"

Ethan continued to smile. "When I was in the service, my commanding officer was always telling me to stop smiling. I didn't realize I was doing it. They used to call me 'Smiley' because they said I always have a smile on my face. When my C.O. would get pissed at me and make me do pushups, I would just smile right through hundreds of them."

"What service were you in?"

"The Army. Reserves."

Kyla discreetly looked at her watch. If she left now, before they ordered, she could get home in time to watch the Saturday night movie on HBO.

"Yo, Kyla," Ethan said, his smile broadening, "have you been to any of the Afro-American history seminars at the Community Experience Hall in Florissant?"

"No. I've only been in town for a couple of months, and now that I'm settled in, I'll be spending most of my time job hunting."

"That's a shame. I was hoping to take you sometime. It would really help you reconnect with your blackness."

"It seems to have done wonders for you," she sighed under her breath.

Ethan called the waiter back to their table. "Do you mind if I order for both of us?" he asked Kyla.

"Actually, I—"

"What can I get for you, miss?" the waiter asked Kyla as he stepped up to the table.

"I'd like the grilled vegetable plate," she began, "with red peppers, artichoke hearts, yellow squash and Vidalia onions." She glanced at Ethan. "And garlic. Lots and lots of roasted garlic."

"Hold up, man," Ethan said, dropping the "d." "Naw, man, I'm orderin' for me an' my lady."

Kyla cringed as he gave his pants legs a tug and stroked his thumb across his nose. "Say, brotherman, hook us up with some black-eyed peas, smothered cabbage, and some 'a that fine fried chicken Mama be cookin' up 'round back. An' slap some 'a that barbequed pulled pork on us, too."

"I'd like to slap something right now," Kyla grumbled.

"You and me both," the waiter chuckled quietly.

His deep, resonant voice struck a familiar chord. "You're an actor," Kyla said as she folded her menu.

"If six years suffering in the Los Angeles Shakespeare Company makes me an actor, then I guess I am."

"Antonio." Kyla sat up straighter. "I didn't recognize you without the tights and codpiece."

The waiter tossed his head, throwing his long braids and nearly whipping Ethan across the face. "You saw me in *The Merchant of Venice*? Good memory. That was four years ago."

"You were wonderful. The whole cast was great. Are you in anything now, here in St. Louis?"

"I'm in a show with the St. Louis Black Repertory Company through the end of the month. Come February, I start rehearsals for an Alvin Ailey production in—"

"Yo, man," Ethan broke in. "You mackin' on my girl? That ain't right, an' you know it ain't right."

Kyla stole a long look at the waiter. He was tall, lean and his sculpted dancer's musculature was evident in his tight white shirt. He might have been earning a living as a waiter, but he was built like a professional athlete, one who could easily snatch off Ethan's lips and shove them in his ear. Kyla half hoped that he would, so Ethan could hear how stupid he sounded.

"What would we like to drink, Ethan?" she asked, attempting to diffuse what could have become an ugly situation.

"You got some orange sodee, man?"

"Orange what?" the waiter snapped.

"Soda," Ethan said quickly, pronouncing the word correctly.

The waiter jotted the order on his notepad with a sorry shake of his head.

"Blind date," Kyla said.

"Has to be," the waiter laughed as he walked away.

Ethan stood up so abruptly, he sent his chair crashing into the person behind him. "Oh, it's like that, man? You got a problem with me being with this fine Nubian goddess?"

The waiter stopped and slowly turned around. The crowded restaurant went silent, but for Ethan's ranting and exaggerated posturing. "You just anotha brotha hatin' on losin' a fine black sistah to the great white colonial master!"

The waiter laughed out loud. "Are you kidding?"

Outraged, Kyla bolted from her chair. "You mother—!" She bit her lip before she lapsed into the very racial stereotype Ethan seemed to want her to project. She grabbed the vase of flowers from the tabletop and would have clubbed him with it if the waiter hadn't leaped between them. Kyla was ready to drag Ethan to the curb and administer a ghetto beatdown with her shoe that would have left him bloody, and in a sick sort of way, probably pleased.

"Calm down, sister, calm down," Ethan urged. He glanced furtively at the diners staring at them. "All I wanted was to get with you, and have a nice dinner."

" 'Git wit choo?' " Kyla repeated in fury, pronouncing the words the way Ethan had. "I have four siblings, you moron, and you ain't one of 'em!" she yelled. "Don't call me sister, I'm not your damn sister!"

"Don't be a hater, Kyla."

"You make it so easy, I can't help it!"

Ethan sat. "Ain't no woman of mine gonna make a fool outta me when I'm the one payin' for the meal. Now sit down, Kyla."

After a long beat of silence, Kyla, the waiter, the Irish kid, and everyone else in the restaurant burst into laughter.

"May I?" the waiter offered, taking Kyla's coat from the back of her chair.

She nodded and he helped her into it.

"That's right, go on," Ethan said. "Take your walkin' papers and go. You can forget you ever met Ethan Ault!"

If only it were that easy, Kyla thought as she walked through the door the waiter held open for her.

"Your StinkShooters are in a plastic bag inside a paper bag in a Tupperware container inside a garbage bag in the garage," Ciel said to Cady as the two helped Kyla carry plates of food into the kiddie room. "I confiscated them from the Grim Reaper on Halloween."

"Did he use them on The Gooch?" Kyla asked.

"He tried." Ciel set a plate in front of Clarence. "Did you like the StinkShooters, honey?"

Clarence shuddered violently. "They smell like skunk."

"He activated them, just to see what they smelled like," Ciel said. "He'd still be stinking if Christopher hadn't cooked up a batch of hydrogen peroxide, dish detergent and baking soda for him to bathe in."

"I'm surprised that concoction didn't take his skin off," Cady shuddered.

"It's harmless, unless you get it in your eyes," Ciel said. "All it did was turn the sulphuric acid in the StinkShooter into sulfonic acid. At least that's what Christopher said it would do."

"He's such a sweet talker, that Christopher," Kyla remarked sarcastically.

"Those StinkShooters really stink, Aunt Cady." Ella reached across the table to grab a dinner roll. "They smell like sweaty old feet and rotten eggs."

"And vomit and dog poop," C.J. added.

"No, they smell like armpits and—"

"Is this really what you want to be talking about before you eat?" Kyla asked them.

"We could talk about your date last night instead," Abigail suggested. "Mommy says she found you a jackass."

"Don't talk with your mouth full," Ciel shot at her oldest daughter.

"But I'm not eating anything."

"Then just be quiet," Ciel snapped on her way out of the room.

"Wait one minute, Ciel." Kyla pursued the sister responsible for her night of hell at Hazel's Soul Food Kitchen.

Ciel took a seat between her husband and Troy at the dining table. At Abby's hurried direction, Kyla circled to the other side to sit opposite Ciel. "You knew Ethan Ault was a StinkShooter, and you set me up on a date with him anyway?" she charged.

Choosing her words as carefully as she did in the courtroom, Ciel said, "I knew he was a jackass. I did not know that he was a StinkShooter."

"The perma-smile was bad enough, but when he started copying everybody's accents, I was ready to clock him one upside the head."

"That almost got him fired last year." Ciel spooned spiced beets onto her plate. "We were meeting with one of our Asian clients, and Ethan kept switching his 'r's' and 'l's,' saying 'Herro' instead of 'Hello' and so on. The saddest part is that our client was Asian *American*. The guy was a California surfer dude and sounded exactly like Keanu

Reeves, and Ethan was speaking to him in this insane Charlie Chan accent."

"I met Ethan at your holiday party last year, didn't I?" Lee asked.

Her mouth was full, so Ciel nodded.

Lee laughed into his napkin. "I thought he was a comic hired for the party. He came up to me and Ciel and says, 'So you're the lucky brother married to our Afro Sheen Queen.'"

"I filed a complaint with Human Resources over that one," Ciel said.

"People actually hire him to represent them in court?" Kyla picked through a helping of Clara's oyster dressing, separating out the pieces of oyster.

"He's a professional second chair," Ciel said. "He's a good researcher, but his people skills are completely retarded. The firm would have cut him loose a long time ago, if he wasn't Justin Fuller's nephew."

"Who's Justin Fuller?" Kyla asked.

"One of my firm's founding partners," Ciel said.

"You and Clara should be ashamed of yourselves, fixing me up with two complete chumps."

Clara hid a laugh in her shoulder. "We did the best we could. All the good men in this world seem to be taken already."

Kyla's appetite vanished and she shoved her plate away. "I should have canceled the date with Ethan and just gone ahead and married Zweli."

The clatter of cutlery and jovial conversation ceased as all eyes turned to Kyla. "He proposed," she reported sullenly. "Again."

Abby, who was making the rounds with a fresh basket of knotted rolls, halted and dropped the basket on the table. "And you said no? Again?" She pursed her lips and patted the top of her head with her right hand.

Kyla pinched back a smile at the sight of her mother's distinctive gesture of annoyance.

"Well, now I know why he said he had other plans when I invited him to dinner," Abby said with a long sigh. "You're killing that man, Ky."

"He's the one who keeps proposing with every full moon," she argued.

"Zweli's a good guy," Lee said, "and you're not getting any younger."

Ciel elbowed him in the side. A cold surge of angry indignation washed through Kyla, and she excused herself from the table even as Lee tried to explain that he was only kidding.

"What did you hit this week, Troy?" Lee asked his nephew, by way of changing the subject.

"You just go from bad to worse," Ciel chastised her husband.

Kyla went into the library-turned-kiddie room and sat down in the one dark leather armchair that remained.

"Who're you mad at, Aunt Ky?" Ella asked.

"I'm not mad." Kyla sank deeper into the chair and picked at a worn spot on the rounded armrest.

"You look mad," Abigail said. She had two forks in her left hand and was using them like chopsticks.

"A person can look mad without being mad," Kyla said.

"It's called acting," offered C.J., who polished off a broiled lamb chop in one hearty bite.

"Are you mad at Zweli?" Danielle asked, picking up where Ella left off.

"Why would you think that?" Kyla turned her eyes to the volumes packed in the floor-to-ceiling bookcases lining one wall. "He's not even here."

"You're always mad at him."

Kyla weighed her niece's observation. "No, I'm not." And with the denial, she reassessed her feelings about him and his latest proposal. She reluctantly accepted that what Ella and Danielle mistook for anger was something far more explosive. "Do you think I should marry Zweli?"

"Yes," Danielle, Ella and Abigail said in concert with C.J.'s and Clarence's "No." Having no opinion on the matter, the twins slipped out of their booster seats and onto the floor under the table.

"You should marry Zweli because he's nice." Abigail punctuated each word with a bounce of her forks.

"And because he's so cute," Danielle gushed.

"I might marry Zweli," Ella decided.

Clarence rolled his eyes. "Zweli is *not* going to marry anybody in kindergarten."

"Why do you guys think I shouldn't marry him?" Kyla asked her nephews, both of whom were poised to dash from the room.

"You might have babies if you marry him," Clarence answered as he gnawed on a clump of macaroni and cheese stuffed into a dinner roll he'd hollowed with his front teeth.

"What about you, C.J.?" Kyla asked.

He shrugged a bony shoulder.

"You said no quickly enough. Tell me why you think I shouldn't marry Zweli."

He grabbed a baked chicken wing from his plate and inched closer to the door. "He keeps asking you and you keep saying no, so I guess you shouldn't marry him because you don't really want to."

C.J. and Clarence made good their escape while Kyla pondered the simplicity of her nephew's words. *But I do want to marry him,* she told herself. *I've wanted to be with him all along.*

"Aunt Kyla, maybe you should just say yes the next time he asks you."

Kyla stared at Danielle, amazed that at eleven years old, she already had the Winters ability to make any suggestion sound like a commandment.

Cady sat on the floor of the attic with Clarence, Keren, and the twins while Kyla looked down on them from her perch in the nearby windowsill. Claire and Sammy, covered in dust, played with the Matchbox and Hot Wheels cars that Cady had collected when she was Clarence's age. A sleek black convertible zoomed across the scuffed floorboards, and Kyla stopped it with the toe of her sneaker. She picked it up and squinted at the tiny embossed letters on the bottom.

"It's a 1963 Lincoln Continental," she read aloud. "Nice car. Didn't work out too well for Kennedy, though."

"I see you're in just as pleasant a mood now as you were during dinner," Cady said cheerfully.

"Why don't you finish corrupting Clarence?" Kyla fired back.

"Oh, right." Cady turned back to her nephew. "The Sword of Damocles might be worth a try. The next time you have lunch lady cake at school, take a piece of it into the bathroom while The Gooch is in there."

"What's lunch lady cake?" Keren moved from his uncomfortable squat on the floor to share the dusty windowsill with Kyla.

"It's that dark chocolate cake with the snow-white buttercream frosting that they make in those big sheet pans in public schools," Kyla explained. "We always called it lunch lady cake."

Clarence loudly slurped. "I love lunch lady cake."

"The Sword of Damocles is when you take pieces of lunch lady cake and toss them up to the bathroom ceiling." Cady lowered her voice in the quiet of the attic. The sunlight played in her multicolored curls as she leaned closer to Clarence, tightening their circle of nascent mischief. "The best time to do it is when you know The Gooch is in the stall next to you, because the cake won't stay up there for very long. As soon as you hear him going to the bathroom, pop the cake to the ceiling, frosting side up. It'll stick for a few seconds. While you're running out of the bathroom, the cake will fall right down on top of The Gooch."

Clarence's eyes glimmered. "Will it really work?"

"It worked for The Three Stooges," Cady assured him.

"Tell me how to do the Stink Chair," Clarence begged, greedily rubbing one hand over the other.

"You can use almost any kind of raw meat, but seafood works fastest," Cady started.

"Are you sure you should be teaching this particular child the chaotic arts of The Three Stooges?" Kyla asked.

"The Stink Chair isn't the Stooges. I invented it myself."

"You're in so much trouble when that one starts kindergarten," Kyla said to Keren with a nod toward Sammy, who was trying to negotiate a spider into his mouth as the tiny creature skittered over his hand and forearm.

"It's Claire we'll have to worry about," Keren said. "She's the quiet schemer who orchestrates Sammy's shenanigans. She gave him that spider."

Kyla shivered as she watched Claire gently jostle a shoebox she was using to imprison a pair of dainty sac spiders.

"Zweli had to work today, or else he would have been here," Keren said softly.

Kyla studied her thumbnail. "Did he ask you to tell me that?"

"Nope. I just thought you should know."

Lee was the jester of the husbands while Christopher and Keren were the strong, silent ones. If Keren had something to say, especially about her relationship with Zweli, Kyla felt obligated to listen. His eyes never left Cady as he said, "I hated her."

"Who? Cady?"

He nodded. "I was minding my own business one day and suddenly, there she was. The most obnoxious, willful, won't-take-no woman I'd ever met." He fondly gazed upon the patch of sunlight currently bathing his wife and the children. "I hated her so much I could feel it pulsating it in my chest. And she hated me right back."

"Uh…how romantic?"

"Cady and I had so much chemistry the first time we met, we didn't know what to do with it." He spun slightly to face Kyla. "I wasn't used to such an onslaught of feeling."

"You worked it out quickly enough. You guys met and married inside of seven months."

"We knew it was right. We knew we were meant for each other. Same as Zweli knows you're meant for him."

"Maybe he wasn't meant for *me*," Kyla said stubbornly. "Has anyone besides me considered that? I lov—" She caught herself. "I like Zweli a lot, but I've got a lot of things going on right now. My life is too complicated already without adding a serious relationship into the mix. I don't want to burden him, and I—"

"Used that speech the first time he proposed to you," Keren broke in. "Zweli is the only man I've ever seen you smile at. I don't mean that fake, pageant-contestant smile you use, but a real smile, the kind that originates here." He touched his knuckles to his chest.

Kyla hugged herself. "Zweli is not a one-woman man."

"He's a right-woman man."

"Don't you mean a right-*now* woman man? If I went back to California today, he'd be sweet-talking a sorority house tomorrow."

"What would you have him do, Kyla? Pledge unwavering celibacy to you in your absence? Is that what you did while you were in California?"

"Is it weird to talk about your sex life with your brother-in-law?" Kyla asked sarcastically. "I'm just wondering."

"Keren, Grandma's got a tin of chocolate stars in the living room," Cady said. "Why don't you take the twins downstairs and find it?"

"I can find it!" Clarence eagerly volunteered. "I know right where it is."

"I think your auntie figured you might," Keren said as he corralled the twins and steered them toward the staircase.

Kyla watched Clarence bolt past his cousins while Keren spotted them as they scooted down the stairs on their backsides. Once the children were out of sight and earshot, Cady moved to sit at her sister's feet. "Who did you sleep with in California, Kyla? You can talk about your sex life with your sister, can't you?"

She spent a moment silently calculating.

"That many, huh?"

"That few, actually."

"How few?"

"None," Kyla exhaled. "Not since Grandma died."

Cady's eyebrows arched. "Not even once in three, almost four years?"

"I was busy working." Kyla massaged her temples with her fingertips. "When I wasn't working, I was taking acting classes, or auditioning, or training in the gym, or making public appearances and generally being alone and miserable. I just…" *Never met anyone like Zweli*, she finished in her head.

Kyla didn't like the sly look on her sister's face as Cady said, "You know what I think?"

"I'm not sure I want to," she said warily.

"I think that you just haven't met the right person yet."

Kyla blinked in surprise. "Huh?"

"Zweli is smart, personable, handsome…he's a catch. But he's not the only shark in the water. Maybe there's someone better out there for you. I think you just need a chance to test that."

Kyla threw her arms up in grateful relief as she dropped to the floor to sit with Cady. "You're the only one who understands what I'm trying to do! It would have been so easy to come back home and just pick up where I left off with Zweli, and that's what I wanted, but it's been a long time. He's a different person now, so much better than he was when I first met him. And I *know* I'm a different person. We enjoy each other's company, but that doesn't mean we're compatible in any long-term, meaningful way." She leaned against the wall and hugged her knees to her chest, which suddenly felt full of bitingly cold air. Her tone softened as she said, "Zweli is so generous and kind. He's patient, understanding and capable." She turned toward the window and stared at the sun until her eyes watered. "He's so beautiful. He deserves someone who's focused and successful, not an unemployed actress whose claim to fame is her inability to grow beyond 'Kati, with an "i.""

Cady's intent, empathetic expression stopped her words. "I'm counting on you," Kyla said when Cady gave her arm a meaningful pat. "You know me better than anyone. You'll find someone special for me, right?"

Cady leaned over and gave her a big hug. "He'll be amazing, kiddo. I promise I won't stop looking until I find a fella who'll make your toes curl."

Kyla buried her face in her big sister's shoulder. She was so eager to turn her worries over to someone else, she didn't heed the warning flares ignited by the saccharin sweetness of Cady's vow.

"Where've you been keeping yourself these days?"

Zweli looked up from the flat-screen monitor on his desk at the sound of Keren's voice. A grilled chicken Caesar salad sat untouched at Zweli's elbow, wilting in its clear plastic container. Keren took one of the comfortable leather and brass wing chairs facing Zweli's desk. "Your absence in the cafeteria has been missed," he said. "The chocolate amaretto cheesecake is piling up."

Zweli set his wireless keyboard on his desk and shoved his work aside. Now that Keren mentioned it, he realized that it had indeed been awhile since his last visit to the hospital cafeteria, where grandmotherly food service matron Myrtle Huckabee always pressed him into accepting her most expensive á là carte dessert, on the house. "I figured Myrtle would have found a new pet by now."

"You might want to stop and see her sometime," Keren said. "She treats me as if I'm holding you hostage somewhere."

Zweli made a noncommittal grunt.

"She won't give *me* any free cheesecake until you come back," Keren complained.

Zweli stretched in his chair, the seasoned leather creaking against his movements. "I've just had too much work up here to take lunch lately. Things always get busy right before the holidays."

"Is that all?"

He knew it was futile to try to hide anything from Keren. "I just don't have the stomach for it anymore." He sat back in his chair and absently swiveled from side to side. "It used to be fun, you know? Like a mini Spring Break in the middle of every day. I never went there for food. You never seemed to notice it much, but it's a jungle down there, man, and I was the king of beasts with my pick of women from every corner of this hospital. I could schedule breakfast with one of those El Salvadoran beauties in housekeeping, lunch with a physician's assistant, drinks with a nurse, dinner with an administrator and a late-night something-or-other with just about anyone else."

"When was your last something-or-other?"

"A good week or so before you cornered me in the hallway and told me that Kyla was back in town."

Keren made a low noise of awe. "Man, you're sprung."

Zweli banged his fist on his desk and leaned forward. "It's worse than that, Keren! She made a pass at me on Halloween, and I let it go. I didn't want her there in the park, like a couple of damn teenagers with no place else to go. I wanted her in my home, in my bed, with the whole rest of our lives stretched out in front of us." He sat back, slightly embarrassed by his confession. "It was an incredible night, K. Like something out of a movie. I thought I had a clear shot and I couldn't *not* propose to her. And damn if she didn't refuse to marry me again."

Keren started to speak, but he only got as far as opening his mouth.

"I don't get her," Zweli said emphatically. "She'll have sex with me but she won't marry me? What the hell kind of ass-backwards nonsense is that? The real question is why I won't just take her up on it. What's gotten into *me* lately? I feel like I'm possessed."

"I know it's easy for me to say, but try not to think about her," Keren suggested.

"*HA!* That was your wife's advice, and look where it's got me. Kyla's *dating*. I tried ignoring her, but it's hard when I see her everywhere I turn. She's picking through the Chilean plums at Harold's Market, she's sweating on the Gravitron at Buddy's Gym, she's running on the Forest Park side of Kingshighway…" He hung his head over the back of his chair, closed his eyes and laced his fingers over them. "I didn't realize St. Louis was such a small town."

"Why don't you come to the house for dinner tonight?" Keren asked. "Cady's been working on a section of her book that concentrates on one of her ancestors from Louisiana, and she's been cooking Creole feasts for the past three days."

Zweli sat forward and logged off his computer. "That's got to be better than that Irish phase she went through. I never ate so much soda bread."

"It's been almost a month since they've seen you," Keren said. "They miss you, Z."

"Who? The twins?"

"Everybody," Keren said. "Abby, Clara and Ciel, Christopher and Lee, Troy—"

"Does that litany end with 'Kyla?'"

"Yes," Keren smiled. "Whether she wants to admit to herself or anyone else. Can I tell Cady to expect you tonight?"

"I really wish I could, but I have plans tonight." He gathered his documents and neatly stacked them before replacing them in an olive drab hanging folder. "What?" he said, noticing Keren's curious stare.

"Nothing," Keren grinned as he stood to leave. "Your business is your business."

"It's nothing exciting," Zweli said. "I'm meeting a real estate agent at seven."

"Oh yeah? What's her name?"

"*His* name is Max Carrick and he's showing me a house."

Keren's dark eyes brightened. "You're thinking of buying a house?"

Zweli rounded the desk, dropped his neglected salad into the trashcan, and started out with Keren. "I'm thinking of buying a home. There's a difference."

"You love that swingin' bachelor pad of yours. Why do you want a house all of a sudden?"

"I like gardening," Zweli said dryly, and he turned off the lights.

CHAPTER SEVEN

Zweli's head lurched forward with the abrupt movement of the car, his upper body restrained by his tight seatbelt and his knees wedged against the dashboard of Troy's 1987 Chevy Nova. "Sorry, Sway," Troy said earnestly for the hundredth time. "I didn't mean to do that."

"It's okay." Zweli's left hand loosely rested on the emergency brake between the bucket front seats. "It's better to jerk it than to stall out completely."

Troy giggled.

"I'm serious, man," Zweli said. "When's your winter formal?"

Troy stopped laughing. "Seventeen days."

"Then that means you have sixteen days to learn to drive this thing without jerking and stalling. Do you want your date to throw up all over the dashboard?"

"No," Troy grimaced.

"You have to provide a smooth ride for your lady when you drive a five-speed." After checking the church parking lot one more time to make sure that it was empty, Zweli gave Troy the go-ahead to start the engine. "Now very slowly, engage the clutch as you give the car a little gas. Just a taste now. This isn't a rodeo. You don't want the car to buck to a stop."

Troy followed Zweli's instruction. "Thanks for coming out with me. Mom won't get in the car with me anymore, and Dad only takes me out on weekends."

"You're welcome, but pay attention to what your feet are doing." Zweli, his hand still braced over the emergency brake, tensed as Troy maneuvered the car across the deserted parking lot. "Drive over there, into the exit lane."

Excited, Troy turned to Zweli. "Are we going onto the street?"

"Hell no," Zweli chuckled. "I want you to drive a few laps on the lot. You have to get used to starting and stopping on an incline. Once you can do that without stalling, you're good to go, kid."

Troy headed for the gentle incline at the southern border of the lot. "Should I brake now?"

"Brake at the top of the incline."

Four seconds later, Troy slammed on the brakes, once more pitching Zweli's head toward the windshield and stalling the car. "Sorry," he said.

Zweli rested his right elbow on the door of the car and pinched his chin between his thumb and forefinger. "Troy, why did you buy a five-speed?"

He shrugged one shoulder in the noncommittal, dispassionate way of his younger brother. "It was a bargain. It's old, but it only has thirty-three thousand miles on it. The engine is tight, the brakes are good and the upholstery is in perfect condition. The chassis's got some rust damage around the tire wells and the rear bumper, but that's just cosmetic. The previous owner wanted one thousand dollars for it, but she agreed to take six hundred if I shoveled her walk this winter and mowed her lawn in the summer. I thought it was a good deal."

"You negotiated the deal yourself?"

Troy nodded. "After the details were worked out, I presented the written agreement to Mom and Dad. They agreed to let me take the money from my savings account, and Dad signed off on the title."

"You're a smart kid."

Troy beamed under the praise. "My aunt's a lawyer. I learned a few things."

"Ready to roll?"

Troy gripped the steering wheel. "Ready."

The sky had darkened to a flat, moonless purple by the time Troy was able to bring the Nova to an easy stop at the top of the incline, and then start again without throwing Zweli's neck out of joint. Zweli was starting to believe that the Nova's original clutch would survive Troy's driving lessons when a parade of automobiles zoomed onto the barren church lot. Teenagers hooted and laughed as they stood in the cabs of the trucks and hung from the windows of cars painted in blue and white and adorned with blue and white crepe streamers.

"Stick to the tree line over here," Zweli said, directing Troy away from the other cars. "It's Wednesday. Is there a church parade tonight?"

Troy looked at the gathering of circling cars. "Those are Wilderberry High fans, judging by their colors. Wilderberry plays Easton in the Thanksgiving Football Classic tomorrow. They're asking for it, riding around here in Easton territory." He turned back to Zweli. "Are you coming to Thanksgiving dinner tomorrow? Grandma wants you to."

"I know. She's left three messages on my voicemail at home and at the hospital."

"Aunt Kyla's going to be there," Troy said with a bounce of his eyebrows. "She was going to take me driving today, but she had to cancel because she's got Aunt Cady's date tonight."

"Cady's what?" Jealousy flared in Zweli's chest.

"Mom says that Aunt Cady fixed Kyla up with some guy named Hippolyte."

Zweli grunted a laugh. His jealousy evaporated in his certainty that a man named Hippolyte would hold no more appeal to Kyla than Sterling Bancroft or the other character Keren had told him of. "Your aunts must really hate Kyla," Zweli chuckled.

"It's more that they really like you," Troy said.

Zweli got out of the car and studied the Wilderberry processional a little more closely. The kids weren't just high on their Thanksgiving vacation from school. Big coolers in the cabs of two trucks had turned them into wet bars, and just about every kid in attendance had a can or a bottle of beer. A young girl, her upper body hanging from the passenger side of a black sports car, sprayed her cohorts with bottles clutched in both hands as the vehicle sped around the lot in ever-widening circles.

"Cut the engine, Troy," Zweli said. "I'm ready to drive you home."

They switched positions, and as Troy buckled himself into the passenger side, Zweli adjusted the driver's seat to accommodate his longer legs. "I'm not your father, Troy, but I'm telling you right now, if I ever hear of you behaving like those idiots when you're driving, I might ground you for life myself. Understand?"

"I understand."

Zweli fastened his seatbelt. "I hate working ER shifts because not a weekend goes by when we're not treating some dumb-ass kid who decided to get loaded and then get behind the wheel of a car." He began adjusting the rearview mirror. "The worst is when the drunk driver hits someone else, and it almost never fails that the drunk is the one who gets a scratch while the other party ends up in a body cast or a coffin." He turned to Troy once more. "Do you ever drink?"

"No," Troy said firmly, meeting Zweli's gaze squarely.

"Honestly?"

Troy's gaze shifted to something beyond Zweli's left shoulder. His eyes flew open wide, his arms stiffened and he awkwardly threw his back against the passenger door as he hollered, "No!"

Alarmed, Zweli turned to see what had so frightened Troy, and at that moment, the black sports car crashed into the driver's side of the Nova.

"Troy?"

Zweli picked himself up off Troy, the slim distance between the front seats narrowed by the collision of the black car, which was inching away from the Nova in a rattling cloud of white smoke.

"Troy!" Zweli shook him, and the boy's hands slowly fell from his face.

"Is it over?"

Zweli gave him a cursory visual exam before grabbing Troy's chin and guiding his face toward his. *Pupils even, reactive,* Zweli told himself. He turned Troy's head, and saw no obvious trauma to his neck, face or cranium. Troy was visibly shaken, but uninjured. "Can you walk?" he asked.

Troy nodded.

Zweli unfastened his seatbelt and unlocked the car door. He had to batter it with his left shoulder three times before the crumpled door would open, and the force of his movement almost toppled him onto the asphalt.

"Dude, I am so sorry, I can't even tell you," the Mohawk-sporting driver of the black car said as he approached Zweli.

"He only had a few beers," one of his young companions hastily explained. "It's not like he was drunk or anything."

"Are you hurt?" Zweli asked the driver. He was only vaguely aware of Troy's voice, speaking the location and name of the church into his cell phone.

The kid swallowed hard and backed away a step. "No, I'm good." He looked at his car and almost crumpled to his knees. He grabbed his head and rushed to the front end, which looked like an accordion. "My folks are gonna kill me!" he cried.

"You're worried about your car?" Zweli shouted, using his right hand to swipe moisture from his forehead. "You could have been killed! Your friend there could have been killed." He had a hard time focusing on the somber faces that now surrounded the accident site. "I'm a doctor. Is anyone hurt?"

Troy approached him, his eyes glassy with fear. He took Zweli's right wrist and raised his hand, displaying it palm up. "You are." His voice broke over the last word.

Zweli's gaze shifted from Troy's face to his own hand. The creases and lines of his palm were filled with blood, and for a long moment, he couldn't figure out how it had gotten there. "Is this mine?"

"Do you know where you are, Sway?" Troy asked, his voice more firm but sounding as though it were coming through a tin can on a string.

Zweli patted himself down but couldn't locate the source of the blood. When he raised his head to address Troy, a bead of wetness trickled over his left eyebrow. He touched his fingertip to it, and it came away with a crimson cap of blood.

"Oh man, I'm getting out of here," the driver of the sports car whimpered as he watched two of the other cars peel out of the parking lot.

"I've called 9-1-1 and I gave the dispatcher your license plate number, so you'd better be here when the police get here," Troy said as he took Zweli by his shoulder and elbow. "Sway, an ambulance is coming, too."

"Who needs an ambulance?" he asked. "Is someone hurt?"

A blonde girl in blue and white face paint moved to the front of the thinning crowd of onlookers. "He's really out of it. I've got some aspirin in my car, if that'll help."

"No," Troy said. "Aspirin could make his bleeding worse."

Zweli tried to pull away but Troy stopped him. "You have a head injury, Sway. It's bleeding a lot. I think you should lie down and wait for the paramedics."

He wanted to argue, but his powers of speech had suddenly deserted him. Troy held his head in line with his neck and shoulders as he helped him into a horizontal position on the asphalt.

"Is his neck broken?" the panicked driver asked.

"I don't know what all's wrong with him, but it doesn't hurt to protect his neck, just in case." Troy took off his sweater and used the sleeve to apply pressure to Zweli's wound. "Is there any ice in either of those coolers?"

"I'll get it," offered the girl with the painted face, and she ran off to do so.

Zweli fought to keep his eyes open. "I'm so sorry about your car, Troy."

"It wasn't your fault," he said. "I'm more worried about you."

I'm fine, Zweli wanted to say. But the pain in his head would have made a liar out of him. His hearing seemed to fade in and out as he listened to the voices around him in the growing darkness.

The one voice he recognized belonged to Troy. "We weren't driving," he said, holding his cell phone in one hand while maintaining steady pressure on Zweli's wound with the other. "We were about to leave when they crashed into us…I'm okay…honestly…I don't know. It's taking so long for them to get here and Zweli doesn't look good, Mom… Okay…I'll call you back when the police get here…Don't worry, Mom… Okay, I hear the sirens now. I gotta go."

Me too, Zweli thought, and for him, the sound of the sirens faded into silence.

"Should I call your mother, honey?" Abby asked. Zweli didn't have the heart to tell her to stop fussing over him. As she moved about his bed, tucking in his scratchy sheets and thin blanket, she filled his room with the scents of the herbs and spices she'd been using in the pre-Thanksgiving dinner preparations she'd dropped to rush to his side.

"No, Mrs. Winters," he said. "She would just drive herself crazy with worry over nothing. Or even worse, she'd drive here from Indianapolis and drive *me* crazy."

Abby leaned over him, armed with a Styrofoam cup of ice chips and a plastic spoon. Zweli drank in her aroma of rosemary and cloves, but he passed on the ice chips.

"He's got a bump on the head, Mama," Clara said. "He's being kept here overnight for observation, not to deliver a baby. Why are you giving him ice chips?"

Abby set the cup and spoon on Zweli's bed table. "If you're allowed to eat real food, I'd be happy to go home and get something for you."

"It's getting late, Mrs. Winters," he said. "I appreciate the trip you made all the way out here. I wouldn't think of having you make another one. I'm still feeling a little nauseous anyway, so I think I'll save my appetite for tomorrow. The ice chips will hold me tonight."

"I'll have plenty to give thanks for tomorrow," Abby said with a short sigh of relief. "I'm so glad neither of you was hurt worse."

"I don't have a scratch on me," Troy said. "Zweli took the entire hit."

"That's a solid little car you have there, Troy, even without airbags," Christopher said, giving his son's shoulder an affectionate squeeze. "Zweli could have been hurt much worse."

"Can the car be salvaged?" Zweli asked.

"We're not sure just yet," Christopher answered. "The other kid's insurance will cover it, but Troy might be better off just getting another car. Anything automatic."

"But I like my Nova," Troy protested.

"What about the drunk driver and the girl who was in the car with him?" Zweli asked.

"They were examined and released," Keren volunteered. He turned off the lightboard near the door and pulled Zweli's X-rays from it. "The driver's blood alcohol level was three times the legal limit. The police arrested him right there in the emergency room. Zweli, your CAT scan verified that you haven't suffered any permanent damage. That laceration above your left eye was fairly nasty, and you have a mild concussion, but I'm sure you'd be released you if you came home with me. Cady and I can keep an eye on you, make sure you don't pop a pupil or start convulsing. Why did you want to keep these?" He handed the films to Zweli.

"Troy wanted them." Zweli put the pictures of his skull into a large brown envelope, which he then gave to Troy. "He was a real professional tonight. He knew exactly what to do, both from medical and criminal standpoints. He secured the scene single-handedly and he kept me calm and immobile. Getting the ice from the drunks was a stroke of genius. And before the crash, he was really starting to get the hang of driving a stick-shift."

Clara proudly kissed her son's temple, and Troy blushed so hard it swallowed up his freckles.

"Do you want to leave tonight?" Keren asked Zweli. "These suburban neighborhood hospitals are a lot cushier than down and dirty Raines-Hartley, but it's still a hospital. You might be more comfortable at my place. You know Cady would wait on you hand and foot."

"I'll be fine here for one night," Zweli said, but what he really meant was that he didn't want to be a bother. And if he had his choice of Winters nursemaids, Cady and Abby would be second and third on his list.

"You need a shirt on, Zweli," Abby said. "Why are you laying up here half naked?"

"The nurses don't seem to mind." Troy jerked his head toward the doorway where a cluster of young women lingered, staring furtively and giggling.

"My shirt is drenched in blood," Zweli said. "And I won't be caught dead in one of those assless dresses hospitals love so much."

"Well, you still need to put something on," Abby insisted. "You'll catch a chill."

"How do you catch a chill?" Clara asked. "What does that actually mean?"

Abby turned to Keren for help. "You're a doctor. Explain to this woman what a chill can do to your health."

"It makes you cold, Clara," Keren said flatly.

"Cold can give you a cold," Abby said. "It's a documented fact."

"No, it isn't," Clara said.

"Yes, it is," said Abby.

"No, it's not," Keren said.

Abby stubbornly set her jaw. "I said it is."

An older, less impressionable nurse entered the room with a tiny plastic cup containing two white capsules. "Actually, it isn't," she said. "It's an old wives' tale that chilly weather gives you a cold. Cold weather doesn't transmit the bacteria that causes the common cold."

"I've been a mother and a teacher for longer than you've been alive, and I've seen how a chill can make someone sick," Abby said loftily. "A chill will give Zweli a cold."

"No, it won't," said the nurse. She watched Zweli pop the capsules into his mouth and follow them with a long swallow of water.

"Excuse me," Zweli cut in before the argument could pick up more steam, "but would you mind taking this debate elsewhere? I have a little bit of a headache."

Keep walking, keep walking, keep walking, Dear God, please make him keep walking.

Kyla's desperate prayer went unheeded as the man in a full-length patchwork rabbit fur coat raised his oversized sunglasses, zeroed in on her, and made a beeline for her table. He smiled, and the muted chandelier light bounced off the gold in his mouth. His shoulders bounced, and he led with the left one as he neared Kyla, giving himself a peculiar sideways gait. His gold-plated incisors glinting, his hands loosely fisted and one eye closed in an exaggerated wink, the man came to a halt before Kyla.

This can't be happening, she thought. It was inconceivable that this man, this nightmarish caricature from *J.D.'s Revenge*, was her date for the evening. *Maybe he just needs the time*, she hoped.

"Excuse me," he said loudly enough to draw the attention of every patron within the austere sophistication of La Mirage, "but can I ask you a question?"

Kyla calmed a little. She half expected and half hoped that his question would be the one strangers typically asked her: "Haven't I seen you on television?"

Before she could answer yes or no, the man fired off with, "Sugar, how'd you get so fly?" With a blush of embarrassment stinging her cheeks and the tips of her ears, Kyla lowered her face and grabbed the tail of the linen swan propped on the gold-etched charger plate before her. The swan collapsed into an embroidered napkin as Kyla drew it to her face.

Laughing at his own cleverness, the man took off his coat with a flourish that left the diners nearest him picking follicles of rabbit hair from their crystal goblets of white Beaujolais. Kyla's jaw dropped at the sight of his fuzzy black ensemble: a double-breasted jacket with wide, notched lapels and straight-leg pants with flared cuffs. A matching fedora and ankle boots perfectly accessorized the outfit.

"Sugar Girl, you're mo' fine live and in person than you are on the *boob* tube," he said jovially as he sat in the empty chair opposite Kyla. He peered over the top of his sunglasses and fixed his gaze on the revealing oval cutout in the bodice of her amber-gold silk dress, the Kara Saun original that Cady had insisted she wear tonight. "I'm Hippolyte." He extended a hand heavy with chunky gold rings glittering with crushed diamonds.

With the entire restaurant as her audience, Kyla felt she had no choice but to shake it. "I'm Kyla. Pleased to meet you," she said weakly.

"Mmm, mmm, mmm!" Hippolyte grunted. "Sugar Girl, you are scrumdillyicious!" His eyes still riveted to her bosom, he said, "You're the Dairy Queen and I'm read' to be your king."

Kyla was deciding how to extract herself from Hippolyte's company when, to her astonishment, he managed to draw even more attention to himself by briskly rapping the thick ring on his pinky against the tabletop. "Waiter?" he called. "Can I get a li'l potent potable over here?"

Stop my heart, Lord, Kyla silently prayed. *Pop an aneurysm deep in my head.*

"You know, this is the first date I've been on in a long time," Hippolyte said. "I'm going to have to think of something real special to do to pay your sister back."

"Me, too," Kyla said darkly as the waiter approached.

The waiter maintained his impassive, professional demeanor as he took Hippolyte's order for an orange juice with a jigger of gin and Kyla's request for an entire bottle of wine.

It suddenly occurred to her that this wasn't for real, that it had to be one of Cady's more elaborate practical jokes. Sending her to a place like La Mirage to meet a man like Hippolyte…this was the stuff of the old sitcoms Lee liked so much.

"So Hippolyte," Kyla began, tossing caution and good sense to the wind with both hands, "what do you do for a living?"

He leaned farther back in his chair, his left leg hanging over his right and sticking into the aisle between tables. His eyes darting around the restaurant, he said, "A li'l a' this, a li'l a' that. You know how it is."

"I can only imagine, although I had a job interview this morning that might pan out into something worthwhile."

"An interview?" Hippolyte scoffed. "Cady said that you were an actress."

"There's really not much acting work for me here in St. Louis." Kyla looked past Hippolyte, hoping to see the waiter approaching with her wine.

"Then what'd you come back here for, Sugar Girl?"

The last thing she wanted was to discuss her reasons for moving back home, but she had to admire Hippolyte's courage to pry. "I like your suit, Mr. Hippolyte." She deftly changed the subject. "Is that…velvet?"

He proudly took hold of his lapels. "Nah, baby, this is burred suede. It's imported from France." He made the most ungodly screeches with the legs of his chair as he scooted over the marble tiles to sit closer to Kyla. "I like all things French. French dressing. French fries. French kiss—"

"Is that my cell phone?" Kyla loudly cut in.

He picked up his swan, shook it out, and then draped the huge napkin over his knee. "What's good here? I've had a hankerin' for a good piece a' pork all day. Where's the menus?"

"The waiter is bringing our drinks," Kyla said. "He'll recite the menu."

The waiter neatly sidestepped Hippolyte's foot as he presented two wine glasses and a decanted French white, a highball of orange juice and a shot glass of gin. The nattily dressed waiter poured a sample of the wine for Hippolyte, who was busy pouring the gin into his juice. Kyla made a subtle gesture with her hand, which the savvy waiter caught. He filled the glass and set it before Kyla, and then filled a glass for Hippolyte.

His spine erect and his hands clasped at his waist, the waiter began presenting the menu. "Tonight, La Mirage offers a celeriac soup with *crème fraiche* and white truffles, and tuna *tartare* with cucumber and sea urchin—"

"Sea what?" Hippolyte almost hollered. "Listen here, Chilly Willy, ain't you got any nice, thick pork tenderloin back there?"

The waiter continued his soft recitation of roasted chicken with *chanterelles* and sirloin with braised beef cheeks, *foie gras*, bone marrow and consommé. He'd reached the dessert point of his spiel when Kyla tactfully interrupted him after the coconut tapioca and fig Napoleon.

"Would you excuse us for a moment?" she said with royal aplomb.

The waiter nodded and retreated once more. "Mr. Hippolyte," Kyla said, not quite believing what she was about to say, "would you like to go somewhere else?"

He downed the rest of his drink and stood up. "Sugar Girl, just lead the way." He reached into his pocket and withdrew a gold money clip thick with folded bills. He peeled off a few of them and let them drift onto the table. "This oughta help Chilly Willy buy a li'l personality."

"Let me get this," Kyla said. She thought it only fair, since she was the one who'd ordered the pricey wine.

"It's on Cady," Hippolyte said. "She said this place was steep, and she wanted us to have a real good time."

Kyla had to smile when he went to the back of her chair, pulled it for her, and then offered his elbow. She took it, looping her arm through his. Heads turned as Hippolyte led her away from the table, then doubled back to grab the bottle of wine. With his rabbit fur trailing behind him, he seemed unaware of the wide-eyed shock his presence brought to the faces of La Mirage's elite clientele as he escorted Kyla toward the exit. Or perhaps he was aware of it, because he paused and offered the wine to Kyla. What started out as a complete farce turned into fun as she took a healthy swig from the bottle right there in the middle of the dining room.

Hippolyte carried their shared tray to a pair of stools at the counter lining the windowed front wall of the restaurant. Mindless of the intoxicated stare of the heavyweight diner sitting three stools away, Hippolyte drew a black satin handkerchief from his outer breast pocket and snapped it across one of the stools before he allowed Kyla to sit upon it. He draped his hankie over the stool two places away from Kyla before setting his hat on top of it. Once he had the attention of the entire restaurant, he removed Kyla's faux mink stole and neatly propped it on a stool of its own.

"Now this is more like it." He sat beside Kyla and faced his array of twelve steaming square hamburgers. He pulled one from its cozy cardboard box, and with his pinkies sticking out, he ate more than half of it in one bite.

He was so comfortable, Kyla wondered how often he combined *haute couture* with White Castle.

She took a deep whiff of her own trio of White Castles. The distinctive aroma hadn't changed one bit, unlike so many other things from her childhood. It uncovered one of her most deeply buried memories, one of the few she had of her father.

Hippolyte gave her a nudge with his elbow as he dribbled wine into his tall paper cup of orange soda. "What's on your mind, Sugar Girl?"

"My father."

"I'm old but I ain't that old," he remarked.

"No," Kyla hastily began to explain. "It's been so long since I last ate here. I gave up fast food a long time ago. I don't think I've eaten a White Castle hamburger in ten years." She took a burger from its box and partially peeled the delicate bun from the thin square of steamed beef. She took another whiff of the onions atop the patty. "My father used to bring me and my sisters to White Castle on Saturday afternoons, when we would be driving my mother crazy. Chiara was a baby and she couldn't nap with all of us running around the house, screaming and fighting." She bit one corner of the burger. "Holy Heaven, they taste exactly the same," she giggled. "My father could eat thirty of these things at one sitting."

"Little girls love their daddies. Even when they get to be big girls."

Kyla watched him chew up two more burgers in three bites. "Do you have children, Mr. Hippolyte?"

"Yep. Four girls, three boys."

Kyla almost choked on an onion ring. "That's a lot of kids. How do you afford…uh," she caught herself before her intrusive inclinations got the best of her, "the time to spend with them?"

"It's easy." He pointed to Kyla's onion rings. When she pushed the carton toward him, he took three of them. "They ain't mine. They belong to my lady friends. I help out however I can, when I can. It ain't easy raisin' kids on your own these days. It takes a village. A village and a whol' lotta dinero."

"How old are they?" Kyla leaned forward to accommodate the gregarious bunch of high schoolers passing behind her.

Hippolyte reached into his jacket and pulled out a thick wallet bound by red rubber bands. When he pulled the bands off, the wallet sprang open and spit out a long strand of photos. "This here," he pointed at the first photo with his pinky finger, "is Nikema. She's the baby of the bunch. She'll be nine next month. This is her brother, Jaden. He's twelve and he's as bad as they come. He got kicked outta school last year for writing on the bathroom walls."

Kyla couldn't imagine the sweetly smiling, bright-eyed boy in the photo doing anything naughty. "What did he write?"

"The lyrics to an old 2 Live Crew song he overheard somebody singin' 'round the house one time."

Kyla chuckled. "Somebody like who?"

"I wasn't even thinkin' 'bout the actual words," Hippolyte explained. "Some of the dirtiest songs got the catchiest little tunes. Me and Jaden both learned our lesson. I tell you, you gotta be careful 'round kids."

She listened attentively as he went through all of his photos, extolling the virtues and decrying the faults of each of "his" children. "Most real fathers don't know as much about their own children as you do about these guys." She tapped the stack of photos.

"I was too busy messin' up to find a good woman and settle down when I had the chance," he said. "I take my kids where I find 'em now, and I love 'em like they was my own."

"Now I can see why Cady and you are friends," Kyla smiled.

"It wasn't obvious from the get go?" He barked a short laugh. "Cady wouldn't ever put you in harm's way. She's worried about you and she wanted you to have a good time tonight." He looked at her over the tops of his shades. "You are havin' a good time, ain't ya?"

With a quiet chuckle, Kyla nodded. "Actually, I am."

"Good." Hippolyte pulled her cold onion rings to his side of the tray. "Maybe now you can step outta your funk."

"I'm not in a funk."

"Cady said you ain't been on any auditions since you hit town. That sounds like a funk to me."

"I go on interviews now, not auditions."

"You an actress, ain't ya?"

"Yes. No. I'm…" She set her cup down a bit too sharply. "There aren't the same opportunities here in St. Louis that exist in L.A.," she blurted.

"How do you know? You ain't even tried to see what's out here."

"I already know what's here. It's what I went to L.A. to get away from when I graduated from college," she argued. "I could do fitness testimonials, telling desperate housewives how I lost forty pounds in just two weeks by using an exercise machine that looks like something from a medieval dungeon. Or maybe I could sign on with a home shopping network and pose in burred suede casual wear for women."

"A'ight now, Sugar Girl," Hippolyte said, "no need to get personal."

"Sorry. But I'm off acting. I just want to get a real job and be a regular person from now on."

"Maybe you ain't meant to be a regular person." He looked her up and down, smiling with both rows of teeth. "You don't look the least bit regular to me."

Hippolyte's gaze shifted from her face to a place beyond her left ear. "Can I help you, brother?" he said as Kyla turned to see what held his attention.

A man stood behind her, and he took Hippolyte's inquiry as an invitation to move closer. His neutral trousers and dark coat were so nondescript, Kyla was forgetting what he looked like even as she stared at him. "How much?" the stranger asked.

Kyla shook her head in confusion.

The stranger leaned farther over her to whisper to Hippolyte. "How much?" he repeated. "For her."

"For...*what*?" she shouted, his meaning dawning on her.

Hippolyte gave her a quiet nudge. He grabbed the man by the crewneck of his sweater and yanked him close enough to whisper in his ear. Horrified, Kyla watched as the man took out his wallet and discreetly took several bills from it. He pressed them into Hippolyte's hand before scurrying out of the restaurant with his balding head hunched into his shoulders.

"What did you just do?" Kyla asked as Hippolyte licked his thumb and sorted through the cash. "That little pervert thinks I'm a hooker and you're my pimp!"

"Well," Hippolyte drawled, "we are a tad overdressed for this particular establishment."

Kyla couldn't argue. Their apparel did indeed stand out amid the yards of denim, fleece and plaid flannel covering the bodies of most of the other diners. "How much did that guy pay you?"

He stood and took up his hat. "You would be flattered, Sugar Girl." He grabbed his handkerchief and tucked it into the pocket of his coat. "Let's be on our way."

"What about that...client?"

"What about him?" Hippolyte folded a few bills, pinched them between his index and middle fingers, and offered them to Kyla. "The way I see it, that fool just contributed to the Hippolyte Child Support Fund. Anything else would be illegal, wouldn't it?"

Kyla closed his fingers around the money, urging him to keep it before she stood and took up her stole. Draping it over her shoulders, she took the arm Hippolyte offered. "I have a feeling that things like this happen to you fairly often."

"Sugar Girl," Hippolyte grinned in a flash of gold, "life ain't worth livin' if it ain't interestin'."

"Hey, Keren," Kyla said after he answered the phone. "I had a date tonight."

"Oh yeah? How'd it go?"

"I can sum it up in one word." She paused. "Hippolyte."

"It's for you," she faintly heard him say right before Cady came onto the phone.

"Hello?" Cady said.

Kyla kicked off her gold mesh heels and pitched them into her bedroom before turning toward the kitchen. "I had a very interesting date."

"Did he wear the black velveteen?" Cady asked.

"Actually, it's burred suede," Kyla corrected. "From France."

"Did you have fun?"

"As a matter of fact, I did."

"I told you he would be special. Did he give you a nickname?"

"He gave everyone he met a nickname. The waiter at La Mirage was christened Chilly Willy over a glass of gin and juice."

"Well, the waiters at La Mir do sort of look like penguins in that black and white livery they have to wear."

"He called the coatroom girl Fi' Dolla."

"What language is that?" Cady asked.

Kyla took a bottle of water from her refrigerator and started into the living room. "It's Hippolyte. As in, 'That woman got on so much makeup, she look like a fi' dolla ho.'"

"He calls me Piddy Ting."

"Pity what?"

"Piddy Ting. That's Hippolyte baby talk for Pretty Thing. What does he call you?"

"Sugar Girl." Kyla took a long drink of the water and plopped down on her overstuffed sofa. "Cady, how do you know Hippolyte? He's a walking stereotype of a stereotype. In what world would you have ever met a man like that?"

"I see him every Friday. We sort of struck up a friendship over the past two years."

"Does he work at Raines-Hartley? Don't tell me he works at the newspaper."

"Hippolyte sells stuff from the trunk of his car outside the Gas 'N Go where I buy my lottery tickets."

"I can't believe you set me up with him."

"You said you had fun."

"He wasn't fake and he wasn't crazy, but Cady, come on…he graduated from high school ten years before I even started."

"He's got character," Cady said. "He's my friend and I like him."

"Oh really? How many times have you had your good friend Hippolyte over for dinner?"

"Four, but only on the nights Keren works late. Ciel and Lee—or Black Aphrodite and Apollo Creed as they came to be known—met him the last time he came over. Keren doesn't like him."

"I like him just fine," Kyla heard Keren say in the background. "I don't like the name he calls me."

"What is it?" Kyla asked.

"Mandingo," Cady whispered.

"I don't know why I couldn't be Chocolate Zeus or something," Keren grumbled in the distance. "Black Kojak would've been nice, too."

Kyla laughed and started to choke on a swallow of water.

"How was dinner?" Cady asked after smoothing her husband's feathers. "Had you ever been to La Mirage?"

"No, and we didn't stay." She wiped her mouth with the back of her right hand. "Chilly Willy mentioned sea urchin and Hippolyte almost lost it."

"It's close to midnight," Cady said. "What did you end up doing?"

"We went to White Castle. We had belly bombers and the sixty-dollar bottle of wine Hippolyte took from Chilly Willy Ville. Thanks for paying, by the way. Hippolyte came out about three hundred dollars ahead on the night if you count the money some john paid him to have sex with me."

"I think we're going to have to discuss this date in a little more detail when I see you tomorrow. But I'm glad you at least had a decent time," Cady said.

"This is the first date I've been on where I wasn't thinking about Zweli the whole time," Kyla admitted.

"Speaking of," Cady said, "he's in the hospital."

Kyla felt as though she'd been kicked in the stomach. "Wh-Wh… " she stuttered.

"He was teaching Troy to drive a stick shift and a car full of high school boozers crashed into them. Troy's fine but Zweli got a bad knock on the noggin. He's at Kirkwood Medical Center. They're keeping him overnight, but his injury isn't serious. He didn't even get stitches, just a little glue."

Kyla's mouth was so dry, she couldn't speak.

"Ky, are you there? I promise, it's nothing serious. Are you okay?"

"Fine," she managed. "I'm sure he's in good hands."

"Visiting hours are over, but you could give him a call. I don't have the phone number handy, but he's in room 319."

"Why didn't they take him to Raines-Hartley?" Kyla left the sofa and went into her bedroom.

"R-H was too far away," Cady yawned.

Kyla slipped out of her dress. "You said it wasn't serious."

"He was dazed and slightly incoherent when the paramedics got to him, but his CAT scan came back relatively clean."

After wrestling her pantyhose off with one hand, Kyla opened the top drawer of her bureau and grabbed a pair of socks, and then sat on the foot of her bed and tugged them on. "What does 'relatively' mean? That still sounds bad."

"He has a concussion. It's no worse than the one I got when I fell out of Grandma's mulberry tree when I was fifteen."

"Your eyes were crossed for two days!" A jolt of panic seared its way through Kyla. "Why didn't you call me and tell me that Zweli and Troy had been in an accident? They could have been killed."

"But they weren't."

Kyla wrapped an arm around her belly, which churned with nausea. Zweli could have been killed. Just like that, while she was sucking down expensive French wine and cheap hamburgers, Zweli could have been lost. She found her legs and went to her closet, where she took a pair of jeans from an overhead shelf.

"He's okay, Ky. Honestly. Keren or Mama would have stayed with him if there had been anything to worry about."

"Okay," she said automatically, not really hearing her sister's words. "Cady, I gotta go. I'll see you tomorrow at Mama's."

"Goodnight, kiddo, and try not to worry about Z. He'll live to fight with you another day."

Kyla hung up the phone. She clutched it to her chest as she paced through her tiny apartment, doing the one thing Cady had told her not to: worry about Zweli. His accident might not have been serious, but the feelings it brought out in her certainly were.

"I could have missed my chance," she whispered to herself. "If I had lost him tonight…" She closed her eyes and swallowed back the grief such a thought invoked. In that moment, none of their past bickering mattered, none of his past relationships mattered. The only thing of importance was that Zweli was safe and well cared for at Kirkwood Medical Center.

She threw on a loose-fitting sweater and went into the bathroom. She quickly washed the makeup from her face before brushing out her movie starlet waves. She was securing her hair into a ponytail as she headed for the living room, when she stopped in her tracks.

"What am I doing?" she asked as she opened the closet in her tiny foyer and took out her coat. "I can't rush to him at midnight like a scene out of *All My Children*."

She hadn't spoken to him since Halloween. They'd seen each other around town, but Zweli had always been heading in one direction and she in another. What would he make of her flying to his side in the middle of the night after she'd spent the evening with another man?

Probably the same thing she'd thought that first time she'd seen him in Harold's Market with Dr. Shute.

She hung her coat back up. Enough of her family had seen to Zweli, and his injury wasn't life threatening. There was no need for her to disturb him in the middle of the night just to put her mind at ease. She'd given up that right along with his last proposal.

Zweli woke up thirsty in the dark of his room. He rolled over toward his bed table and reached for a pink plastic pitcher of water. An arrow of light from the overhead fixtures in the corridor pierced the blinds on his door, and he fell back onto the bed, squinting against the blinding burst of brightness. Too groggy and achy to move again, he lay on his back and draped a forearm over his eyes. He made a mental note to ask the duty nurse who'd come on at midnight to close the blinds the next time she came in to wake him.

He thought she was already there when an indistinct shape emerged from the shadowed half of the room to pour a cup of water for him.

"Kyla," he exhaled, his voice sleep-deep and gravelly as he raised himself on one elbow.

She sat on the edge of the bed and handed him the water. "Drink this," she said, her voice a silky part of the darkness.

He gulped it down and accepted a refill. "What are you doing here? It's late."

"I know." Her fingertips grazed the bandage covering his forehead above his left eye.

He took her hand and brought it from his face to his chest. "It's not serious."

"I know."

"My head is as hard as a hickory nut," he tried to reassure her.

"I know."

"I'm glad you're here."

"I know."

Her soft, quiet voice was like a lullaby, and when she opened her arms he readily went into them. However long this display of tenderness lasted, he resolved to enjoy every second of it. He pushed aside the bleak knowledge that the only woman he'd ever loved was the one in his arms now, the same one who repeatedly refused to have him. He hugged her close, pulling her onto the bed with him so he could feel her warmth through the bed coverings. "My head hurts," he murmured into the top of her head.

"I know." She snuggled into him, drawing one of her legs over both of his.

"I'm sleepy, too."

"I know."

"The painkillers make it hard to stay awake."

"Then go to sleep."

His eyelids grew heavier by the second, but he fought to stay awake. "Can I ask you a question?"

She nodded against his shoulder.

"Why did you come?"

"Because I love you," she barely whispered. "Now sleep."

Her presence assailed his senses, dosing him with the very best medicine. With her weight and heat beside him, he inhaled the spicy, floral scent of her hair as he closed his eyes and tried to fall asleep to the whisper of her soft breathing.

When he was awakened a few hours later by a neurologist and the duty nurse, he sat up alone in bed, refreshed and eager to go home.

"Did you sleep well?" the neurologist asked as he removed a penlight from the breast pocket of his white coat.

"Very well." Zweli looked around for Kyla.

The neurologist examined his pupils and reflexes, and gave him his home-care instructions before signing his release forms. "I had a visitor last night," Zweli said as the doctor left and the nurse set a fresh bandage on his bed table. "I don't suppose you've seen her roaming the halls?"

"I've been on shift since midnight, Dr. Randall," the nurse said. She put on a pair of sterile gloves and peeled off Zweli's old bandage. "You didn't have any visitors."

"Yes, I did," Zweli insisted. "We talked. I—"

"Head injuries are funny things, Dr. Randall," the nurse said. She stood close enough for him to see the individual hairs comprising her faint mustache. "They play strange games with the mind. I once had a patient with a skull fracture who said he played for the Blues. He talked about the hat trick he'd scored, and his teammates and all the cities he'd traveled to for games." She gently applied a fresh bandage to his wound. "Come to find out, the guy was a tow-truck driver who didn't even know how to ice skate. A good bump on the head was all it took to make his fantasy a reality."

Zweli threw back his covers and swung his feet to the floor. He sat on the edge of the bed, still not totally convinced that he had crafted Kyla's visit from wishful thinking and a concussion. He rubbed his face with both hands and thought back on the wee hours of the night when he'd held Kyla, and he'd breathed her scent and she'd told him that she loved him.

His shoulders slumped. " 'I love you,' " he said somberly, repeating Kyla's words. "That proves it was only my concussion talking."

CHAPTER EIGHT

Cars lined both sides of the rain-glossed street and the Winters house was packed with family and friends from church, Abby's school, Clara's lab, Ciel's law firm, Cady's newspaper, and Raines-Hartley. Extra tables and chairs had been set up in the living room and in Abby's enclosed rear patio to accommodate all the guests. Thanksgiving dinner itself would be a buffet-style affair comprised of three twenty-pound toms—one smoked, contributed by Clara and Christopher; one deep-fried, courtesy of Ciel and Lee; and the one Abby roasted—and a record thirty-one side dishes, more than half of which had been brought by Abby's guests. The library, which traditionally doubled as the kiddie room for ordinary Sunday dinners, found still another use as the dessert room. Sixteen desserts lay in wait. Abby and her daughters had made pumpkin, apple and sweet potato pies from scratch, but their guests had contributed a wider variety of sweets, everything from plates of homemade turkey-shaped sugar cookies to a chocolate silk torte speckled with flecks of genuine 14K gold.

After having spent seven hours being ordered about the kitchen by their mother, Clara, Ciel, Cady and Kyla joined Abby in her hostessing duties once the dinner guests began to arrive. Kyla assumed the role of bartender while her sisters entertained in the living and dining rooms.

"Put a little more bourbon in Reverend Kurl's iced tea," Abby directed.

"It's practically all bourbon now." Kyla waved her hand over the glass to diffuse the scent of the strong liquor.

Abby took the neck of the bottle and sloshed a bit more bourbon into the tall glass, which was garnished with fresh mint and a lemon slice. "I'd rather he fall asleep before he gets warmed up enough to give a sermon. Let him save it for Sunday."

Given her mother's reasoning, Kyla would have tipped even more bourbon into the glass if Clara, Ciel and Cady hadn't hustled into the kitchen like a flock of geese to grab Kyla and Abby. They pulled them to the kitchen door and opened it a tiny crack. Five pairs of eyes in varying shades of brown lined the narrow opening and peered into the dining room.

"Who's the guy in the black sweater?" Ciel asked. "He's not one of my guests."

"He's not mine, either," Clara said.

"None of my guests are that cute," Cady said. "Everybody else in St. Louis is here today. Maybe he just wandered in off the street."

"He's one of mine," Abby said primly, stepping away from the door and returning to a ceramic pitcher of spiced apple cider. "He's a speech and language therapist at my school."

Clara and Ciel went to the counter Abby worked at. Clara began slicing Macintosh apple rings into the pitcher while Ciel propped cinnamon sticks in the mugs lining a wicker tray. Kyla stayed at the door with Cady and continued to eyeball the attractive young man.

"What's his name?" Kyla asked.

"Who, dear?" Abby asked as she carefully poured the cider into the mugs.

"Your speech guy."

"Evan Stewart."

Kyla heard the smile in her mother's voice as she studied Evan. He stood near the windows, chatting amiably with Lee and Christopher. He was tall, if not six feet then close enough to it, and had flawless honey-brown skin. He wore jeans but dressed them up with a stylish black sweater and black leather uppers. He laughed at something Lee said, and then turned toward the kitchen. Kyla had to smile, too, when she saw that his laugh reached his brilliant dark eyes.

"He's cute," Cady said. "In a sexually non-threatening, Shemar Moore kind of way." She left the door to retrieve juice boxes from the refrigerator.

"Well, I thought I'd toss my candidate into the ring." Abby defiantly lifted her chin and smoothed back a tendril of hair loosened by the steam of the cider. "I want my baby girl to find someone to love." She scowled at her older daughters. "Not end up on *Unsolved Mysteries*."

"Mama," Cady whispered, "you know we've been doing our best to make sure that Kyla ends up with the right man."

Kyla kept her eyes on Evan but strained to hear the hushed conversation behind her.

"You people act like you haven't known Kyla all her life," Abby said in a low voice. "You can't force rhinestones on her to make her see the diamond-shine of Dr. Randall."

"What are you up to, Mama?" Clara asked.

Still at the door, Kyla leaned backwards to better hear her mother's quiet response. "Same thing you all are, only with good sense," Abby said. "Kyla's stubborn. She needs a big, shiny, glittering hunk of cubic zirconium like Evan Stewart. Now let's go feed some folks and see how this plays out."

Abby took up the cider tray and enlisted Clara and Ciel to grab the other trays. Kyla held the door open for them before following them. She entered the dining room in time to see Keren ushering a bandaged Zweli to the table. Her whole body swelled in happiness and relief to see him, but she forced it back before it could take the shape of a smile. Her eyes met his for an instant before Abby used the edge of her tray to shunt her toward the opposite side of the dining table.

"Everybody take a seat so the Reverend can say grace," Abby said loudly, so everyone could hear her over their conversations and the noise of the children. After setting her tray on the table and taking Kyla by the hand, she dragged her against the traffic flowing into the dining room and shoved her into a chair on the window side of the table. She then grabbed Evan and brusquely deposited him beside her. Abby stood behind them, a hand braced on the back of each of their chairs.

Evan offered Kyla his hand along with a smile full of perfect white teeth. "Hi. You must be Kyla."

"Why do you say that?" she asked suspiciously, her eyes still fixed on Zweli, who sat near the head of the table with Keren and Cady.

"Because I've met Clara, Ciel, and Cady, and your mother said that Chiara was overseas on business. You're the only one left. And I recognize you from your television show." He treated her to a quiet, unassuming smile that made the best use of his dimples and the bright sparkle in his eyes. Kyla might have been completely disarmed, had her gaze been on Evan rather than Zweli. "I bet you get that a lot," Evan said.

"I do," she vacantly agreed.

"Quiet, everybody, the Reverend is starting grace," Abby announced.

A wave of silence worked its way through the house as Reverend Kurl cleared his throat. "Brothers and sisters, we give thanks today for the blessings God has bestowed upon us." He cast an eye toward the living room, where attorney Ariel Horowitz and virologist Elihu Nassar stood with bowed heads. "However you call Him, we thank God for the delicious gifts we are about to receive from Sister Abigail, who once again has opened her home to family and friends."

"Amen," murmured one of the deacons from Abby's church.

"We thank you, Lord," the Reverend went on, gathering steam, "for sparing Doctor Zweli and Troy. You could have taken them from us yesterday, but you didn't, and we want to thank You for it."

Reverend Kurl began bouncing on his heels and swinging his arms as he fell victim to the sound and rhythm of his own voice. "We want to thank You, Lord, yes we do, for blessing Cady and Keren with another baby. And Lord, I don't think Cady would mind if You made it a single instead of a double this time."

Kyla, wide-eyed, stared at Cady, who stood near the kitchen door glaring at Reverend Kurl.

The Reverend was reaching his crescendo. "Lord, Lord, Lord!" he proclaimed joyfully. "We thank You for giving Sister Clara a promotion to lab director, and we thank You for helping C.J. come out with an 'A' on his algebra mid-term. We thank You Lord, for sparing Brother Lee's position at Lewis & Clark Financial, now that they've been bought by that German banking firm. And Lord, we ask You to forgive little Clarence for the youthful indiscretion that got him suspended from school, and we ask You to also forgive the sinner that seduced him into puttin' his foot on the path toward the Stink Chair."

Cady loudly snorted.

"Do you tell him *everything*?" Kyla hissed over her shoulder at her mother.

Abby gave her a little pinch.

After two more minutes of gossip disguised as thanks to the Lord, the Reverend spoke his final amen and was the first in line at the buffet. Kyla excused herself from Evan to join Clara and Ciel in confronting Cady in the kitchen.

"I only told Mama yesterday," Cady started before her sisters could pounce. "She's the reason I took a pregnancy test. She suspected it long before I did, when she saw me dipping her cheese sticks in mayonnaise a couple of months ago. I wouldn't have told her if I'd known that she'd blab to Reverend Kurl."

"Outed by the Reverend," Kyla said. "That stinks."

"How far along are you?" Clara asked.

"Ten weeks." Cady grabbed a stray stalk of celery from the cutting board atop the center prep island. "I wanted to wait until I was at twelve weeks before I told everybody else." She crunched into the celery before asking her sisters, "Is it much different having three than two?"

"It's logarithmic, not linear, in terms of the work load," Clara laughed lightly.

"Yes," Ciel said, translating for her math-challenged sisters. "It's a lot more work. And a lot more fun." Clara and Ciel congratulated Cady and enveloped her in a big hug.

"I'm happy for you, Cady," Kyla said. She left the kitchen before her sisters could call her on how unconvincing she sounded.

"Hey," Evan greeted when Kyla stepped out of the kitchen and into his path as he stood in line for the buffet.

She mustered a smile. "You again."

"I came for the girl but I'm staying for the food," he joked. "I'm so hungry, I could eat an entire turkey. Everything looks so good."

She assumed he was still talking about the food, even though his gaze flitted over her face and hair. "Is that a line?"

"I didn't mean for it to be, but if it works, then yes," he chuckled. "I'm not usually into blind setups but I think I'm going to enjoy this one."

She inched forward with the flow of traffic in the crowded dining room. "No one told me that I was being fixed up today."

"We're single and on the verge of thirty," Evan said. "People treat us like pandas. They put us in a room together and hope for the best."

Kyla laughed in spite of herself, and her eyes landed on Zweli as he was leaving the dessert-filled kiddie room with Keren. The bandage near his hairline was no bigger than a business card, but it filled Kyla with a renewed sense of doom. *I could have lost him*, she fretted inwardly.

Evan was speaking to her, and laughing softly at whatever charming remark he had just made, but Kyla didn't hear a word of it. "Evan, I'm sorry." She held up her hands as if to ward him off. "On most days, I'd be delighted with your company but…" People shuffled past her to get to the buffet, and in that moment, the number of guests in the house overwhelmed her. "I'm not a panda." She shoved past Evan and pushed her way into the kitchen. But her mother, sisters, and their husbands monopolized that room. They crowded around the small telephone table between the back and basement doors, where Abby had Chiara on speakerphone.

"Hey, it's Carlton the Doorman!" Lee directed at the speaker.

"Not funny, Lee," came Chiara's sweet laugh.

"Where are you, baby?" Abby asked. "You sound so far away."

Kyla watched her mother hover over the phone, as if it would bring her even a tiny bit closer to her youngest child.

"I'm in Hong Kong, Mama," Chiara said. "I'm part of a seven-person sales junket. U.S.I.T.I. wants to sell software to investment firms here. John's here, too. He's demonstrating some of the programs."

"Mahofro!" Cady called, singling out John Mahoney, an old Winters family friend. "What's up?"

"Hi, everybody," John said. "Happy Thanksgiving."

"I saw your mother at Soulard Market last weekend," Abby said. "She looked really good. She's cut her hair, and I think she's lost a few pounds."

"I'll tell her you said so the next time I talk to her," John chuckled.

"What time is it over there?" Abby asked. "Is it still Thanksgiving?"

"It's almost five A.M. on Friday, Mrs. Winters," John said. "Thanksgiving is over, for us. We spent it at the American Embassy."

"Oh, that must have been so exciting," Abby said. "Did you meet the president?"

"Of what?" Chiara asked.

"Of—" A new thought preempted Abby's old one. "It's awful late for the two of you to be together making long distance phone calls."

"Is that what the kids are calling it these days?" Lee teased.

"You all have a nice holiday, okay?" Chiara said, speaking loud enough to drown out Abby's further inquiries. "My cell battery is dying, so I have to go. Bye!"

"Chiara?" Abby took up the receiver. "Chi, honey?"

"She's gone, Mama." Clara hung up by pressing the TALK button. "She sounded good though, didn't she?"

"I wish she'd just quit that job and come on home." Abby busied herself with the strings of her apron. Her voice shook with unshed tears as she said, "I miss my little girl."

Clara took her mother in an embrace. "She'll come home." She kissed Abby's forehead. "We all do, eventually."

"We forgot to tell her about Cady," Abby said.

"I'll e-mail her," Cady said. "At least there's one person left in the world for me to surprise. Come on, Mama. Let's get back out there and make sure everybody's got enough to eat and drink."

Abby led the way with her daughters and sons-in-law in tow. Left alone in the kitchen, Kyla took advantage of the moment, and disappeared.

Zweli's head began to ache from the effort it took to search a house crammed with people. In her black Donna Karan heels, Kyla was the tallest woman in the house and she should have been easy to find in her off-the-shoulder black top and the flowy black skirt that emphasized the pretty lengths of her legs.

She wasn't in the living or dining rooms. He would have spotted her, most likely in the company of Evan Stewart, who'd done his best to stay Velcroed to her right hip. She wasn't in the attic, where Troy, under the chaperonage of his nosy cousins Abigail and Ella, regaled his big-eyed girlfriend with the tale of his brush with death. The Reverend was on the enclosed back patio, sermonizing between catnaps, and it was too cold and rainy to be outside, so that left only one place for Kyla to hide out.

Danielle and Clarence were in the kitchen using Red Delicious apples, mini marshmallows, cranberries, and toothpicks to make turkeys, so Zweli waited for them to finish and leave before he opened the door to the basement. He quietly pulled it shut behind him and moved stealthily down the steep, carpeted staircase. At the bottom, he stepped onto the thick, colorful squares of rubbery foam that he had helped Christopher, Lee, and Keren install to give the twins a safe place to fall when they were in the basement "helping" Abby fold the laundry. That half of the basement was the most inviting, with the washer, dryer, and drying racks on one end and a giant toy box on the other. In between sat a table on which rested five baskets of freshly folded laundry. Most of the clothes were black, which led Zweli to believe that Kyla was using her mother's house as her personal Laundromat.

ONLY YOU

The basement ran the length of the big house, and the half of it away from the stairs was used primarily for storage. The light from the laundry area scarcely penetrated the aisles formed by dozens of plastic storage bins with neat labels, and the mountain of bulk paper products, soap, canned soup, and pudding snack packs Abby always had on hand.

Dressed in black with her back to him, Kyla was a corporeal part of the darkness in the shaded and undisturbed side of the basement. She stood beneath the dust-covered awnings of giant cobwebs near the back wall, next to a graveyard of broken appliances and clothes in need of mending, and a giant deep freezer containing a surplus of chickens, roasts, and hams that Abby purchased on sale for future Sunday dinners.

Zweli took a few steps in her direction, but remained in the clean, well-lit place where the foam puzzlework mat cushioned the floor. "How was your date?"

Kyla flinched at the sound of his voice. She spun to face him, the hem of her skirt sweeping the dust from the boxes nearest her. He stood under the overhead fixture, the light bathing him in a warm nimbus of gold. The sleeves of his white shirt were rolled up and his hands were in the pockets of his tawny wool trousers. Inwardly, Kyla was pleased that he'd found her, but his question raised her fur.

"Are you on medication?" She crossed her arms over her chest and remained in the shadows.

"Why?"

"You sound strange."

"How was your date last night?" he repeated.

"I had a wonderful time," she said with a perky tilt of her head. "It was the best one yet."

"Good." He nodded. "At least now I know where I stand with you."

"My dating has nothing to do with you," Kyla protested.

"Hah."

"Jealous?" she taunted.

"You're damn right I'm jealous."

His impassioned calm drew her a few steps forward. "I was ready to dive over the table and snatch the smile right off of Evan Stewart's face," he admitted. "Is he the one you're down here hiding from?"

She took note of Zweli's hopeful tone. "There are too many people up there for me. It's like being at one of the *Lifeguards* conventions. Evan was actually okay, but some of the other men…" She shook her head.

"They look at you like you're a part of the buffet."

She nodded.

"You looked like you were lost up there. Who did you invite? All your sisters have about ten friends here. Which ones are yours?"

She shrugged a shoulder. "I didn't invite anyone. I don't really have any friends in St. Louis."

"You grew up here. You went to college here and you don't know one single person?"

"Maybe I should have invited Javy the pizza guy," she said snidely. "He delivers a soy cheese special every week, whether I've ordered it or not." She dropped her gaze to the cement floor and the acid left her tone. "I was never very popular in school. Not like my sisters."

"You seem fairly popular now," Zweli said wryly.

"Why did you become a doctor, Z?"

"What's that got to do with anything?"

She stepped out of the shadows to hover at the edge of the light. "Just answer the question."

"I was inspired by my undergraduate biology professor at Northwestern," he said.

"He showed you the beauty of science?"

He moved closer to her. "*She* was a beauty, and when she left to take a research position at Johns Hopkins Medical School, I decided to apply there."

"So you went to medical school just to be with that professor?"

"She was really beautiful."

"Why did you become a cardiologist?"

"When I was a resident, I met this Greek girl who had the most beautiful green eyes. When she chose cardiology as her specialty, so did I."

"Was this in Baltimore?" Kyla snapped.

"Yes. At Mercy Medical Center."

"What brought you to St. Louis?"

"Dr. Albert Raines recruited me. I visited Raines-Hartley and met the good doctor's granddaughter at a reception. She convinced me to stay, and I've been in St. Louis ever since."

Kyla's body tensed with frustrated anger. "So just about every major decision you've made in life has been motivated by your pursuit of women?"

He dropped his head. "You make it sound so shallow."

"Well, it's not deep," she fired back.

"It's not like I haven't tried to find...depth."

She snorted.

"I tried with you, Kyla, and you know it."

"I'm sorry." She stalked toward the stairs, the clack of her heels against the cement floor like gunshots. "Your life is your business and I have no right to pass judgment on it."

Zweli reached out and took her upper arm, stopping her escape. "You're the only one who has the right because you're the only one whose judgment matters to me. I can't stop wondering why you keep saying no, why you won't even consider marrying me." He swung her to face him and held her in place by her upper arms. "Is it because you suspected what I just confirmed? That there have been a lot of pointless, meaningless relationships before you?" His hands moved to cup her face and he lightly touched his forehead to hers. "Or is it because you realized what I knew the moment we first met? That you're the woman I was looking for all along. That you're the only woman for me."

"You're ridiculous," she argued weakly as she tried to pull away from him.

Zweli tightened his grasp. "Why is it so hard to believe that I love you?"

"Stop it." She twisted her head from his grasp. "Just stop it."

"This isn't about me or my past." His gaze bored into her hers, but she kept looking away. "This is all you."

She shrugged out of his hold.

"I love you, Kyla."

"Shut up," she hissed.

"I haven't been free of you for one day since you left."

"Would you please just stop it?" She paced in a tiny circle on the edge of the shadowy half of the basement.

"It's the worst late at night, or when I'm tired. I think about you and it's impossible to get you out of my head again."

Tears stung the backs of her eyes, and she suddenly wanted to punch him, to kick him and hurt him, until he felt as horrible as she did.

He approached her, but he didn't try to touch her. "Remember the time we had Thanksgiving dinner in Cady's hotel? You gave me a tour of the place, and somehow we ended up having a foot race in the corridor."

"I'm not listening to this anymore." She tried to push past him, but he nimbly stepped into her path.

"I know what it was. We were testing your theory about hotel décor. You said hotels deliberately choose carpeting with a pattern that makes you feel like you're staying in one place, even when you're moving. You have such a unique way of thinking about things. It's one of the things I first fell in love with about you—"

"*SHUT UP!*" Her arms went rigid at her sides, her fingers splayed, and the veins in her neck stood out from the force of her voice. "Just shut up! You proposed to me after six weeks, as if you could know me in that amount of time, and now I'm supposed to believe that you *still* love me? Time and…and…lust have probably forged your memories of me into something you want me to be, something that I'm not. You love me? You don't know me. You don't know what I am, because if you did, you'd run out of this house right now and never come back."

"What I know is that you measure yourself against every other woman I've ever been with," Zweli said evenly. "And that you think you fall short." He laughed sadly. "That's it, isn't it? You don't think you're good enough. For me or anyone else."

She turned her back to him and hugged herself, determined to keep her tears to herself, but failing. "I'm a failure, Zweli," she whispered. "I'm good at just one thing, and I couldn't make a success of it."

His hands hovered above her shoulders for a moment before closing into fists and returning to his pockets. He wanted to comfort her, he ached to, but he couldn't. He had made all the overtures he possibly could, and now she had to meet him partway. Even if it was just one step, he'd rush the rest of the way to her.

"I can't stand to hear you cry," he said, and his tenderness made her sob all the more. "I want to hold you, but I can't. You have to give me something too, Kyla, just one step, honey, and—"

"Do you know why I wanted to be an actress?" She struck tears from her cheeks with both hands before whirling on him.

He shook his head.

She winced as she said, "I hated being me."

"Ky—"

She spoke over him. "You don't know what it's like to be number four of five, to follow in the footsteps of Clara, Ciel, and Cady Winters. Did you know that when she was ten, Clara skipped from the fifth to the seventh grade? Last year, she helped isolate a new strain of bacteria, and it's going to be named after her. Ciel graduated college in three years and law school in two. She was asked to head a presidential advisory committee on racial profiling, but she turned it down because she didn't want to uproot her kids. And Cady…Cady's never failed at anything. She's been freelancing for three years and already she's got colleges inviting her to teach journalism courses. Her stories have won awards and she gets tons of letters from people who've benefited from her articles. She's got the best husband in the world, gorgeous kids, and now she's got another baby on the way.

"Then there's me, the actress. Kyla with an 'a.'" She laughed bitterly. "What have I got? What have I done that matters?" She aimlessly wandered into the laundry area. She kicked off her shoes when the heels sank into the foam rubber. "Who have I helped? I should have done what Chiara did and just disappeared halfway across the world and found my own life out of the blinding light of my sisters' accomplishments." She hid her face in her hands and wept in earnest. "If I dropped off the earth right this second, it wouldn't make one bit of difference to anyone."

Zweli clenched his jaw. "Damn it, Ky, this melodramatic bull is infuriating. Now I see why Cady calls you Susan Lucci." He grabbed her and gave her a hard little shake. "Since you need to hear it, I'm going to say it, but you'd better listen because I won't say it again." She tried to pull away, but Zweli held her in place. "You matter." His gaze sought hers. "You matter to so many people. You think the rest of us see you the same way you view yourself, but we don't. Your only failing is that you're too damn selfish to realize how much we all need you. How much I need you." His hands moved over her arms and her shoulders before coming to rest in her hair. "What do I have to do to make you believe how much I love you, how much I want you? Tell me, sweetheart, because I'll do it."

"Go upstairs and leave me alone," she choked over her tears.

His hands fell away from her and he took a step back. "You're a mess, Kyla."

"You know what they say," she said with a cruel lift of her lovely eyebrow, "men are attracted to women like their mothers."

The warmth of Zweli's green eyes chilled as he lightly ran his fingers over his bandage. "You aren't a thing like my mother. Even when she was dead stinking drunk, she was there when someone who loved her needed her. You're not capable of that, are you?"

"I went to you last night, you nincompoop!" she hollered.

He blinked and spent a moment floundering for words. "You…are you sure?"

"I'm not the one with the brain damage," she sniped. "Of course I'm sure."

"Why?"

"I told you why."

"Tell me again."

"Why do you think?" She gave her nose a rough swipe with her sleeve. "What could possibly make me speed to Kirkwood Hospital at one A.M. and sneak into your room behind the back of a big ol' nurse with a mustache?"

"Just say it, Kyla. Please."

A fresh torrent of tears blurred the image of him as he stood before her, his arms open.

"You wear me out," he sighed when she made no effort to respond. "I'm too tired to fight you anymore, and I love you too much to give up the fight." He turned and took one step toward the stairs before the weight of her hand on his shoulder stopped him.

"I love you, Zweli."

He caught the second syllable of his name on her lips as he turned and swept her up in his arms. His hands moved deep into her hair, mussing her loose chignon to hold her head in place as he smothered her with his kiss.

Kyla melted against him, and her weight forced his back to the dryer. She ran her hands over his forearms, delighting in the tickle of his golden-brown hair against her palms before she clasped his wrists and turned her face to kiss one of his hands.

The tracks of her tears evaporated in the heat of her hunger for his kisses. He gripped her torso and she cradled his head as his lips traveled over the smooth skin of her exposed shoulder and collarbone.

She grabbed his head and raised his face to hers. "You aren't going to push me away again, are you?"

He watched the rapid flutter of her pulse at the base of her throat as her heart tripped along, beat for beat, with his own. "Why would I do that?"

"You've turned me down twice." She brought her mouth to his ear and gave his earlobe a teasing nibble. "I don't think I could stand it a third time."

"I didn't want to touch your body until I touched your heart." He slipped his hands beneath her loose-fitting top and slowly raised it, exposing her upper body to the bare yellow light. She gently shook her hair out as he braced a hand in the middle of her back. His other hand whispered over her jaw line to her chin, along her throat and down to her sternum before coming to rest along the outer curve of her breast. As his thumb stroked the caramel bud, tipping it into rigid life, he studied her face. Her eyes managed to look sleepy and alert at the same time as she took the corner of her lower lip between her teeth. Her breathing halted for a moment, but then she took a choppy breath as she curled one hand around his neck and placed the other over the hand sweetly tormenting her breast.

Her head fell back, her long hair sweeping over his hand, and he needed no further invitation to continue his exploration of her body. He brought his head to her breast, and her flesh jumped when the moist heat of his mouth made contact. The gently savage pull of his mouth contrasted wonderfully with the tenderness of his caresses as he sampled her flesh, tasting and testing the limit of her restraint.

She swung forward, locking her arms around his neck as she hopped up and wrapped her legs around his waist. Through her skirt, Zweli ran his hands along her strong, supple thighs and he moaned into her hair as she positioned the center of her heat over the hard bulge behind his fly. She used her chin to nudge his head up, to claim his mouth in a kiss that left no doubt that she wanted him as much he wanted her, that she was willing to surrender her whole heart to him.

Kyla reached between them and released the mother-of-pearl button fastening his trousers. Following the quick hiss of his zipper, her hand burrowed into his pants and freed the straining length of him. The silky heat of her touch almost made his knees buckle, and it was all he could do to spin around and prop her backside on top of the dryer.

Her fingers went to his shirt buttons, and her hands shook as she unfastened them. She gasped and clamped her eyes shut when he pinched her earlobe between his lips and suckled it. When he came away for breath she slipped his shirt from his body and sank her teeth into the meaty muscle capping his left shoulder. She raised her knees, bracing his trim hips between them and he hunkered over her, branding her flesh with hot kisses that left her gritting her teeth.

The slinky black fabric of her skirt pooled around her hips when Zweli pushed it up to hook his thumbs under the skinny waistband of her thong panties. One tug and the tiny triangle of damp black silk was sailing over his shoulder. Kyla arched her back and leaned on her elbows when he bent over her and draped her skirt over his head like a magician's cloak.

She inhaled sharply as his mouth worked its own brand of special magic between her legs, leaving her thighs quivery with the desire rising within her.

He taunted her mercilessly, bringing her to the edge of an explosion, then drawing away to kiss her inner thigh. In the farthest recesses of her mind, she was aware of the voices in the kitchen, and the play of light and shadow their footsteps made as people moved on the other side of the unlocked basement door. As much as she wanted to cry out, to beg Zweli to carry her to the zenith of pleasure, she kept her silence, afraid that the slightest noise would invite a parade of nosy sisters.

Zweli clutched handfuls of Kyla's skirt. He wasn't sure what fueled his own fires more, her taste, the sweet musk of her scent, the softness of her skin or her eager response to him. He decided that it was a delicious recipe of all four as he once more delved into her most secret darkness. Her hips rose to meet each soft rasp of his tongue, each pull of his lips. She grabbed tight fistfuls of her skirt when he took the engorged pink pearl at the heart of her pleasure tenderly between his teeth. His name creaked from her lips with a shudder of her thighs, and he pulled back to rest his forehead on her lower abdomen.

He fought to control himself, and the effort left him weak. He was dumbfounded. He had always taken great pride in his powers of control, never hesitating to show off for his partners by asking them to tell him when they wanted him to reach completion. It was the boudoir equivalent of Babe Ruth pointing to the stands before hitting a home run, and he had never failed to hit his mark.

His resolve was already in shreds, and he'd barely touched her. He was desperate for her, so much that his teeth chattered, and he struggled to get himself under control. He bought a few seconds by turning to the laundry table. He tugged the cord of the overhead light, plummeting them into semi-darkness, and then he spilled the folded contents of the laundry baskets onto the floor mat. Like a cavemen he used one foot to kick the clothing around to form a nest upon which he carefully placed Kyla. She wriggled out of her skirt and helped him slide off his pants and briefs. He kissed her fingers and eased his weight on top of her before once more taking her mouth.

They exposed everything to the mounting darkness, filling it with breathy moans, the sounds of teeth against teeth and moist skin against skin. They took mastery of one another, their need primitive as they wasted no time satisfying their desire. They knew there would be another time to take their time, to leisurely explore and enjoy. This coupling would be no less loving, no less satisfying, but this current urge demanded immediate satisfaction.

Kyla smiled, slightly embarrassed about having been so stingy with her feelings. The journey that had begun three months ago with Nigel's slap had finally ended in the place where she'd wanted to be all along. In truth, she had to admit that the trip had been much longer, closer to four years. Even if she wanted to, she could no longer deny that she belonged to Zweli. And she was as close to believing that he truly belonged to her as she would ever be.

The muscles of Zweli's abdomen and upper arms trembled as he rose above Kyla, and then entered the snug heat of her welcoming body. He spent a moment with his forehead touched to hers, willing his flesh to cool just enough to make their union last long enough for him to give Kyla the pleasure she deserved. She took the initiative and clasped the solid rounds of his backside, drawing her knees higher and wider to start a rhythm that eroded his determination.

Bracing his weight on his forearms, he pumped his hips, deepening his loving invasion under Kyla's guidance. She winced in exquisite surrender, widening her legs and curling her hips upward, inviting more of him. They laced their fingers together, joining their bodies as tightly and completely as possible, yet still wanting to be even closer.

They existed in a world of insensate pleasure, joined as if for the first time with their missing halves. Zweli had demanded her heart and found himself giving no less in return, and it made all the difference. He'd had plenty of sex in his life, his statistics hovering somewhere between Usher's and Wilt Chamberlain's. He stared into Kyla's eyes and lost himself in their whisky-gold depths. As he realized that he was making love for the first time, the experience nearly drove him to tears as he crested the summit of pleasure buried deep within her.

He stiffened with her clinging to him, and then he shuddered in her embrace as he buried a cry in the warm place where her neck met her shoulder. His hips still pumping his heat into her, he curled over her, bringing his head to her bosom. His mouth captured her right breast while his right hand slipped between them. The first glance of his fingers over her oversensitive flesh made her bark in rapture. Zweli caught her cries of release with his mouth as pure pleasure exploded within her. Her body locked around him with such force, Zweli bit his tongue. Kyla knocked her head against the foam mat and bucked her hips as her body milked every twitch of hot tension from him that it could.

For a long moment after, she lay in Zweli's arms, delighting in the aftershocks of bliss that issued from her body wherever his skin touched hers. She wasn't aware of the chilliness of the basement until the furnace blared, startling her deeper into Zweli's embrace.

"Mama must be clearing the house," Kyla said as Zweli grabbed the edge of a bed sheet beneath them and pulled it over them. "She always turns the heat up when she wants people to leave."

"Won't the heat just make them sleepy?" He smoothed her hair from her face. The only illumination came from the windows built close to the ceiling, and the light from the stormy sky painted Kyla in somber blues and grays.

"That's the point. Everyone gets sleepy and wants to go home. Mama's probably making coffee right now. Sleepiness drives 'em out the door and the coffee helps them get there safely."

"Your mother thinks of everything."

After a beat of silence, Kyla said, "I wish she'd thought of buying a case of condoms to go in her price-club shopping section down here."

Zweli didn't know what to say. This was the first time in his lengthy sexual history that he'd ever neglected to protect himself and his partner. "I'm sorry, Kyla. I should've—"

She stopped his words with two fingers to his lips. "I'm a big girl. I could have stopped you, if I'd wanted to."

"Still, I should've—"

"Do you regret what we just did?"

Her hair was a tousled mane of auburn silk and he used a thin tress of it to tickle the end of her nose. "No," he finally said, his gaze on her kiss-swollen lips. "Not one bit."

"Good." She smiled, draping an arm over his shoulder and pulling him half atop her. "Then let's do it again."

Full dark had come and the footsteps from upstairs had lessened. Kyla and Zweli quietly listened to the hushed voices on the kitchen side of the closed basement door.

"Do you think they're down there?" came Clara's voice.

"Their cars are still here, so they didn't leave," Ciel said. "The basement is the only place we haven't looked."

"What are they doing in the basement?" Abby said.

Cady must have been on her hands and knees, because her voice seemed to shoot straight under the door. "I hear something..."

"What?" Clara asked.

"Why don't you hens flock back into the living room and leave other people alone?" Lee said loudly. He was answered with a round of loud, hissing "Shhhs!"

"What is it, Cady?" Ciel asked. "Are they talking?"

"It's..." Cady listened harder. "The dryer." Her voice faded a bit as she stood and moved away from the door. "They're doing laundry."

"Is that what the kids are calling it these days?" Lee teased.

Kyla started to laugh, and Zweli gently clapped his hand over her mouth.

"That must be what they call it," Abby said skeptically, "since I did Kyla's laundry yesterday."

CHAPTER NINE

Thanksgiving Sunday dinner at the Winters home was a casual affair that served primarily to finish off the last of the leftovers from Thursday's feast, so no one missed Kyla and Zweli when they abandoned their turkey sandwiches and retreated into the kitchen for twenty minutes.

Or so they thought.

"You're really not fooling anybody, you know."

Kyla and Zweli leapt apart like guilty teenagers at the sound of Danielle's high-pitched voice behind them. They turned to see her knowing dark eyes looking up at them over the tops of her glasses. "Did you want something, Dani?" Kyla asked, her heart pounding from the thrill of Zweli's kisses and the sudden shock of Danielle's presence.

"No." In perfect imitation of her father, Danielle used her middle finger to shove her glasses higher up on her nose. "I just wanted to see what you were doing."

"We were, uh…" Zweli licked his lips. Tasting Kyla on them, his made-up excuses fled, and he squatted in front of Danielle. "You won't tell anyone that you saw me and your Aunt Kyla kissing, will you?"

"No," Danielle grinned shyly. "But can I tell Abigail and Ella? They know anyway. Mom and Dad said that you and Aunt Ky were doing laundry in the basement the other day, but we all know you were down there kissing."

Flames of embarrassment singed Kyla's cheeks and stuck her tongue to the roof of her mouth.

"You tell whoever you want, whatever you want," Kyla said once she pried her tongue loose, "but remember, Santa Claus doesn't like snitches."

Danielle peered over her glasses once more. "There isn't any Santa Claus. I figured that out two years ago, when I woke up and saw Mom and Dad putting together the bike I asked for. They were drinking wine and listening to some old music on the CD player."

Kyla braced her hands on her knees and bent over to face her sassy little niece. "There's no Santa? Who do you think left the bike? Do you really think that Santa has time to personally assemble bikes?"

"The bikes should be already made by the elves," Danielle argued.

Kyla straightened. "So you believe in elves but you don't believe in Santa?"

"Elves are just an old-fashioned name for dwarves."

"Is your mother aware of how ignorant you are?" Kyla muttered. "Look, Dani, you can't believe in elves and not believe in Santa Claus, and you shouldn't not believe in something unless you can prove that it doesn't exist."

Danielle's mouth drooped open slightly. "That doesn't make any sense." She turned to Zweli for help. "It doesn't, right?"

"Actually, your auntie makes a good argument here," Zweli said. "If you can prove that Santa doesn't exist, then it's okay for you to not believe in him."

She spent a moment wrestling with her own personal belief and Kyla's convincing argument before giving her glasses an emphatic shove. "I won't tell anybody you were kissing, even though everyone knows that's what you were doing."

"Thank you, Dani." Zweli gave her a kiss on the forehead and a hug that left her glasses sitting crooked across the bridge of her nose. A blush rose to tint her cheeks as she scurried out of the kitchen, her braids dancing behind her.

"I suppose we've been in here long enough," Kyla said as Zweli stood behind her and wrapped his arms about her middle. "I'd better get back out there and draw a name before the more experienced inquisitors come in and pick up where Dani left off."

"I'll grab a few beers for the boys since we told them we were coming in here for drinks anyway." Zweli kissed the side of her neck and the curve of her ear before he drew away and went to the refrigerator.

Cady burst into the kitchen and dealt slips of white paper to Kyla and Zweli. "You've got Clara," she told Kyla. "And you got Lee this year," she said to Zweli.

"You started without me?" Kyla asked, offended.

Cady smiled wickedly. "You were gone so long, we thought you and Zweli were doing some more laundry. So yes. We started without you."

"You put me in the hat this year?" Zweli stared at the name on his paper. He'd been a fan of the Winters tradition of drawing names for Christmas on Thanksgiving Sunday. It only made sense, since buying gifts for everyone in a large family could put a sizeable drain on a holiday budget. Zweli had spent enough time with Cady and Keren to know the rules: there was a fifty dollar minimum on the gift, the sisters drew among the sisters, husbands drew among husbands, children drew among children, and adults shopped for all the children.

"You're a member of this family, aren't you?" Cady gave Zweli's chest a solid pat before she left the room.

Kyla threw her arms around Zweli's neck. "This is going to be the best Christmas!"

Joy washed through Zweli, and he had to agree with her. This would be Kyla's first Christmas at home since the first one he'd spent with her, the year her grandmother died.

"It feels so nice not to be working through the holidays." Kyla drew away enough to play with the collar of Zweli's Armani sweater. "I get to wake up on Christmas morning and personally deliver my presents to everyone instead of FedExing them a week early. I won't have to pull a Chiara and phone my holiday in."

"You're shopping for everyone? Did you get that position you interviewed for at Brighton Public Relations on Wednesday?"

"No," she said matter-of-factly. "They said that my so-called fame would be a distraction, but that they'd love it if I hired *them* to rebuild my 'crumbling popularity.' No thanks. I'll get something else. If worse comes to worst, I'll give up my apartment and move back in with Mama. Or I could borrow a few thousand from Keren and Cady," she laughed. "I plan to kill my savings this Christmas. I want to spoil my mother and my sisters. When I first moved to California, they took care of me after my nest egg ran out. Cady and Ciel paid my rent, Clara had groceries delivered to me, and Chiara wrote the most incredible letters, telling me how much she believed in me. She always told me not to let the chumps get me down. Those letters got me through more than the money did, and they really made me feel good, especially when the biggest chump of all knocked…" Her eyes were on Zweli, but she seemed to look inward as she quieted. "What are you going to get Lee?" she asked, clumsily redirecting the conversation.

He would have steered her back to their previous topic if Lee, Christopher, and Keren hadn't invaded the kitchen.

"Yes, Zweli," Lee said, crossing his arms over his Irish sweater. "What are you gonna get me?"

"Welcome to the brotherhood of brothers-in-law," Christopher said.

"You're jumping the gun, fellas." Zweli handed the bottles of beer around.

"You do laundry with a Winters woman, and you're in the brotherhood," Lee said with a wink. "I got my ticket in when Ciel and I were changing the toilet paper roll. Chris, you and Clara almost got caught changing spark plugs in the garage, right?"

Lee moved out of the path of the door's swing when Abby rushed into the kitchen holding a sofa cushion. A damp spot darkened the pale cream and gold floral pattern. "Time and time again, I've told Cady not to give juice boxes to Sammy in my house. He squeezes them and hoses down the furniture."

"It's just juice, Mama." Kyla joined her mother at the sink, where Abby vigorously rubbed at the juicy patch with a clean, dampened sponge.

"What was it for you and Cady?" Zweli asked Keren under his breath.

Keren pretended to study one of the dozens of coupons pinned to the refrigerator by Danielle's junior varsity cheerleading magnet. "We were looking for old toys in the attic."

"This is fruit punch and it's gonna set," Abby declared, giving up her effort. She displayed the pillow. "Do you think this is too big to go in the washer?"

With a sly glance at Kyla, Lee scratched the underside of his chin. "I don't know, Mom. Kyla, you and Zweli are the experts on laundry. What do you think?"

"Oh for Heaven's sake," Abby said, swatting the pillow at Lee. "Sometimes I wonder if any of my girls know what a bed is for. Lord knows, they have the most peculiar taste in men." Hugging the pillow under one arm, Abby went into the basement.

"I'll just go and get the hairspray, so Mama can treat her stain," Kyla volunteered before hastening out of the kitchen.

The husbands—and Zweli—stood in silence for a moment before bursting into laughter. "I have never been able to get anything past that woman!" Lee said. "Not one damn thing in twenty-some years."

"What do you guys want to do about Christmas?" Christopher asked, pushing his glasses higher up on his nose. "Same thing as last year?"

Lee and Keren nodded their agreement. "What did you do last year?" Zweli asked. "I'm new to this."

Lee took a swig of his beer. "Well, for the first five years of this name drawing thing, we gave each other gift cards to the hardware store, the lawn and garden center, or a bookstore. Three years ago, we decided to cut out the middle man, so to speak."

"We buy a gift card for ourselves and just keep it," Keren said. "It's a logical system."

Zweli uttered a noncommittal grunt. "So a case of 2002 Véro Pinot Noir is out of the question," he aimed toward Christopher, whose ears perked up enough to send his glasses slipping a half-inch down his nose.

"Véro 2002?" Christopher echoed longingly.

"It's such a pretty red." Zweli stared at the ceiling as though he could see the beauty of the wine etched into the blades of the ceiling fan. "The bouquet has amazing notes of cherry and raspberry with a nice, peppery back note." He turned back to Christopher. "I would have recommended decanting it before serving, to really aerate it and bring out the rich berry flavors. But since we aren't exchanging real gifts…"

"Maybe we should rethink our decision," Christopher considered with a push of his glasses. "Christmas is a time for giving, after all."

"When Cady gave me your name, the perfect gift came to mind," Zweli said, lining up Lee in his sights. "The boxed DVD set of *The Best of Norman Lear.*"

Lee staggered back. *Bullseye*, Zweli thought merrily. "*All In The Family,*" he said wistfully. "*Maude. Good Times. The Jeffersons.*"

"George and Wheezy," Lee muttered reverently, his eyes nearly glazed over.

Zweli went for the kill shot. "Don't forget *Sanford and Son.*"

Lee clutched at his heart and slumped against the sink. "I wanted to name my first born child Rollo, but Ciel used her veto power." He offered his beer in a salute to Zweli. "Here's to the fair exchange of Christmas gifts, man."

Sensing a point of discord, Zweli looked at Keren, whose mouth was pinched in a scowl. "What?" Zweli chuckled uneasily.

"We had a perfectly good system here, and you had to come along and ruin it," Keren complained. "What were you going to get for me?"

"A unicycle."

Keren laughed in spite of himself. "What for?"

"Do you already have one?"

"No."

"Then that's why."

Keren raised an eyebrow. "Cady would be so surprised if I wheeled up on a unicycle at the twins' next birthday party. 'Course, I almost killed myself the one time I wore roller skates for her."

"It's settled then," Lee said. "Men?" He raised his bottle in a toast.

Zweli, now a Winters man all but in official title, brought the neck of his beer to the trio formed by Christopher, Lee and Keren.

"All for one and one for all," Lee said as they clinked their bottles together. "May God bless you as you battle in the malls."

"And God help *you* if you buy me another Easy Bake Oven," Christopher said, lowering his beer. "Lee's the reason we set the fifty dollar minimum. The first year we drew names, he gave me an Easy Bake Oven."

"I've explained that again and again," Lee protested with a weary roll of his eyes to the ceiling. "Ciel wrapped the presents and she tagged the wrong box."

"If you cared, you would have wrapped my present yourself," Christopher pointed out.

"Man, that was years ago," Lee said. "Every Christmas, you bring up the wrapping. What is it with you and the wrapping?"

"All I'm saying is that if you only have one person to shop for, the least you could do is wrap the gift with your own hands," Christopher said, his calm further irritating Lee.

Zweli and Keren inched toward the door, leaving Christopher and Lee to rehash their annual argument as they made a quiet escape.

"Promise you and I won't ever get like that," Zweli laughed.

"Like what?" Keren asked.

"Like an old married couple."

The Winters sisters formed a line as they moved along the glass display cases encircling the grand oak tree growing in the center of The Curiosity Shop. One of their favorite window-shopping destinations in the West End as teenagers, the five-story glass dome of The Curiosity Shop appealed to them even more as adults, now that they could share it with their own children and afford the beautiful, one-of-a-kind pieces of jewelry for which the shop was known.

ONLY YOU

The shop was most famous for the live oak around which the store literally had been built. With a trunk circumference of twelve feet and a height of forty feet, the tree was a local landmark, and as the tree's dress changed with the season, so did the store's décor. July shoppers found the store a cool haven against the hot and humid St. Louis summer, with the oak providing nature's original system of air conditioning. It wasn't unusual for shoppers to suffer a blow by or two from the sparrows that nested in the tree. October was a glorious time to shop with the oak's foliage in a riotous display of natural fireworks, but the store was closed the entire month of November, to allow professional groomers to dispose of the oak's leaves as efficiently as possible.

The first Saturday in December marked the shop's annual grand holiday re-opening, and the owner, a Russian émigré who went by the single moniker of Zazu, turned the tree into the center of a magical winter wonderland.

Every display case was made of glass, and each seemed to sparkle with a kiss of real frost. Zazu's love of color and shine was more evident during the holidays than at any other time of year, and every surface and corner was occupied by something that caught the eye in both color and texture. Fuzzy alpaca scarves in every color from white to midnight were draped over dress forms throughout the store. Live plants and cut flowers were packed in one corner of the shop, as though it were perfectly normal to purchase flowers, diamond rings, and vintage clothing all under the same roof. Everything in the store was adorned with fringe, streamers, ornaments, or feathers in dark, passionate shades of purple, navy and burgundy, or twinkled in metallic gold, silver and platinum. Real icicles glittered in the front windows, and Zazu refused to tell Cady how she got them to survive indoors.

"It's magic," Zazu said in heavily-accented English with a wave of a hand full of rings.

"Zazu's been here for twenty years," Cady said. "How is it possible that we've all aged and she still looks the same way she did the first time we walked into this store?"

" 'Eet's mah-zheek,' " Kyla repeated, deepening her voice to mimic Zazu's accent once the sylphlike woman had glided to the other side of the tree.

"Shh!" Cady whispered sharply. "You think she won't cast a spell on you?"

"Zweli says that magic only works on you if you believe in it," Kyla said as she peered closer at the gems and baubles decorating a bed of dark blue velvet.

"He'd know," Cady said. "His people come from New Orleans. That's Mystical Mojo Central, U.S.A."

Kyla looked up at her sister, who was trying on a pair of cat's eye sunglasses dotted with Swarovski crystals. "Have you ever met his family?"

"One of his brothers came up once." Cady took the glasses off and replaced them on the head of a bald, bodiless mannequin. "Yawu, the youngest one. He seemed kind of moody."

"Keren moody or Christopher moody?" Kyla asked.

"Keren is brooding, not moody, and he doesn't do so much of that anymore. Between work and the kids and me, he doesn't have the time or a reason to brood."

"And Christopher is just quiet," Clara said in defense of her husband. "It's not easy for him to get a word in edgewise when Lee's in the room."

"What's that supposed to mean?" Ciel asked.

"You know what it means." Clara circled around her sister to look at a case of necklaces and pendants. "Lee's not exactly a shrinking violet."

"He has to be so serious and sedate at the brokerage firm," Ciel said. "He likes to cut loose when he's at home and with the family. By the way, Kyla, Lee said that he saw your manager on *E!* the other night."

"*Former* manager," Kyla corrected. "I didn't renew my contract with him before I left the West Coast. What the heck was he doing on *E!*?"

"Being charged with possession of a controlled substance," Ciel said. "They showed him in an orange jumpsuit at his arraignment."

"They must be really desperate for news if they have air time to burn on a chump like Nigel," Kyla said.

"Did you know he used drugs?" Clara asked.

"I don't think he does," Kyla said in grudging fairness. "He's too conceited about his body and too much of a control freak to do drugs. He's too cheap, too. I don't know the story, and I don't care. Whatever he did, I hope they give him the death penalty."

"I'm sure Lee will keep us posted." Ciel tapped the glass above a selection of necklaces and waved for Zazu. "I get my news from *CNN*. He gets his from *E!*"

"We were televisionaholics when we were kids, but Lee is ridiculous," Kyla laughed lightly.

Ciel leaned on one elbow on the glass countertop and faced Kyla. "He was an only child and he was a latchkey kid. Television kept him company when he was in the house alone. It's like an old friend to him. Some men drink, some do drugs, some stay out 'til all hours and cheat on their wives. My husband comes home to me and his children every night, and if he wants to watch a *Dukes of Hazzard* marathon, he's welcome to it. He deserves it."

"Guess it should be called a therapy box instead of an idiot box," Clara said.

"Television is an idiot box only if you're an idiot to start with," said Cady.

"Maybe he could take up boxing with Keren and Zweli," Kyla suggested. "They go about twice a week."

Ciel scoffed. "Lee's too short."

"Yes, but he's wide," Cady said. "He's got that bruisin' bulldog physique."

Ciel turned to Cady. "Do you remember Dick the Bruiser and Bulldog Bob Brown, from *Wrestling at the Chase*? I used to love watching him on Sunday mornings before the Abbot & Costello movies."

"Isn't that what you and Lee did on your honeymoon?" Cady said. "You went to an Abbot & Costello Festival in New York City?"

"We went to New York City but the Festival was only one small part of our trip." Ciel smiled at Zazu, who had finished helping another customer and was now ready to serve her. "Could we see that gold chain there, the plain one?"

The full sleeves of Zazu's navy velvet robe slipped over her hands when she reached into the case and withdrew the jewelry form bearing the necklace. Danielle, Ella and Abigail must have smelled the scent of gold because they scurried to the counter from the stand of three-way mirrors before which they had been trying on crystal tiaras. They crowded close to their aunts to study the item their mother had requested.

"Oh that's not plain at all," Kyla observed.

The chain was actually comprised of three threadlike strands of 24-karat gold mesh braided around a filament of white gold. Teardrops of precious gems hung from the white gold, adding their own color and shine to the airy sparkle of the chain as Zazu lifted it from the display case and set it on the counter before the sisters.

Clara sucked in a quiet breath and pointed to a gem that changed from blue to violet as the light above it changed. "This is beautiful. What stone is this?"

"It's a sapphire," Zazu said. "The Ayurvedic birthstone for August. It's supposed to have mystical powers to promote clear thinking."

Kyla used the nail of her pinky finger to point out a white stone with an unusual bluish sheen as she rattled off a string of squishy, guttural syllables.

Cady gave her a nudge. "Show off."

"Your Russian is very polished," Zazu said, before she responded in her native tongue.

"Moonstone," Kyla translated for her sisters. "In India, it's a sacred stone that brings good fortune."

"Is it a birthstone?" Ciel asked.

"Yes, for September," Zazu said.

"Is it possible to have this item customized?"

Zazu smiled. "Every piece I sell is an original and made to order to your specifications, within reason."

"Could we get this chain but with specific birthstones placed on it?" Ciel conferred with her sisters for a moment. "This would be perfect for Mama this year. We could put all of our birthstones on it, plus the stones for our kids."

"Excellent idea," Clara said.

"Cool with me." Cady, who cared as much about jewelry as she did about lima beans in Peru, inched away to look at a display of ornate temporary tattoos.

Zazu unlocked a drawer under the display case and withdrew a wide, flat case that had been sectioned into at least fifty one-square inch compartments. A variety of exotic jewels glimmered beneath the glass lid. She opened it, and set it before Ciel and Clara.

"This is like a pirate's treasure," Abigail said hungrily.

Ella crowded close at her sister's elbow. "Are these real?"

"They are real and they are samples of every birthstone—traditional, modern, mystical, and Ayurvedic—that I use in my work."

"I've never seen one like this." Ella pointed to a bluish stone with reddish-orange spots.

"That's bloodstone," Zazu said. "The spots are thought to represent the blood of Christ. This is the Ayurvedic birthstone for March."

"That's you, Mama," Abigail said to Ciel before turning back to Zazu and the stones. "I was born in November and so was my Aunt Cady. What's our birthstone?"

Zazu plucked a pale pink stone from its velveted pocket. "You and your Aunt Cady are topaz." She set the stone in Abigail's palm. "This is a natural pink topaz, the most rare color. It represents strength in all things."

"I was born in June," Danielle said eagerly. "Do I have a rare birthstone?"

"This is yours." Zazu pointed to a glistening white orb. "This is a natural silver pearl from the Gulf of Manaar. They are thought to be the tears of God. It is the 'queen' gem to the diamond, the 'king.' "

Clara, who was born in June, listened intently to Zazu's lesson on the black garnet and Kyla was captivated by the properties of the transparent amethyst and the Australian black opal that represented February and October, the respective birth months for herself and Chiara.

"How much is this gonna cost?" Kyla wondered aloud.

"The sky's the limit, Zazu," Cady piped in. "Nothin' but the best for our mother. She's like a raccoon when it comes to jewelry, the shinier the better."

"Easy for you to say," Kyla snorted. "Mrs. Dr. Moneybags."

"Zweli's a doctor, too," Danielle reminded her. "Is he a money-bags?"

"Zweli uses all of his money on clothes," Kyla said dryly. "This necklace is for your grandma. I'm using my own money to pay my share of it, not Zweli's."

"But you're getting married to him, aren't you?" Abigail said.

Zazu clapped her hands under her chin and beamed a smile upon Kyla. "Congratulations, my dear!" she said, after first offering congratulations in Russian. "You have two purposes here today then, to find a present for your mama and to look at engagement rings, yes?"

Kyla had been happy to spend a Saturday morning shopping for their mother's Christmas present. In years past, Ciel would do the selecting and then collect equal shares from each of her sisters to pay for it. Kyla was all for talking about what to get Abby, but she would have preferred keeping her own business, her own business.

Zazu didn't wait for her to answer before she reached into a nearby display case and drew out a velvet-covered tray of engagement rings. Their atypical settings and stones caught and held Kyla's eye. "Tell me," Zazu said, resting her elbows on the counter and leaning toward Kyla, "about this fiancé of yours."

"He's not," Kyla said, her eyes moving over the rings.

"Not *yet*," Cady interjected. "He needs to get a ring. And to propose. *Again*."

Zazu picked up a ring with a platinum band and a fat, bright ruby centered between two yellow diamonds. "Have you considered a non-traditional engagement ring? Rubies are symbols of passion and constancy."

"You had a ring here a long time ago," Kyla said. "It was shaped like vines with little gold berries, and—"

Zazu raised a finger, silencing Kyla. She dropped behind the counter once more and unlocked another drawer, this time bringing a palm-sized jewelry case to the counter. When she opened it, Kyla's mouth dropped open.

"Is this the ring?" Zazu asked.

Kyla picked it up with a trembling hand. "This can't be…"

Zazu's crystalline blue eyes crackled. "Something is wrong?"

"No, th-this is it," Kyla gasped. Cady went to her while Zazu excused herself to help a customer who wanted to purchase a marabou and peacock feather boa.

"What's wrong?" Cady asked. "You look like you're going to faint."

Kyla swallowed hard. "This is the ring." She displayed it for Cady. "This is my ring."

She turned it, learning anew the features she'd memorized fifteen years ago when she was a sophomore in high school scooping spumoni after school at Marc Antony's, the Italian ice cream store across the street from The Curiosity Shop. So many of her little paychecks had been spent on Zazu's precious knickknacks, her *tchotchkes*, back then, but the one thing she'd most wanted was the ring now pinched between her right thumb and forefinger. The tiny band was made of platinum shaped to resemble two twisting, entwined vines. Beads of 18-karat gold formed berries and tiny pink and yellow diamonds looked like sparkling flowers. The ring looked alive and different from every angle, and that was what Kyla had liked most about it. During the grisly summer Saturdays when she was literally up to her elbows in gelati, she would fantasize about the ring, and the Prince Charming she hoped would someday present it to her.

"Did you make more than one of these?" Kyla asked Zazu as she bid her customer goodbye.

"I make only one of everything," Zazu said. "This ring was always one of my favorites. It's always harder to part with pieces like this. I stopped displaying it once you stopped coming to visit it."

"I went to college," Kyla explained. "I left my romantic notions behind."

"And now it must be time to pick them up again."

"Zazu?" Ciel said. "We've made a list of the stones we'd like in our mother's necklace."

"It's a beautiful ring," Cady said, drawing closer to Kyla once Zazu went to help Clara and Ciel.

"This is the ring I've always wanted," Kyla said. "Why is it still here? It doesn't make sense that someone else, in all these years, hasn't come along and bought it."

"I don't know," Cady grinned. "Maybe eet's mah-zheek."

Cady never met an arts and crafts store she didn't like, and when they passed Katy-Lynn's Fabrics on the way home, she insisted that they stop in to look at material for a Christmas dress for her daughter. Their grandmother Claire had taught all of them how to sew, but Cady was the one who seemed to love it and practiced the skill most often.

Kyla knew how to sew in theory, but she'd never had the desire to prove it to herself or anyone else. Her skill at the domestic arts began and ended with the B. Smith and Martha Stewart books sitting unused on her bookcases. She sat between her nieces at a long, angled table beneath a glaringly bright fluorescent light and leafed through the pages of pattern books with her sisters. Cady, who for years had sewn without patterns, stood behind her and peered over her shoulder.

"Evening and formalwear, huh?" Cady adjusted the two bolts of soft, wintery white fabric braced against her hip.

"I'm just looking," Kyla said lightly. She opened the book to a two-page spread of wedding gowns. "Are these Vera Wang?"

"Yep." Cady set the bolts on a chair next to Ciel. "Lots of designers have patterns out. You, too, can wear a Wang at your wedding. If you know someone who sews. And you do."

"This would look so good on you," Danielle gushed, shoving her glasses up and pushing her head in Kyla's view to look at the backless, floor-length gown. "When I get married, I'm going to wear a long, strapless Calvin Klein." She stood up abruptly, nearly knocking over her plastic chair. "My husband will ask me to marry him in Paris."

"How old are you again?" Cady asked.

"Why Paris?" Kyla wondered aloud.

"Because I'll be a model living there when I'm twenty."

"Oh really?" Clara said dryly.

"I'm going to tell my husband when to marry me," Abigail said.

"Like mother, like daughter," Cady said.

"I didn't propose to Lee," Ciel said without looking up from a magazine devoted to knitting. "He proposed to me."

"That's not how I remember it," Clara said. "You were still in law school, and we were doing the dishes after Sunday dinner one night. Lee was over, and you told him that the two of you were going to get married on the last Saturday in June, three weeks after you graduated."

Ciel raised the magazine to her face, to better see the complicated stitch involved in a poncho pictured there. "The first time Lee asked me to marry him was at our tenth-grade winter formal. We were dancing to…to…" Her gaze went to the ceiling as she tried to remember the song. "I think it was 'September.' "

"September's not in winter," Danielle said.

"Earth, Wind & Fire's 'September,' " Ciel clarified. She set down the magazine and smiled fondly at the memory. "We were both sixteen, and your father just screamed a proposal out on the dance floor. He was so silly back then."

"Daddy's still silly," Ella said.

"Daddy's not silly," Abigail said. "Daddy's goofy."

"Well, then that makes you half goofy because he's your father," Ciel pointed out. "He proposed to me all the time, until we were in college and I told him that I'd let him know when I was ready to marry him."

"Aunt Clara, how did Uncle Chris propose to you?" Abigail asked. Clara closed her pattern book and stood. Her sisters followed suit, and Danielle offered to carry one of Cady's cumbersome fabric bolts as they started for the cutting table.

"Our decision to get married was a practical one made by two people who loved each other very much," Clara answered.

"That's amazing," Cady said.

"What is?" Clara asked.

"How you can make something sound so romantic and sterile at the same time." Cady paused to run her hand over a bolt of furry pink panne.

Kyla and everyone else kept walking. "You and Chris are so much alike. Both so scientific and serious."

"Chris and I are very different people," Clara argued.

"You were the only one who laughed when Christopher toasted you at your wedding," Ciel said.

" 'Like two bonded electrons, we journey together into the next phase of our evolution,' " Kyla said, imitating Christopher's austere delivery.

Cady jogged up to them. "You and Chris are a severe case of like liking like, as Grandma would say," she told Clara.

"Zweli and I are such opposites," Kyla said. "Like Lee and Ciel."

"Ha!" Cady said derisively as she set her heavy bolt on the cutting table. "You guys are too much alike. That's why you fight all the time."

"How much of this would you like?" the cutter asked Cady as she unwound a white wool jersey a few turns.

"Four yards, please," Cady said.

"Where are you going to have your wedding, Aunt Kyla?" Danielle asked.

"Oh, how nice, a wedding," the cutter said as she measured out four generous yards of the jersey. "This is the perfect fabric for a winter wedding gown. It's light and it's warm, and it perfectly matches your complexion." She directed her last comment to Kyla. "Brunettes always look best in pure white. Leave the ivories and shell whites to the pale English roses, I always say."

"This is for my daughter's Christmas dress," Cady said politely. "She's a brunette, too."

"But she isn't getting married," Ciel said.

"I can't wait to get married," Danielle said dreamily. She leaned on the cutting table and caressed the soft fabric. "I want it to be special when my husband proposes to me, like at a party. And I want to be surprised."

"Done it," Kyla said.

"I want mine to be private," Abigail said. "Just me and my husband and someplace pretty."

"Done it," Kyla said.

"Yet you've managed to come out the other side unengaged both times," Cady said as she handed over her second bolt of fabric.

"Unengaged or disengaged?" Clara wondered aloud.

"All that's in the past now," Kyla said. "Zweli and I have a new understanding of each other. If he asks me to marry him again, I'll take the good advice I was given by my darling nieces, and I'll say yes." She winked at her Abigail and Ella.

"If?" Cady questioned. "Since when is there an 'if' involved?"

Kyla watched the cutter measure out four yards of white wool gabardine. "I thought he would ask on Thanksgiving, but he didn't. Maybe he didn't think the timing was right."

"Or maybe he's planning something special," Ciel said. "Zweli likes his surprises."

"Are you going to have a wedding like Aunt Cady's?" Danielle asked. "That was so much fun."

"Your wedding was the biggest carnival in St. Louis since the World's Fair," Kyla said.

"I'm sure your wedding was lovely," the cutter said, defending Cady against a perceived attack. "Don't you let anyone say it was a carnival. Families behave in strange ways at weddings. When my youngest got married, her brand new father-in-law got drunk and started singing 'I'm Your Boogie Man' by KC & the Sunshine Band, and—"

"My sister's wedding really was a carnival," Kyla explained. "After the church ceremony, chartered buses took everyone to Forest Park for the reception. My brother-in-law had rented a Ferris wheel and a merry-go-round."

"And a Super Slide and Scrambler," Danielle said. "And everything was free. It was so fun."

"Don't forget the sword swallower and the fire-eater," Clara added.

"There were game booths and cotton candy, caramel apples, snow cones and funnel cakes," Kyla went on. "Dinner was a Cajun buffet and it was served under a striped big top tent. The chef came from my sister's favorite restaurant in Cambridge, Massachusetts, and he offered to pay his own way just so he could be the one to cater the affair."

The cutter tapped her chin. "That was a few years ago, wasn't it? I heard about that wedding." She handed Cady her folded cuts of fabric. "That was your reception? I think my grandchildren were there."

"We opened the carnival part up to whoever happened to pass by," Cady said. "My husband and I met at Raines-Hartley, which is right across the street from the park, and we wanted to make the reception accessible to all of our friends there. It worked out very nicely."

"Are you planning a big wedding like that?" the cutter asked Kyla.

"I'm not planning a wedding at all," Kyla said uncomfortably. "I'm not even engaged."

Cady thanked the cutter and gathered her neatly folded fabric.

"Lee still talks about the bachelor party Zweli organized for Keren," Ciel said as they headed for the checkout counter. "They started the day at a Cardinals-Cubs game, then went to dinner at

Keren's favorite steak house. They were supposed to go back to Zweli's for live entertainment flown in specially from Chicago."

"Zweli still accuses me of sabotaging it," Cady said.

"You did," Kyla told her. "You canceled his exotic dancers and replaced them with a baboon from Clever Creatures."

"It wasn't a baboon," Ciel recalled. "It was a monkey, one of those little black ones with the white fur around its face."

"A capuchin monkey," Cady said. "They're very smart."

"Christopher said it was the funniest thing he'd ever seen." Clara laughed at the memory. "The monkey drank beer and spit it between its teeth, danced to Snoop Dogg songs and picked pockets. I wish I'd been there to see it."

Cady paid for her purchase, thanked the cashier, and hung an arm over Kyla's shoulders as they walked toward the exit. "Better a monkey with a hand in your groom's pants than a naked lady, I always say," she whispered.

Dressed in a sheer, white cotton knit camisole and matching bikini briefs, Kyla sat tucked into one side of her sofa, mesmerized by her awesome view of moonlit Forest Park. Her left hand cradled a purring Cicely Tyson while her right moved over the corduroy upholstery of her sofa. After three months it still seemed brand new, thanks to the amount of time she spent away from her apartment. She'd enjoyed the solitude of her new place, at first. There was something to be said for being able to walk around in her underwear, or play music as loud as she wanted.

But there was also something to having someone to talk to, which was why she'd gradually spent more and more time at her mother's and the livelier homes of her sisters.

This Saturday spent with her sisters and nieces would hold her for another few days, so she'd turned down their dinner invitations. She'd come home, microwaved one of Javy's pizzas, and settled in the living room to eat it as she watched the moon climb higher in the night sky. She thought of her sisters and marveled at how easy they made their lives look. They each had successful careers, gorgeous children with no major dysfunctions, and the town of Stepford couldn't have programmed better husbands.

Sitting with no company other than Cicely Tyson, who stood on her lap to greedily lap crumbs from her pizza plate, Kyla might have sunk fast into a morass of self-pity. But her thoughts of Zweli kept her afloat. Better than that, they kept her spirits bobbing somewhere between the clouds and Heaven. She drew mental images of him around her as she would a homemade quilt, only they warmed her from the inside out. He was in Indianapolis this weekend, visiting his family since he planned to spend Christmas in St. Louis, and she couldn't wait to see him when he came back.

So delighted that Zweli was spending Christmas with her, she almost started dancing before her spectacular view. As Ciel had said, Zweli liked his surprises, and Kyla had the strong suspicion that he was planning one for her, for Christmas. She wondered what it would be, and the possibilities seemed limitless.

His first proposal had taken place on New Year's Eve, in front of a penthouse full of his exciting friends, most of whom were far too cosmopolitan for sedate St. Louis. Moonlight and a magical October night had packaged his second proposal, which had taken place at the Tower Grove Park ruins. Either one of them should have done the trick, and Kyla conceded that she'd blown two very good chances. She smiled and scratched Cicely Tyson's ears as she nestled her shoulders into the back of the sofa and brought her bare heels to the seat.

All of a sudden the reason why Zweli hadn't proposed again occurred to her. "He wants to make it even more special than the first two," she murmured to the kitten, who paused in her personal grooming to give Kyla a disinterested stare.

Kyla knew that had to be it. Zweli didn't do anything halfway, and he didn't do it before every bell and bow was in place. He was the only man she knew to be as cunning and creative as her sister Cady, and he was the only man who'd ever professed to love her in such a way as to make her believe it. The next time he proposed, it would be special…and not just because she planned to scream "Yes!" from the treetops.

Kyla's right arm snaked out of the warm burrow formed by her eiderdown comforter. By the second loud ring of the rotary phone on her nightstand, her hand made contact with the receiver. Before the phone could ring a third time, she'd dragged the heavy black receiver into the toasty cocoon of her bedcovers.

"Let me guess, Cady," she mumbled, her voice growly with sleep. "You found a potato chip that looks like Al Sharpton, or one of the twins just recited the Gettysburg Address. Whatever it is, I'm sure it can wait until morning."

"It's not Cady," Zweli said apologetically. "I'm sorry I woke you."

Instantly awake, Kyla sat up and tossed the comforter off her head. "Hi."

"Hi."

"Are you back?" She glanced at her alarm clock. The big, green digitized numbers flashing at her confirmed that it was officially the middle of the night.

"Not yet. I'm on my way, though. Illinois just officially thanked me for visiting."

"You're on the road?"

"Yep," he sighed heavily.

"You sound odd." She turned on the tiny reading lamp on her nightstand.

"I'm tired. I have early rounds in the morning and I missed a lot of work when I took off on Friday." His voice became louder and clearer once he silenced the Isley Brothers CD he'd been playing. "But I didn't wake you up to talk about work. How was your shopping date with your sisters?"

"It was like when we were kids." Kyla leaned against her headboard and drew one knee up to her chest. "Even though we're all adults now, when we're together for more than ten minutes we seem to revert back to the ages when we were most annoying to each other. Clara gets quiet, Ciel gets bossy, Cady gets nutty, and I just sort of fade into the background."

"Was it really that bad?"

"It wasn't bad at all, actually. I didn't realize how much I missed spending time with them. We had a lot of fun. How's your family?"

Zweli sighed again. "Kwaku and his kids are doing well, and my parents are fine. Everything was going along well until Yawu showed up."

"Cady says he's moody." Kyla patted her bed when she noticed Cicely Tyson sitting in the doorway between the bedroom and the corridor. The little cat stared unblinkingly and ignored the unspoken invitation into the bed.

"That's one way to describe it," Zweli said. "Another way would be to say that he's a straight up jackass."

"What happened?"

"Nothing worth talking about." Then, changing his mind, Zweli said, "He lost his job last week. He got into a fight with a co-worker."

"It must have been a pretty serious fight."

"Little Mike Tyson Randall broke the other guy's nose right there in his office. It probably would have been chalked up to boys being boys and blowing off steam if the other guy hadn't been Yawu's boss."

"What started it?"

"He wouldn't tell us. It could have been anything. Yawu almost got into it with Kwaku over a game of chess. It doesn't take much to set him off these days. I don't want to talk about him anymore. Tell me what we're doing for Christmas."

Kyla perked up. "Christmas dinner's going to be at Mama's, of course, and we're decorating the tree on Christmas Eve. She's putting it up late this year."

"That works out great. I can bring all my gifts for the Holtz, Clark, and Winters-Bailey clans to your mom's."

"You've already shopped for them?"

"No. I figured we could do that together this week."

"I'd like that." She suddenly felt as goofy as a junior high school girl sneaking late-night phone calls.

"Me, too. Your sisters are hard to shop for. They already have everything, and they're so creative with their gifts. Last year, your sisters went in together and gave me a day at the spa. I thought it was a joke. Kyla, I'll deny every word if you ever tell anyone I said this, but it was fantastic. The facial made me feel a little stupid, and I don't think I'll ever take another dip in a tub full of hot dirt and enzymes, but the hot rock massages made it all worthwhile. The food was pretty good, too, and I really enjoyed the time I spent with your sisters."

Kyla picked at a tiny feather poking out of her comforter. "They never told me that they hung out with you."

"There's lots you miss when you're a thousand miles away. Do you know what Ciel gave Lee for Christmas last year?"

"No, what?" Kyla pulled the feather out and blew a puff of air at it. An enraptured Cicely Tyson tried to catch it as it floated crazily to the floor.

"She took his last name. Well, she hyphenated her last name, like Cady."

"I knew she'd hyphenated, but I didn't know that it had been a gift to Lee. That's romantic, for them. Ciel's always been very proud of being a Winters."

"What about you? Are you going to hyphenate?"

Kyla grinned and trembled with excitement. This was it! Just as easily as breathing, it had come up, and now, with Zweli cruising down the interstate in his big SUV while she was bundled in bed in her tiny apartment, she was about to become engaged. She closed her eyes and began forcing herself to remember every mundane detail of the moment. She tried her best to sound innocently ignorant as she said, "Am I going to hyphenate what, Zweli?"

"Your name. When you get married."

A cold, leaden sensation killed her exhilaration. *Did I hear him right?*, she wondered. Her stomach began to hurt just a little bit. *When you get married...*saying it like that was so impersonal, so uninvolved, as if he wouldn't have a thing to do with it. Her panic was reaching a crisis point when his voice cut through it.

"I don't mind the hyphen," he said. "Kyla Winters-Randall has a nice rhythm to it."

Tiny bells of joy pealed in Kyla's head.

"What do you want for Christmas, Kyla?"

"I saw a r—" She stopped herself. As much as she wanted to tell him about the ring at The Curiosity Shop, she thought better of it. She wanted him to propose again, but not because he thought she was dropping clumsy hints to prod him into it.

"You saw a what?"

"Actually, I think I'm getting exactly what I want. I don't like Christmas Day so much as I like the hubbub leading up to it. I can't wait for the tree decorating and gift-wrapping to start. Christopher and Lee bought Mama's tree yesterday with the boys while the rest of us were shopping. The tree is in a kiddie pool of water on the patio until we move some of the furniture out of the living room."

"I love the high ceilings in your mom's house," Zweli said. "How tall is the tree this year?"

"Twelve feet," Kyla laughed. "Mama almost had a heart attack, because it's really full and bushy, too. It'll be a Seuss tree unless Christopher cuts a little off the trunk to keep it from bending against the ceiling. I'm supposed to invite you over to decorate it with us on Friday night."

"What time?"

"Whenever. You know how it is at Mama's. Come when you can."

"I missed you," he said.

"This weekend?"

"Yes. And while you were in California."

Kyla gripped the phone a little tighter. "It seems like a whole other life ago. Lately, I've found myself wondering why I ever went out there in the first place."

"You had to go there or to New York if you wanted to seriously pursue your acting. You couldn't stay in St. Louis. You were too good for St. Louis."

"And not good enough for L.A."

"You weren't patient enough for L.A. Or maybe you didn't have the right management."

"You ain't whistlin' 'Dixie' about that," Kyla laughed uneasily.

"Have you been in touch with him since you left California?"

Kyla felt a little sick to her stomach. "No, and I don't intend to. Why? Are you trying to get rid of me already?"

"Not at all."

"Then why the sudden interest in my career? Or lack of it?"

"I don't want you to give up. That's all."

"What brought this on?" Kyla knew the answer before the question had fully left her mouth. He'd just spent two days at home with his family, and Kyla knew from experience how unflinchingly enlightening such visits could be. *I won't do what your mother did*, she wanted to say. *I wouldn't be sacrificing anything to be with you.*

"I don't like hearing you doubt yourself," Zweli said. "You weren't like this when we first met. What happened to that ballsy tiger lady who stole my heart and left me ruined?"

"She woke up one day and realized that there were other dreams worth pursuing."

"Like what? A glorious hop to the bottom rung of public relations?"

"Like you."

Zweli moaned low in his throat. "I think I'm going to be late for rounds."

"Why?"

"I have one more stop to make before I go home."

Kyla glanced at her window to see the pink of the sunrise fringing the gray edges of dawn. "Is it that important?"

Her doorbell rang, startling Cicely Tyson into scurrying for cover under the bed. Kyla heard it in stereo, from her living room and through the receiver at her ear. She dropped the phone, tumbled out of bed, tiptoed across the cold hardwood to the front door, and squinted an eye at the peephole. Zweli was on the other side, his tiny cell phone held to one ear.

She tossed off the chain, unlocked both deadbolts and flung open the door. She leaped at Zweli, wrapping her arms around his neck and her legs around his waist, her momentum forcing him back against the wall of the corridor. She kissed him deeply, reveling in the warmth of his kiss and the scent of new car and December cold on his coat.

He locked his hands under her bottom, supporting her as he carried her into her apartment. "You're right," she purred between kisses, "you are gonna be late this morning."

Laughing, Zweli kicked the door shut behind him.

CHAPTER TEN

"I never knew that you guys got together like this." Zweli sank onto the overstuffed cushions of the sofa in Christopher's home office. The cozy room was located off the garage, which had been expanded to accommodate the family automobiles and Christopher's carpentry. Along with the sofa, the office contained twin recliners and a large desk and shelving unit, both of which were prime examples of Christopher's skill at woodworking. Zweli studied the stately cherrywood pieces, admiring the lines reminiscent of Hepplewhite's work as Christopher opened the doors enclosing the center cabinet of the shelving unit.

"It's been a few years since we called one of these special meetings," Lee said. He clutched the necks of two beer bottles in each hand. After handing one to Christopher, Keren and Zweli, he claimed one of the recliners and spread out on it. "When was our last meeting?"

"Shortly after Keren got engaged to Cady." Christopher dropped into the oak and leather banker's chair at his well-ordered desk. He pushed his glasses up the bridge of his nose as he aimed a remote control at the television housed in the shelving unit. The Rams appeared onscreen, stampeding onto the field for their battle against the Philadelphia Eagles.

Zweli sat forward. "W-Wait a minute, guys." His wary gaze shifted to Keren, who had used the football game to lure him to Christopher's. "Kyla and I aren't engaged yet. And I know how to handle a woman, if that's what this get together is about."

"Oh, we know you know how to handle a woman." Lee shot out the footrest of his recliner. "You need to learn how to handle a *wife*."

"Uh, perhaps 'handle' isn't the best verb to use," Christopher suggested.

"A wife *is* a woman," Zweli said.

"Kyla's going to cannibalize him before the honeymoon," Christopher predicted quietly.

"There's a saying, Zweli," Lee said. "If Mama ain't happy, ain't nobody happy." He tipped his bottle to Zweli. "Remember that, rookie."

Zweli propped his beer on one knee. "You're really jumping the gun on this, guys. Kyla and I aren't married. I'm just auditing this gathering. I'm not a husband." He sipped his beer and sputtered a sudden laugh.

"Want to let us in on what's so funny?" Keren asked.

"It's just the idea of being someone's husband." Zweli laughed a little harder. "I figured I'd win a Nobel Prize in medicine before I'd ever jump the broom." He wiped tears of mirth from his eyes, and laughed until no sound came from him except a high-pitched wheeze.

Christopher peered into his beer. "I think I got a regular one. What's Zweli drinking?"

"You're losing it, Zweli," Keren said calmly, his eyes on the football game.

"No, I'm not," Zweli managed. "I've *found* it. It's Kyla. It's all her." His laughter faded to a peaceful smile. "I never understood why otherwise intelligent people would want to get married, and then Kyla came along. I can't picture my life without her. When I think back to the first time I met her, I feel…" He searched for the right word.

"Connected," Christopher said.

"Happy," said Lee.

"Saved," Keren said.

Zweli snapped his fingers. "Punished."

"You're kidding, right?" Lee said.

"No, really. I felt like God was punishing me for having been such a dog. I thought Kyla was one of His mysterious ways, you know? Putting the most amazing woman I'd ever met out of reach to teach me a lesson."

"Did it work?" Christopher asked.

"Yes." Zweli rested his elbows on his knees. "And no. I felt like a restaurant critic who'd lost his sense of taste. I still carried on, but it just wasn't fun anymore."

Keren harrumphed. "That yoga instructor you dated last year looked like fun."

It took Zweli a long moment to remember the woman's name, and even then he couldn't decide if it was Laura or Linda. She was a sweet girl with a bubbly personality, and she'd done the pursuing after he'd attended one of her classes with Cady, who'd bullied him and Keren into taking the class with her. Keren had hated it, never to return, but flattered by Laura or Linda's attentions, Zweli had gone back twice more. By their second date, he'd learned that Laura or Linda could move her body in ways that would have embarrassed the authors of the *Kama Sutra*. But he ended the relationship soon after with 'It's Not You, It's Me.' And it had been the truth. Mostly. To be totally honest he would have had to re-name the break-up speech 'It's Not You, It's That You're Not Kyla,' since he'd been thinking of her the whole time he was with Laura or Linda.

"I love Kyla," Zweli said. "It's that simple."

"We know you're good at proposing," Lee said, "but are you really ready to get married?"

"Is that a trick question?"

"It's more like the preface to a pop quiz," Keren said.

Lee reached over to the desk and grabbed a sheet of paper offered by Christopher. "Question One," he said, reading from it. "Your wife asks you to pick up a few things at the grocery store. She asks for a specific brand of, say, chocolate cake mix, but the store is all out. What do you do?"

"I'll just get her another brand," Zweli said easily. "Cake mix is cake mix."

Christopher chuckled. "Maybe we should make this multiple choice."

"Why?" Zweli said. "Was that the wrong answer?"

"Do you A," Lee began, "bring home another brand, thinking that one cake mix is just as good as another; B: Drive to another store to find the cake mix she asked for; or C: Do you call her from the first store and list the available brands of cake mix, and let *her* decide which one, if any, she wants?"

After a moment of quiet, serious thought, Zweli said, "B."

"Is that your final answer?" Lee asked.

" 'A' might piss her off and 'C' is what a servant would do. B. Final answer."

Christopher and Keren applauded. "Well done, doctor," Lee said.

"Question Two," Christopher cut in. "When you change the toilet paper roll, do you allow the free end of the new roll to hang under or over the body of the roll?"

"What difference does it make?" Zweli asked.

"You'd be amazed at how much difference it makes," Christopher muttered.

"Why?"

"Why does the wind blow?" Lee responded. "Why is water wet? It's one of those mysteries of married life that only women can explain."

"What's the answer?" Zweli asked.

"Over," the married men answered as one.

Keren took the quiz paper. "Question Three," he read. "Your wife works all day and she's with the kids all night. She asks you to take them out on Saturday so she can get a few things done. Do you A: Take the kids to the library for an hour…"

"Stop right there, K." Zweli warded off his question with an upraised hand. "We won't be having children right away. You're asking advanced questions now."

"B," Keren continued. "Take the kids to Abby's house. She loves being with them and you could use some of that 'me' time. It's not like you don't work all day, too. Or C: You take the kids to the park and run them in circles until they're so tired, they're thanking you for telling them to go to bed early."

Zweli tapped his fingers on the arm of the sofa as he pondered his answer. He remembered how cranky a sleep-deprived Cady had been in the weeks immediately following the birth of the twins. Keren hadn't taken no for an answer when she'd told him that she was too tired to attend one of his medical functions, and she'd spent the evening addressing him as her "first husband." "C," Zweli said with certainty. "Final answer."

Lee bowed his head toward Zweli. "Excellent, Grasshopper. No matter how much time you spend with the kids, never forget that your wife already has forty weeks deposited in the Bank of Who Takes Care of the Kid before you even get a chance to meet him. You owe both her and your children your time."

"Now it's time for the speed round," Christopher said. "Laundry goes *in* the hamper, not on the floor next to it."

"The toilet seat always goes down," Keren said. "Seat up is for single men."

"Don't ask her to smell things you think have gone bad," Christopher advised. "A woman's sense of smell is twenty times better than a man's, but that doesn't make her a bloodhound. Clara, however, can identify dozens of molds and bacteria by smell alone. My wife is quite a remarkable woman."

"I know this is off the tutorial," Zweli said, "but how did you and Clara end up together, Chris?"

"Basic Chemistry, I suppose."

"You met her and you felt that zing of instant attraction?" Zweli suggested.

"No, actually, in college we were both assigned to be teaching assistants in Basic Chemistry. We became friends."

Zweli waited for more. When Christopher didn't offer it, he said, "Is that it? You met, became friends, and got married?"

"Well, we began spending quite a lot of time together. We had classes of our own together, we were TA's together, we were both on the cross-country team. We both really enjoyed visits to the Theoretical

Physics lab at Argonne National Laboratory in Argonne, Illinois. When it comes to deuterons, hadrons and nuclei, you really can't beat—"

"You and Clara fell in love over deuterons, hadrons and nuclei?" Zweli cut in. "How is that even possible?"

"Oh, Clara and I don't believe in love."

Keren and Lee chuckled. Confused and astounded, Zweli stared at Christopher as though seeing him for the first time. "This is the good part of the story," Lee remarked.

"Clara and I share the same belief that love, at least the hearts and flowers Hallmark variety, is a fallacy. It establishes a completely unreasonable standard that human beings aren't equipped to maintain over long periods of time. Falling in love in that sense would be like shooting off a firework and expecting that color, heat and excitement to last forever."

"As opposed to burning hot for a second before fizzling out," Zweli said.

"Exactly," Christopher agreed.

"So how did you and Clara end up married?"

"We were always together. Once we began to map out our futures, I suppose it ultimately became a matter of compatibility. When I met Clara, I was a gangly, redheaded science geek who understood more about the world of things we can't see than the world around me. Clara was a beautiful, proud, smart woman who treated me as though I were her equal. We come from totally different backgrounds, but we connected. We were a good match." Christopher spent a moment staring vacantly at the floor, and Zweli wondered if he was seeing the moment when he first met Clara Winters.

"It's like when two otherwise dissimilar atoms collide and discover that they can successfully share electrons," Christopher added, retreating to the territory he knew best. "Like when oxygen meets hydrogen, or sodium meets chloride. A molecule is created that neither atom desires to break. It creates something new, something better than what they were when they were apart."

"Did you ever date any other women?" Zweli asked.

"I never had time to date. I was always studying, working, or with Clara."

"Well, did you ever *want* to date other women?" Zweli persisted.

"How many women do you think are out there who know the difference between a strange quark and a charm quark?" Christopher laughed. "No, we never dated. Dating was a nightmare. Clara and I used to compare it to a punctuated equilibrium, where speciation only occurs—"

Lee spoke over him before he got too deep into his complicated metaphor. "That right there is why Chris and Clara are together. They're the only two of their kind on this planet."

"So in spite of molecules, equilibriums and basic chemistry, you and Clara never fell in love?"

"Nope," Christopher responded.

Zweli wasn't fooled. "You can't live without her, can you?"

"Absolutely not."

Lee and Keren laughed out loud. Zweli was certain that every man in the room knew exactly how Christopher felt, whether they called it love or a successful collision of molecules.

"Do you guys have any other pearls of husbandly wisdom to impart?" Zweli asked.

"Wash both sides of a dish," Lee advised, "and not just the surface you ate off."

"Do not ever go into your wife's purse," Keren warned, "and if she invites you to retrieve something from it, don't ask her any questions about anything you may have seen in there."

"If you're going to be more than an hour late coming home from work, call and tell her, so she doesn't meet you at the door in tears thinking that you've been killed on the highway, because it never occurred to her that you were so inconsiderate as to not call when you knew you were going to be late," Lee said. "Think you can remember all this, rookie? Maybe you should have taken notes."

"I can remember." Zweli glanced at the television, but he wasn't seeing the Rams celebrating a touchdown.

"You'll be good for Kyla," Lee said. "We're just messin' with you."

"No, you guys have given me some really good advice." He looked at the thick dark carpeting beneath his feet. "You've given me some things to think about."

"Like what?" Keren asked.

"Like the fact that I can give Kyla everything except the one thing she most wants."

"Which is?" Christopher hit the mute button on the remote.

"Validation." Zweli regretted the way he was killing the fun in the room, but he appreciated the help his future brothers-in-law could offer. "She wants…*needs*…to prove herself professionally."

Lee puffed his cheeks and slowly exhaled. "I've known Kyla since she was ten years old. She was a quiet little thing with these long, thick pigtails and big teeth. She was always off drawing or playing with dolls. She never talked."

"Maybe there was no one listening," Zweli said.

"Clara and Ciel were little mothers to Kyla," Lee said. "Cady tried to kill her a few times, but when they were young, those two could really push each other's buttons. They were like Shaggy and Scooby one day and Tom and Jerry the next. Chiara was Kyla's competition. She was the new baby who came along before Ky was tired of being the baby. Abby once said that Kyla never forgave her for giving birth to Chiara. Kyla might have needed more attention as a child, but she never lacked attention. Abby, Claire and Hank Winters treated all of the girls the same."

"You watch more television than anyone I've ever known," Zweli said to Lee. "Do you think Kyla's a good actress?"

Lee hesitated. "Personal feelings aside?"

Zweli nodded. "Of course."

"She's one of the best I've ever seen. It's a shame she never got a real chance to show what she could do. She should have gotten new representation instead of quitting Hollywood altogether."

"She's got an interview at Ciel's firm this week, doesn't she?" Keren asked.

"Yes," Lee answered. "There's an opening in human resources. It's mostly filing, answering phones, that sort of thing. If she gets it, I give her two weeks before she goes nuts. Or before she rips out Ethan Ault's tongue and staples it to the company bulletin board."

Kyla tried her best to hold the fat blue spruce steady while Christopher kneeled on the deck at the trunk end, sweating as he used a hack saw to take ten inches off its base. The soft, bristly branches gently battered the sleeves of her black parka, and Kyla took a deep breath of their pungent pine scent.

"Could you trim a few short branches from the bottom of the tree for me?" she asked when Christopher stopped to push his glasses up. Sweat darkened the fringes of his red hair and he used the cuff of his flannel shirt to swipe his forehead.

"Are you going to make a wreath?" Christopher asked, his breath condensing in the cold air of twilight. "The branches near the top of the tree are more pliant."

"I just want to stick them in my car," she explained. "I figured I'd take advantage of the natural, seasonal air freshening properties of Mama's tree."

"That's so Martha Stewart." Christopher sat back on his heels. "You and your sisters should get together and create your own lifestyle show."

Kyla let go of the tree to zip her coat up to her neck and to pull on the faux fur lined hood. "That's not a bad idea. The whole family could get in on it. Clara could do health and beauty, Ciel could give hair and fashion tips. Cady could do sewing, cooking, and party planning. You could do a woodworking-slash-furniture making segment once a month, Zweli could do manscaping—"

"Man what?" Christopher chuckled.

"Unibrow waxing, knuckle and ear hair plucking," Kyla said. "Manscaping. Zweli's the most well-groomed straight man I've ever met."

"That's actually more than I ever cared to know about Zweli." Christopher used the hacksaw to finish sawing the trunk. "What would your specialty be, Kyla?"

"Directing the segments." She stared at the toes of her boots. "Those who can't do, and all." She turned her face toward the sky. "I don't want to act anymore. I'm past that phase of my life. I've got something way better now."

"Oh?" Christopher uttered expectantly.

"Zweli," she giggled. "He's all I need."

Christopher stood up and grabbed the middle of the tree trunk. He set the shortened tree on its end in the kiddie pool and gave it a bounce to shake off any loose needles. "You had an interview…yesterday?"

"Yes, and it was my bad luck to encounter the one red-blooded American male human resources director who hated *Lifeguards*. He practically laughed me out of the office when he read my résumé."

"I suppose it's not every day that Kati with an 'i' comes into his office looking to file documents and answer phones."

"I filed and handled the phones in the student services office as part of my work-study in college," Kyla said defensively. "It's not like I didn't have any experience at all working as an administrative assistant. The guy didn't want to give me a chance. He thought I was just a pretty face."

"How could you tell?"

"I can always tell. He all but admitted that the only reason he was interviewing me was because he was scared of Ciel." Kyla planted a hand on the wood railing of the deck. "That's one of the things I like best about Ciel. She's so regal and elegant, yet at the same time she inspires terror in her underlings. She's like Henry VIII. Before the syphilis and obesity, of course." She looked out over the backyard, where the swing set Christopher and Lee had installed years ago seemed to rest in quiet hibernation. "Maybe I should just become a professional volunteer at

Raines-Hartley or something. It's not like Zweli and I need two incomes to get by."

"Has he asked you to marry him again?"

She uncomfortably cleared her throat. Zweli hadn't mentioned marriage, an engagement, or anything even remotely related to matrimony since his return to St. Louis early Monday morning. He was in Abby's living room with the rest of her family unpacking Christmas ornaments, and the reason she'd left him there to join Christopher out on the deck was because she couldn't stand being with him while his unspoken question hung between them.

"No," she said. "He hasn't. I think he's holding out for Christmas. He's staying in St. Louis this year instead of going home to Indianapolis, so I'm pretty sure he's got something pretty important planned." A nervous smile played at the right corner of her mouth.

"You could ask him, you know."

"Ask him what?"

Christopher slipped the blade cover onto the hacksaw. "To marry you."

"I want an old-fashioned proposal. Man to woman, and I want to be swept off my feet."

"The first two weren't sweeping?"

The darkening winter sky was the same deep cobalt blue as Christopher's eyes. Kyla's gaze moved from one to the other as she answered him. "Zweli gave me the kind of proposals that women dream of. I've put him in an awkward position. I think he feels that he has to top himself."

"I don't think that's the problem." Christopher took off his glasses and cleaned them with the tail of his shirt.

"There's a problem?" She crossed her arms over her chest and stood closer to him. "What kind of problem?"

"Don't panic. I shouldn't have used the word 'problem.' It's more of a concern."

"Spill it, Chris," she ordered.

He stuck his hands in the pockets of his jeans and leaned against the deck railing. "I really miss the lab, Kyla. I love being at the house when Troy, C.J., and Danielle get home from school, and I even like the fact that my house is the one all the kids' friends flock to on the weekends. I count myself lucky to be able to earn a decent living working from home while performing my duties as a Mr. Mom. But sometimes, I miss the lab so much I have to steal away and spend a day at the Washington University Physics Lab just to get the craving out of my system."

She pursed her lips and wrinkled her brow. "I'm very sorry to hear that, but what's that got to do with me and Zweli?"

"When your grandma Claire died, Clara took it very hard. She needed to move back here, to be near her family. She knew that she could find work here with no problem. As a matter of fact, her position at the medical school is better than the one she left in California. My work, on the other hand, was slightly more specialized. I can't do it just anywhere."

Kyla nodded. St. Louis wasn't exactly a hotbed of opportunity for particle physicists.

"I enjoyed teaching at Stanford, but my wife's happiness meant even more. I loved being in the lab, but I love carpentry just as much."

"I'm still not seeing what this has to do with me and Zweli." She stamped her feet to warm them up.

"My respect for your sister's wishes inspired me to trade one passion for another, and I've never been happier. I just wanted to let you know that it can be done. That you can find happiness, as long as you're being true to yourself."

"That's why I want to marry Zweli. To be true to my heart. I'm willing to sacrifice just about anything to be with him. He knows that."

Christopher propped opened the patio doors and wrapped his gloved hands around the trunk of the tree. "Maybe that's his concern," he said as he wrestled the tree into the house.

Kyla sat on the arm of Zweli's chair and watched her nieces and nephews tear into the mountains of presents surrounding the freshly decorated tree dominating one corner of the big living room. Many hands had made quick work of the trimming, and Kyla wanted to bask in the comfort and joy the sight of the finished tree usually gave her. There was no particular motif or theme to the decoration. A flour, salt, and water dough snowman made by Clarence shared a fragrant bough with a Hallmark Oscar Meyer Weinermobile that issued the famous jingle. A tin train that her grandmother Claire had owned as a child dangled prettily beside a polar fleece gingerbread girl that Cady had made from a scrap of fabric left over from one of her many sewing projects. Fresh Bob's candy canes provided splashes of red and white in the upper portions of the tree. The children had long since stolen away the candy canes in the bottom half. Kyla spied her favorite ornament, a wooden drum whittled from a single piece of soft pine, hanging near the top of the tree, well out of the children's reach.

She nudged Zweli, and he slipped an arm around her hips as he looked up at her from the chair. "See that little drum there?" she said, pointing to it.

"That's a drum? It looks like Winnie the Pooh's honey pot."

"You've been spending way too much time with the twins," Kyla chided. "That ornament is the oldest one we put on the tree. My great-great something or other—"

"Grandfather," Abby piped in as she hustled past carrying a tray of warm molasses-clove cookies and hot cinnamon tea. "I think."

"His name was Jacob Winters and he's the only ancestor I have that ever showed an interest in the performing arts," Kyla said.

"Jacob was a doctor," Cady said. She sat on the Persian rug with the twins, working to disentangle them from the long strands of ribbon that had been used to wrap their gifts. "So was his sister, Zacadia. Jacob was the first black doctor to practice in Juniper Falls, Missouri. He opened his own practice in 1889."

"I knew the tribal historian could fill in the blanks," Kyla allowed graciously. "Grandma Claire used to tell me about Jacob's music."

"What did he play?" Zweli asked.

"What didn't he play?" Abby said. She handed Zweli a holly-printed paper plate with two cookies and a dollop of freshly whipped cream sprinkled with lemon zest and sandy crystals of turbinado sugar. "Jacob was truly gifted when it came to musical instruments."

"Grandma used to say that Jacob never met an instrument he didn't teach himself how to play." Kyla was speaking to Zweli, but with the exception of the twins, everyone quieted to listen to her share the legacy of her great-great grandfather. "He loved music. As a child he started with the harmonica and penny whistle, and by the time he finished medical school, he'd taught himself the piano, flute, clarinet, trumpet, saxophone, oboe, and accordion. A few years before he died at eighty-nine, he was teaching himself to play a Gibson ES-150 electric guitar he'd ordered by mail after falling in love with the instrument during a Charlie Christian performance."

"Who's Charlie Christian?" C.J. asked.

Kyla smiled at her nephew, who was silently fingering the keys of the electronic keyboard Cady and Keren had given him for Christmas.

"Charlie Christian was probably the first great electric guitar player," Kyla told him. "He played jazz, the blues...everything."

"They say he could make his guitar sing as though it had a voice," Zweli added.

"Cool," C.J. said, his fingers picking out imagined notes.

Zweli pulled Kyla onto his lap and wrapped both arms around her. "Is that why you like that drum so much? Because Jacob was a musician?"

"It's my only tangible connection to someone who succeeded at the thing he was most passionate about," Kyla said. "He liked medicine but he loved music. He performed at the 1904 World's Fair. He played the piano before hundreds of people. Do you know how fearless he would have had to be? And how happy he probably was once it was all over, and all those people were clapping for him and appreciating his talent?"

Zweli gave her thigh a supportive squeeze. "You're fearless, too. Once you realize that, you'll be able to do what Jacob did."

"Jacob had his moment of stardom, and I suppose I have, too." Kyla raised her mug of tea in a half-hearted salute. "Here's to Kati and her 'i.' May she rot in syndication hell while I get on with the rest of my life. Maybe I'll color my hair and put on fifty pounds so no one ever recognizes me again."

Zweli watched Kyla stare into her mug. Tendrils of steam curled into the air just under her nose. The serious set of her mouth and the dull light in her eyes contrasted sharply with the bright merriment of the family gathering around her. He knew from experience that such somber quiet typically signaled the onset of one of Kyla's sarcastic, splenetic storms.

"Why don't we get going?" he asked quietly. "I have a surprise for you."

She raised her eyes to see Clara and Ciel helping Abby gather up black trash bags full of crumpled and torn wrapping paper. Christopher and Lee, shaking their heads at all the toys and gifts their children had received, tried to prod the recipients into helping them collect everything and bundle it into bags for easier transport to their cars.

"Can I drive us home?" Troy pleaded with his father as he removed the snazzy black leather driving gloves Zweli had given him. "Please?"

Kyla smiled in spite of her darkening mood. Troy had been the best of drivers since the accident, even though he still didn't have use of his Chevy Nova. He had spent most of the past month wheeling and dealing with his aunts and uncles for use of their cars until Abby had taken pity on him and lent him the beet-red Chevette that had been enjoying a peaceful retirement in her garage since the day its last owner, Chiara, graduated from college. The old puddle jumper wheezed, sputtered, and belched Troy to and from school, and Kyla admired the way he cared for the car as though it were a beloved, elderly relative. In some ways, it was. Cady had purchased the used car with her babysitting money during her senior year of high school, and it had been passed down to Kyla and then Chiara.

Troy had been delighted with the loaner, but Kyla smiled as she imagined how much happier he would be the next morning when he woke up to find his freshly pimped out Nova in his driveway. His aunts, uncles and Zweli had chipped in to have the Nova fully repaired and upgraded with a new sound system, clutch, and airbags. The new and improved Nova was currently hiding in Abby's garage even as Troy clasped his hands under his chin and begged his father to let him drive their Expedition home.

"If Troy drives the big car," C.J. asked, "can I drive the Chevette home?"

"Boy, you're only fourteen," Clara said.

"And you're a bad driver," chimed Danielle, who obsessively arranged the onyx and ivory pieces of the hand-carved chess set Cady and Keren had given her.

C.J. scowled at his sister. "You've never seen me drive."

"Yes, I have." Danielle nestled her onyx queen in its cushy bed of black velvet. "You drove in the Crazy Karts at Clarence's birthday party. You crashed into everything."

"You're supposed to crash into everything, dookieneck." C.J. would have accompanied his insult with a tug of his sister's braid if his cousin Abigail hadn't intervened.

"C.J., you can't drive a car," she said with a haughty flip of her long, blue-black hair. "You're just a kid."

"My dad lets me drive up and down the street in front of the house early Sunday mornings. I'm a good driver, aren't I, Dad?"

Clara, who had been trying to force C.J.'s new keyboard back into its box, straightened and set a hand saucily on her hip. "Is that what you and your father are doing when you're supposed to be going out for donuts and the Sunday paper?"

Christopher's cheeks went as red as his hair, and he gave his glasses a nervous push. "Given Troy's track record as a fledgling driver, I assumed that as soon as possible would be early enough to start teaching C.J. the basics of good driving."

"Well, if you put it that way." Clara smiled in spite of herself.

"C'mon, Dad." Troy stole back his parents' attention. "Let me drive home tonight. The roads are clear, traffic is light, and Mom's been letting me drive the Expedition to and from the supermarket some-times."

With a sack of her children's gifts in her arms, Clara jetted out of the room.

"Okay," Christopher sighed. "We'll leave the Chevette here overnight."

"I'll go put it in the garage," Troy offered.

"No!" cried his mother, father and Abby.

"Fine," Troy said warily, backing slowly away as though afraid they might pounce.

Kyla covered her mouth with her hand to hide her laughter.

"Ready to go?"

A pleasant tingle coursed through Kyla at the sound of Zweli's voice in her right ear. She nodded and followed him when he stood and took her right hand to pull her to her feet.

"Do you need any help cleaning up, Mrs. Winters?" Zweli asked.

Abby spent a moment surveying the room. But for a few scraps of wrapping paper and the rumpled appearance of the skirt beneath the Christmas tree, the room was in good order. "I think I can handle it from here. You go on and get Kyla home."

He gave Abby a warm hug and a kiss on the cheek. Kyla stood in the archway between the living room and the foyer, talking with her mother while Zweli made the rest of his goodbyes.

"Are you okay, baby?" Abby asked.

Kyla kicked at the faded gold fringe of the Persian rug in the foyer. "I just feel a little out of place. I'm the only one here who isn't a wife. I wish Chiara had come home. Spinster aunts are supposed to come in pairs, right?"

"What's a spinster?" asked Abigail, who appeared from nowhere.

"Girl, someone needs to tie a bell around your neck," Abby remarked as she gave her young namesake a gentle shove toward the living room.

"A spinster is someone who minds her own business," Kyla called after her niece.

Abby took Kyla by the shoulders. She leaned slightly to one side to spy on Zweli in the foyer beyond Kyla as she spoke. "I know you're looking for something special these days, but do yourself a favor…don't try to rush anything. Everything happens the way it's supposed to, in its own good time."

"I just want everything to be settled," Kyla mumbled impatiently.

"Why are you in such a rush lately?"

"I'm not. I…" She pressed her hand to her forehead. "I'm just tired of being in a holding pattern. I'm ready to move forward and build the kind of life Clara, Ciel, and Cady have."

"You won't ever have their lives because you aren't them," Abby advised. "Take the time to enjoy the moments you're living in, honey." She turned Kyla toward the foyer, and stood beside her as they watched Zweli help Danielle into her coat. "When it comes to husbands and children, the days are long but the years are short. Be patient and enjoy this time with Zweli. Don't try to rush anything."

Kyla tried to take her mother's advice, but it was hard as she watched Zweli drive into the darkness of Interstate 64. He wore a quiet smile as he stared at the road, his right hand resting on hers. Nat King Cole's rendition of *The Christmas Song* issued from the CD player, and Zweli contentedly hummed along. Kyla slid across the seat and lifted his right arm so she could snuggle into him. He kissed the top of her head and hugged her into his side.

"I feel like a teenager," he said. "Driving my girl home after McDonald's and a movie."

"It kinda feels like you're just driving." Her hand moved into his lap and she smiled when he sat up a bit straighter. "I live fifteen miles in the opposite direction."

"I told you. I have a surprise for you."

"It's almost midnight." She traced the inseam of his wool slacks until her hand came to rest over the bulge behind his fly. "I was hoping you could come over and help me put out some treats for Santa."

He removed her hand and kissed it. "If you keep that up, you're gonna make me crash."

"I'll be nice," she promised. "Until you take me home, and then I plan to be naughty."

"Santa won't bring you any presents," he teased.

"Santa ain't the man who's got what I want this year."

He eased into the right lane and cruised down the exit ramp. "What is it that you want?"

She opened her mouth to answer, but found a pinch of patience. "I'll tell you tomorrow at dinner. By then I'll know if I got it or not."

"I think the kids liked the gifts we picked out for them." He slowed the car as he drove the darkened residential streets of West St. Louis County. "Clarence went nuts for that Foam Fighter."

"I forgot to tell Ciel that *you* picked that out," Kyla said, sitting up. "I don't want her coming after me when Clarence fills her house with soap suds." She saw nothing but trees and sprawling dark lawns when she looked out of her window. "Zweli, where are we going? Another Christmas Eve party?"

"Sort of." He turned left onto a gated street, and drove over five distantly spaced speed bumps before making a second left onto the smooth, blacktop driveway leading to the only house that had lights burning in every window. With the engine idling, he turned to her.

"Is this what you wanted to show me?" she asked.

"What do you think of it?"

His green eyes burned with anticipation as he watched her face, hoping to gauge her honest reaction. Kyla unlocked her door. "Do you know who lives here?" she asked. "I want to get out, but I'm afraid someone might release the hounds on me."

"I don't think the owner will mind if you have a look around." Zweli got out of the car and hurried around to the passenger side to get her door.

"Wow," she exhaled, her eyes on the house as she exited the car. Each house on the private street had its own unique architectural design, and this two-story brick house had clearly been styled after a French country manor. The white patina on the brick gave the house an ancient look and matched the white shutters opened wide at the numerous windows. A single candle burned in each window, and Kyla had to squint to see that the candles flickered with electricity rather than fire. Wide garlands of red, green, and gold ribbon intertwined with fresh evergreen boughs adorned the windowsills.

Pulling her hood on, Kyla walked farther up the driveway and peered around the back of the house. The property went farther back than she'd first assumed, with the darkness enveloping what looked like a pool house. The front lawn was as big and wide as a soccer field and the backyard seemed to go all the way to the edge of a body of water glittering with moonlight.

"This place is enormous," Kyla whispered, sure that if she spoke any louder, she would trigger a security detail that involved helicopters and nets shot from cannons. "Do you know how much something like this would go for in California?"

She got no response from Zweli, and turned to see that she was alone. She ran on tiptoe to the front of the house to find him standing on the doorstep. "I do not want to be arrested on Christmas Eve again!" she whispered urgently. She took his arm and tried to pull him away. "Let's go before the rich people look out of their windows and realize that we aren't just a pair of big, brown elves!"

"It's okay, Kyla, really," he gently insisted as he pulled her onto the doorstep. "Do you like the place so far?"

She faced him, and he used both hands to lower her hood. "I love it," she said. "The only thing missing is a little bit of snow to really give it the Hallmark stamp."

As she gazed into the clear green of his twinkling eyes, tiny white flakes began fluttering between them. She laughed and threw out her mittened hands. "Are you kidding me?" she asked, her face upturned to the dark sky. "Did you plan this?"

"Nope," he chuckled. "But if I could, I'd make all your holiday wishes come true." He wrapped his arms around her waist. "Want to see the inside of the house?"

"It's the middle of the night."

He displayed a pair of keys. "The owner won't mind."

A wide foyer tiled in cream Italian marble provided a showroom for a double staircase leading to the upper floor. Kyla took a hesitant step deeper into the house, staring up at the chandelier dangling from the twenty-foot ceiling. It was big, easily four feet across, but its simple three-tiered design gave it a merry, unobtrusive sparkle. Kyla peeped into the empty formal dining room to her right and the living room to her left. After whistling under her breath at the high gloss of the hardwood floors, she noticed Zweli's cherished Le Corbusier sofa and Noguchi cocktail table, the only furniture in the living room.

She whirled on him. "Since when do you have a house?"

"Since a couple of weeks ago. I saw it and I just had to have it. It used to belong to the chief of endocrinology at Raines-Hartley. He offered it to me for a great price, and we closed the deal without a realtor."

"You dump the Alfa Romeo for a carpool-friendly SUV, and now you've traded the swingin' bachelor pad for several green acres in the 'burbs. People are gonna talk."

"Oh yeah? What are they gonna say?" He followed her as she made her way through the dining room and into what would likely be turned into a library or sitting room. Two sets of French doors accessed the rear patio, and through the polarized panes of glass, Kyla spotted the huge in-ground pool, cabana, tennis court, and lake.

"That you've been domesticated," she mumbled. "I love this house, Z. Do you know what something like this would go for in California? Only plastic surgeons can afford a house like this."

"Thank God for Missouri, where there's more land than people." He took her hand and pulled her toward another doorway. "Want to see the kitchen?"

She gave him a noncommittal shrug and sighed, "Okay."

"You don't like cooking much, do you?"

"I don't like measuring and mixing and stirring and standing over steaming pots and pans. That's Clara and Cady's thing. I'm more of a peel it, slice it, season it and eat it raw kind of person. Cady calls it cooking without cooking. I love food, don't get me wrong, but I have to be careful about what I eat. I might not have to be in front of cameras anymore, but I do intend to stay in shape. Cady thinks I should write down some of my recipes. She says that some of them taste so good, you'd never know they were health—"

Mid-word, her tongue adhered to the roof of her mouth when Zweli turned on the lights. She tried to take in everything at once, but the kitchen was just too big. Stainless steel appliances along one wall gleamed in the soft track lighting, a center preparation island housed a huge grill and a double sink, and a glassed-in section on the opposite side of the kitchen formed a gorgeous casual dining area. "Wow," she finished. She took off her mitten and ran her fingers along the polished blond wood of a cabinet door. "I don't think I've ever seen a kitchen big enough to rollerskate in. You could film a cooking show in here. Your dad could do *Zweli's Cajun Kitchen,* and your mom could do dessert segments."

"Or *you* could," Zweli suggested. "Why don't you pitch the idea to one of the cable channels?"

"Can I see the upstairs?"

He'd touched a nerve and decided not to pursue the television idea further. Kyla gave him a grateful smile when he again took her hand and walked her through the kitchen, to another staircase. Her boot heels clattered over the bare bird's-eye maple as she climbed two flights of stairs and ended up in a wide rotunda overlooking the potential library.

Five opened doors revealed the rooms branching off the open space. "Those are the small bedrooms." Zweli pointed to the two doors nearest the safety railing above the library, and Kyla peeked into them.

"Small?" she coughed. She went into one of them and spun in a circle, her arms outstretched. "This room is bigger than my whole apartment." The bathroom caught her eye and she skipped over to it, flipped on the lights, and noticed the second small bedroom adjoining the bathroom on the other side. "Zweli, this is so sweet! This is what just Cady and Keren need, for the twins when they get bigger."

"This is what Cady and Keren need *now*, with number three on the way." Zweli waved Kyla back into the atrium, where he showed her a bedroom with a view of a dormant rose garden and a tiny piece of the lake.

"This room really would make a nice nursery." Kyla walked the hexagonal perimeter by the dim moonlight. "It's not too big, it's not too small." She opened the double doors of the closet and gasped at how large and deep the empty space was. "My car could fit in here. You could put the baby's clothes on one side, and have a hideaway library on the other side, for books and toys." She closed the doors and walked to the window. "The crib would be good here, so the baby could see the garden." She rapped on the window. "Is this tempered glass? The window is so low, I know Junior's gonna be leaning on it and throwing toys at it, and you don't want it to break."

"Yes, it's tempered." Zweli bit back a smile. "And it's polarized, so the morning glare won't wake him up."

He listened to Kyla plot out the rest of the furnishings, and in his mind the dark room was transformed into a place of sunlight and pastels, a room filled with toys and books, and at its center, a doting mother who cradled her baby in her arms as she rocked him to sleep.

"It would be so nice to rock the baby to sleep looking at the lake," Kyla sighed dreamily. She shook herself and looked away from Zweli, but not before the intense longing in her tone registered. "I mean, it would be so nice for Cady. She, uh, really likes putting the twins down for bed. She says it's the one time of day that she can really see what her babies look like." She uneasily cleared her throat. "Show me the rest of the place."

He had deliberately saved the best for last, and stepped into the master bedroom suite before her, to witness her reaction. The bedroom was empty but for the wall-to-wall, triple-padded blue-grey carpeting, a few unopened plastic bags of new bedding, and pillows bound with paper tape. "I figured I'd wait until after the holidays to move the rest of my furniture," he explained as Kyla peeped into the master bathroom, "since I'm still using the condo as my home base. I was hoping you could provide the bed for this room, and—"

Kyla turned on the bathroom light and screamed, drowning him out.

She ran into the bathroom and froze inside the entrance, her hands splayed, her eyes wide and her mouth hanging open. "Do you like it?" Zweli chuckled.

Nearly drooling, she managed to nod. He had owned the house for only a few weeks, and apparently had spent all of that time focusing on the bathroom. She took off her parka and let it drop to the champagne marble tiles. The room was long and began with what could only be considered a mini foyer with a deep, wide linen closet filled with thick towels on one side and a sculpted marble toilet with gold fixtures on the other. She passed through a high archway and into the main body of the bathroom. A giant bay window with a view of the treetops rounded out the wall on her left, and a counter with lots of drawers and cabinet space ran the long length of the right wall. The marbled basins of the His and Her sinks in the counter boasted gold fixtures, wall-mounted swivel mirrors and several modes of lighting, including delicate crystal dishes of vanilla and plumeria scented votive candles.

On either side of the counter stood His and Her dressing areas. Kyla caressed the full-size, folding triple mirror and oohed out loud at the clothes steamer on the Her side. Zweli approached her from behind and rested his hands on her shoulders. "There's a dry cleaning system built into the laundry room in the basement," he whispered near her ear.

"Mmmm, dry cleaning," she hummed hungrily.

The glass walls of the shower stall revealed six heads mounted at varying heights, and the bathtub, which doubled as a whirlpool, caught Kyla's eye next. A tiny pip of joy bubbled from her lips as she lunged at the tub to sit on its edge. Deep and wide, it would easily accommodate two people, and the adjustable nozzles set in it convinced her that those two people could have scads of fun once the bathing began.

She climbed into the tub and lay flat in the bottom of it. "My tub at home is so small, I have to bathe in the fetal position. And the view…" She pictured a tiny, paint-encrusted window, a torn screen and the dumpster outside it. "Let's just say this one's much, much better."

Lying in the tub, Kyla noticed that the ceiling above it was one-way tinted glass that made her feel as though she owned the patch of night sky above her. The snow had picked up and fat, fluffy clusters of it dropped heavily onto the angled panes of glass. She laced her fingers and used them to pillow her head as she crossed her legs at the ankles. "You know what I'd like to do right now?"

Zweli sat on the edge of the tub and looked down at her. "I can't even imagine."

"I'd love to take a bath."

"Okay."

A loud, powerful rush of warm water hammered Kyla's feet as Zweli, at the touch of a button in a console at his hip, began filling the tub. "Zweli, damn it!" she laughed as she scrambled into a sitting position. She grabbed his arm and pulled him off balance. Too late he tried to right himself, and he fell across her lap. She laughed as she gathered her hair and wound it into a loose knot at the back of her head.

He shifted off her to gather her into the embrace of his arms and legs. "If you wanted me to take a bath with you, all you had to do was ask."

"I like to give as good as I get," she giggled. "Nice trick with the water."

"You can program whatever temperature you want, so that every time you use the tub, your water will be ready to go. You can even set the power level and number of the whirlpool jets, too."

With the water rising around them, and still fully dressed, Kyla settled deeper into his embrace, nuzzling his neck and clasping his hands in hers. "So this is your new home."

He kissed her forehead and the end of her nose. "It is now," he said, his lips finally meeting hers.

While Kyla had peeled off her soggy clothing and added a splash of sage and citrus bubble bath to the running water, Zweli had gone to the kitchen for the only food he happened to have in the house—a bottle of Veuve Clicquot and a pint of fresh strawberries. The empty bottle and a heap of strawberry stems sat forgotten against a backdrop of snow and stars as Zweli and Kyla faced each other in the middle of an island of fragrant bubbles.

Candles burned on the counter, their dancing light reflecting in the mirror, the windows beside and above the tub, and in Kyla's wet skin. Zweli pressed his lips to her shoulder, and then her collarbone, and her head fell back as she pressed her torso tighter to his. Under the water, his hands moved along her thighs, encouraging her to fasten her legs tighter about his hips. Smiling, she made a low noise of pleasure when he stroked her wet hair, laying it along her spine. His touch gave her goosebumps even as the heat of the water warmed her, and she kissed him as her long, strong thighs began a rhythmic pulse that elicited a throaty moan from Zweli. Hands clasped, bodies melded and water churned as they shared the same air and seemingly the same skin.

Zweli worshipped every inch of her body, and Kyla went from watching the stars to seeing them. Throwing her head back and facing the skylight, she felt as though they were bathing in the velvet darkness of space, on a planet of their own where warmth, water, flesh, and passion collided to send her soaring beyond the heavens.

Her responses shattered his arrogance as he humbly succumbed to her power over him. Her breathy panting in his ear, the quiver in her supple thighs and the clench of her darkness around him shattered his every pretense of mastery, over her or himself, and he surrendered with a deafening groan. Still joined and still working to catch his breath, he reclined against the built-in backrest with Kyla cloaking him. Blanketed in warm water and a thick layer of bubbles, Kyla shifted to rest her head on his shoulder.

He traced aimless patterns in the dampness on her back as he said, "May I ask you a question?"

Her whole body perked in excitement. Zweli had given her stars, snowflakes, bubbles and a bath, yet she wanted more. She wanted a ring. More importantly, she wanted everything the ring represented. Delighted that he had actually managed to top himself, she trembled and forced herself to maintain an even tone. "Sure. Ask away."

"Kyla, will you— Are you cold?"

"Yes!" So primed to answer the question she assumed was coming, she wasted her enthusiasm on the wrong question. "What?"

He made a move to stand. "You're shivering. Let's get out and get dressed."

She shoved him back down, pinning him in place by lying atop him. "I'm fine. Is that all you wanted to ask me?"

His fingers danced over her shoulder blades as though she were a fine musical instrument. "No. There was something else."

"Good." She laced her fingers together on his chest and rested her chin upon them. "Talk. *Ask*."

With his index finger, he traced the cute slope of her nose. "I'm not sure how you're going to feel about this, and I've seriously debated whether I should ask, given the way things stand. I don't want to rock the boat."

"Rock." She smiled so hard, her cheeks ached. "Rock away, Z."

The intensity of his gaze started her heart tripping along so fast that she was sure he could feel it through her skin. Her heart surged painfully when he dropped his gaze to her shoulder and said, "Will you appear in a Raines-Hartley commercial?"

Her smile vanished. She sat up. "Are you frickin' kiddin' me?"

"I know it isn't glamorous, but the director of publicity wanted me to invite you to take part in a promotional trailer for R-H." His fingertips grazed her spine as she sat forward and hugged her knees. "She thinks you'd lend credibility and celebrity all in one shot. It hasn't been announced yet, but Keren and Cady are giving the hospital the money to fund a residential living facility for the families of children undergoing long-term treatment at R-H. It'll combine hotel amenities with R-H's top-notch healthcare."

"You sound like a press release." She stood, and Zweli watched rivulets of water and soap bubbles slide along the graceful lines of her body as she climbed the three deep steps to exit the tub. She grabbed a towel from the warmer between the tub and the shower stall and wrapped it around herself. A trail of wet footprints marked her path as she went into the master bedroom.

Still pulling a freshly cooked towel around his hips, Zweli hurried after her and put a hand at her waist. She tensed and turned around. It was so hard to stay mad at him when all he had to do was touch her to make her crave him all over again.

"I'm sorry, I should have asked you before I brought your name up to the development team," he started. "Cady and I thought it would be a good idea to involve you."

She crossed her arms over her chest. "I'll do your promotional thing," she snapped.

"They'll pay whatever you ask."

"It's for Keren and Cady and a bunch of sick kids." She put her hands on her hips. "I'll do it for free."

"Why are you so upset?"

She opened and closed her mouth twice before answering. "I thought you wanted to marry me."

He started back to the bathroom. "I thought we worked this out on Thanksgiving Day."

"So did I." She marched toward him. "I want to marry you, Zweli."

From halfway across the room, she saw the wicked sparkle in his eyes as he said, "Then ask me. I'll probably say yes." She ran after him and he darted into the bathroom. She tackled him and her weight carried him into the countertop. "Why do you want to marry me, Ky? Tell me."

She settled into his arms but still had a hard time removing her frown. "Because I love you."

He swallowed hard. "Is that the only reason?"

"Isn't that enough?"

"For me, it's all I wanted. For you…I'm not so sure."

"So now all of a sudden, you *don't* want to get married?"

He took her hand and walked her back into the master bedroom, coming to a stop at a patch of wall between the two bay windows. "That's your Christmas present, but it's what *I* want," he told her, with a nod of his head directing her to the framed print mounted on the wall.

She read the placard beneath it. " 'Mommy Playing in the Sun with Her Children.' "

She wasn't much of an art connoisseur, but she recognized a masterpiece when she saw one. The print was more than art. It was a promise that tied together every room and mood of the house. She stared at the print and imagined herself going into the Jack and Jill suite to deliver goodnight kisses. She saw herself making lunches every morning in the showroom kitchen, and hosting birthday pool parties in the backyard. Blinking tears over her lower lashes, she looked back at Zweli.

"Do you like it?" he asked, his tone unmistakably hopeful.

Nodding, she went into his arms and kissed him. Tears clogged her voice. "If that's all you want, I can give it to you."

He used both hands to smooth her damp hair from her face as he peered into her eyes. "Are you sure?"

Openly weeping, she could only nod, and the beauty of her sincere emotion forced Zweli to blink back tears of his own. "When I ask you to marry me, you'd better say yes," he warned. "Because when I ask, I'll mean it. I don't want you to have any doubts about anything."

"That's fair," she sniffled.

"And I won't be asking just because you want me to now. I'll ask when I'm good and ready, preferably when you least expect it."

"You like your surprises," she chuckled through her tears.

He peppered her forehead with kisses before planting a loving one on her lips. "Your nose is running."

She tugged at his towel and brought it to her nose, which she blew heartily. "Thank you." She handed it back, and he used a clean corner of it to wipe the moisture from her cheeks.

"Merry Christmas, Kyla," he said, pulling her to his naked body.

Even though she hadn't gotten the one thing she wanted, she realized that it truly was a merry Christmas because Zweli had done one better, and given her what she needed.

CHAPTER ELEVEN

"You have a phone message."

Abby's accusatory greeting came as Kyla was still trying to wedge her leather jacket onto the packed coat tree in the foyer of her mother's house. "Merry Christmas to you too, Mama," she responded. Abby's body language was all wrong. Her arms crossed over the chest of her festive red sweater, and one slippered foot jackhammered a rhythm of consternation. "I didn't forward my calls here, if that's what's got you cranky."

"Why is—"

Zweli entered the house, stamping snow from his Timberland boots and forcing Abby to curb her question and turn her inquisitive scowl into a happy holiday smile. Zweli greeted her with a hug that lifted her off the braided welcome mat.

"Merry Christmas, Mrs. Winters," he said, setting her back on her feet. Blushing, she wished him the same and then offered to take his coat to the closet.

Kyla's jacket sprang off the overly full coat tree and slid to the floor. "Take mine while you're at it. Please," she added sweetly.

"Let me," Zweli offered. He took Kyla's coat and started for the narrow closet built into the space under the stairs.

"Thank you, Zweli." Abby took Kyla's arm and pulled her toward the kitchen. "Kyla, a moment, please?"

Once in the kitchen, Abby, her voice low, was all scowls again. "Why is Nigel Chamberlain calling you at my house? Is there some reason you didn't give him your current phone number and address?"

Kyla stiffened to fight off a shudder. She swallowed back the hard lump that had lodged in her throat at the sound of Nigel's name. "Yes. And I don't want to talk about it."

Abby took a step back, her expression softening into concern as she studied Kyla, who pointedly avoided her mother's stare. "I saved it for you," Abby said. "It's still on the answering machine."

Kyla anxiously worked one hand over the other. Knowing that Nigel had called her mother's house made her feel a whole lot less cheery in the comfy red chenille turtleneck Cady had given her for Christmas.

She played with the big gold hoop at her left ear and turned her attention to the platters and dishes of food lined up on the countertops and center island. "Let me help you carry this out to the buffet, Mama." She went to the cabinet under the sink, tugged an apron from one of the hooks attached to the inside of the door, and tied it around her hips. "It looks like you spent the whole day in the kitchen. Do you know if Clara is bringing that apple and walnut salad Zweli likes so much? He's been looking forward to—"

"Kyla." Abby took her hands. "I knew you were unhappy out West, and I wanted you home so much, I didn't ask too many questions when you decided to come back. I know you said you retired, but is work really the reason you left California?"

She chewed the inner left corner of her lower lip, a nervous habit she thought she'd overcome after years of comportment lessons. Her mother had always been able to read her feelings no matter how hard she tried to cloak them, so she made no effort to camouflage her unease when she said, "I left because I want something more." She looked down at their joined hands. "It would have been nice to get a film role like the one Nigel presented before I left. But it would have meant being around him for a few more weeks. I couldn't afford that."

Her forehead creased in concern, Abby cupped Kyla's face, her eyes searching. "Baby, what did he do to you?"

She hugged her mother's hand to her face. "Nothing I didn't do right back to him."

Tears rose in Abby's eyes, her mouth stiffened, and Kyla acted quickly to diffuse her mother's anger. "It wasn't anything serious, Mama. Just a broken nose and a little bruising."

Abby's left hand shot out and fastened around the handle of the ten-inch chef's knife lying innocently on the prep island. "That son of a bitch broke your nose?"

"I broke his." Kyla backed up a step, toward the answering machine on the telephone table. "Did he say what he wanted?"

"He only said what he had to, I guess." Still clutching the knife, Abby crossed her arms over her chest in a defensive posture worthy of a prizefighter.

Kyla spent a pensive moment staring at the bright red winking eye of the answering machine before she hit PLAY. The volume was turned up too high, and her skin crawled when Nigel's voice barked from the answering machine.

"I'm so sorry to disrupt your holiday, Mrs. Winters, but I've been trying to contact your daughter Kyla for some time now." Kyla cringed. She'd known Nigel for seven years, and she wasn't fooled by his affable introduction. He had spoken to Abby in the same tone he'd always used on her when they were in public together and he wanted to bully her into doing something she didn't want to do. "My change of address card must have gotten lost in the mail," he said around an empty laugh. "I have an exciting property that has Kyla's name all over it, and I'm quite anxious to present it to her. As I'm sure you're aware, my contract with her expired several weeks ago, and since we're no longer official, I'm not at liberty to divulge the nature of this project. I feel comfortable saying that it's really a once-in-a-lifetime opportunity." Another hearty guffaw turned Kyla's stomach. "Please let your daughter know that I called. I've relocated my office since Kyla went on vacation, so I have a new phone number. It's 310—"

She stabbed the ERASE button with her finger, and the machine tape seemed to screech in pain as it rewound.

"Maybe you should call him," Abby suggested.

"A second ago, you wanted to fricassee him through the phone." Kyla shouldered past her and went to the refrigerator for a bottle of water. "Now you want me to call him? No, but thanks."

"He's got work for you." Abby set down the knife. "Just let him tell you about his big secret project. You can get it without him, can't you, once you know what it is?"

Kyla leaned back against a counter and sipped at her water. "Nigel won't make it that easy. He won't tell me about it until he's signed me. No project is worth that."

Abby steeled herself for battle. "I want to know what happened in California."

"It's Christmas, Mama. I don't want to talk about it."

Abby stared at her intently, as if she were still capable of making Kyla confess everything through the force of her gaze alone. Kyla looked away, just to be on the safe side.

"It won't be Christmas tomorrow, little girl," Abby warned her. "You and I are going to have us a nice little sit-down."

Kyla never got a chance to decline or accept her mother's commandment because Cady and Keren, each carrying a twin, knocked on the back door. Stomping snow from their shoes, the Winters-Bailey family shuffled into the warmth of the kitchen, the twins leaving wet footprints as they ran straight into their grand-mother's waiting arms.

The bad feeling fled Kyla at the sight of the twins in their fleece snow outfits. Claire wore a red jacket, blue pants, and a red pointed cap; Sammy was dressed in a blue jacket, red pants, and a blue pointed cap. On their feet were the pointy-toed, brown leather boots Chiara had sent them from Thailand.

"They look like a pair of lawn gnomes," Kyla said.

Cady pursed her lips and surreptitiously tipped her head toward Keren, who was hanging their coats on pegs near the back door. "They look adorable and you know it." Under her breath, she added, "Be nice. Keren dressed them. He doesn't know any better."

"Zweli would've known better. He's got the best fashion sense of any man I've ever seen. He's got a good eye for home decorating, too. Wait 'til you see the master bathroom of our new house. It's…" The wide-eyed stares of her mother and Cady stifled her. She loudly cleared her throat. "It's Zweli's house, actually. Just Zweli's. Not mine. And…" She eyeballed Keren. "And you don't seem surprised that I'm talking about Zweli's house, K."

Cady turned on her husband. "Zweli bought a house? And you knew about it?"

"I knew he was buying Dr. Pelham's old place," Keren said. "I didn't think he'd closed on it already."

"Closed and half moved in." Kyla raised her water bottle in a salute. "The man moves fast, when he wants to."

"You've seen it?" Cady rounded up the twins, who were accepting tiny chocolate Santas from Abby, and herded them toward Keren. "Take these two into the living room and change them into the outfits in their diaper bag. Mama, why don't you help him? Thanks, y'all." Cady crowded Kyla. "Talk. Start at the minute you left the house last night, and don't you dare leave out a single detail."

"I think I'll wait for Clara and Ciel to get here with their entourages. I don't want to have to tell the story two more times."

Kyla's head bobbled and water splashed on her black skirt as Cady took her forcefully by the shoulders. "Spill it, Ky. I've got Christmas Eve in the pool, and I want to know if I won."

"What pool?"

"The proposal pool." Cady flattened a hand at her abdomen and her back and turned sideways to model her clingy black dress. "Am I starting to show? I looked paunchy with the twins by the second month."

"You look great and who's in this pool?"

"The usual suspects." She grabbed Kyla's water and took a swig of it. "Clara, Christopher, Lee, Ciel, me, Keren, and Mama. We let Troy in, too. If he's old enough to drive and sit at the grown-up table, he's old enough to pay into the pot."

"What's the pot?"

"Everybody except Troy put in fifty dollars. We cut the kid a break and he only had to pay ten. But the winner has to apply the money toward your bridal shower. We figured it would be in bad taste to profit from your third proposal."

"Great." Kyla took back her water. "Only trouble is, there has to be a proposal before a proposal pool can pay off."

Cady's curls seemed to bounce in surprise. "He didn't…"

Kyla glowered. "Do I look like he did? He showed me his house, we played Up Periscope in the bathtub for two hours and then he asked me to be in the commercial for your sick-kid hotels."

"You didn't get a ring?"

"I got pruney."

When Cady put an arm around her shoulders, Kyla slumped into her. "He's going to ask you, you know," Cady said. "If I knew why he was stalling, I'd tell you. But don't let it get you down. I'm the one who should be sad. As of midnight last night, I'm out of the pool."

"I'm not upset about not getting a ring last night." She withdrew from Cady and turned toward the wide window above the sink. "I got a phone message from someone I was hoping I'd never hear from again."

"Who?"

"My old agent-slash-manager."

"Nigel the television coke head?" Cady laughed.

"Nigel the bully," she whispered through a sudden stream of hot tears. She'd never been able to keep her true feelings secret from Cady, and to her sister's credit, she didn't press for more. Cady hugged her from behind, and Kyla clung to her as though she were the lifeline between the comfort of her mother's kitchen and the knuckle side of Nigel Chamberlain's fist.

"Are you deliberately trying to torture her?"

"Who?" Zweli asked.

"Ky—*Ouch!*" Keren whirled on Danielle. He was sitting on an ottoman in the living room with Danielle standing over his shoulder and her new 100-piece body art set propped open on the seat of the wing chair behind her. "Are you using the colored pencils?"

"I wanted to see if they would show up."

"Do they?" He rubbed the stinging spot on his bald head where she had just tried to carve something into his skull.

"No."

"Would you mind sticking to the oil sticks and the washable markers?"

"I think I'm done." She stepped around him to examine her work head on. With a push to her glasses, she studied his dome from several angles.

"I think you missed a spot, there above his right ear," Zweli offered helpfully.

"How do I look?" Keren asked.

Zweli chuckled. "Like an 11-year-old girl just tagged your whole head with butterflies and rainbows." He peered closer at Keren's head. "Who's Keith Ketsenburg?"

The apples of Danielle's cashew-blonde cheeks instantly reddened. Rather than risk further interrogation, she fled the room, joining her cousins and siblings in the dining room for the dessert buffet.

"Keith Ketsenburg is Dani's latest flame," Keren said.

"I figured. The little purple and red hearts around the name gave it away." Zweli reached across the coffee table and grabbed a few cocktail napkins from a stack beside Abby's onion dip. He handed them to Keren, who scrubbed them across his cranium. "Now why were you asking me about torture?"

"Did you propose to Kyla last night?"

"No." Zweli sat forward, slightly lessening the distance between himself and Keren. From his vantage point on the sofa, he watched Kyla help Sammy safely navigate a spoonful of banana split cake into his mouth. Proud of himself for not spilling, he puckered his lips and waited for a kiss from his aunt, who happily obliged him. Zweli's chest filled with so much love for Kyla he had trouble breathing through it. "She wanted me to. I had the ring right there in the house, and I almost did, but…" He worked one hand over the other in a rare display of nerves. "I couldn't."

If any other man had been sitting before him with his head covered in a young girl's psychedelic renderings, Zweli would have laughed until his spleen exploded. But Keren's serious expression, which was even less humorless than usual, kept him stoic. "Do you still want to marry her?" he asked. "Or is it time for 'We're Better as Friends Than Lovers?' If it's talk time, I'll give you a ten-minute head start before I let Cady and the rest of the sisters loose on you."

"Just ten minutes? Man, I thought we were friends." Zweli mustered a weak smile. "All kidding aside, I still want to marry her. I can't stop wondering if she wants to marry *me*. She's a good actress, K. What she says she wants and what she actually wants might be two different things. I don't want to be her excuse for not living her life out loud."

"She wants a life with you, Z. Plain and simple."

"She also wants to perform. She seems to think that she has to choose one or the other. All I want for Kyla is what I want for myself."

"What's that?"

"Everything. Love, children, career…all of it. You've got it. Christopher and Lee have it, and I want it, too. I won't settle for less and I won't let Kyla settle, either."

"She's not settling. She's made her choice, and she's comfortable with it."

Zweli shook his head as he stood up. Kyla was looking at him, and her smile sent a current of electricity crackling through his veins. "That's what scares me the most. Comfortable isn't good enough."

Kyla stood in the lobby of her building, her face practically pressed to the glass door as she watched for Zweli's car. A bulging black suitcase slumped against her leg, a leopard-printed handbag hung from her shoulder and she clutched the thick pile of Friday afternoon junk mail to her chest. Zweli was supposed to pick her up at one o'clock for their drive to Indianapolis. He was only five minutes late, but her anticipation of the New Year's trip dragged out each second.

She was just as curious about Zweli's family as she was eager to spend a weekend away with him. The last time they'd spent a New Year's together, he'd asked her to marry him. She hoped for a repeat this holiday, but it was no longer a burning, anxious desire. What concerned her now was the reason for his reluctance. So many times she'd caught him looking at her, questioning her without words, and no matter what she said or did, she couldn't remove the doubt or curiosity or whatever it was from his eyes.

When she spotted his Explorer drawing to the curb in front of her building, she smiled and shoved her mail into her handbag, hoping that this weekend would put whatever troubled him to rest.

He left the car idling with its hazard lights on as he trotted over to Kyla. In a shearling coat, black turtleneck, and jeans, he looked so good that Kyla wanted to drag him into the lobby and pin him to the wall behind the potted plastic palms. She settled for meeting him on the pavement, throwing her arms around his neck and kissing him.

"I guess you're ready for the weekend," he mumbled into her ear once she allowed him to come up for air.

She drew slightly away and framed his face in her hands. "Aren't you?"

Smiling stiffly, he looked somewhere over the top of her head. "I'm looking forward to introducing you to my family. I'm not sure how I feel about going home, though."

"You were practically just there."

He reached around her to take her suitcase. "Yeah. Once a year is usually my limit." He started for the car, but Kyla took his hand and drew him back.

"We don't have to go, if you really don't want to," she offered. "I'm really looking forward to meeting your people, though."

He cupped her face, stroking a thumb across her cheek as he said, "I know. Just don't expect them to be like your family. Okay?" He didn't wait for her to respond before he took her luggage to the car and set it on the backseat. He opened the passenger door for Kyla and graciously helped her climb in.

"It's going to be fine, Zweli," she told him. He gave her a brief look before he turned away, his breath condensing in the cold air to create a gauzy haze. "I make a really good first impression, when I want to. And I want your family to approve of me."

A sharp pain moved through Zweli's chest, and he knew guilt was at the heart of it. "Baby, it's not you I'm worried about."

"Then what's the matter?"

Still avoiding her gaze, he shook his head. "It's nothing. Let's just get on the road. The sooner we get there, the sooner we'll be on our way back." He shut the door and went around to the driver's side.

"How long does it take to drive to Indianapolis?" Kyla asked once he'd pulled the car into traffic.

"A little under four hours."

"And we're leaving Saturday afternoon?"

"I have early rounds on Sunday."

She turned in her seat to lean against the door. His left elbow propped on the window ledge of his door, Zweli stared straight ahead, his forehead creased in serious thought. "How was your day today?" she asked brightly.

"Fine."

"I think my interview with the publicity director at your hospital went well. It was really low-key and friendly. She seemed really excited about my fluency in Spanish and Russian."

"Um," Zweli grunted.

"Stop the car."

Zweli sat up straight. "Why? What's the matter?"

She unfastened her seatbelt and unlocked her door. "Stop the car. I'm getting out."

He cut across one lane of Lindell Boulevard to get to the curb before Kyla opened her door. The car had barely rolled to a stop before she hopped out of it and opened the back door. She was dragging her suitcase onto the sidewalk by the time Zweli rounded the passenger side of the car.

"What the hell is this about?" he shouted. "You're a stuntwoman now, jumping out of a moving car?"

"I'm not spending another second in that car with you, Dr. Zombie." With a sharp snap, she extended the end handle of her suitcase. She dragged it behind her as she started back the way they had come.

"Kyla…dammit!" He hurried after her, taking her by the arm.

"You're the one who invited me to your parents' for New Year's, and now you're acting like you'd rather be anywhere than in that car on the way to Indiana."

"I would!" He scrubbed a hand over his head in exasperation. "I…" He softened his tone. "I'm sorry."

She let go of the suitcase handle to give him a little push. "Why are you having second thoughts?"

"I don't like going home," he blurted. "It's…"

"Zweli," she spoke over him. "Are you ashamed of your family?"

He dropped his gaze to a spidery crack in the sidewalk. "No."

"Are you ashamed of me?" she asked tenderly.

"Of course not." He pulled her into a rough embrace and kissed her left temple.

"Then stop expecting the worst and start having fun. This is our first road trip, and you're ruining it for me."

He hugged her closer. "I'm sorry, and you're right."

"I'm with you, Zweli. No matter what happens this weekend, I'm on your side."

The cold wind pasted a thin lock of her hair to her face and he gently brushed it aside as he stared into her eyes. He couldn't ask for a better ally than the woman in his arms, and he thanked his lucky star for her. "You are with me, aren't you?"

"Yep." *'Til death do us part,* she added silently.

CHAPTER TWELVE

The Explorer quietly idled in front of a white, two-story gambrel with crisp, black shutters. Cars parked bumper to bumper in the long driveway on the left side of the house spilled their occupants, who trooped across the lawn to the front door. The dark purples and blues of the early twilight were warmed by the golden light from the door and the windows, which wore a holiday dress of evergreen garlands and tartan bows with long tails that gently danced on the cold breeze. Showing a level of patience she hadn't felt since she and Zweli had hit Marion County, Kyla waited for him to cut the engine, a sure sign that he planned on staying at least through the night.

Although he'd remained attentive and interested in conversation during the four-hour road trip, he'd grown progressively more tense, so much so that he now gripped the Explorer's steering wheel with white knuckles as he fixed a feral stare on his parents' house.

Kyla already knew that the picture-perfect gambrel wasn't the house of Zweli's childhood. The gambrel was just over twelve years old, and had been the realization of Jackson Randall's dream. At the tender age of twenty, he'd promised his wife a big house, and decades later, soon after he'd earned his accounting license, he'd delivered on that promise. His construction project had triggered the revitalization of N. Kenwood Street, and what had once been a region of economic depression was now a thriving community dominated by young, family-oriented professionals.

The Randall ancestral estate, as Zweli had called it, was situated a good 200 feet in back of the gambrel. The one-story, five-room brick house in which Zweli had grown up looked familiar to Kyla. She'd seen hundreds like it dotting the roads near the citrus orchards of Southern

California. Such boxy little residences provided temporary housing for migrant workers.

Kyla wondered why the Randalls hadn't turned the weather-beaten building into a mother-in-law suite or carriage house. Upon closer inspection, she had noticed the debris-clogged rain gutters and drab curtains drawn behind grime-dulled windows, and concluded that the house was all but abandoned.

Which begged one question: Why hadn't the old house been razed? It was an eyesore, but even that didn't account for the sense of unease the old place gave Kyla. The longer she stared at its dark, curtained windows, the more it seemed like the house was scowling.

Kyla kept her curiosities to herself, unwilling to risk an inquiry that might spur Zweli into throwing the car into drive and stomping on the accelerator. "Are we going in?" she asked softly.

His mouth shaped into a no but before he could issue the syllable, their attention was stolen by the merry chime of jingle bells affixed to the tassels of the front door wreath. A woman exited the house, her right hand clasping the neck of a black sweater draped over her shoulders. Smiling, she hurried along the red brick path and down the four stairs leading to the sidewalk. She seemed to look past Kyla, and right then Kyla knew that she was about to come face to face with Zweli's mother.

And she wasn't a thing like Kyla had imagined.

Mrs. Randall wasn't the fearsome, robust woman whose victories over her personal demons made her larger than life and triumphant. Kyla saw nothing of the shrewish, mean drunk Zweli had known as a child in the doll-like woman with the bright eyes and smile hurrying toward the car. Mrs. Randall was tiny, at least a foot shorter than Zweli, who had finally left the car, met his mother at the curb, and was lifting her from the ground in a long hug. She pulled away only after Kyla got out of the car.

Zweli, his hand at the small of Kyla's back, handled the introduction. "Mom, this is Kyla Winters. Kyla, this is my mother. Niema St. Lucien Randall."

The anxiety had left his voice and he sounded proud and eager when he introduced her, to Kyla's relief. She turned on her most winning smile as she offered her hand. "I'm so happy to meet you, Mrs. Randall."

Mrs. Randall ignored Kyla's hand, instead taking her in a tight hug that startled the breath right out of Kyla. In the practiced way of all mothers, Mrs. Randall reached up and cupped Kyla's face. "You are even prettier in real life than you are on the television," she said.

Never one to pass up a chance to add to her considerable voice talents, Kyla soaked up Mrs. Randall's mellifluous, cultured dialect and sunny tone. Thirty-eight years in Indiana had done nothing to temper the lilt of the bayou in Mrs. Randall's accent, and it was literally music to Kyla's ears.

"I'm glad to finally get to meet you. Zweli's been promising to bring you here, but I could never pin him down to a when." Mrs. Randall's mouth pursed the littlest bit as she slanted her light brown eyes at her son.

"You're meeting her now, Mom," Zweli said. "She's only been back from California for three months."

Mrs. Randall propped her dainty fists on her hips. "Three months? You've been talking about Kyla for three years, and it's about time you settled down and—"

"It's freezing out," Zweli spoke over his mother. "Let's get you ladies inside and I'll come back out for the luggage."

"I'll have your daddy get the bags," Mrs. Randall said. "The party's already started and everyone's waiting to see you and Kyla."

"I was just here a couple of weeks ago." Zweli stepped to his mother's left, placing her between him and Kyla as they walked to the front door. "Are you sure it's not *just* Kyla everyone wants to see?"

Mrs. Randall took Zweli's hand and surprised Kyla by taking hers as well. "Everyone wants to see you *with* Kyla," she clarified.

Ordinarily, Kyla was good with names and faces, but so many people populated the Randall home she couldn't keep half of them straight. Mrs. Randall had given her and Zweli just enough time to freshen up and get Kyla's bag settled in a spare room before she bustled them into the Randalls' New Year's Eve party.

Kwaku and his family were already there, and Kyla immediately liked his wife, Akiba, who owned a whole-foods health store.

"Kwaku was a little apprehensive when I told him that I wanted to open a whole-foods store in Indianapolis," Akiba told Kyla. "He was afraid that there wouldn't be a consumer base for jicama and golden beets in an area where canned asparagus is the most exotic vegetable most people come across. We got a great location, near Indiana University-Purdue University in Indianapolis. We get every international student from both universities, plus all the foot traffic from all the restaurants and museums near us. You should come down and see the place before you head back to St. Louis."

Kyla eagerly accepted the invitation. "I'd absolutely love to. That's one of the things I miss the most about California, easy access to fruits and vegetables I just can't get in St. Louis. Harold's Market is probably the best one going in St. Louis, but the staff isn't as knowledgeable as I'd like. They had ackee fruits a while back, but they weren't even close to being ripe."

"You have to be so careful with ackee," Akiba cautioned. "Unripe ackee can kill you because of its toxicity."

"That's the problem with a lot of health and whole-foods stores I've been to," Kyla said. "They can get so many interesting things, and you assume that they're safe because they're right there on the shelves. I get so frustrated when the produce clerk looks at me cross-eyed and says, 'I dunno,' when I ask about a fruit or vegetable I've never seen before. A few times I've bought things and then looked them up in books or on the Internet."

"Maybe you should write a book of your own," Zweli interjected, reminding the women of his presence. "You know as much about healthy foods as any nutritionist I know."

"And you're a walking testament to the effectiveness of a whole foods diet." Akiba gave Kyla an appreciative head-to-toe visual assessment. "I haven't had a body like yours since my first child was born."

"Neither have I," Kwaku winked, earning a soft punch from Akiba.

With their mutual love of food and fitness, Kyla and Akiba might have formed their own splinter party if Kwaku and Zweli hadn't ordered them to exchange phone numbers and e-mail addresses so they could continue their discussion at another time.

To Kyla's eye, Kwaku was handsome, but not as handsome as Zweli had led her to believe that night in the ruins. His dark eyes held sadness even when he smiled, but the easiness and frequency of his smiles muted it. But Zweli hadn't exaggerated Kwaku's height. At six feet, four-and-a-half inches, he and five-foot-six Akiba were an adorable mismatch.

Jack, Sierra, Clio and Merlin—Kwaku's beautiful and well-mannered children—ranged in age from twelve to sixteen. Sierra and Clio had the Randall green eyes, and twelve-year-old Jack's were a soft shade of grey that gave the mischievous boy the gaze of an angel. At sixteen, Merlin was the spit and image of his father, only he was five inches shorter and his brown eyes laughed even when he was being quiet.

Zweli had made the initial rounds with Kyla, introducing her to the people he knew from the neighborhood and his parents' church, and whispering in her ear about the people he didn't know, mostly his parents' business associates and Kwaku's friends. Once his mother became occupied with her guests, Zweli guided Kyla to a less crowded section of the sitting room, where they could watch the party from a distance without seeming aloof as they sipped seltzer water and nibbled on mushrooms stuffed with bread crumbs, asiago cheese, and andouille sausage.

Kyla had enjoyed mingling with the guests, answering the inevitable questions about whether or not she knew Will or Denzel, and harmonizing on choruses of "with an 'i'," all while keeping a subtle eye on Mrs. Randall. In her gray wool trousers, collared white silk shirt and genuine pearls, Mrs. Randall had the spry elegance of the black debutante she had once been. Kyla suspected that she colored her hair, but with her smooth, caramel complexion and bright eyes, she carried it off well. With her short, flirty haircut, Mrs. Randall resembled Leslie Uggams in her heyday, and she worked the room, entertaining and catering to her guests with an earnest sincerity that impressed Kyla.

She also noticed that twice Mrs. Randall had excused herself, put on her coat, and ventured to the old house. The first time she had returned with a plastic-covered tray of hors d'oeuvres and the second time she'd come back empty-handed.

"Parties are always hard for her," Zweli explained. "She might be using the spare refrigerator they keep in the old place, but I think she goes over there so that she won't forget."

"Won't forget what?"

"Where drinking takes her." He finished off his tumbler of water and set the empty glass on the small table beside him. "Will you excuse me, Kyla?" he asked, and without waiting for her response, he left her and began weaving his way through the guests toward his mother.

Kyla watched him, and the stiffness of his posture worried her. Zweli usually took to parties the way an eagle took to the stratosphere, and on the surface, this looked like the perfect gathering. But underneath, as her gaze moved from face to face, a current of tension seemed to curl around Kyla's ankles with the same soft stealth as Cicely Tyson.

"Are you enjoying yourself?"

Startled by the unexpected voice at her side, Kyla jumped and sloshed seltzer water on her black turtleneck and the top of the antique satinwood flower table beside her.

"I'm sorry, I didn't mean to scare you."

Once she turned and looked at her surprise companion, her heart stopped throbbing in her throat. She'd met everyone else in the house, except the man who'd built it. The man who looked at her with his son's twinkling green eyes. "Mr. Randall," Kyla smiled. "Hi. It's a pleasure to finally meet you."

He took Kyla's proffered hand in both of his. His hands were so huge that her hand disappeared past her wrist. "I'm sorry I didn't greet you sooner," Jackson Randall said, returning Kyla's hand to her. "I had to divert a marinated crab claw catastrophe in the kitchen. One of my crew left a case of them on the counter for too long, so we had to dump the whole batch. It was easy enough to substitute broiled scallop skewers. Remember that, Kyla. When you find yourself in a pinch entertaining, you can always rely on scallops."

She chuckled as she committed his dialect, which was slightly sharper than his wife's, to memory. A simple white shirt, sleeves rolled up, stretched over Mr. Randall's belly, which slightly overhung the waistband of his black dress pants. The trousers were a bit too long and their creases a bit too sharp, leading Kyla to believe that they had been purchased specifically for the New Year's party, and that Mr. Randall would have been more comfortable in jeans and a sweater. Zweli had his mother's fashion sense, and now in his father Kyla discovered the source of Zweli's ability to speak to any stranger as though they'd already been having a lengthy conversation.

"Zweli told me that you were a good cook, but I had no idea that your talents ran to catering, too," she said.

"Well, I don't know about catering, but I can feed a few dozen folk in my own house," Mr. Randall laughed. There was a friendly bearishness to the deep, gruff sound that seemed to roll from the soles of his feet, which were almost six feet from his head. Kyla easily saw how the large and rough-hewn Jackson Randall had snared the heart of the coolly elegant and privileged Niema St. Lucien.

"Now that I've met you, Yawu's the only mystery left," Kyla told him. "Is he here tonight?"

Mr. Randall crooked the fingers of his right hand and scratched them vigorously behind his right ear. It was a variation of one of Zweli's nervous habits. "He was here earlier," he said uncomfortably. "He might've left."

"Well, he's missing a great party. I wish we'd gotten here sooner. I think Zweli planned it on purpose, getting here so late. He was probably worried that your wife would corner me and show me all of his baby pictures."

"Oh, Niema won't spare you the baby pictures. There's plenty of time for that between now and midnight. Zweli's got nothin' to worry about. He was the prettiest li'l baby, and he acted like he knew it, even when he was small enough to sit in my cupped hands."

Contentment flowed through Kyla as she listened to Mr. Randall extol the beauty of Zweli as a baby. There was nothing more attractive than a man in love with his babies, even when the babies were full-grown men. If she hadn't already known what kind of father he was, Kyla wouldn't have been able to form a mental picture of the rugged giant hemming his sons' pants or soothing away a hurt.

She set down her glass and looped her arm through his. "Who else haven't I met? Now that Zweli's run off, I'd love it if you introduced me."

He patted her hand. "Everybody knows who you are, honey. You're the reason everyone we invited showed up tonight."

"If your friends were expecting a television star, I hate to tell you, but I fall pretty short of that mark," Kyla laughed.

"Television's got nothin' to do with it," Mr. Randall said. "You're the first woman Zweli's ever brought home. Everybody turned out for that."

"Are you sure?" Kyla teased. "They might've come for the food."

Laughing, Mr. Randall escorted her back into the main body of the party.

In the earliest hours of the new year, Zweli rolled over in the double bed in his bedroom and squinted against the light pouring from the opened bathroom door. The emptiness beside him had roused him from a shallow sleep, and after a brief pinch of panic at Kyla's absence, he enjoyed a burst of relief at knowing that she was only in the bathroom.

He watched her run a quiet stream of cold water into a small glass, and then stand at the sink as she gulped it down. She could have been posing for a modern-day Vermeer, with her tousled dark hair spilling over her shoulders and her brown skin standing in warm contrast to the startling whiteness of the bathroom. She rinsed the glass before overturning it and setting it on the counter, and she ran her fingers through her hair to smooth it from her face before she flicked off the light and started back to the bed. Zweli raised the snowy white comforter and welcomed her.

"Did I wake you?" she whispered.

"No." He winced when she snuggled into his embrace and began toasting her cold feet against his warm ones.

"What would your parents think of me being in here with you instead of in the guest room they fixed up for me?"

"It's three in the morning. They're sleeping. They're not thinking anything."

"How do you know that they're not doing what we did a little while ago?" She kissed his chin, giving it a little nip.

"Aw, Kyla," he groaned. "Man, don't make me think about things like that."

"You think about sex all the time," she giggled.

"Not between my parents. How would you feel if I started talking about Abby gettin' busy with Reverend Kurl? I wonder if that lustful cat daddy takes his socks off when he's gettin' busy."

Abruptly sitting up, Kyla tossed off the comforter, sending a rush of cold air over Zweli's naked body. "I need the bathroom again. I think I'm going to be sick."

He pulled her back into his arms and drew the bedclothes over them once more. "I take it back, and I apologize. I shouldn't say things like that about your mother, even in jest."

She rested her head on his shoulder and traced tiny circles around his belly button with the tip of her index finger. "Zweli?"

"Hmm?"

"Why didn't Yawu come to the party?"

He exhaled heavily and her hand rose and fell with the movement of his taut abdomen. "He was there. He just wasn't in the big house with everyone else."

"Where was he?"

"I don't know."

"Yes, you do. You left me to go find him, didn't you?"

He took her hand and settled it lower, atop the awakening arrangement of flesh between his thighs. "I don't want to talk about Yawu right now, if that's okay with you," he murmured in her ear.

"Can we talk about it tomorrow, then?"

He tried to distract her by suckling her earlobe, but Kyla steered him back on track with a squeeze that caught and held his attention. "Yes!" he squawked. "Tomorrow. We'll talk about anything you want. Just…just don't bruise the peaches."

She loosened her hold on him. "I'm keeping you to your promise. Don't make me use the Iron Claw again."

"You ought to be apologizing for that Iron Claw."

She rolled onto her hands and knees and backed under the covers. Her silky hair whispered over him from his chest to his upper thighs, and a low moan escaped him as he arched his head back into his pillow. "Ky, what are you doing to me?" he exhaled softly.

"Apologizing."

The muffled word was a moist puff of air on his recently aggrieved flesh, and he barely managed to acknowledge it before her apology left him blinded by the New Year's fireworks shooting behind his closed eyes.

Yawning and squinting against the mid-morning sunlight flooding the bedroom, Kyla enjoyed a long, sibilant stretch that shifted her bedclothes. She came to rest against a nest of fluffy pillows. Smiling, she gazed out of the window, the bottom half of which was closed off by ecru chintz café curtains. She closed her eyes and lightly ran the fingertips of her left hand over her throat and collarbone, her skin still humming with the memory of the stolen hours she'd spent in Zweli's room.

Their last New Year's together had ended in terrible awkwardness within the first few minutes. In front of a penthouse full of people, Zweli had proposed at the stroke of midnight. Fifteen minutes later, Kyla was in a cab on the way to her mother's house and she presumed Zweli was where she'd left him: in his bedroom suite with a marquis-cut pink diamond in his lax hand and her 'My Life Is Too Complicated' speech ringing in his ears.

She smiled at the ceiling as she thought back on how much better this New Year's was, for both of them. Zweli hadn't attempted a proposal, but he'd done one better, by introducing her to his family. Knowing that she was the only woman he'd ever brought home to meet his parents was, in some ways, even better than a proposal. With a contented sigh, she sat up and debated whether or not she should risk sneaking back into Zweli's room. She was stroking her hair from her face when she saw him, the man sitting in the rattan chair opposite the foot of the bed.

"I guess Zweli got rid of the take-a-number machine in his bedroom in St. Louis?"

Under almost any other circumstance, Kyla might have spent a moment appreciating the well-defined musculature of his bare chest and torso. She might also have noticed the scruffy nubs covering his head where his dreads had been recently shorn, and she probably would've enjoyed studying his oddly bright eyes and the way their color gleamed more gold than brown. His strong, square Randall jaw marked him as a native, but before her brain registered that fact, Kyla's mouth opened wide and issued a ragged, siren-like shriek that probably startled her mother out of bed in St. Louis.

The sonic power of Kyla's voice must have paralyzed the stranger, because his hands locked on the ends of the armrests and he made no move to protect himself when Kyla, still screaming, began pelting him with the objects she blindly grabbed from the night table. The bounce of a floral cube of tissues off the stranger's head unfroze him, and he stood up in his baggy flannel pajama pants in time to avoid being walloped with an empty champagne bottle. Clutching the white bed sheet to her bare body, Kyla scrambled to her feet in the bed, still managing to pitch the petite clock radio at her visitor as she backed toward the wall.

"Would you kick that noise?" he pleaded, neatly catching the radio in one hand as he stepped within arm's reach of her.

Perhaps misinterpreting his meaning, Kyla dropped onto her butt on the bed and used both feet to give him a donkey kick in the gut that should have sent him flying into the wall. It was like kicking a rock face, and knowing that he was slightly indestructible scared Kyla even more. With the tail of the bed sheet obediently trailing behind her, she rolled across the bed, hopped onto the floor, tossed open the bedroom door and ran smack into Zweli and Mr. Randall. Zweli wore a pair of grey sports briefs and Mr. Randall was dressed in jeans and a sweater, and he still clutched the sports section of Saturday's *Indianapolis Star.*

Tugging the sheet around her with one hand, Kyla pointed an accusing finger. "I woke up and he was sitting there, staring at me!"

"Yawu," Mr. Randall sighed wearily, rubbing his eyes with his thumb and forefinger. "Can I have one Saturday morning of quiet in my own house?" He turned to Zweli, who held Kyla in a protective embrace.

"That's Yawu?" she panted. "Why was he in here?"

"Well, probably because this is his room," Zweli said.

"No, it—" she started, but she shut up once she took a good look at the décor. The french vanilla walls, ecru curtains and natural rattan furnishings weren't in the room she'd been given. The color scheme of the guest room was all white, like Zweli's room. "Oops," she said. "I must have made a wrong turn when I was coming back from—"

"The kitchen," Zweli finished loudly. "Kyla's a big fan of late night snacks."

Yawu smirked, and he looked so much like Zweli had when Kyla first met him. "I got up a little while ago to go to the bathroom, and when I came out, Miss Kyla was cuddling up with my pillows."

"I'm a big fan of *early morning* snacks, too," Kyla fired petulantly.

"It's not early," Yawu said. "It's ten o'clock."

"Quit it, Yawu," Zweli sighed.

"What?" he asked innocently. "You're adults, man. You shouldn't have to lie about where your girl was sneaking from this morning."

"All three of you need to get dressed and come down for brunch," Mr. Randall said. "I can't keep the *pain perdu* warm for much longer, or else it'll dry out."

Zweli spoke quietly to Kyla. "Your door's right there." He nodded toward the closed door that faced Yawu's on the other side of the corridor. "Dad is famous for his Saturday brunch. I'll meet you in the kitchen, okay?"

"You're still hungry?" Yawu asked with exaggerated interest. "Even after your late-night, early-mid morning snack?"

Kyla shoved a hand at Yawu. "It's been a pleasure meeting you, Yawu," she said prettily. "You're everything Zweli said you were."

His flippant smile melted as his jaw clenched. He ignored Kyla's outstretched hand.

Zweli gave Kyla a gentle push toward her door. "Dad, would you mind making some of that Kona coffee I brought? It's Kyla's favorite."

"Sure thing, Son." With a last pained look at his children, Mr. Randall gave Zweli's shoulder a pat before he left them alone.

Yawu crawled onto his bed and reclined against the pillows, lacing his fingers behind his head and crossing his legs at the ankle. "This wasn't my fault," he grinned, clearly enjoying his brother's discomfiture.

"Nothing's ever your fault." Zweli closed the door firmly behind him and stepped deeper into the room. "Have you updated your résumé? January is a good month for job hunting."

Yawu grimaced. "See, this is why I spent all last night avoiding you. This is a holiday, man. You're not supposed to go to work, and I don't want to talk about work."

"Maybe that's your problem."

"Why don't I just move to St. Louis and let you hook me up at the hospital. I could sweep floors. Sponge up blood and piss. Of course, if the human resources director is a woman, I might just end up as chief of staff."

"Awfully sure of yourself these days, Wu."

"You ain't your mama's only player, Zweli. I got a little game, too."

"Why do you talk about her like that? Like she's a stranger."

Yawu swung his legs over the side of the bed and sat with his back toward Zweli. "Why do you talk about her like she's some kind of saint? She's an alcoholic."

"Recovered," Zweli corrected.

"If she's recovered, why can't she have a sip of something once in a while?" He glared at Zweli over his right shoulder. "If she's recovered, why did all the rest of us have to spend last night drinking liquid candy and toast the New Year with sparkling grape juice?"

Zweli eyed the empty champagne bottle that lay in the far corner where it had landed after Kyla had launched it. "Our sparkling grape juice didn't cost one hundred dollars a bottle. You know better than to bring alcohol into this house."

Yawu's head sank between his slumped shoulders. "It wasn't out in the open. It was in my room. No one would have known about it if your lifeguard hadn't been in my bed."

Zweli ignored the pleasure he heard in his brother's last remark. "So you're drinking on the sly? That's how Mom started. Is that why the Pacers let you go? Because of your drinking?"

He whirled around. "I quit the Pacers, and don't ever compare me to your mother!"

"She's your mother, too, and you know better than to be around her when you've been drinking."

"What I do in my bedroom is none of your business. You wouldn't have known about the champagne if your woman hadn't invaded my space." He laughed grimly. "Maybe coming in here wasn't an accident. Have you considered that, Z? If you'd been doing your job right, maybe she wouldn't have ended up in my bed." He stood up and rounded the bed, singing Bell Biv DeVoe's "Do Me." By the second verse, Zweli had grabbed him by the throat and forced him backwards onto the bed, choking off Yawu's song, his thumb and middle finger pressing on his carotid arteries.

Zweli spoke quickly, knowing that Yawu would be unconscious if he kept up the pressure for another few seconds. "It's one thing to disrespect Mom. I'm used to it and so's she. But if you say one more word against Kyla, I'll choke your tongue out." He shoved away from his brother, his fists and jaw clenched.

Yawu jumped to his feet, rubbing his neck. He was a bit broader and bulkier than Zweli, but his size advantage was no match for Zweli's expertise at boxing and anatomy. Zweli knew where and how to strike to render maximum damage with minimum effort.

"If you don't care how your behavior affects Mom, think about what it does to Dad!" Zweli yelled. "You don't disrespect that man in his own house! You owe him at least that much."

"I am so damned tired of you trying to school me on what I owe Pops! He's just a man, Z. For twenty-five years he broke his ass, and all he's got to show for it is high blood pressure and insomnia." Zweli started to interrupt, but Yawu spoke over him. "Oh, I know what you're gonna say now. 'He's got three healthy sons and at least two of them aren't failures.' " He narrowed his eyes and hissed, "And let's not forget his loving wife." Yawu dragged his overnight bag out of the closet and drew a long-sleeved pullover from it.

Zweli crossed his arms over his chest and leaned against the closed door while his brother dressed. Sometimes, attempting to reason with Yawu was like trying to force running water back into the faucet. This was one of those times, but Zweli couldn't leave him alone without asking the one question he most wanted answered. "Why can't you forgive her?"

"Why should I?" Yawu grumbled as he shoved Zweli aside, threw open the door, and disappeared into the corridor.

The curtains had once been orange, but years of dust and neglect had darkened them to a strange shade of burnt umber that closed out all of the afternoon light. Zweli, sitting at the kitchen table, noticed how one set of curtains hung a few inches lower than the other, the mark of his father's handiwork. He'd purchased the curtains and hemmed them himself years and years ago, two days after Niema had accidentally set the old ones on fire one morning after starting a skillet of fried eggs and then blacking out in the very chair in which Zweli now sat.

Zweli could almost smell the stench of the burning bacon fat his mother used for cooking, and the suffocating smog that had resulted when the fat overheated and spat flames at the curtains, which went up in an acrid cloud of cotton and polyester. A cool-headed and quick-thinking Kwaku had hopped over to the stove, slammed a cast-iron cover onto the flaming skillet and turned off the burner before rushing to the sink and starting the water full blast. He'd used the sprayer like a lawn sprinkler, wetting down the curtains, the walls and even his mother, whose duster had caught a few burning bits of debris.

Thanks to a bottle of peach schnapps, Niema had slept through it all, not even stirring when the cold water and smoke hit her. Zweli remembered how his father had come home while Kwaku was mopping up the water and found him and Yawu cowering under the kitchen table.

Zweli ran his hands over the dusty, cracked ice laminated surface of the table, marveling that he and Yawu had ever been small enough to find shelter beneath it. The table was two feet wide and forty inches long, and Zweli's knees touched the underside of it. He ran his hands along the wide polished aluminum edge of the table, silently paying it a long overdue thanks for all the times it had shielded him from his mother's wrath, his older brother's tyranny, and his father's sadness.

Neither he nor the table had been able to do much about Yawu's tears. Zweli peeped under the table and half expected to see stains from the lakes of tears a terrified Yawu had cried beneath it. So many times, Yawu had sought refuge by scrambling under it and pulling the chairs in on all four sides. The chrome legs were the perfect thickness for his little hands, and he would hold onto them, stopping his mother from going in after him, as though his life depended on it.

Zweli picked at an ancient knife gouge in the table. He couldn't remember how the gouge had been made, whether it had been his father in the process of cutting through a watermelon, or his mother, who had once flown into a gin-induced rage that had ended with the flinging of a chef's knife. The knife had ricocheted off the table before landing perilously close to Zweli, who'd been hiding in the narrow space between the stove and the refrigerator.

The old kitchen looked almost exactly as it had twelve years ago, when the gambrel had been completed and his parents had moved into it. Every time Zweli came home he promised himself that he wouldn't go into the old house, but his curiosity always got the better of him.

Today, as he'd done on every visit home, he'd come into the old house to see if his mother's colander was still sitting in the drying rack.

He stared at the overturned blue and white speckled colander. When his parents moved into the gambrel, they'd literally left everything behind, and everything had been left where it had last been used. The fragment of a bar of soap still sat in the rubber-nubbed dish in the bathroom. A neatly made trio of bunk beds waited for three boys that had become men since their last night spent in the room. The 11 x 12-foot space of the master bedroom had the most history to tell. Jackson had patched and repatched walls after Niema had damaged them again and again by throwing anything within reach, once even breaking a window with the basketball trophy Kwaku had brought in to show her.

The bed sat a good foot away from the wall, which had been Jackson's way of hiding a section of carpeting that had been burned when Yawu was playing with matches next to Niema, who'd been in a drunken coma on the bed.

From the kitchen, Zweli could see straight into the living room, and his gaze landed on the sofa lining the wall shared with the front door. Like an old, broken-down beast of burden, the sofa slumped in the middle, from years of his father's weight upon it. Zweli had only the most vague memories of his parents sharing a bed. It had become Jackson's way to come home from work and settle in on the sofa, so as not to awaken his wife, he'd tell them.

Looking back, Zweli knew better. Jackson slept on the sofa because he couldn't bear the sight and smell of his drunken wife in his bed.

Today, when he'd first come over to the old house, Zweli had felt a chill at the sight of a clean blanket and fresh pillow on the old sofa. He'd first thought that his father had been sleeping on the old sofa, until he'd noticed the size thirteen EE basketball shoes tucked under the edge of the sofa.

That was when Zweli realized that Yawu hadn't been in the bathroom when Kyla mistakenly went into his room. He'd been in the old house, and Zweli instinctively knew that by spending the night there, Yawu was attempting to defy his hurts, to spit in the face of his painful memories.

Zweli covered his face with his hands in a futile attempt to blot out the image of his baby brother lying in the dark of the old house, drunk on champagne, trying to fit his six-foot-three adult frame into the uncomfortable depression of the old sofa. His chest grew heavy and tight with the weight of melancholy he suddenly felt with the flicker of understanding of his troubled brother.

"My God," he whispered. "He can't forgive her because he can't let go."

Niema had started drinking when Yawu was a baby, so he never knew the gentle, loving mother that he and Kwaku had known. Until he was almost ten, Yawu had known his mother only as a mean drunk, and his first impression of her was the one he chose to believe.

On the tail of that flash of knowledge, came another revelation, that of Zweli's own reasons for venturing into the old house. He didn't care about the colander or the bunk beds or the gouged tabletop. He didn't visit the old place to reaffirm how far his parents, his mother in particular, had come.

He'd come to the old house to test himself, to see if he'd gotten past the past, or if it still had the power to hurt him.

As he rested his head on his folded arms, he realized that it did. Bitter emotion flooded his chest and he took deep, hard breaths, trying to force it back.

Zweli's memories began to crush him, and he couldn't muster the strength to rise from the chair and leave, to return to the light and laughter, and the shiny, happy lives his parents now lived. The close, musty scent of the old place, the even coating of dust that gave everything an unsettling sameness of color, and the odd angles of the walls and floor held him prisoner now, just as they had when he was a boy cringing in fear.

The gentle weight of a hand on his right shoulder rescued Zweli from the cycle of remembered hurt. He raised his head, his eyes stinging from the pressure of tears, to find Kyla standing over him. In a loose white sweater and matching, flowing skirt, she looked like a most unlikely angel. She sat on the edge of the chair adjacent to him and took his hands.

"Baby," she sighed, her eyes searching his. Zweli seemed to be feeling the way the old house looked, and Kyla suppressed a shudder. Tears shone in his eyes, and his jaw was so tense it felt like stone when she cupped it.

"I hate this place."

His voice was almost too low for her to hear, but there was no mistaking the misery in it. She stood and took him in her arms, folding herself over him to shield him from his memories, his past, from whatever put the woeful hurt into the beautiful eyes of this man whom she loved with her whole heart. "Then let's go home," she murmured. "Let me take you home, love."

His arms tightened around her to the point where she couldn't breathe adequately. She softened his grip with whispery kisses to his forehead and eyes, and when her lips met his, he rose from the chair and kissed her hard, his tears dampening her cheeks. His hands roamed over her with an unfamiliar urgency, and when he unsnapped his jeans, Kyla laid herself on the table, inviting him to seek solace. The old chrome and aluminum table became the altar upon which she helped him exorcise the demons of his childhood. He sank into the dark warmth of her body, drawing comfort and strength from her strength and touch.

If every moment he'd lived in the old house had made him the man he was, and had led to this moment with Kyla, then it had all been worth it. And with her at his side, he could walk away from it. This wasn't his home, not anymore, and neither was the gambrel.

Without words, without reservation, Kyla welcomed him home, her soft breath filling his ear.

CHAPTER THIRTEEN

"Did you see Zweli on your way up?" Kyla led Cady into the living room, Cicely Tyson gamboling at her feet.

Cady scooped up the little cat and draped it over one shoulder. "What do you feed this animal? She's the friendliest cat I've ever met."

"For now," Kyla said. "She'll go back to her usual, self-centered ways in a little while. I just got back from Indianapolis a few minutes ago, and she's not finished missing me yet. I'm surprised you didn't see Zweli in the lobby. He just left."

"I saw him, but I don't think he saw me. He didn't look like he wanted to talk. Your left hand looks a little naked, so I'm guessing that he didn't pop the big one?" Cady dropped her leather satchel onto the floor at her feet and curled up on the sofa. Cicely Tyson daintily slipped into her lap.

Kyla took a detour into the kitchen, and came out with a bag of taro chips and two bottles of spring water. "It was a strange trip." She plopped onto the opposite end of the sofa. "Now I know why Zweli likes being with our family so much. His family's like something from a Faulkner novel." She rolled down the edge of the plastic bag and offered the chips to Cady.

"No, thanks." Cady sharply turned her face from the bright, salty-sweet chips. "I'm off yellow and orange foods again."

"Like when you were pregnant with the twins?"

"Yes, but worse. I can't even drink orange juice this time. I like blue foods, though."

"I've got fat-free blue corn tortilla chips in the kitchen, too," Kyla offered.

"Thanks, but I'm not hungry. Everything I eat gives me the worst indigestion."

Kyla crunched into a taro chip. "Are you going to dinner at Mama's tomorrow night?"

"Of course. And I almost forgot. She asked me to give you this." Cady used her foot to gently lift Cicely Tyson from her satchel before she picked it up and unbuckled the wide flap. She reached into it and pulled out a battered, catalog-sized envelope covered with Priority Mail and forwarding address stickers. "This came to Mama's house. It looks important."

Kyla took the envelope and had no trouble recognizing the handwriting of the return address. Her light and crispy taro chips turned to lead in her belly. She used a perfectly manicured thumbnail to open the envelope, and she said nothing as she withdrew the folded pages and began reading them.

"Ky?" Cady said after a long moment of silence. "Is everything okay?"

"Before I left California, Nigel had a movie lined up for me. This is the contract from Miraculum Films." She held up a thick sheaf of legal-sized papers bound with blue tape. "And this is Nigel's contract." She showed Cady another set of legal papers, this one bound in yellow tape. "I have to sign with Nigel for three years before he'll allow me to read the script."

"Can't you get the script directly from the production company?"

"Nigel brokered the deal. It would be shady for me to try to go around him to get the movie behind his back. It would be a breach of Hollywood etiquette."

"There's such a thing?"

"Yes, believe it or not."

"Is it a good movie?"

Kyla nodded. "But not good enough to make me sign three more years of my life away to Nigel."

"Well, you know what Grandma used to say. If you don't get the thing you really wanted, it just means that there's something better waiting for you."

"I'm not sure I want something better." Kyla balled up both contracts and tossed them onto the floor. Cicely Tyson viciously attacked them, as though they were hiding weapons of mass destruction. "I want what's here. I want Zweli."

"You don't want to be an actress anymore?"

"I stopped being an actress the second I left California."

"I'm a writer even when I'm not writing, Ky. You can't just turn off what makes you *you*."

"I can in this case. All I want is right here in St. Louis. And Zweli needs me more than I realized. I can't leave him again. I won't."

Keren, his left foot forward, held the big, red, heavy bag in place as Zweli peppered it with sharp, quick jabs. Each punch traveled through the bag and into Keren's chest, inching him backward blow by blow. "Zweli," Keren said, glancing over his shoulder at the boxer working the heavy bag behind him. "Take it down a notch."

His chin to his chest and sweat dripping into his eyes, Zweli gave the bag a series of lightning-quick jab-right-cross combinations that forced Keren ever nearer the neighboring pugilist.

"Time out, Z." Keren dropped the bag and stepped out of the way. He pulled the Velcroed straps of his training gloves and peeled the sweaty mitts off his hands. Grunting, Zweli gave the bag a few more solid blows before he reluctantly turned his back on the bag and started for the locker room.

"We missed you at dinner Sunday," Keren said, falling into step beside him. "Kyla was kind of vague when we asked after you."

Zweli used his teeth to unfasten his practice gloves as he walked into the locker room. The gym was crowded for a Saturday morning, and he bumped shoulders with another man as he made his way toward his locker. Squeezing his right glove between his left arm and side, he pulled his hand free. "I've spent the past week trying to chase down my brother Yawu by phone. When he finally returned my calls, we had it out. I haven't been fit for polite company since New Year's Day."

"You had a bad visit with Yawu?"

Zweli sat heavily on the floor-mounted bench in front of his locker and took off his other glove. Unwinding the protective tape from his wrists and hands, he said, "You know, my mother gave up everything to be with my father. Twice. Once when she was nineteen and again when she was thirty-three, when my dad offered her her freedom. Yawu flat-out refuses to see that she's changed. That she's the woman she was meant to be. It really hit me on this last trip home that trapped inside that big, angry man is the scared little boy who used to sneak into my bed at night when Dad was at work."

Keren leaned back against the lockers, his arms loosely folded across his chest. "I have no idea what you're talking about, Z."

Zweli punched a series of numbers into the digital keypad on his locker. Once the latch disengaged, he opened his locker and withdrew a clean white towel, which he used to mop sweat from his face. "My brother and I used to be so close. And now…" He shook his head and looked away from Keren. The last thing he wanted was for Keren to read him as easily as Kyla had, for him to see the heartache he felt lately whenever he thought of Yawu.

"Yawu's a grown-ass man." Keren turned to open his own locker. "He can take care of himself."

"Not lately. I think his drinking is getting out of control."

Keren paused, then sat beside Zweli. "Are you sure?"

"He lost his job last month, he's been drinking in my parents' house when he knows better than to bring liquor anywhere near our mother, and he's been staying in the old house."

"You said the old house was a shanty."

"It's got running water, and electricity. That's about it."

"Maybe it's time for your folks to get rid of that place once and for all," Keren said. "It might make it harder for history to repeat itself. Alcoholism can run in families."

"It seems to be taking a leisurely stroll through mine, at any rate." Zweli took off his sweat-soaked T-shirt and tossed it into the duffel bag on the floor of his locker. "I can't think about Yawu right now. I have a date with Kyla tonight, and I don't want my brother lurking in the back of my mind. I need to be on point."

"Oh? Why's that?"

"Because tonight, I am going to ask your sister-in-law to be my wife."

Keren stood and gave Zweli a high five. "Congratulations, man! It's about time. Can I tell Cady?"

"You were going to anyway, weren't you?"

"Of course. Mind if I ask what you've got planned?"

"First, we're going to see *Aida* at the Fox. This is the Elton John-Tim Rice *Aida*, not Giuseppe Verdi's. The tickets were a gift from Kyla for Christmas, so she won't suspect what's coming afterward." Zweli's spirits floated as he gave Keren an account of how he expected the evening to proceed. "After the matinee, I'm taking her to the Linnaen House at Shaw's Garden. A seven-piece string ensemble from the St. Louis Symphony Orchestra will meet us there, along with a table set for dinner for two, catered by Currier & Chives. There, surrounded by the most beautiful camellias in the world, I'm going to ask Kyla to marry me. And if she says no, I think I might go on some kind of a spree."

Keren chuckled. "I don't have to tell Cady about this, do I? I ought to be asking her what's going on."

"How do you figure?"

"Currier & Chives is based in Boston," Keren said. "Cady and I were going to use them for our wedding, until the chef at Magnolia's offered up his services."

"Well, I had to have an accomplice if I wanted to pull this off, and no one knows Kyla better than Cady."

"I wish you luck, man." Keren gave him an amicable slap on the back.

Zweli laughed. "Thanks. I can't help feeling that whether she says yes or no, I'm going to need it."

Zweli raked his hand through his hair as he trotted into the lobby of Kyla's building. His hair was still damp from his shower at the gym. He hadn't had time to dry it properly before stopping at Fiori Flowers to pick up Kyla's orchid corsage. He wanted to drop it off at her apartment while she was at a yoga class with her sisters.

Whistling to himself, he left the elevator, turned the corner and traveled the corridor to Kyla's apartment. The whistling tapered to just plain air when he caught sight of a short, brown-skinned man with dark hair reading a sheet of paper in front of Kyla's door. Zweli maintained a casual pace, and as he neared Kyla's apartment, the smaller man smiled guiltily and shoved the paper into a large white envelope.

"*Buenos tardes*," he said with a nod to Zweli, his right arm shooting out to tape the envelope to Kyla's door.

Kyla's apartment was at a closed end of the corridor, and Zweli blocked the small man's only escape route as he said, "You don't live here."

"I-I don't live here, specifically, you know, mister, but…uh…"

"I know you don't live here because my girlfriend lives here." Zweli glanced at the letter dangling from Kyla's door. Her name was written on it in a bold, masculine script.

"Look, man," the small man pleaded, "I wasn't snoopin' into Kyla's business. Well, I was, but not the way you think. I'm worried about her. She's being stalked."

Zweli's facial muscles hardened.

"Not by me," the small man quickly clarified. "By some guy who keeps sending her flowers and stuff."

The bad feeling Zweli thought he'd left on the floor under the heavy bag at the gym resurfaced in the form of blind jealousy. "How do you know so much about Kyla's life?"

"I bring her pizzas every week." He opened his fleece-lined denim jacket to reveal the Angelo's Pizzeria T-shirt with the JAVY nametag he wore underneath. "It used to be soy cheese with buffalo chicken, but now she's into the Mediterranean Maestro. It's a tasty pie, with black olives, feta cheese, spinach—"

Zweli cut him off. "What do you know about a stalker?"

"I was droppin' off a pie Tuesday night and she was trying to lug a vase of flowers down the hall to the garbage chute. The whole thing was so big I almost couldn't see her behind it. She looked like she'd been crying. I offered to get rid of them for her. I took the card out and gave the flowers to my old lady."

"Did you read the card?"

"Well...yeah," Javy admitted.

"Who were the flowers from?"

"Some guy named Nigel. I remembered it because Nigel's the name of the snake on this show I used to watch when I was a kid, *Villa Alegre*." Javy began snapping his fingers and la-la-laaing the peculiar, rock-and-roll mariachi theme song.

Zweli was in no mood for a sing-a-long. "What makes you think that Nigel's a stalker?"

"My old lady's got two other bouquets of flowers and a big box of Godiva chocolates from him that came this week." Javy jerked a thumb at the letter. "Guy can't seem to take no for an answer."

Zweli snatched the letter from the door. He wanted to read it, and came the closest he ever had to deliberately violating someone else's privacy. At the last second, he squatted and shoved the letter under her door. He set the boxed corsage on the carpeted floor.

"You did the right thing, man," Javy told him. "You should never violate your lady's privacy."

Javy started down the corridor and Zweli walked out with him. "You read it, didn't you?" Zweli said once they reached the lobby.

"She's not my lady," he chuckled. "You know, man, I wouldn't be violatin' anything by telling you why Nigel wants her."

They halted near the wall of tiny mailboxes just inside the lobby doors. Zweli's curiosity and respect for Kyla wrestled for a moment. He knew that she'd tell him, if she wanted to, what was in the note, once she read it. But then she hadn't said one word to him all week about the rest of Nigel's attempts to contact her.

"You may as well hear it from me before you see it on *Entertainment Tonight*," Javy said, making Zweli's mind up for him.

He exhaled sharply. "Talk," he commanded.

"I saw Heather Headley and Adam Pascal perform *Aida* in Los Angeles, and the performance stayed with me for weeks." Kyla raised her wine glass and took a sip of the rich, smooth red wine Zweli had requested for dinner. "It was so evocative. You did like the show, didn't you?"

"It was wonderful." Zweli took her hands over the small circle of their dining table. Beautiful music expertly played in a room filled with beautiful flowers, and Kyla was the loveliest blossom of all. Her backless black dress had a plunging neckline and was as simple and sexy as the white orchid gracing her slender wrist. Her dark hair fell over one shoulder, and with every movement its natural red highlights crackled in the candlelight.

Her smile made his heart flip-flop, and if she was feeling at all disturbed by Nigel's letter, she did a masterful job of hiding it. But even if she could ignore what was in it, Zweli couldn't.

Kyla curled her fingers through his and gave them a squeeze. The late matinee had been her present to Zweli, yet he had taken the date and turned it into something else, something so awesomely special that she dared to suspect that it meant only one thing: that he was finally going to ask her to marry him. His timing couldn't have been better, given the way her week had progressively gone from bad to worse.

Unsatisfied with having his letters forwarded to Abby's house, Nigel had managed to get Kyla's address. It wasn't so hard to do, not with Internet services willing to sell her out for less than fifty dollars. She had no idea when he'd arrived in St. Louis, but she knew that he'd come as evidenced by the hand-delivered letter she'd received while she was out with her sisters.

After tearing the letter into tiny pieces, she had forced Nigel out of her mind and concentrated on her date with Zweli. Glad that she hadn't spent the day fretting and worrying, she did little to hide her eagerness regarding the purpose of their ultra-romantic dinner.

"Only you could find a tropical paradise in the middle of winter in Missouri," Kyla told Zweli. "I think you've truly topped yourself this time."

"I'm glad you like it." His left hand tenderly caressed her right one. "There's something I want to ask you, Ky. I hope...well..."

Ask, she begged silently, her feet beating a nervous rhythm beneath the table. *Ask me!*

Underneath the table, Zweli's hand sweated around a tiny blue ring box. The thrill of excitement he'd felt while standing with Cady at the counter of The Curiosity Shop, selecting the ring Kyla had wanted from her prince, had completely vanished. Apprehension filled him as he said, "Will you move in with me?"

Her smile became brittle enough to crack and her hands stiffened in his. "Will I...Zweli?"

He dropped his eyes to avoid the pained confusion flashing in hers. "I think it would be a logical next step for us. The house is certainly big enough for both of us, and—"

Propping her elbows on the table, Kyla gripped the sides of her head. "I think I'm going to be sick." Her chest tightened. No matter how hard she breathed, she couldn't seem to pull air in deeply enough to satisfy the needs of her lungs.

"Think about it, Ky," Zweli implored. "It's the best thing, for now. In a year or so, we can reevaluate where we are and...things might change."

She lifted her face and silky tendrils of her hair fell into her face, drawing his gaze to the tears suddenly shimmering in her eyes. Her chin quivered as she said, "Why are you doing this?"

He swallowed hard and sat back in his chair. "I don't know what you mean."

She abruptly stood, knocking over her chair, and the string quartet stopped playing on a series of discordant notes. "You're sitting there in your best tux, you pulled strings to get the Linnaen House and the St. Louis Symphony Orchestra, you sent halfway across the world for an orchid that lives three weeks out of the year and you got a caterer to come from Boston to prepare Lobster Thermidor just so you could ask me to shack up with you?" Her whole body shook with anger and indignation. "Is this some kind of joke?"

"Kyla, I…" He stared into her eyes, mutely pleading with her to understand him even though he'd given her no cause or reason to. "I just want what's best for both of us."

Ignoring the pain she saw in his face, she sang a broken note of disbelief. "I'm going home, Zweli. And for the record, the answer is no. I do not want to live with you unless I enter that house as your wife." She paced a tiny circle, and each second that passed felt like an hour. "Let me ask you a question, Zweli," she demanded. "Do you still want to marry me?"

"Yes," he said.

She angrily crossed her arms. "*Will* you marry me?"

He couldn't force words from his mouth, so he slowly shook his head.

"Is this because of New Year's?" Her voice broke as she struggled to hold back tears of fury.

"No."

"Have I done something wrong?"

Again, he shook his head.

Her temper reached its boiling point. "Forget it, Zweli. Just forget it, okay? If this is some game or some way of working out your family drama, then you're not the man I thought you were. I love you." Those three words triggered a waterfall of tears down her cheeks, and she roughly swiped them away. "But I don't ever want to see you again." She grabbed her tiny purse and clutched it in her fist as she hastened to the exit. Without a look back, she pushed open the door, and was gone.

Zweli sat at the table, staring at the stars of light glinting off the bowl of his half-filled wine glass. His whole body felt numb, and he was sure that if he tried to move, he'd vomit all over the table. The Currier & Chives attendants manning the nearby chafing dishes and the musicians looked uncomfortably at one another, unsure how to proceed now that their services appeared to be needed no longer.

A violinist, an older man with a handlebar mustache that seemed extremely appropriate within the confines of the 120-year-old greenhouse, approached Zweli. "Dr. Randall? Shall we play, or...not?"

His joints ached with a pain borne of misery as Zweli pushed his chair back and slowly stood. He dropped his linen napkin onto his unused dessert plate. "Play," he sighed. "By all means, play."

Zweli spent a quiet moment listening to the lilting strains of Puccini's 'Nessun Dorma' before he blew out the candles and walked alone into the night.

Kyla sobbed into her pillow. With her bedroom curtains drawn, she couldn't tell what time of day it was. Even though it felt as if she'd spent an entire week crying, she knew it had been only a few long hours because Cady was sitting over her, stroking her back and pleading with her to come to Abby's for Sunday dinner.

"Obviously, there's something going on that you two need to work out," Cady said. "I honestly don't think that Zweli was trying to hurt you last night."

"You weren't there, Cady," Kyla wept. "You didn't see him. He was like a robot sitting there, asking me to live with him."

"You said no to him twice before," Cady reminded her. "Maybe he got cold feet and thought you were going to say no again."

Kyla pounded the bed with her fists. "No, no, no! He knew that I would say yes!"

Cady locked her jaw to stifle a yawn. "We've been going back and forth on this all night, and I'm tired. Let's take a nap and then go to Mama's, and Clara and Ciel can help us figure out what to do next."

"I already know what I'm gonna do." Kyla rolled off the bed and snatched a couple of tissues from the box on her nightstand. She noisily blew her nose, balled the tissues up, and tossed them into the corner, where her wastepaper basket overflowed with gooey balls of used tissue. "I'm gettin' the hell outta St. Louis. I'm going to pack my car and head east."

"East is a big place." Cady dragged a dry pillow to her side of the bed and snuggled into it. "Can you be more specific?"

"You know people in Boston." Kyla dropped to the floor and dragged a big suitcase from under her bed. She plopped it onto the foot of her bed, making Cady cough on the cloud of dust that rose from it. "Isn't there someone from your old paper I could stay with until I found a job and a place of my own?"

"You'd hate Boston. You hate cold and snow, you don't like traffic, and everybody talks funny."

"I'm an actress, Cady, remember? I can act like I like Boston. I can act like I was *born* there." She threw open the top drawer of her bureau and grabbed handfuls of bras and panties, which she shoved into the suitcase.

"Bawstin can't be all bad," she said with forced lightness. "You lived there for years. I picked up the language the last time I visited you. Remembah when we stopped for haht dahgs and we had to take the looza crooza to the Sox because it was too fah to wok? It was wicked pissa, Cady, until you accidentally dropped your pockabook into the barrel outside Fenway when we were in line at the bubblah."

"Only people from Southie talk like that. And I've never heard anyone refer to a bus as a 'looza crooza' or a water fountain as a 'bubblah.' "

"Well, I guess I'm one step up on you in the lingo department." Kyla made a move toward the closet and almost tripped over the hem of her evening gown. Without her heels on, the garment was perilously long. "Maybe I should change before I leave."

"Wash your face, too," Cady advised. "You look like a damp possum."

Kyla slipped the dress off her shoulders and tugged on a plain white T-shirt and a pair of loose-fitting sweats. They were much too long, and she realized that the worn grey pants were Zweli's. Hot, fresh tears began trickling from her eyes and she threw herself on the bed, almost landing on Cady.

"You're going to die of dehydration if you don't cut this out," Cady soothed, taking Kyla in her arms. "Is this really necessary?"

"I just feel so bad. Something's wrong and I don't think I can fix it. I don't know if it's me, or his family, or—"

Loud knocking on her front door abbreviated her speculations. "Maybe you're about to find out," Cady said. "I'll bet that's him. Who else would be pounding on your door at eight o'clock on a Sunday morning?"

Kyla used the hem of her shirt to blot her eyes and nose as she padded to the door in her bare feet. With no pretense of calm or aloofness, she threw open each deadbolt and slid off the chain before flinging the door open. Fully prepared to forgive Zweli anything, it took her several heartbeats to realize that the man at her threshold wasn't him.

"Woman, you have run me ragged," Nigel greeted.

He seemed taller than she remembered, and leaner. Or perhaps hungrier. He wore a dark Armani suit that had seen better days, but it was the wild shine in his eyes that sent warning bells ringing in Kyla's ears. She slammed the door, but Nigel's scuffed Bruno Magli loafer stopped it from settling home. "I just want to talk," he insisted. "Give me two minutes, that's all."

"I've got nothing to say to you," Kyla grunted as she tried to force the door home with her shoulder. "You might as well leave."

"Be reasonable, Kyla." He put his two hundred pounds behind a push that forced the door all the way open and sent Kyla flying into her living room. He coolly sauntered in and closed the door. "You left me no choice but to come here, and believe me, it wasn't easy to track you down. I spent five hundred dollars on a private investigator who came up with your address twenty minutes after I spoke to him." He tossed his arms open wide. "The wonders of the Internet. Live and learn, I guess."

Kyla slowly backed away from him, maneuvering so that the sofa would remain between them. "You're not welcome here. Get out, before I call the police. I'm sure the California authorities will be very surprised to find that you've left the state."

He laughed. "So you know about my little brush with the law in Los Angeles." He wagged a finger at her. "See, now that's your fault too, Kyla. When you left, I was forced to take on a few clients that weren't quite as savory as I'd have liked. One of them was up for the whole-some hero lead in a thirty-million dollar picture that he would have lost if he'd been caught with dope on him during a routine traffic stop."

"So you took the fall for him?" she guessed.

"The things I do for my clients," he grinned.

"The things you'll do for your percentage," she fired back.

"There was no percentage, sweetie. The kid got pinched for a misdemeanor hit and run the day before he was supposed to sign the contract. The studio dropped him like a bad habit. That brings me back to you." He reached into his breast pocket and Kyla cringed, half expecting him to draw a weapon on her. It didn't put her at ease when he pulled out a sheaf of papers. "I want you back, Kyla. I need you to come back. There's a fat role in a good movie waiting for you, and I need you to take it. I told you all about it in the letter I taped to your door yesterday. There's no nudity, there's not even a cuss word in it. It's a feel-good sports flick and you're perfect for the part. The producers from Miraculum Films have been bangin' down my door for you since you left, girl. Sign on the dotted line, and I'll let bygones be bygones."

"My sister is in the next room." This was her hardest acting job yet, trying to sound calm and fearless while her knees shook inside Zweli's ill-fitting sweatpants. "She's probably called the police already. If you leave now, I might just tell them that the call was a false alarm."

Nigel ran his hand along the edge of the sofa back. As he moved to his right, Kyla eased to hers, maintaining the distance and obstacle between them. "That's the oldest trick in the book. The ol' 'someone's in the next room calling the cops' trick." He raised his foot and kicked at the sofa, shooting one end of it out at an odd angle and startling a short scream out of Kyla. "Don't try to play me for a sucker, Kyla."

"Mr. Chamberlain?"

He whirled toward the bedroom door at the sound of Cady's voice.

"Or may I call you Nigel?" Cady didn't wait for an answer before raising the cordless phone she'd been gripping at her hip. "His name is Nigel Chamberlain and he refuses to leave the apartment. He's threatening my sister and—" Cady listened to the voice on the other end of the line. "Yes, that was her screaming…great. Thank you." She hung up the phone. "It's an old trick, but it's a good one, especially when it's not a trick. The police will be here any minute. If I were you, big fella, I'd snake my ass on out of here while I still can. Unless, of course, you want your nose broken. Again."

"Cady," Kyla whispered sharply.

"I was wrong about you and your sisters, Kyla," Nigel muttered through clenched teeth. "I thought you were the only one who was a bitch."

"Actually, I'm a Scorpio," Cady said.

Kyla moved to stand near her. "Please leave, Nigel, before the police come."

"I'm not going anywhere until you sign this contract." He pulled a ballpoint pen from his breast pocket and started toward Kyla.

Cady stepped in front of her younger sister. "Are you deaf or just dumb? She said no."

"Am I talking to you?" Nigel shouted, his hot spittle dotting Cady's face. "Back down before I knock you down." But before Cady could make a move, Nigel grabbed the front of her baggy sweater and threw her aside. Her hip struck the corner of a lamp table and she hit the floor hard.

"Cady!" Kyla cried, lunging for her.

Nigel grabbed her around her waist and twisted one of her hands behind her back. "If I'm going to be arrested I may as well do something to deserve it. I owe you a broken nose, don't I, Ky?" He wrenched her arm up high between her shoulder blades, and she cried out in pain.

Cady ran to the foyer closet for Kyla's emergency defense system, a Louisville Slugger. Gripping the thing tightly with both hands, she ran at Nigel and swung it, smashing it into the back of his knees. With a whoop of pain and rage, he crumpled to the floor, releasing Kyla. Cady took another swing, this time aiming for his back. He spun and caught the blow against his forearm and managed to grab onto the bat. He shoved it at Cady, driving it into her right shoulder and sending her to the floor.

Kyla dashed between Cady and Nigel. "She's pregnant, Nigel!" she yelled when he raised the bat.

"She should have thought of that before she started a fight she couldn't finish," he sneered.

Kyla screamed and folded herself over Cady, protecting her from a blow that never came. A pair of armed police officers burst into the apartment, their weapons trained on Nigel, each of them barking orders at him. One officer broke away to check on Kyla and Cady while the other forced Nigel to place his hands on his head. An officer was reading Nigel his Miranda rights when another man rushed into the apartment. In all the ruckus, Kyla assumed that he was another policeman, until she noticed his tuxedo.

"Zweli," she gasped, a sob catching in her throat as she let him gather her in his arms.

"I was pacing around the lobby trying to decide whether I should come up here, and these cops came flying by talking about Kati with an 'i,' " he said. "They wouldn't let me ride in the elevator car with them so I had to wait for the next one." With an arm around Kyla, he went to Cady, who was striking dust from the legs of her jeans. "Are you okay? Did that son of a bitch hurt you?"

"I'm all right, I think." Cady rubbed her shoulder and made circles with her elbow. "I'll probably pay for this tomorrow, though."

"I'm not the criminal here," protested Nigel, who now sported a shiny pair of silver bracelets. "I'm the one who should be pressing charges for assault and battery. They came at me with a baseball bat!"

"It was self-defense after you tried to break my arm," Kyla spat.

After speaking to Kyla for a moment, the officers led Nigel away. "Was that your old manager?" Zweli asked her.

She nodded. "He tried to force me to sign with him again so he could make me do some damn movie."

"The one being made by Miraculum Films?"

She tipped her face up to his. "How did you know who made the offer?"

"Your friend Javy told me."

"How did *he* know?"

"He read the letter you got yesterday."

"So you knew about the movie when we went out last night. Is that why you didn't ask me to marry you?"

"I didn't want to put you in a position where you had to choose between marrying me and taking that movie."

"So you tried to force me into it by giving me no choice at all."

"I didn't want you to enter into a marriage that you might end up resenting later."

"Don't make this about the way your parents' lives turned out. You didn't propose because you assumed that I'd pick the movie over you."

He held her by her upper arms. "I don't want you to marry me unless it's what you truly want. I won't be your alternative to taking one more big chance on your dream. I'm not a consolation prize and I'm not a rival to your career. Why can't you have me and the movie, too? For God's sake, Ky, I'm so greedy and selfish, I want a movie star wife. I want you to be both."

Kyla held his gaze. "You honestly think I can do it, don't you?"

"Yes."

She narrowed her eyes in suspicion. "And that's the only reason you haven't asked me to marry you?"

"The only one."

She thought back on their failed dinner, and this time she focused on Zweli rather than herself. He hadn't been happy, or even eager to ask her to move in with him. He'd been miserable, as though he'd just lost his best friend. Kyla suddenly threw her arms around his neck.

"What you did last night was the most selfless and generous thing you've ever done for me," she said softly into his ear. "I'll never forget that you were willing to sacrifice your happiness just to make me happy. That film is the kind of work I always dreamed of doing, but my dreams have changed. I don't need this movie or any of the others. I want you, Zweli. Only you. Ask me, and I'll say yes."

He pried her arms off and drew back to face her. The fingertips of his left hand lightly danced over her cheek. "Kyla Winters, will you—?"

"Yes." She laughed and cried at the same time as she leaped on him. "Yes, yes, yes, yes!"

Cady slapped her forehead and sighed in relief. "Thank God!"

EPILOGUE

Kyla stood on the flagstone patio and looked out at the faces of her entire family: the one she was born into, and the one she'd married into. Her sisters and their husbands occupied the brand new floral patio furniture at the sheltered end of the beautiful in-ground pool Jackson and Niema had installed over the site previously occupied by the old house.

Most of Kyla's nieces and nephews splashed in the pool. Now nearly three years old, Claire and Sammy received the lion's share of attention from their older cousins, even though the pair swam like guppies. Cady's eleven-month-old, Virginia, was the only child on the patio when Kyla and Akiba called the adults to attention.

"Zweli and I asked you all here today to introduce you to the project that I've been working on all year." Kyla moved closer to the cloth-draped sandwich board propped on an easel at the edge of the pool. "As most of you know, I watch what I eat and try to maintain a balanced, healthy, whole-foods diet."

"It really shows," Lee snickered, poking fun at the generous swell of Kyla's abdomen.

"When you see her from the back, you can't even tell that she's almost nine months pregnant," Akiba said in defense of her sister-in-law.

"With that, I give you *Ugly Food*." Kyla drew away the cloth cover to reveal a blow-up of a book cover. White lettering and an arrangement of dewy vegetables were pictured against a pale matte background. KYLA WINTERS-RANDALL was printed at the bottom of the book cover, and underneath in a smaller font was "With Akiba Randall and Jackson Randall."

"*Ugly Food: Cooking Without Cooking* is my new cookbook," Kyla explained. "The premise is that the so-called ugly foods are the ones that make you pretty, and with a minimum of peeling, chopping, slicing and seasoning, you can make complete, health-conscious meals in minutes. Candy and chips and all the foods that are bad for you come in pretty packages full of color and crinkly noise. Put them side by side, and a cabbage doesn't stand a chance against a bag of Cheetos."

"Can I have some Cheetos, Mom?" Jack called from the pool.

Akiba ignored her son's request.

"The foods we label as 'ugly' aren't really ugly, but you get the point I'm trying to make," Kyla said.

"Who's your publisher?" Christopher asked. He moved to adjust his glasses before realizing that he wasn't wearing them. Lasik surgery had recently corrected his vision, but it would take more than surgery to get rid of his old habit.

"Cady hooked me up with her publisher," Kyla said.

"All I did was give her the name of an editor," Cady said as she rested Virginia on her shoulder and gave her a gentle burping. "Kyla did all this on her own."

"Why didn't you tell us that you had a book contract?" Clara asked.

Kyla gave her big sister an enigmatic smile. "I didn't want to jinx it."

"When is your book coming out, Cady?" Mrs. Randall asked. "I can't wait to read about your grandmother."

"It's supposed to drop in September," Cady said. "It's not about my grandmother so much as her whole side of our family."

"Ahem," Zweli said pointedly. "Mrs. Winters-Randall has the floor, if you all don't mind terribly."

"I think now would be a good time to adjourn to sample some of the recipes in *Ugly Food*," Akiba said. "Kyla and Jackson and I were in the kitchen all morning, working on an *Ugly Food* feast."

"Are you sure you want to call the book *Ugly Food*?" Abby said to Kyla as the group adjourned to the buffet table set up poolside under a sun umbrella. "People might not want to eat things called ugly."

"Mama, the Road Kill Café in Maine has a cookbook," Kyla said. "*Ugly*'s a lot more palatable than *Road Kill*."

Kyla was pleased to see her mother's reservations falling away as she moved down the buffet tables, sampling such "ugly foods" as baked sweet potato chips, seared turnips, spicy cucumber salad and shallot-sautéed green beans.

"Thank you," Kyla said quietly to her father-in-law. She took his arm and rested her head on his shoulder. "They put my name in big print on the book cover, but I couldn't have done it without you and Akiba. She's the food expert, you're the chef, and I'm just a face with a little recognition."

"That book was all your idea, honey, and you know it. You did all the research, you came up with all the recipes. You did the hard part. We're all very proud of you."

The sharp crack of glass on glass made Kyla jump. She and Jackson turned to see Yawu, the only one not in a bathing suit, pouring a foamy beverage from a brown paper bag into the tall glass he'd just set on the tinted glass top of a patio table. "Here's to you and your culinary success," he mumbled, raising his glass to Kyla. She caught the sent of beer before he took a long drink of it and noisily smacked his lips afterward. "Ah, that hits the spot," he said.

Kyla let go of Jackson and searched the crowd for Zweli. She caught his gaze and he read the SOS in her eyes.

"Can't we just have a nice afternoon with the family?" Jackson asked his youngest son.

"That's all I'm trying to do," Yawu answered.

"Hey, Wu," Zweli said, approaching his brother. "Glad you could make it."

"I couldn't miss the big unveiling." Yawu wouldn't meet Zweli's eyes. "Isn't there someone missing? You're one sister short."

"Chiara's in South Korea on a sales trip for U.S. IntelTech, Inc. She says she'll try to make it home after the baby's born," Kyla explained.

"Hmm," Yawu grunted. "I look forward to meeting her. But then I suppose you all do, given that she hasn't been in the United States for more than a visit in what…six, seven years?"

"How much have you had to drink today?" Zweli asked. "I'm guessing you're on your third or fourth now. You always get mean after a few beers."

"Like mother, like son," Yawu muttered before walking away with his bag and glass.

"Let him go." Kyla took Zweli's arm when he started to go after his brother. "Don't let him ruin the party."

Kwaku caught Zweli's eye and nodded toward Yawu. The brothers mutely understood one another, and Zweli watched Kwaku go after Yawu. The old house was gone, finally, but something still needed to be done about Yawu, whose attitude and surliness had grown worse in the year since the wedding. Zweli had taken a chance and asked Yawu to be his best man, and everything had gone fine until the reception, when Yawu made the first toast, clearly after having had a few drinks on the sly.

"To Zweli and Kyla," Yawu had said, slightly weaving on his feet. "I'd wish you luck, but I know you don't need it." To anyone other Zweli and perhaps Kwaku, the toast had seemed like a generous compliment, but Zweli knew Yawu better than that. The toast had been one more display of Yawu's jealousy of Zweli's happiness, and Yawu had been cool to him ever since.

"You've done everything you can for him, Zweli," Kyla assured her husband. "He has to meet you partway, remember? And he will." She looked around the pool and saw Yawu splayed over a lounge chair on the far side of it. He exchanged a few animated words with Kwaku, and then shoved his brown bag into his big brother's hands. Kwaku hastily concealed the bag in the towel that had been draped over his lounge chair, but he continued to speak calmly to Yawu, who ignored him.

"When he gets lonely enough or sad enough or drunk enough, he'll let you help him," Kyla said in a soft voice. "He'll let *us* help him."

Zweli studied his wife's concerned face and reluctantly let go of his worries for Yawu. This was a happy day for him, and more importantly, it was a happy day for Kyla. She had embarked upon a new career, their first child would soon arrive, and she'd made him the happiest man in the world. He couldn't let Yawu's drama infect his wife's day. He ran his hands over her white bathing suit and silky sarong and was moving in to kiss her when Kyla stopped him with a gentle finger to his lips.

"There's one more thing I wanted to announce today, but I need to discuss it with you first," she said.

"You sound serious."

"I am. It is. It's something that could change our lives."

"Well, what is it?" Zweli swallowed back a lump of panic. "Is there something wrong with the baby? It's not twins, is it? I'm not Keren. I don't want to be surprised in the delivery room."

"It's not twins," Kyla grinned.

Zweli's eyes widened. "Triplets?"

"Now you're getting carried away," she chastised. She took his hand and led him through the gambrel and up to the room they were staying in. She sat Zweli on the edge of the bed, opened her purse, and withdrew a certified letter. "Before I give this to you, you have to promise to read it all the way through before you say anything about it. Okay?"

"Okay," he agreed warily.

She set the letter in his hands.

He read the return address. "This is from your publisher." He looked up at her. Her serene smile should have allayed his worry, but he still had to ask, "Is there a problem with the release of your cookbook?"

"Just open it and read what's inside," she gently insisted.

The unsealed outer envelope contained still another envelope, one Kyla's publisher had forwarded to her, and this time the return address sent a cold lump of dread plummeting into Zweli's gut. It was from a production company called Miraculum Films.

His eyes fixed on the letter, Zweli barely noticed Kyla's weight easing down beside him. "It's for a movie," she said.

"I know." Zweli's mood darkened. "The last time you got an offer from Miraculum Films, it came with a psychopath attached to it."

Nigel Chamberlain had been sentenced to two years in jail for violating the probation of his drug charge by leaving California without the court's authorization, and another four years had been stacked on top of that for his assault on Cady and Kyla. In order to do his assault and battery time in California rather than Missouri, he'd agreed to serve the sentence without the chance for parole. Zweli was galled by the possibility that Nigel had sent a contract to Kyla's publisher, who'd then forwarded it to her.

"It's not from Nigel," she said. "It's from the Miraculum producers. They want me for a part in the film they're doing about a female Negro Leaguer." She re-read the accompanying letter. "They said they've had pre-production on hold for almost a year because they were hoping to get me. For the lead, Zweli." He stared at her, wide-eyed in shocked amazement. "They saw a write-up of *Ugly Food* in the *Los Angeles Times* and they got a press release from my publisher. They're soliciting me directly. Nigel Chamberlain has nothing to do with it. The only problem is that I have to give them an answer by the end of the month, or they're going to recast with their second choice."

"B-But you're pregnant," Zweli faltered. "They have to know that, if they read your press release. Do you think they can they hold off a few more months?"

Moisture welled in her eyes as she shook her head. "They rewrote the beginning of the script. The character is seven months pregnant at the beginning of the story."

A smile slowly bloomed on Zweli's face, and he wrapped Kyla up in a tight hug. "Kyla Winters-Randall—mother, author, movie star. It has a nice ring to it, doesn't it?"

She grinned up at him. "So you think I should take the part?"

A bark of laughter hit her in the face. "Don't *you* think you should take the part? Why are you so calm about this? This is what you've always wanted."

"It's what I thought I wanted," she said. "Because I didn't have anything else. I know better now." She eased onto her back. Zweli positioned himself across the bed to lean over her without crushing her belly. "I don't need that movie. My life is perfect the way it is."

Zweli tenderly pressed his lips to her forehead, then her lips, and then he pulled back to stare into her eyes. "That's the most ridiculous thing I've ever heard," he said sweetly. "Woman, you can do anything, and this proves it." He snatched up the envelope and looked at the postmark. "You've been sitting on this for a week and you're only just now telling me about it? What's the matter with you?" Kyla laughed, her belly bumping into Zweli. "I'm going to get the phone, and you're going to call Miraculum and tell them that you'll be in L.A. with bells on."

"You only want me to take this part because you want a movie star wife," Kyla accused with a laugh.

"I want a happy wife. If writing cookbooks, or having babies, or acting in movies make you happy, then that's what I want for you."

Kyla searched his eyes, and despite the sincerity she found there, she couldn't resist one more jibe. "There has to be something in it for you, Zweli. What do you want?"

He held her gaze and lovingly caressed her face. "All I've ever wanted is you. Only you." And if she wasn't convinced by his words, Zweli bowed his head and gave Kyla a kiss that left no doubt in her mind whatsoever.

ABOUT THE AUTHOR

Only You is the newest contemporary romance by Missouri native **Crystal Hubbard**, who resides in Massachusetts with her husband and children. When she isn't busy writing, caring for her children, maintaining her household or hiding out from door-to-door magazine salesmen, Crystal enjoys paintball, bowling, and Po-Ke-No.

2006 Publication Schedule

January

A Lover's Legacy
Veronica Parker
1-58571-167-5
$9.95

Love Lasts Forever
Dominiqua Douglas
1-58571-187-X
$9.95

Under the Cherry
Moon
Christal Jordan-Mims
1-58571-169-1
$12.95

February

Second Chances at Love
Cheris Hodges
1-58571-188-8
$9.95

Enchanted Desire
Wanda Y. Thomas
1-58571-176-4
$9.95

Caught Up
Deatri King Bey
1-58571-178-0
$12.95

March

I'm Gonna Make You
Love Me
Gwyneth Bolton
1-58571-181-0
$9.95

Through the Fire
Seressia Glass
1-58571-173-X
$9.95

Notes When Summer
Ends
Beverly Lauderdale
1-58571-180-2
$12.95

April

Sin and Surrender
J.M. Jeffries
1-58571-189-6
$9.95

Unearthing Passions
Elaine Sims
1-58571-184-5
$9.95

Between Tears
Pamela Ridley
1-58571-179-9
$12.95

May

Misty Blue
Dyanne Davis
1-58571-186-1
$9.95

Ironic
Pamela Leigh Starr
1-58571-168-3
$9.95

Cricket's Serenade
Carolita Blythe
1-58571-183-7
$12.95

June

Cupid
Barbara Keaton
1-58571-174-8
$9.95

Havana Sunrise
Kymberly Hunt
1-58571-182-9
$9.95

2006 Publication Schedule (continued)

July

Love Me Carefully
A.C. Arthur
1-58571-177-2
$9.95

No Ordinary Love
Angela Weaver
1-58571-198-5
$9.95

Rehoboth Road
Anita Ballard-Jones
1-58571-196-9
$12.95

August

Scent of Rain
Annetta P. Lee
158571-199-3
$9.95

Love in High Gear
Charlotte Roy
158571-185-3
$9.95

Rise of the Phoenix
Kenneth Whetstone
1-58571-197-7
$12.95

September

The Business of Love
Cheris Hodges
1-58571-193-4
$9.95

Rock Star
Rosyln Hardy Holcomb
1-58571-200-0
$9.95

A Dead Man Speaks
Lisa Jones Johnson
1-58571-203-5
$12.95

October

Rivers of the Soul-Part 1
Leslie Esdaile
1-58571-223-X
$9.95

A Dangerous Woman
J.M. Jeffries
1-58571-195-0
$9.95

Sinful Intentions
Crystal Rhodes
1-58571-201-9
$12.95

November

Only You
Crystal Hubbard
1-58571-208-6
$9.95

Ebony Eyes
Kei Swanson
1-58571-194-2
$9.95

Still Waters Run Deep –
Part 2
Leslie Esdaile
1-58571-224-8
$9.95

December

Let's Get It On
Dyanne Davis
1-58571-210-8
$9.95

Nights Over Egypt
Barbara Keaton
1-58571-192-6
$9.95

A Pefect Place to Pray
I.L. Goodwin
1-58571-202-7
$12.95

Other Genesis Press, Inc. Titles

A Dangerous Deception	J.M. Jeffries	$8.95
A Dangerous Love	J.M. Jeffries	$8.95
A Dangerous Obsession	J.M. Jeffries	$8.95
A Drummer's Beat to Mend	Kei Swanson	$9.95
A Happy Life	Charlotte Harris	$9.95
A Heart's Awakening	Veronica Parker	$9.95
A Lark on the Wing	Phyliss Hamilton	$9.95
A Love of Her Own	Cheris F. Hodges	$9.95
A Love to Cherish	Beverly Clark	$8.95
A Risk of Rain	Dar Tomlinson	$8.95
A Twist of Fate	Beverly Clark	$8.95
A Will to Love	Angie Daniels	$9.95
Acquisitions	Kimberley White	$8.95
Across	Carol Payne	$12.95
After the Vows	Leslie Esdaile	$10.95
(Summer Anthology)	T.T. Henderson	
	Jacqueline Thomas	
Again My Love	Kayla Perrin	$10.95
Against the Wind	Gwynne Forster	$8.95
All I Ask	Barbara Keaton	$8.95
Ambrosia	T.T. Henderson	$8.95
An Unfinished Love Affair	Barbara Keaton	$8.95
And Then Came You	Dorothy Elizabeth Love	$8.95
Angel's Paradise	Janice Angelique	$9.95
At Last	Lisa G. Riley	$8.95
Best of Friends	Natalie Dunbar	$8.95
Beyond the Rapture	Beverly Clark	$9.95
Blaze	Barbara Keaton	$9.95
Blood Lust	J. M. Jeffries	$9.95
Bodyguard	Andrea Jackson	$9.95
Boss of Me	Diana Nyad	$8.95
Bound by Love	Beverly Clark	$8.95
Breeze	Robin Hampton Allen	$10.95

Other Genesis Press, Inc. Titles (continued)

Broken	Dar Tomlinson	$24.95
By Design	Barbara Keaton	$8.95
Cajun Heat	Charlene Berry	$8.95
Careless Whispers	Rochelle Alers	$8.95
Cats & Other Tales	Marilyn Wagner	$8.95
Caught in a Trap	Andre Michelle	$8.95
Caught Up In the Rapture	Lisa G. Riley	$9.95
Cautious Heart	Cheris F Hodges	$8.95
Chances	Pamela Leigh Starr	$8.95
Cherish the Flame	Beverly Clark	$8.95
Class Reunion	Irma Jenkins/John Brown	$12.95
Code Name: Diva	J.M. Jeffries	$9.95
Conquering Dr. Wexler's Heart	Kimberley White	$9.95
Crossing Paths, Tempting Memories	Dorothy Elizabeth Love	$9.95
Cypress Whisperings	Phyllis Hamilton	$8.95
Dark Embrace	Crystal Wilson Harris	$8.95
Dark Storm Rising	Chinelu Moore	$10.95
Daughter of the Wind	Joan Xian	$8.95
Deadly Sacrifice	Jack Kean	$22.95
Designer Passion	Dar Tomlinson	$8.95
Dreamtective	Liz Swados	$5.95
Ebony Butterfly II	Delilah Dawson	$14.95
Echoes of Yesterday	Beverly Clark	$9.95
Eden's Garden	Elizabeth Rose	$8.95
Everlastin' Love	Gay G. Gunn	$8.95
Everlasting Moments	Dorothy Elizabeth Love	$8.95
Everything and More	Sinclair Lebeau	$8.95
Everything but Love	Natalie Dunbar	$8.95
Eve's Prescription	Edwina Martin Arnold	$8.95
Falling	Natalie Dunbar	$9.95
Fate	Pamela Leigh Starr	$8.95
Finding Isabella	A.J. Garrotto	$8.95

Other Genesis Press, Inc. Titles (continued)

Forbidden Quest	Dar Tomlinson	$10.95
Forever Love	Wanda Thomas	$8.95
From the Ashes	Kathleen Suzanne	$8.95
	Jeanne Sumerix	
Gentle Yearning	Rochelle Alers	$10.95
Glory of Love	Sinclair LeBeau	$10.95
Go Gentle into that Good Night	Malcom Boyd	$12.95
Goldengroove	Mary Beth Craft	$16.95
Groove, Bang, and Jive	Steve Cannon	$8.99
Hand in Glove	Andrea Jackson	$9.95
Hard to Love	Kimberley White	$9.95
Hart & Soul	Angie Daniels	$8.95
Heartbeat	Stephanie Bedwell-Grime	$8.95
Hearts Remember	M. Loui Quezada	$8.95
Hidden Memories	Robin Allen	$10.95
Higher Ground	Leah Latimer	$19.95
Hitler, the War, and the Pope	Ronald Rychiak	$26.95
How to Write a Romance	Kathryn Falk	$18.95
I Married a Reclining Chair	Lisa M. Fuhs	$8.95
Indigo After Dark Vol. I	Nia Dixon/Angelique	$10.95
Indigo After Dark Vol. II	Dolores Bundy/Cole Riley	$10.95
Indigo After Dark Vol. III	Montana Blue/Coco Morena	$10.95
Indigo After Dark Vol. IV	Cassandra Colt/	$14.95
	Diana Richeaux	
Indigo After Dark Vol. V	Delilah Dawson	$14.95
Icie	Pamela Leigh Starr	$8.95
I'll Be Your Shelter	Giselle Carmichael	$8.95
I'll Paint a Sun	A.J. Garrotto	$9.95
Illusions	Pamela Leigh Starr	$8.95
Indiscretions	Donna Hill	$8.95
Intentional Mistakes	Michele Sudler	$9.95
Interlude	Donna Hill	$8.95
Intimate Intentions	Angie Daniels	$8.95

Other Genesis Press, Inc. Titles (continued)

Jolie's Surrender	Edwina Martin-Arnold	$8.95
Kiss or Keep	Debra Phillips	$8.95
Lace	Giselle Carmichael	$9.95
Last Train to Memphis	Elsa Cook	$12.95
Lasting Valor	Ken Olsen	$24.95
Let Us Prey	Hunter Lundy	$25.95
Life Is Never As It Seems	J.J. Michael	$12.95
Lighter Shade of Brown	Vicki Andrews	$8.95
Love Always	Mildred E. Riley	$10.95
Love Doesn't Come Easy	Charlyne Dickerson	$8.95
Love Unveiled	Gloria Greene	$10.95
Love's Deception	Charlene Berry	$10.95
Love's Destiny	M. Loui Quezada	$8.95
Mae's Promise	Melody Walcott	$8.95
Magnolia Sunset	Giselle Carmichael	$8.95
Matters of Life and Death	Lesego Malepe, Ph.D.	$15.95
Meant to Be	Jeanne Sumerix	$8.95
Midnight Clear	Leslie Esdaile	$10.95
(Anthology)	Gwynne Forster	
	Carmen Green	
	Monica Jackson	
Midnight Magic	Gwynne Forster	$8.95
Midnight Peril	Vicki Andrews	$10.95
Misconceptions	Pamela Leigh Starr	$9.95
Montgomery's Children	Richard Perry	$14.95
My Buffalo Soldier	Barbara B. K. Reeves	$8.95
Naked Soul	Gwynne Forster	$8.95
Next to Last Chance	Louisa Dixon	$24.95
No Apologies	Seressia Glass	$8.95
No Commitment Required	Seressia Glass	$8.95
No Regrets	Mildred E. Riley	$8.95
Nowhere to Run	Gay G. Gunn	$10.95
O Bed! O Breakfast!	Rob Kuehnle	$14.95

Other Genesis Press, Inc. Titles (continued)

Object of His Desire	A. C. Arthur	$8.95
Office Policy	A. C. Arthur	$9.95
Once in a Blue Moon	Dorianne Cole	$9.95
One Day at a Time	Bella McFarland	$8.95
Outside Chance	Louisa Dixon	$24.95
Passion	T.T. Henderson	$10.95
Passion's Blood	Cherif Fortin	$22.95
Passion's Journey	Wanda Thomas	$8.95
Past Promises	Jahmel West	$8.95
Path of Fire	T.T. Henderson	$8.95
Path of Thorns	Annetta P. Lee	$9.95
Peace Be Still	Colette Haywood	$12.95
Picture Perfect	Reon Carter	$8.95
Playing for Keeps	Stephanie Salinas	$8.95
Pride & Joi	Gay G. Gunn	$15.95
Pride & Joi	Gay G. Gunn	$8.95
Promises to Keep	Alicia Wiggins	$8.95
Quiet Storm	Donna Hill	$10.95
Reckless Surrender	Rochelle Alers	$6.95
Red Polka Dot in a World of Plaid	Varian Johnson	$12.95
Reluctant Captive	Joyce Jackson	$8.95
Rendezvous with Fate	Jeanne Sumerix	$8.95
Revelations	Cheris F. Hodges	$8.95
Rivers of the Soul	Leslie Esdaile	$8.95
Rocky Mountain Romance	Kathleen Suzanne	$8.95
Rooms of the Heart	Donna Hill	$8.95
Rough on Rats and Tough on Cats	Chris Parker	$12.95
Secret Library Vol. 1	Nina Sheridan	$18.95
Secret Library Vol. 2	Cassandra Colt	$8.95
Shades of Brown	Denise Becker	$8.95
Shades of Desire	Monica White	$8.95

Other Genesis Press, Inc. Titles (continued)

Shadows in the Moonlight	Jeanne Sumerix	$8.95
Sin	Crystal Rhodes	$8.95
So Amazing	Sinclair LeBeau	$8.95
Somebody's Someone	Sinclair LeBeau	$8.95
Someone to Love	Alicia Wiggins	$8.95
Song in the Park	Martin Brant	$15.95
Soul Eyes	Wayne L. Wilson	$12.95
Soul to Soul	Donna Hill	$8.95
Southern Comfort	J.M. Jeffries	$8.95
Still the Storm	Sharon Robinson	$8.95
Still Waters Run Deep	Leslie Esdaile	$8.95
Stories to Excite You	Anna Forrest/Divine	$14.95
Subtle Secrets	Wanda Y. Thomas	$8.95
Suddenly You	Crystal Hubbard	$9.95
Sweet Repercussions	Kimberley White	$9.95
Sweet Tomorrows	Kimberly White	$8.95
Taken by You	Dorothy Elizabeth Love	$9.95
Tattooed Tears	T. T. Henderson	$8.95
The Color Line	Lizzette Grayson Carter	$9.95
The Color of Trouble	Dyanne Davis	$8.95
The Disappearance of Allison Jones	Kayla Perrin	$5.95
The Honey Dipper's Legacy	Pannell-Allen	$14.95
The Joker's Love Tune	Sidney Rickman	$15.95
The Little Pretender	Barbara Cartland	$10.95
The Love We Had	Natalie Dunbar	$8.95
The Man Who Could Fly	Bob & Milana Beamon	$18.95
The Missing Link	Charlyne Dickerson	$8.95
The Price of Love	Sinclair LeBeau	$8.95
The Smoking Life	Ilene Barth	$29.95
The Words of the Pitcher	Kei Swanson	$8.95
Three Wishes	Seressia Glass	$8.95
Ties That Bind	Kathleen Suzanne	$8.95
Tiger Woods	Libby Hughes	$5.95

Other Genesis Press, Inc. Titles (continued)

Time is of the Essence	Angie Daniels	$9.95
Timeless Devotion	Bella McFarland	$9.95
Tomorrow's Promise	Leslie Esdaile	$8.95
Truly Inseparable	Wanda Y. Thomas	$8.95
Unbreak My Heart	Dar Tomlinson	$8.95
Uncommon Prayer	Kenneth Swanson	$9.95
Unconditional	A.C. Arthur	$9.95
Unconditional Love	Alicia Wiggins	$8.95
Until Death Do Us Part	Susan Paul	$8.95
Vows of Passion	Bella McFarland	$9.95
Wedding Gown	Dyanne Davis	$8.95
What's Under Benjamin's Bed	Sandra Schaffer	$8.95
When Dreams Float	Dorothy Elizabeth Love	$8.95
Whispers in the Night	Dorothy Elizabeth Love	$8.95
Whispers in the Sand	LaFlorya Gauthier	$10.95
Wild Ravens	Altonya Washington	$9.95
Yesterday Is Gone	Beverly Clark	$10.95
Yesterday's Dreams, Tomorrow's Promises	Reon Laudat	$8.95
Your Precious Love	Sinclair LeBeau	$8.95

Order Form

Mail to: Genesis Press, Inc.
P.O. Box 101
Columbus, MS 39703

Name _____
Address _____
City/State _____ Zip _____
Telephone _____

Ship to (if different from above)
Name _____
Address _____
City/State _____ Zip _____
Telephone _____

Credit Card Information

Credit Card # _____ ☐ Visa ☐ Mastercard
Expiration Date (mm/yy) _____ ☐ AmEx ☐ Discover

Qty.	Author	Title	Price	Total

Use this order

form, or call

1-888-INDIGO-1

Total for books _____
Shipping and handling:
 $5 first two books,
 $1 each additional book _____
Total S & H _____
Total amount enclosed _____

Mississippi residents add 7% sales tax